Praise for Jonathan Maberry and His Acclaimed Pine Deep Novels

"I first met Jonathan when he was a teenager, and I predicted great things then. And look, he has achieved great things. Jonathan Maberry is writer whose works will be read for many, many years to come."
—**Ray Bradbury**

"Maberry has the unique gift of spinning great stories in any genre he chooses. His Pine Deep vampire novels are unique and masterful."
—**Richard Matheson**

GHOST ROAD BLUES
Winner of the Stoker Award for Best First Novel

"Jonathan Maberry rushes headlong toward the front of the pack, proving that he has the chops to craft stories at once intimate, epic, real, and horrific."
—**Bentley Little**

"Reminiscent of Stephen King . . . Maberry supplies plenty of chills in this atmospheric novel. . . . This is horror on a grand scale."
—*Publishers Weekly*

"Every so often, you discover an author whose writing is so lyrical that it transcends mere storytelling. Jonathan Maberry is just such an author."
—**Tess Gerritsen**, *New York Times* bestselling author of *The Mephisto Club*

"*Ghost Road Blues* is a hell of a book—complex, sprawling, and spooky . . . with strong characters and a setting that's pure Americana Halloween hell. A satisfying chunk of creepy, visceral horror storytelling—I'd recommend this to anyone who loves the works of Stephen King."
—Jemiah Jefferson

"Reading Maberry is like listening to the blues in a graveyard at the stroke of midnight—the dead surround you, your pounding heart keeps steady rhythm with the dark, melodic prose, and the scares just keep coming. You find yourself wondering if it's the wind howling through the cold, foreboding landscape of gray slate tombstones or whether it's Howlin' Wolf's scratchy voice singing 'Evil.' "
—Fred Wiehe

"Get ready to be totally hooked, because it's all here: incredible atmosphere, characters you truly care about, and a level of pure suspense that gets higher with every page. Jonathan Maberry is writing as well as anyone in the business right now, and I'll be counting the days until his next book."
—Steve Hamilton

"Maberry's *Ghost Road Blues* leads with a hard left hook and never lets up, full of good, strong writing and complex characters who step right off the page and into readers' heads. It's a lyrical, frightening, and often astonishing read. Although Pine Deep is not a place you'd like to call home, you'll feel as if you've been there before. A wonderful novel from a fresh new voice in the genre."
—Nate Kenyon

"Maberry weaves words of mesmeric power. Gruesome, scary, and bloody good fun."
—Simon Clark

"Riveting, bristling with scares, rich with atmosphere . . . brings to mind early Stephen King. Highly recommended!"
—**Jay Bonansinga**

"Without a doubt this prolific author is the next Stephen King. Maberry deserves more then a Bram Stoker Award for this; he deserves Bram Stoker to rise from his grave and shake his hand."
—**Chad Wendell**

"A must for anyone who enjoys a literary roller-coaster ride with a deliciously grotesque streak."
—**Litara Angeli**, *Dark Realms* magazine

DEAD MAN'S SONG

"Maberry takes us on another chilling roller-coaster ride through the cursed town of Pine Deep. You might want to keep the night-light on for this one. Really."
—**Laura Schrock**

"A fabulously written novel that grips you from its first line to its last. Jonathan Maberry's writing runs from dark and beautiful to sharp and thought-provoking, and his books should be on everyone's must-read list."
—**Yvonne Navarro**

BAD MOON RISING

"One of the best supernatural thrillers of recent years."
—**John Connolly**

GHOST ROAD BLUES

A Pine Deep Novel

JONATHAN MABERRY

KENSINGTON BOOKS
www.kensingtonbooks.com

KENSINGTON BOOKS are published by

Kensington Publishing Corp.
119 West 40th Street
New York, NY 10018

All Kensington titles, imprints, and distributed lines are available at special quantity discounts for bulk purchases for sales promotions, premiums, fund-raising, educational, or institutional use. Special book excerpts or customized printings can also be created to fit specific needs. For details, write or phone the office of the Kensington sales manager: Kensington Publishing Corp., 119 West 40th Street, New York, NY 10018, attn: Sales Department; phone 1-800-221-2647.

KENSINGTON and the K logo are Reg. U.S. Pat. & TM Off.

ISBN-13: 978-1-4967-0539-6
ISBN-10: 1-4967-0539-4

First Pinnacle Mass Market Printing: June 2006
First Trade Paperback Printing: June 2016

10 9 8 7 6 5 4

Printed in the United States of America

First Electronic Edition: June 2016

ISBN-13: 978-1-4967-0542-6
ISBN-10: 1-4967-0542-4

As always . . . for Sara Jo!

Ghost Road Blues: An Introduction

BY JONATHAN MABERRY

Ten years.

That's how much time has passed since my first novel, *Ghost Road Blues*, was published.

In some ways it feels like ten minutes, and in others it feels like this is the sort of thing I've always done. Write fiction, I mean.

It's not, though. When I sat down to write this novel it was my very first attempt at fiction. I had no idea if I was going to be any good at it. Hell, I didn't even know if I was going to *like* writing novels. Prior to that I'd written nonfiction going all the way back to my college days. Thousands of feature articles and how-to articles for magazines, mostly on topics like jujutsu, self-defense, travel, bartending, skydiving, relationships, science, music. I did reviews and op-ed pieces, then I shifted gears and began writing college textbooks (on judo, archery, martial-arts history, etc.) and mass-market nonfiction, again mostly about martial arts. Until something odd happened in 2000.

That was the year I published a book on a subject I'd never before written about, although it was a subject that had always fascinated me.

The supernatural.

I wrote a huge nonfiction book on the folklore of supernatural predators from around the world and throughout history. It was the final book in a four-book contract with a small press. And since the first three books had been about—you guessed it—martial arts, the editor assumed that's where I'd go again. I didn't.

You see I've always been fascinated by the things that go bump in the night. Monsters, in all their varied aspects and guises, filled my young dreams and my waking speculations. That process started with my grandmother, who was a wonderfully spooky old lady. She believed in *everything*. All of the monsters, spirits, devils, demons, ghosts, and faerie folk were part of what she called the "larger world." That was her world. She read tea leaves for the other ladies in the neighborhood—a fiercely blue-collar, low-income part of Philadelphia. The stuff she believed in scared the bejeezus out of my siblings and, quite frankly, a lot of her neighbors. She was the crazy old woman down the street.

I loved her.

She taught me to read tarot cards when I was eight, told me stories about ghouls and goblins . . . and vampires. Werewolves, too. Because of her, I knew the folkloric versions of these monsters long before I saw the Hollywood versions and before I read the literary takes on them.

So I wrote a book about it. *The Vampire Slayers' Field Guide to the Undead*. My publisher feared that my martial arts readers would think I'd lost my marbles; he insisted I publish it under a pen name. And so it came out with Shane MacDougall as the author.

Suddenly Shane MacDougall was getting more attention than Jonathan Maberry. More people were talking about his vampire book than had about the dozen or so nonfiction books on other subjects I'd written previously.

It was because of that book that I met some of the people in the horror community—other writers, but also readers. It encouraged me to go back to reading horror fiction, which was something I'd drifted away from over the years. I rediscovered old favorites: Bram Stoker, Shirley Jackson, Sheridan Le Fanu, Mary Shelley, Robert Bloch, H. P. Lovecraft, Richard Matheson, Stephen King, Peter Straub . . . so many others. And I encountered the newer breed, among them Graham Masterton, James Herbert, Brian Keene, Bentley Little . . . well, the list goes on and on.

I read everything I could get my hands on, and the more I read the more I loved the subtlety and variety in the genre.

Somewhere along the way—I think it was around 2002—I began toying with the idea of trying my hand at horror fiction. Although I'd written plays and poetry, which are a kind of fiction, I'd never tackled prose fiction with any enthusiasm. I always assumed I had too orderly a mind, a journalist's mind. Fiction was something magical that only other, better writers could manage and who the hell was I, anyway?

While I mulled over it, I began scouting around for horror fiction that drew on the folkloric monsters rather than retreaded the Hollywood versions. I looked and looked, and found very little. I began grousing about the paucity of such fiction. I became vocal about it. Which is when my long-suffering wife, Sara Jo, finally said, "Well, stop complaining about it, and write the damn thing."

Which I did.

Ghost Road Blues was written to get it out of my system. In part. Mostly, though, it was written because it was a story I wanted to read. It was real people in a practical and pragmatic version of the world encountering monsters. And the monsters in question were variations of vampires, werewolves, and ghosts that appeared in old legends. I wrote the book that was conjured in my boyhood dreams and fed by my love of horror.

In the writing I realized a couple of things.

First, it became very apparent that the story I wanted to tell was not going to fit in one volume. Not even in one very large volume. I love stories with ensemble casts, stories that have an epic feel to them. So I broke the story into three parts, set at the beginning, middle, and end of one very unlucky October.

The second thing I realized was that I rather enjoyed writing fiction. It felt natural, comfortable. It felt right. It felt so right, in fact, that I had to wonder why I'd waited so long to try it. I sold my first magazine features in 1978. My first nonfiction book was published in 1991. Why had I waited until almost the new millennium to try writing a novel?

No clue at all. Maybe I just wasn't ready.

The third thing I realized was that I had to get an agent. When you write articles and textbooks you don't need a literary agent. You do need one—and ought to find a good one—when you write novels.

I did my homework and I found a good one, Sara Crowe, originally of Trident Media and since then of Harvey Klinger, Inc. Even though Sara is not a fan of horror, she saw something in *Ghost Road Blues* that made her want to take it, and me, on. She shopped it and surprised the living hell out of me by selling it—and its two sequels—to Michaela Hamilton at Pinnacle, an imprint of Kensington Publishing.

The first of what was to become the Pine Deep Trilogy debuted in June 2006. I doubt any of us had high expectations. It was a paperback original, and a horror novel, published during a period of tragic decline in horror fiction. I was warned that the book would probably enjoy a few months on the shelves and then quietly fade away. Maybe it would sell a few extra copies when each of the sequels came out, but maybe not.

Something different happened.

People started buying *Ghost Road Blues*. Reviewers began talking it up. There was message board chatter about it (this was way before Facebook and Twitter). Jonathan Maberry began getting invited to speak at the same events where Shane Mac-Dougall had formerly been a guest.

And then something that was totally out of the blue happened. The book was nominated for the main award in the horror industry, the Bram Stoker Award. It was nominated twice, in fact. Best First Novel and Best Novel.

In that latter category I was up against Stephen King. He trounced me—fair enough—because he's Stephen King and his book that year was the beautiful and nuanced *Lisey's Story*, which deserved to win.

In the Best First Novel category I was also up against serious talent—and what's fun is that they've all since become good friends. Those other books were killer. Absolutely killer.

But *Ghost Road Blues* won the Bram Stoker.

I was at the Stoker Awards banquet, held in Toronto that year. I vaguely remember them reading the names of the winning book and author. I remember kissing my wife and stumbling up to the podium to give an acceptance speech. God only knows what I said. I sure as hell don't remember.

At that point I had no real plans in fiction beyond the three books of the Pine Deep Trilogy. I expected to go back to nonfiction—and I did, kind of. I wrote five more nonfic books on supernatural folklore, this time under my own name. But something had changed in me. Through a process I've never quite been able to define I had changed from being a nonfiction writer to a novelist.

Novelist.

That was something I never expected to use as a self-defining word.

Now, though, that's mostly who and what I am. And most of what I write is horror. The experience of writing the Pine Deep Trilogy left a curious mark on me. I fell in love with the characters—Malcolm Crow, Val Guthrie, Terry Wolfe, Iron Mike Sweeney, Ferro and LaMastra . . . they've become friends. And the tragic, confused, but well-intentioned ghost, the Bone Man. I even like the villains in the way one can like a villain. Karl Ruger, the utterly vile Vic Wingate, Jim Polk, and Ubel Griswold are fun to write even if they are loathsome in every practical way.

Since the books came out in 2006, '07, and '08, they've remained in print. They've become popular in audio. I've revisited the town in quite a few short stories that have gone into the series' prehistory and also revealed what happened after the end of the third book. The town of Pine Deep remains as a second home for me, troubled as it is.

At this writing, with October 2015 about to start, I am writing the pilot for a possible Pine Deep TV series. I'm also writing my twenty-fifth novel since I tried my hand at this weird "fiction" thing. Writing number twenty-five, and I have seven more presold and stacked up behind it, with no end in sight. I write some articles and I write comics for Marvel, IDW, and Dark Horse, but when I pick a single word to define who and what I am, it's "novelist."

And it all started with *Ghost Road Blues*. A book I wrote because it was the horror novel I wanted to read. A book that changed the course of my professional life, and—despite the appalling things that happen in its pages—has made me a happy man.

In the succeeding volumes of this tenth anniversary printing I'll talk more about the content of these books. The legends behind the novels. The horror inside the horror.

For now, though, I wanted to share the story of how I chose to write my first novel.

So, old friend or new reader, turn the page and go visit the troubled little town of Pine Deep, Pennsylvania. I hope you enjoy your stay. But . . . don't go wandering alone in the dark.

Del Mar, California
September 2015

PROLOGUE

One Month Before Halloween This Year

I have wrought great use out of evil tools.
—Edward George Earle Lytton Bulwer-Lytton,
first Baron Lytton, *Richelieu*

Every evil in the bud is easily crushed;
as it grows older, it becomes stronger.
—Cicero, *Philippicæ*

I got to keep moving, I got to keep moving
Blues falling down like hail, blues falling down like hail
Mmm, blues falling down like hail, blues falling down like hail
And the day keeps on remindin' me, there's a hellhound on my
trail Hellhound on my trail, hellhound on my trail.
—Robert Johnson, "Hellhound on My Trail"

The last thing Billy said was, "Oh, come on . . . there's nothing out there."

And then two sets of bone-white hands arched over the slat rails on the wagon and seized him by the shoulders and the collar and dragged him screaming into the darkness. He tried to fight them, but they had him and as he rasped along the rail, feet flailing and hands scrabbling for some desperate purchase, other white figures closed in and he was dragged away.

Claire screamed at the top of her lungs. Everyone else screamed too. Even the guy driving the tractor screamed.

Billy screamed louder than all of them.

Claire launched herself forward from the hay bale on which she'd been sitting just a moment ago holding Billy's hand; she leaned out into the darkness beyond the rails, her fingers clawing the air as if that could somehow bring him back. Thirty feet away six figures had forced Billy down to the ground and were hunched over him, their white hands reaching down to tear at him with hooked fingers, their black mouths wide with slack-jawed hunger, their bottomless dead eyes as vacant as the eyes of dolls.

"Billy!" she screamed, and then grabbed at the others around her, pulling at their sleeves, slapping at the hands that tried to pull her back. She wheeled on them—on eighteen other kids, most of them from her own high school, all cringing back against the wooden rails of the flatbed, or trying to hide behind bales of hay—she begged them to help. A few shook their heads. Most just screamed. One boy—a big kid who looked like he might be a jock—made a halfhearted attempt to move forward, but his girlfriend and his buddies dragged him back.

Claire spat at them and spun back, screams still ripping from her throat as she watched Billy's thrashing arms and legs. She looked up at the man driving the tractor, but he was white-faced with shock and was frozen in a posture of near flight, half out of his seat.

Then one of the white-faced *things* bent low toward him and because of the angle Claire could not see what he was doing, but Billy gave a single high, piercing shriek of absolute agony and then his legs and arms flopped to the ground and lay still.

The moment froze.

Slowly, the creature raised its head from Billy's body and turned toward the tractor with its towed flatbed of schoolkids. It snarled at them—a low, menacing growl, the kind a dog would give when another animal came close to its food. The creature's white skin peeled back from its teeth and there, caught between those yellow teeth, was a drooping tube of purple meat that trailed back to the red ruin that was Billy's stomach.

Claire's scream rose up above the darkened road, above the vast seas of whispering corn on either side, far up into the swirling blackness that spread like a shroud from horizon to horizon. Flocks of nightbirds cried out and took to the air. The driver stamped down on the gas and the tractor's engines made a guttural roar as the flatbed was jerked forward.

Three of the creatures rose at the sound and turned to face the tractor, their faces painted with crimson, their jaws working as they chewed. As the tractor inched forward, the wheels still churning in the mud that had stalled it there a few minutes ago, the creatures began moving toward the smell of fresh meat. Of living flesh.

Everyone screamed again and they shouted and cursed at the driver to move, move, *move!* The man at the wheel kicked down harder and with a great sucking sound the wheels tore free of the mud and the whole mass—tractor, flatbed, and kids—lurched forward, picking up speed with every second. The white-faced ghouls staggered out into the road and began to follow. Slowly, awkwardly at first, and then faster as they saw their prey gaining ground.

"Move!" the jock roared, and others shouted with him.

The ghouls were trotting now, their awkward gait becoming more orderly as they gained momentum. They were gaining.

Up ahead, the road bent around past a stand of old weeping willows and the driver shifted gears and kept kicking the gas pedal.

"They're coming!" Claire shrieked.

The tractor was moving faster and faster now, the cold air whipping past the faces of the kids. The ghouls were thirty yards back. Twenty-five.

Twenty.

The jock was mumbling, "This isn't happening . . . this isn't happening . . ." over and over again as he clung to his girlfriend.

The tractor took the curve as fast as the driver could manage it, with the flatbed canting sharply to one side and all the kids screaming again as they were pushed one against the other.

It cleared the curve and there in the distance were the lights of the main building. Everyone was still screaming as the tractor roared down the last hundred yards toward the big barn where scores of people stood, each of them caught in a posture of surprise, turned toward the sound of the big engine and the constant screams.

Claire turned and looked back, but the shadows along the road had closed over the leading ghoul. It was gone. Maybe . . . maybe it had given up.

She sank back against the nearest person, clutching the stranger's sleeve and weeping brokenly. "Billy!" she kept saying. "Billy . . ."

The tractor jerked to a stop by the barn and the crowd surrounded the flatbed. The driver stood up, turned around to the kids on the flatbed, and then gave them a bright grin that stretched from ear to ear.

"And that, kids, concludes our ride," he said, giving everyone a little bow.

The kids on the flatbed stared at him in total, comprehensive shock.

Claire was the first one to stand up. She turned to the other kids, smiled sweetly, took a bow of her own, and let one of the crowd help her down to the ground.

The kids on the flatbed were still stunned to silence.

The driver—a small man named Malcolm Crow who had dark hair, dark eyes, and a wicked grin—plucked his hat off his head and waved it toward the barn. "There's refreshments at the concession stand. And if you haven't had enough for one night, visit our haunted house. Only five bucks and it'll scare the bejesus out of you."

He winked at the shocked-white faces, and then hopped down to the ground.

Two older teens in jeans and black staff sweatshirts that had *Pine Deep Haunted Hayride: the Biggest, the Best—the Scariest!* emblazoned in glow-in-the-dark orange letters stepped up to help the customers down.

The kids on the hayride still didn't move.

The taller of the two staffers turned to the other. "I don't know about you, dude, but I think Crow kinda overdid it with this one."

They glanced at Crow, who was now helping another set of kids climb onto a second flatbed that stood at the far corner of the barn; a third tractor and flatbed was already vanishing into the far distance where the complex maze through the cornfields began. Claire was with him, sipping a Diet Pepsi that someone had given her, and chatting airily to Crow, sharing the highlights.

The shorter staffer said, "Oh, ya think?"

It took them a couple more minutes to convince the huddled teens on the flatbed that everything was all right. It was the jock who broke the spell. He forced a laugh that was supposed to sound like he knew it all the time. "It's all planned," he said. "Those two—the girl, the kid that got killed—all part of the show." He patted his girlfriend's arm. "I knew it all along. It's more fun if you play along."

She looked up at him with a measure of contempt on her face. "Tommy . . . you screamed like a girl."

She hopped down and trotted off to the bathroom on wobbly legs, leaving the jock to try and paste on a look of cool indifference. His expression would have been more convincing if his face weren't gleaming with sweat despite the forty-six-degree temperature.

Over at the barn, Malcolm Crow handed the tractor keys to an older man who wore an ancient Pine Deep Scarecrows ball cap over a perpetually sour face.

"Coop," Crow said, still grinning, "you should've seen the looks on their faces. Jee-sus!" He laughed bent over, hands on his knees, ribs convulsing, shaking his head back and forth like a dog. "Claire and Billy—I'm telling you, Coop, we're not paying those kids enough. I'm talking Academy Award performances. Damn near had *me* going."

Coop just smiled and nodded, but his mouth had a sour twist to it. He wasn't a bright guy at the best of times and generally didn't like extremes. Like some of the other staffers, he thought Crow's latest addition to the Haunted Hayride was a little over the top. He remembered days when the hayride just had kids in fright masks jumping out and going *Boo!* Simple stuff. Not this weird blood and guts nonsense. It meant adding a bunch of new staffers, including three sets of kids from the Theater Department of Pinelands College to play the doomed couple, one for each of the attraction's three tractor-pulled flatbeds.

Coop didn't think the owner, Terry Wolfe, would approve, either, but the problem there was that Mr. Wolfe was also the town mayor and he never—*ever*—came out to the hayride. To him it was just a seasonal cash cow, and he gave Crow a free hand to do with it as he pleased.

Lately Crow seemed pleased only when the kids came back

half a tic away from a genuine coronary. Coop watched Crow laugh it out and when he saw that Crow was looking at him, he measured out half a spoonful of smile.

He said, "What are you going to do if we get some kid from Philadelphia or Trenton who's got a gun tucked down the back of his pants? Half the kids these days have guns. Bang! There's Billy or maybe one of the ghouls shot and killed. That might not be so funny."

Crow rolled his eyes and shook his head. "Never happen. Everyone knows this is a haunted hayride. Things are *supposed* to jump out at you."

"Yeah, maybe."

Crow checked his watch. "I'm probably going to do the nine-fifteen tour and then I'm out of here. Think you can handle it the rest of the night?"

"Have so far," Coop said, trying to convey through his tone that having run the attraction for fourteen years before the owner had made Crow the general manager, he could somehow find it in himself to slog through another night.

If he caught the sarcasm, Crow made no sign. Instead he clapped Coop on the shoulder and went through the barn into the office.

In the office, Malcolm Crow settled into the leather swivel chair behind the desk, propped his crossed heels on the edge of a stack of boxed T-shirts, and tugged his cell phone out of his jeans pocket. He hit a speed-dial number with a thumbnail and held it to his ear.

She picked up on the third ring. "Hey," she said, her voice husky and breathless.

"Mmm," he said, "sounds like I interrupted you in the middle of some sordid sexual adventure."

Val Guthrie's dry snort was eloquent. "Yeah. I'm having wild and crazy sex with my Stairmaster."

"You harlot."

"I think I climbed the equivalent of Mount Rainier. I'm all sweaty, but my buns are like steel."

"Whereas I get my strength through purity."

"Crow, if that's the source of your strength you would be able to bench-press a daffodil."

"So young to be so hardened." He clucked his tongue a few times.

"Are you coming over tonight, or are you going to stay there and increase the therapy bills of every teenager in four counties?"

"I'll be over, baby," he said. "But—you should have heard the screams. That last trap I built—the one with the living dead dragging the kid out of the cart? Man oh man, was that hot!"

There was a slight pause and Crow could imagine her sighing and shaking her head. "You are a very, very, very strange man."

"Your point being?"

"Oh, shut up and come over here so we can engage in something a bit more wholesome than blood and gore."

"Hmmmm," he said, drawing it out.

"I'll take a nice hot shower and I'll be all pink and clean when you get here."

"I don't know, I think I prefer you sweaty."

"I don't mind getting sweaty all over again," she said sweetly, and hung up.

Crow leaned back in his chair and pictured her—slim, strong, with black hair and a crooked nose, and the most intelligent eyes he'd ever seen. Eyes that went all smoky and out of focus when they made love.

Suddenly gore and ghouls had less immediate appeal.

He looked at his watch. Almost time to take out his last batch, and after that it would be off to Val's farm, and maybe a long walk in the cornfield to a spot where they both liked—well away from the house—where they sometimes made love under the stars. Even on cold nights like this one.

Crow got up and shoved his cell back into his pocket as he walked through the barn to the field. The staff would be herding the next group of kids onto the flatbed, but Crow didn't watch them. Instead he turned and looked east. Val's farm was that way. Miles and miles away, across seas of waving corn and knobbed fields of pumpkins. There were no lights at all in that direction, and there would be no spray of stars tonight. The sky was a uniform and totally featureless black that stretched forever.

He felt wonderfully happy. The hayride was a success, even if it did push the limits—a fact he'd never openly admit—and Val Guthrie was the most wonderful woman on earth.

Then, without warning, he shuddered. A deep shudder that raised gooseflesh along his arms and made all the hair on his scalp twitch and tingle. Somewhere beyond the veil of black nothingness he heard the faintest growl of thunder. Just the hint of a coming storm. The thunder sounded a little like laughter. The deep kind, from far inside the chest. Mirthless.

He shivered again.

"Someone walked over my grave," he said aloud.

In the distance the thunder laughed again and there was a single flash of lightning that scratched a deep red vein in the darkness.

Off to his right he could hear the screams of the kids as they encountered monsters. At that moment, Crow didn't like the sound of it.

(2)

That night, after leaving the hayride and driving over to Val's farm, and after taking a moonlight stroll and then making love, Crow drifted to sleep in her arms, the strangeness of the coming storm gone from his mind. But down there in the darkness, even with Val's arms around him and the warm reality of her breath against the side of his throat, Crow sank down into a tangle of an old dream. Not a dream that was so old that he hadn't dreamt it in a while, but a dream that was worn into the fabric of his mind like calluses on a grave digger's hands. Part of the dream was actual memory—the latter parts—but most of the dream was a patchwork of things he had guessed, or pieced together over the years, or intuited. The dream was as ugly and as compelling as the morbid fascination of watching a neighbor's house burn down, and on some level Crow knew that he had to pass all the way through it, relive every bit of memory and supposition, before the dream would leave him alone. Asleep he set his jaw and ground his teeth and floated helpless on the current that took him back thirty years. . . .

(3)

Autumn of 1976

The Bone Man killed the devil with a guitar.

He chased the devil past the crossroads and chased the devil through the corn, and he caught the devil in the hollow between the mountains where the deep shadows live. It was a swamp down there with mosquitoes as fierce as hurt dogs and snakes the color of mud.

Truth is, they chased each other. Sometimes the devil had the upper hand and he hunted the Bone Man, first with a German Luger he'd been issued a long time ago, and then when he ran out of bullets he chased the Bone Man with a skinning knife. Though the Bone Man was skinny and looked sick, he was a strong man with twenty years of fieldwork in his hard hands and a back made of iron slats and old rope. They'd grappled at the top of the hill, down at the Passion Pit where the kids go to neck. They were both filled with blood and rage, but the moon was still down and the devil was still only a man; on equal ground the Bone Man was stronger. The skinning knife went spinning off into a tangle of wild rose and the devil lost his footing there at the edge. He fell and rolled and tumbled and finally overturned back onto his feet and went running the rest of the way down that steep slope into the shadows of Dark Hollow.

The Bone Man stood panting at the top of the hill for just a second, looking west to see the sun dropping toward the tree line and gauging how much day he had left to do this thing. The amount of day was the same as the amount of time he'd had left to live if he didn't catch the devil right now. Once the moon was up, the tide of events would turn, and turn red.

His guitar was still strapped across his bony shoulders—it had jiggled and jounced throughout the chase and the fight but it was still there. Clear beads of cold sweat ran in streaks down his brown face and glistened like splinters of broken glass in his Afro.

Then he jumped over the edge of the hill, dropping eight feet onto the slope, running so fast that he beat the pull of gravity and kept from falling. He wore no socks and around his ankle was a dime with a hole through it strung on a piece of twine. The dime flashed in the dying sunlight with each step, and then he reached the line of shadows created by the angle of the far-thest mountain, and the twinkling dime winked out. His aunt in Baton Rouge had given him that, and even though the Bone Man didn't do vodoun, he was smart enough to keep any charm against evil. The slope was three hundred yards and almost as steep as the inside of a pilsner glass. The Bone Man could hear the devil crashing through the brush in the shadows a dozen yards below.

The Bone Man raced faster, not caring at all when tree branches whipped his face or briars tugged at his ankles. He had to catch the devil before moonrise.

He hit the bottom of the hollow hard enough to jolt him down to his knees and he cried out in pain, but he hauled him-self right back up because crying about it don't get it done. Set-ting his teeth against the pain and setting his heart against the fear, he ran into the shadows, his eyes adjusting to the bad light, searching for the devil and finding him almost at once. The devil had stopped to wrestle with a tree branch, trying to break it off, but the wood was green and didn't want to die.

The Bone Man had no Luger, no skinning knife. All he had was his guitar and without even thinking about it he plucked the strap from his chest and hauled the instrument over his head just as the devil broke off the green branch. As the devil turned to face him, the Bone Man could see the man's eyes *change* from blue to yellow to red. Just like that. The pupils contracted to slits and the devil suddenly laughed, his mouth opening wet and

wide, and there were a lot of teeth in there. The devil looked at
the stick in his hands and as his hands began to change he snarled
with contempt and threw the stick away.

The Bone Man didn't stop, didn't flinch though his heart was
turning to ice in his chest. He gripped the guitar by the neck
and as he raced the last few yards he swung it. The devil was arro-
gant. He was into the change now and he knew what he would
become. He was prideful, was the devil; and pride is a dangerous
thing, even to the devil.

The guitar whistled through the air and the strings hummed
with dark music as it cut around in a tight arc, powered by every
ounce of strength the Bone Man possessed. The body of the
guitar hit the grinning devil in the face and exploded into a million fragments of swamp ash and maple. The strings broke and
twanged, singing chords of anger; the rosewood fingerboard
split in two pieces. In the microsecond before the impact sent
the devil crashing to the ground his face changed from a sneer
of hungry triumph to a look of pure human amazement. He
spun away, crying out in shock and pain, spit and blood erupting
from his mouth as he fell. He wasn't far enough into the change
to be able to shrug that off with a sneer. He was still more man
than wolf.

The devil crashed to the muddy floor of the hollow, his red
eyes flickering like candles, his distorted face a dripping red mask
of hate and pain.

The Bone Man stood over him with only the broken neck of
the guitar in his hands. In the darkness of Dark Hollow there
was no trace of God's sunlight, and somewhere over the mountains the moon was rising. Above them the tips of the pine trees
were turning to silver as the death-mask face of the moon
climbed into the night.

Even now, beaten down and bloody, the devil was about a
heartbeat away from winning. He needed only the kiss of moonlight and the night would be his.

The Bone Man's face was streaming sweat and his eyes were
streaming tears. He was a gentle man, but gentle wouldn't get this

done, and he tried to make his heart turn to stone as he took the
guitar neck in both hands and raised it over his head. The strings
of the guitar and all the tuning pegs touched the moonlight and
turned to silver fire.

"You go back to hell!" he screamed and then slammed the
broken and jagged end of the guitar neck down onto the devil's
back. The Bone Man's body arched back and then bent forward
as he convulsed to use every ounce of strength he had to drive
the wooden spike like a stake through hair and flesh and muscle
and bone; drive it deep, seeking the devil's black heart.

The devil screamed so loud all the crows fled the trees, and
the echo of it slammed off the walls of the three mountains that
formed the hollow. The scream burst through the Bone Man's
ears and he let go of the stake and grabbed his own head and
staggered back. The scream was so loud that in the swamps of
the hollow frogs died and worms turned white and sulfur gas
erupted from the mud. Pinecones rained down and caught fire
as they fell. The Bone Man coughed and blood sprayed from his
mouth and nose.

The devil tried to rise, tried to reach behind him and claw
the stake out of his body, but his arms wouldn't reach. He
screamed again, and again, but now the screams were man
screams, and they were weaker. The red in his eyes drained away
and then the yellow faded and the eyes were an icy blue, but still
they were without any trace of humanity. No love, no fear, just a
cold and enduring hatred that burned into the Bone Man even as
the eyes began to glaze and empty of all light.

The devil collapsed back onto the muddy ground near the
swamp. His mouth opened one more time, but instead of a scream
a dark pint of blood splashed heavily onto the damp leaves.

The Bone Man sank down onto his knees and then toppled
forward onto his palms. Blood dripped from his mouth and nose
and fireflies danced in his brain. He stared at the devil for a long
time, stared at him . . . and watched him die.

Above them the moonlight shone cold and hard on the devil,
but now it was only light and it did no harm.

(4)

The Bone Man went through the devil's pockets. There was some cash, but he left that. He flipped open his wallet and looked at the driver's license. The devil's face stared at him, a small cruel smile caught by the camera. The name on the card was Ubel Griswold, but the Bone Man suspected that it wasn't the devil's real name. He found nothing else that was personal enough, so he just tore out some of the devil's hair, wrapped it in a leaf that had a few spots of blood, and put it in his shirt pocket. When he got back to his sleeping bag, he'd take the hair and blood and mix it in a bowl with some herbs and then bury it in a churchyard. Evil, he knew, is hard to kill, and he wanted to kill the devil on the spirit plane as well as the physical. Else it'd come back.

He dragged the corpse of Ubel Griswold toward the swamp and pushed it down into the steaming mud. He found the green stick the devil had broken off and used it to push the body down into the hungry mud. It took a long time, but eventually the body was completely submerged in the black goo. Now no one would find it except the bugs and the vermin, and the Bone Man thought that was fair enough.

He spat on the stick and threw it into the woods, then wiped his hands on the seat of his work pants.

Then he gathered up the pieces of his guitar—all except the neck, which was still buried in Griswold's back—and dug a fresh hole and buried them. He wept for his guitar. It had been his father's and then his great-uncle's before that. That guitar had played a lot of sweet blues music, from Mississippi and all over the country. Once Charley Patton had borrowed the guitar from his great-uncle and had played "Mississippi Boweavil Blues" on it at a church picnic in Bentonia, laying it on his lap like a Hawaiian guitar and singing in that loud gospel voice of his. Another time the Bone Man's father, old Virgil Morse, had played backup on a couple of Sun Records sides by Mose Vinson. That guitar had history, and even the Bone Man himself—or Oren Morse to those back home—had played it in a hundred clubs and coffeehouses from Pocahontas, Mississippi, to the Village in New York to the smoky black clubs in Philadelphia. Now it was splinters and all its music and magic had fled out.

Still, it had held enough magic to kill the devil, and what more can you ask of a guitar than that?

He covered over the pieces and stood up. The moonlight showed him the way up the hill and he started climbing, his legs aching from all of the running and his heart still hammering with the greasy residue of terror.

He climbed and climbed and almost the only thought that ran through his head was *It's over.*

A dozen times he caught his trouser cuffs on thornbushes and had to pull hard to free himself. He never noticed that one time when he pulled he tore loose the dime on its twine. The old charm fell into the brown grass and was lost to him forever.

He reached the top of the hill just as a flat black cloud cover from the south was being pulled like a tarp over the moon and stars. Even so he could see his way. There was a dirt road that led from the Passion Pit back out to the main road of the A-32 Extension; or he could just cut through the corn to the Guthrie place. All of the corn, far as the eye could see, was Henry Guthrie's, and way over past the fields was the barn and in the barn was the Bone Man's bedroll.

"It's over," he said to the night as he set out toward the corn.

Then the lights came on.

Four sets of car headlights and one set of blue and red police dome lights. All at once he was caught in a circle of light. He stopped, frozen in the moment, as he heard the sounds of car doors opening and shoes crunching down on gravel.

"Hold it right there, *boy.*"

Boy. There it was again. Suddenly he felt as if he was down South again. He knew this was trouble.

He stood there, arms long and heavy at his sides, as seven men walked toward him from all sides, forming a loose ring. Big men, some of them. None of them were strangers. The man with the badge was Officer Bernhardt, a stocky young man with a hound-dog face and little pig eyes. He had his right hand on the walnut grips of his holstered .38, and his left thumb and index finger circled around the handle of his baton where it jutted above the belt ring. He was the only cop.

The others were townsmen. All of them were young, with Vic Wingate at seventeen being the youngest, though he had the meanest face. Vic always called him Nigger Joe whenever they chanced to meet. The Bone Man had always tried never to meet him. The oldest was Jimmy Crow—and that was almost funny, *Jim Crow*—but there was nothing funny about the cold humor in Crow's eyes. Next to him was the biggest of the men, Tow-Truck Eddie. The Bone Man didn't know his last name, but the kid was about twenty and had to be six and a half feet tall. Tow-Truck Eddie never sassed him with race names, though; he was a polite kid, and the Bone Man was a little heartened to see him here because he knew the kid was a regular churchgoer and was often seen in Apple Park, sitting on the bench reading a Bible. The other three were just young guys from town, Jim Polk, who had just started at Pinelands College, and Phil and Stosh, but the Bone Man didn't know their last names.

Seven men with seven hard faces, ringed around him.

The Bone Man had been rousted by cops from every jurisdiction from here to Benoit, so he knew it was always better to wait and find out what the game was.

"You that boy Morse, aintchu?" said Officer Bernhardt. Again the "boy" rankled, coming as it was from a kid ten years younger than the Bone Man.

"Yessir." When he was scared his accent became more that of a southern farm kid. It came out like "Yahsuh."

"Whatchu doin' way out here, Nigger Joe?" said Vic Wingate.

The Bone Man wanted to toss them all down the hill. He also wanted to run. He said, "I was jus' taking a walk."

"Taking a walk?" Jimmy Crow echoed. "Taking a fuckin' walk?"

"Maybe he came out here to peep into some cars and see white kids making out," suggested Polk. "See some white titty." As he laughed he touched his genitals.

"No, sir," said the Bone Man, trying to force the Delta drawl out of his voice. He wasn't going to be Amos *or* Andy to this pack of shit kickers. "I'm not a Peeping Tom. 'Sides, there's no one out here tonight. Ain't nobody been out here for weeks, ya'll knows that." He heard the slip again and almost winced.

"How the hell you know that?" growled Crow.

"'Cause *everybody* knows that. Since them killings started nobody comes out here to neck. Nobody hardly comes out at all."

Vic stepped half a pace forward. "But you go out for evening strolls."

The Bone Man said nothing.

"This is bullshit," said Crow. His face was set and hard. His oldest boy, Billy, had been the third victim of the killer and the hurt of it was in his eyes.

"Why's that, boy?" asked Bernhardt.

Morse tried not to let the rage and humiliation show in his face. *Boy?* What did that fat ass think this was, 1956? It constantly amazed him how much more redneck Pennsylvania was than most of the South.

"I'm not afraid to go walkin'," was what he managed to get past his clenched teeth.

"That's really strange," Vic said. "Everyone else is afraid of the dark, afraid that the killer might get them . . . but you're not. Now, why is that?"

The Bone Man said nothing.

"C'mon, Morse . . . why is that? Why is it that a skinny nigger like you is the only person in this whole town who ain't scared to go out in the dark when there's a killer running round loose?"

Polk snickered. "Maybe he ain't afraid 'cause the killer can't see him in the dark, black as he is!"

A few of the other guys laughed, but Vic didn't and neither did Tow-Truck Eddie. The big man's face was almost thoughtful, but he didn't say a word. Vic on the other hand flapped an arm at the others to shut them up.

"Bullshit, Jimmy. This motherfucker ain't afraid of what might be out here in the dark because *he's* what's out here in the dark."

It took Polk and the others a couple of seconds to sort that out. Tow-Truck Eddie just inhaled and exhaled, slowly and deeply, through his nose.

"What kind of shit is this?" the Bone Man said, staring Vic right in the eye. "That's jus' bullshit and you know it."

"Is it?" barked Crow, and Vic snapped, "Then why you got blood on your shirt?"

The Bone Man glanced involuntarily down at his shirt. It was speckled with blood, though in the darkness it just looked black and wet.

"What'd you do?" Polk sneered. "Cut yourself shaving?"

"Holy shit," murmured Stosh, who had apparently not noticed it until now.

The Bone Man shook his head. "No, man, this is bullshit. I—"

"Is it your blood?" asked Tow-Truck Eddie. He had a soft, deep voice. In other circumstances it would have sounded kind.

"No, but—"

"Then whose blood is it?" Bernhardt asked.

Overhead, there was thunder. The Bone Man looked from face to face and then licked his dry lips. "Look . . . you gotta believe me. . . ."

"What is it you want us to believe?" the big man asked, his voice still mild.

"It's about the killer . . . I found out who it was been cutting those people up." He licked his lips again. "I figured it out."

"You figured it out," Bernhardt said. "You? A corn-picking nigger migrant worker figured it out when the whole police department hasn't been able to find a single fucking clue?" He laughed. "Yeah, I'm ready to believe that shit."

Vic stepped closer, his fists balled at his sides and his eyes suddenly intense. In a tight whisper he said, "And just who do you think it is?"

The Bone Man started to say *Ubel Griswold*. It got as far as his tongue, his lips had just started to form the first sound when Vic hit him with such shocking speed and force that the Bone Man flew backward against Tow-Truck Eddie's chest. It was like hitting a brick wall.

"Fuck you!" screamed Vic. "Whose blood is on your shirt? What the hell did you do?" He was screaming, totally out of control, as if someone had jabbed him with a hot wire. He stepped into the Bone Man and struck him again, and again.

"Is that the piece of shit killed my boy?" Crow yelled, his expression of cruel delight giving way to real rage. "Give him to me, Vic . . ." But Vic was raining down blows on the Bone Man with an insane ferocity.

"Stop!" the Bone Man screamed back, his mouth filling with blood. "Jesus, please make him stop!" He tried to cover his face with both arms the way a boxer does, tried to turn and twist to roll with blows, but even flipped out with rage, Vic Wingate was a good fighter. He used short hooks to claw the Bone Man's arms away and fired straight jabs and crosses to the chest and face and throat. Vic's hands were iron hammers and under the rain of blows the Bone Man could feel his face break and split.

Tow-Truck Eddie wrapped his arms around the Bone Man and spun him away from Vic. The other men, shocked by Vic's sudden rage, felt their own anger dampening down. They milled, confused and embarrassed. Vic threw one more punch and it just bounced off Eddie's huge shoulder.

The Bone Man felt his legs buckle, but he didn't fall. Tow-Truck Eddie took bunched handfuls of the front of his shirt and held him up. He leaned in close, his pale eyes burning with a weird light.

"Mr. Morse," he said softly—so softly that only he, the Bone Man, and Vic could hear him. The Bone Man's head lolled on a loose neck and sunbursts were exploding in his eyes. His ears rang like church bells. "Mr. Morse, tell me what you did tonight. Tell me whose blood this is."

The Bone Man stared through the fireworks and tried to focus on the big man's kind eyes. He looked deep into those eyes, searching for hope, or maybe an ally. "Don't hurt me," he whispered and was immediately ashamed of his cowardice. An hour ago he'd chased a monster down and killed him, and now he was pleading for his life from a group of Pennsylvania rednecks.

"Tell me, Mr. Morse."

"Damn it, Eddie, let me have him!" Vic snarled and tried to reach around the big man. Eddie turned again, blocking Vic's reach with his broad back. He pushed the Bone Man up against the side of Vic's pickup truck and leaned his face close.

"Tell me and I'll stop all of this, Mr. Morse." whispered Eddie.

The Bone Man thought he saw some kindly lights in the big man's eyes. He turned his head and spat blood onto the gravel and then through a tight throat said, "It was Griswold."

The big man's face didn't change.

"What'd he say?" shouted Bernhardt and Crow together.

"It was Ubel Griswold!" the Bone Man said, his voice a faint babble of desperation and pain. "It was *him*, man, swear to God. That farmer who owns the beef ranch down on the other side of the hollow." The Bone Man licked his pulped lips. "He's the one been killing all them kids."

His voice was only a whisper, and only Tow-Truck Eddie heard it. He stared into the Bone Man's eyes for a long time, his face thoughtful. Hope soared in the Bone Man's chest. Then the big man shook his head.

"No," he said.

"Wh . . . what?"

"I said no. That isn't possible. Mr. Griswold goes to my church. He's a righteous man. He believes in God." His eyes searched the broken landscape of the Bone Man's face. "I've never seen you at church, Mr. Morse. Tell me . . . what is it that you believe in?"

"Please . . ."

"Satan is the Father of Lies." Tow-Truck Eddie's eyes were as pale as ice, and looking into them the Bone Man saw that in thinking that salvation lay in the big man's hands he had been terribly wrong. Eddie's face almost looked sad as he said, "Vic's right, it must be you did all those things."

"But I—"

"You're the devil, Mr. Morse, you are the *Beast*," he whispered. "God have mercy on you."

Tow-Truck Eddie hit him. He let go with his right hand, drew it back just eight inches, and punched the Bone Man in the face, turning into the punch with all the massive power of muscle and speed and torque.

The blow exploded in the Bone Man's brain and everything went white as a big bell broke in his mind. His limbs turned to jelly and Eddie let him fall. The Bone Man collapsed onto the gravel by the side of the truck. He flopped there, dazed, unable to speak. His nose was broken, and so was his jaw. The punch had herniated three disks in his neck and upper back, and his throat was filling with blood.

Tow-Truck Eddie turned to Vic and the others. Vic was the closest one and their eyes met and held.

Vic licked his lips in much the same way as the Bone Man had. "Eddie . . . what did he say?"

Their eyes held for a long time. Finally Tow-Truck Eddie's softened and he gave Vic a sad smile. "Only lies, Vic. All he had to say were the devil's own lies."

There was a strange flush of relief in Vic's eyes and he took a second to set his features before he turned to the others. He looked at Jimmy Crow.

"Jimmy," he said, pitching his voice to sound grave, "I hate to tell you this, man, but . . . he's the one killed your Billy. He just told me."

Eddie flicked a glance at Vic and almost said something, but then closed his mouth and stepped away. The eyes of every other man fell on the Bone Man. Eyes that had been confused a minute ago now hardened with purpose. They stared at the bleeding man for nearly fifteen seconds in silence, and then there was the cold rasp as Gus Bernhardt slid the hickory baton from its metal ring.

As Tow-Truck Eddie stepped out of their way, they suddenly rushed past him. After that, it was just a matter of doing the killing.

(5)

No one ever took either blame or credit for the murder of Oren Morse. His body was found tied to a scarecrow post at the crossroads of A-32 and Dark Hollow Road with a piece of paper stuffed in his shirt pocket that had the names of the sixteen people who had been killed that autumn. It was the end of the Black Harvest of 1976, and nearly everyone accepted the fiction that the Bone Man had been the killer. After all, who was he? A migrant farm worker who had told more than one person that he had been dodging the law since he'd dodged the draft in 1970. That made him a criminal already, and few of the farmers saw it as a far leap from being un-American enough to flee from his responsibilities to the war effort to being a killer. Logical progression of thought didn't seem to enter into it.

The body of Ubel Griswold, a farmer and landowner who had settled in Pine Deep eight years before, was never found and was generally believed to have been the last victim of the *Reaper*, the lurid nickname given to the mass-murderer by one of the local papers.

Henry Guthrie—who owned the farm on whose outermost corner the grisly scarecrow was placed, and who had employed Morse as a migrant field worker—took the body down. He was one of the few who did not believe that Oren Morse was the Reaper. Guthrie kept it to himself, though. He had lost a cousin during the massacre, but he didn't believe for a moment that Morse had done the killings.

He and his brother, George, took the body to the old Presbyterian cemetery out by the canal bridge and buried it. The church had burned down forty years ago and no new Presbyterians had moved in to care for the graveyard. No one would know or care if there was a new grave there. The Guthrie brothers didn't tell anyone about it, though; nor would the two children who stood by the brothers during the unbeneficed service. Guthrie's ten-year-old daughter, Val, and her best friend, Malcolm Crow. Malcolm's brother, Billy, had been one of the first townies killed, and though the boy would never know it, his father, Jimmy Crow, had helped stomp Morse to death. Malcolm, of everyone in town, knew for sure that the Reaper hadn't been the bluesman, but his voice had been silenced forever. Weeks later, Morse—or "the Bone Man" as the kids had called him because he was so skinny—had saved Malcolm's life in an incident that had revealed to just those two who the real killer had been.

The kids had loved the Bone Man. They'd worked alongside him in the fields, had learned about the blues from him, and had begged Guthrie to let them go with him to the lonely funeral, promising to keep the secret always.

There had been a lot of evenings during that long summer and longer autumn when the Bone Man had sat on the porch steps and played acoustic blues to keep back the night and the night terrors. The young man had told tall tales of the road, and of unlikely meetings with legendary bluesmen such as Muddy Waters and Howlin' Wolf. Guthrie hadn't known or cared if the stories were true, but the music he played was beautiful and sad and somehow it helped everyone get through the worst season they'd ever had. The Black Harvest, which had started out with a vicious crop blight that had turned half the crops into bug-infested garbage, and then with the series of brutal murders. Somehow the blues and the magic of that guitar were a charm against evil. Now the man was dead and God only knew where his guitar was.

Guthrie bought a stone in another town and set it on the grave, and he read a prayer over the young man's grave, and then he left and never returned. Years later Malcolm Crow would try to find that grave, but he never could remember just where it was.

The blight ended but the sky turned dark and bruised and they had months of heavy rains.

The next year's harvest was normal and the corn was tall and green and the blight was lifted. In time the Reaper faded from everyday conversation; though when the stories were told about it over the following years, the name of "Bone Man" came to replace that of "Reaper," and all of the evil was ascribed to him.

Down in Dark Hollow, the devil's bones lay in the earth like seeds of hate, waiting for another year's harvest.

PART I

Down at the Crossroads

I went to the crossroads, fell down on my knees
I went to the crossroads, fell down on my knees
Asked the Lord above, have mercy now, save poor Bob if you please.
—Robert Johnson, "Crossroads Blues"

Out there at the crossroads,
molding the Devil's bullets.
—Tom Waits and William Burroughs, "Crossroads"

Demons they are on my trail
I'm standing at the crossroads of the hell
I look to the left I look to the right
There're hands that grab me on every side.
—Tracy Chapman, "Crossroads"

Chapter 1

Modern Day

Malcolm Crow pretended to be asleep because that was the only way he could get to see Val naked. He kept his breathing regular and his eyes shut until she got out of bed and headed into the bathroom. Then he opened his eyes just a fraction, until he could see her standing there at the sink, as naked and uninhibited as could be. If she knew he was watching she'd have put on a T-shirt or robe.

It drove him bonkers. She had no problem with nudity when they made love at night, where the shadows hid her—though she underestimated his night vision, which was excellent—but if they made love during the day, even here in her room, she always wore something, even if it was a camisole.

Crow couldn't understand it. At forty Val was gorgeous, tall, tanned and toned from the daily rigors of farm life, even farm life from the point of view of the farm manager. She was strong and slim, with lovely breasts only lightly touched by the gravity of early middle age. Her belly was flat, her thighs, though not thin like a runway model's, were slender and deceptively muscular. Her ass was, according to Crow's intense lifelong study of these particular aesthetics, perfect. She had black hair that was just long enough for a bobbed ponytail, which she usually shoved through the back of a John Deere ball cap. Her pubic thatch was trimmed into a heart—a Valentine gift from earlier that year that Crow had begged her to maintain even though he only got glimpses of it in the dark. The only thing she was currently wearing was a small silver cross on a delicate chain.

There was nothing about Val Guthrie that wasn't perfect, an assessment he reaffirmed as he watched her brushing her teeth, the motion of her arms making her breasts bounce a little and which in turn made Crow's pulse quicken. He felt himself growing erect under the heaped quilts and hoped that he wouldn't be pitching a visible tent, should she look.

Crow knew that Val was self-conscious about her scars, no matter how much Crow tried to convince her that, in the first place *who cared?* and in the second, he thought they were kind of sexy. Fifteen years ago Val had wrecked three motorcycles in as many years, each time taking some dents. She had a four-inch scar across her stomach, a few minor ones on knees and elbows, and a whole bunch of jagged little ones dotting the curved landscape of her left shoulder, left breast, and the upper ribs. Those scars were linked by a few patches of healed burns. The third and last crash had been bad and Val had given up on Harleys and moved on to the relative safety of four metal walls and a roof in the form of a Dodge Viper.

Val finished brushing, rinsed, spat, and then washed her face and hands in the basin. Crow was fully erect now and wished she would come back to bed so he could contrive to wake up out of an erotic dream of her, or something along those lines. He knew he had to wait until she was back in bed before he affected to awaken.

She switched off the bathroom light and paused there in the doorway, checking to see if Crow was still asleep before coming back into the room. Crow did some of his best acting during the next few moments as she assessed, decided the coast was clear, and quickly crossed the broad stretch of hardwood floor to the giant king-sized bed. With smooth and practiced efficiency she slipped under the covers, turned her back, and nestled back against him until her rump encountered his thighs.

And then stopped as she felt something other than the flaccid thigh muscles of a sleeping person.

Crow held his breath, waiting for her to tell him to go take a cold shower or, worse, to just ignore it and go back to sleep herself.

Without turning toward him Val said in a low voice, "Is that a gun in your pocket or are you just happy to see me?" It was supposed to be à la Mae West but it sounded more like Minnie Pearl.

Crow pretended to wake up, but Val elbowed him lightly in the ribs.

"You're a lousy actor, Crow."

"Damn it, Jim, I'm a lover, not an actor." He was convinced he sounded exactly like Dr. McCoy. He was equally mistaken.

Smiling, Val rolled over toward him and kissed him. Chastely. On the forehead. "You were spying, weren't you?"

"Who?" he said. "Me?"

She reached down under the blankets and closed her hand around him. "This is an official lie detector."

"Yikes . . . what'd you do, wash in cold water?"

"Aha! You were watching, you complete sneak!" She was smiling. Her eyes were a brilliant dark blue, darker now under the overhang of the covers. Behind the curtain windows dawn was brightening to a golden intensity and there were late-season birds singing. Crow could hear the rustle of the cornstalks in the fields beyond the window, and it sounded like waves rolling up onto the beach.

Val's hand was still there.

"You caught me, Sheriff!" he confessed. "I throw myself on the mercy of the court."

Val's smile changed from sleepy to devilish. "Sorry, pal, but no mercy for the condemned in this court." And she hooked a warm leg over him and climbed on top. Even then she had the presence of mind to pull a sheet up around her left shoulder.

"If you don't come down for breakfast in the next minute I'm feeding this to the cows!" The voice boomed up from two flights below just as Crow was lacing up his sneakers. Val was still in the shower.

"Your dad's calling," he yelled in through the now closed bathroom door. "Again."

"You go. I've got to dry my hair."

"Love you, baby!"

"Love you, too!"

Grinning, Crow headed out of the bedroom and jogged down the stairs, humming Lightin' Hopkins's "Black Ghost Blues." The song had been in his head for days now and he meant to see if he could download it off the Net later on.

Malcolm Crow was a compact man, only an inch taller than Val's five-seven and built slim without being skinny. He had the springy step of a kid half his age, and when he played basketball he was up and down the court so fast he just wore out the bigger and better players. His black hair was as smooth and black as his namesake's feathers, and it gave him a Native American look that was at odds with his Scottish ancestry. Crow had a lot of white teeth and he smiled easily and often, as he was now as he bounded into the vast kitchen of the Guthrie house.

Henry Guthrie was at the stove using a spatula to stack slices of French toast onto a metal serving tray. Plates of bacon and sausage and a dish of scrambled eggs were already on the table.

"If you're quite through being a bother and a burden to my daughter," Guthrie said sternly, "then see if you have enough strength left to take this over to the table."

"My strength comes from purity," Crow said, hefting the plate. "As well you know."

"Then you must be as weak as a kitten."

"Ouch." Crow thumped down the plate and slid onto one end of a hardwood bench at the far end of the massive oak table. There were enough plates and cups scattered around to show that several people had already eaten and left. Crow knew from long experience that the Guthrie kitchen was in nearly constant use by field foremen and supervisors, the Guthries themselves, and various other people who happened to be passing, from the seed merchant to the milkman. Despite Guthrie's threat of giving the breakfast to the cows, they didn't actually own any.

Guthrie poured coffee for Crow and then for himself and sat down in the big captain's chair at the other end of the table.

"So, what's on your agenda?" Guthrie asked. He checked the hall to make sure Val wasn't looking before adding real sugar and half-and-half to his coffee instead of Splenda and skim milk.

With a mouthful of French toast, Crow said, "Got to go over to the hayride and do some work. Couple of the traps need some repairs." Pine Deep boasted the largest Haunted Hayride in the country. It was owned by Crow's friend Terry Wolfe, but Crow was the one who designed it and kept it in top shape. He personally devised each of the "traps"—the spots where the monsters jumped out at the customers and scared the living hell out of them. Each of Crow's traps was very elaborate. "After that," he said, swallowing and reaching for the bacon, "I guess I'll head into town to open up the shop."

"Business okay?"

"Doing great." Crow's other concern was a small arts and crafts store on Main Street, where he sold art supplies, fancy paper for scrapbookers, even knitting yarn, but which turned into Halloween central this time of year. Even with the crop blight that was hitting the local farms, and the resulting economic slump, Halloween was still the number-one business in Pine Deep.

Munching bacon, Crow assessed Henry Guthrie. Val's dad was getting up there now, and high-tech farming or not, the fields took their toll. He looked every one of his sixty-four years, and perhaps a bit more. His bushy black eyebrows had become wilder and shot with silver, and since Val's mother died two years ago, Guthrie's head of hair had gone completely gray. Even so, his blueberry-blue eyes sparkled with youth and mischief.

"I'm thinking of taking Val to New Hope next weekend. Just to get away for a day or so. Can you spare her?"

"Well," Guthrie said, considering, "without her the farm will collapse, I'll be financially ruined and will have to live in a cardboard box under the overpass, but other than that I don't see why you two shouldn't have some time."

"Cool."

"Oh, I ran into your buddy—His Honor, I mean."

"Terry? Where'd you trip over him?"

Guthrie almost said that they'd met in the waiting room of the psychiatrist they both shared—Henry for grief management and Terry for who knew what?—but shifted into a different lane when he realized he didn't know if Crow knew that Terry Wolfe was in therapy at all. He said, "In town. I had a few errands to run."

Crow grunted, eating more bacon.

"He doesn't look too good these days," Guthrie said.

"Yeah. He says he's been having trouble sleeping. Nightmares, that sort of thing." Crow wasn't looking at Guthrie while he spoke. He was having some nightmares as well, and didn't want Val's very sharp and perceptive dad to see anything in his eyes.

"Well, I hope he takes care of himself. Terry always was a little high-strung."

The batwing saloon doors that separated the kitchen from the main dining room creaked as Mark Guthrie, Val's brother, pushed through. He was a few years younger than Val but was beefy and out of shape, and unlike his father Mark was starting to lose his hair. He wore a gray wool business suit and was reading the headlines of the *Black Marsh Sentinel*.

"Morning, Dad, morning, Crow."

"Hey," Crow said, waving at him with a forkful of sausage.

"It's all on the table," Guthrie said. "Sit down and let me pour you a cup."

They sat there and ate, and Mark gently shifted the conversation to local business, discussing the financial crisis in town without actually mentioning the phrase "crop blight." So far it hadn't hit the Guthrie farm, but some of their neighbors had been devastated by it. Mark, who was a nice but rather pedantic guy, offered his views on how to solve everyone's financial woes by the right investments. Guthrie nodded as if he agreed, which he didn't, and Crow ate his way through a lot of the food. Val's brother ran the student aid department of Pinelands College and therefore held himself up as an expert on anything dealing with finances.

Crow let him talk, grunting and nodding whenever there was a pause, and when there was an opening, he jumped in and said, "Well, fellas, much as I hate to eat and run . . . I'm going to anyway. Mark, see you around. Henry, I'll probably see you later. Val said she's going to make dinner for me tonight."

Both of the Guthrie men stared at him as if he'd just said that blue ferrets were going to pop out of his ears.

"Val?" Guthrie said.

"Cook?" Mark said.

And they burst out laughing.

"If she hears you she will so kick both your asses," said Crow, but they were right. In all the years Crow and Val had known each other she'd only cooked for him a few times and it had always ended badly.

They were still laughing as Crow jogged upstairs, gently pushed aside the hair dryer, kissed Val in a way that made them both tingle, and then ran downstairs again. Now Henry and Mark were exchanging horror stories about some of Val's previous attempts at cooking. Mark was as red as a beet and slapping his palm on the table as they guffawed about something dealing with a pumpkin pie and a case of dysentery.

Whistling to himself, Crow strolled across the broad gravel driveway to where his old Chevy squatted under a beech tree. The song he was whistling was "Black Ghost Blues," though he wasn't consciously aware of it.

(2)

Terry Wolfe rolled over onto his side as if in sleep he was trying to turn away from his dream. It didn't work. The dream pursued him, as determined this morning as it had been for the last ten nights. As cruelly persistent as it had been, off and on, since the season had begun. Since the blight had started.

His face and throat were slick with sweat. Beside him, Sarah moaned softly in her sleep, her dreams also troubled, but in a less specific way, as if the content of hidden dreams tainted hers, but somehow in her sleep she was only aware of a sense of threat rather than of the nature of it.

Terry's hands gripped his pillow with ferocious force, his fingernails clawing at the thick cool cotton as he dreamed. . . .

In dreams Terry was not Terry. In dreams, Terry was something else.

Some.

Thing.

Else.

In dreams, Terry did not lie sleeping next to his wife. In dreams, Terry always woke up and turned to Sarah and . . .

The part of Terry that was aware that he was dreaming cringed as he watched what the dreaming *thing* did. That part of Terry cringed and cried out and wept as he watched the *thing* pull back the covers from Sarah's sleeping form and bend over her, dark eyes flashing as they drank in her curves and her softness and her vulnerability. The watching Terry tried to scream as the *thing* opened its mouth—and the sleeping body of Terry Wolfe actually opened his mouth, too—and leaned closer still to Sarah, teeth bared, mouth watering with an awful hunger.

No! the watching Terry screamed—but the scream only took the form of a choked growl.

It was enough, though. The tightening of his throat and the desperation of his need to cry out snapped the line that tethered him to the nightmare and he popped awake. He lay there, chest heaving, throat raw from the strangled cry, sweat soaking him.

Somewhere behind the curtains morning birds absurdly argued that it was a sunny, wonderful day and all was right with the world. Terry would gladly have taken a shotgun to them.

He sat up, his muscles aching from the long hours of dreaming tension. Sarah was still asleep, curled into a ball, her face buried in a spill of black hair and crumpled pillows. Standing, Terry looked down at her, at her lovely lines, smelling the faintness of her perfume in the bedroom air. He loved her so much that tears burned in his eyes and he wondered—not for the first time—if he should kill himself.

Every morning the idea had more appeal, and every morning it seemed like it would be the best thing he could ever do for her.

Terry wrenched himself away from staring at her and lumbered into the bathroom. He leaned both hands on the cool rim of the sink and stared at his reflection. Every day there was just a moment of dread when he brought his face to the mirror—wondering if today was the day he would see the beast and not the man, if today he would wear the face he wore in his dreams.

It was just his own face. Broad, square, with curly red hair, a short beard that was not as precisely trimmed as it once was. Bloodshot blue eyes that looked back at him, shifty and full of guilt for something he just could not name. He was five weeks shy of forty and normally looked five years younger than that. Now he looked fifty, or even sixty.

He opened the medicine cabinet and selected from among a dozen orange-brown prescription bottles until he found the clozapine, tipped one into his mouth, and washed it down with four glasses of water. The antipsychotic gave him terrible dry mouth. He put another of the pills into a small plastic pill case along with half a dozen Xanax and snapped it shut, feeling edgy and strangely guilty as he did so. He glanced up at the mirror again.

"Good morning, Mr. Mayor," he said, hating the face he saw, and then he set about washing and brushing and constructing the face he needed everyone else in town to see.

(3)

Crow pulled out of the long Guthrie driveway and turned northeast along Interstate Extension A-32, heading to Old Mill Road and the Haunted Hayride that was nestled back in between the Pinelands College campus and the sprawling southern reach of the great Pine Deep State Forest. He had stopped whistling to himself and was now singing along badly to a Nick Cave CD. As his battered old Chevy, Missy, rolled up between corn farms and berry farms, Crow sang his way through the Bad Seeds' raucous and obscene version of "Stagger Lee," a song he could never play in anything like polite company. To Crow, there was nothing particularly strange about starting a lovely late September morning off with a ballad about mass murder and pederasty.

He sang badly and loud and the miles rolled away as the car took the hills and jags and twists of A-32 with practiced ease.

A busload of migrant day workers passed, heading for the Guthrie farm, and Crow tooted to Toby, the driver and crew boss. A few of the workers waved at him and he waved back. Most of them were Haitians and there were half a dozen among them that Henry Guthrie was considering taking on full-time.

Behind the bus were two cars—both with people Crow knew—and beyond them the first of the day's school buses. It was just hitting 7:00 a.m. and already the town was up and about. Nobody sleeps late in farm country.

Crow's cell phone beeped—the tune was "I Got My Mojo Working"—and he flipped it open. "Hello, Miss Beechum's Country Dayschool," he said.

"Hey there," Val said. "I just had a very, very nice flashback."

He turned down the CD player. "Yeah, baby . . . me too. You are the most delicious woman in the world, you know that?"

"Mmm," she purred. "You may be a goofball, Mr. Crow, but the things you do to me. Wow."

"Gotta say that it's pretty darned mutual. Three times between eleven-thirty last night and six this morning. My oh my. It's like being eighteen again."

"I wanted you to know that I'll be thinking of this morning for the rest of the day. Bye-bye," she said, and disconnected.

As he drove, Crow's grin was brighter than the sun that now shone above the distant waving fields of corn.

(4)

In his dreams he was always Iron Mike Sweeney, the Enemy of Evil. In dreams he wasn't fourteen—he was fully grown and packed with muscle head to toe. No one could possibly stand up to him, and no one dared attack him. He was the agent of Order pitted eternally against the nefarious forces of Chaos. He was the quiet stranger who came to troubled towns and brought rough justice with his lightning fists, flashing feet, and cleverly disguised array of ultra-high-tech weaponry. He was the immortal Soldier of Light who carried the torch of reason and understanding through the growing and malevolent shadows of night. Demons fled before him; vampires would wither into noxious clouds of dust as he turned his Solar Gaze on them. The androids of the Dark Order, powerful as they were, could never match the thunderstorm power in his hard-knuckled hands. Iron Mike was the single most powerful warrior this old world had ever seen.

Even now the Enemy of Evil was holding the Bridge of Gelderhaus against the forces of Prince Viktor and his slavering band of genetic freaks, each of them armed with laser swords and shock-rods.

The battle had raged all night but Iron Mike Sweeney was not tired. His sword arm was as strong and steady as it had been when he drew his titanium rune-blade and braced himself, legs wide, at the mouth of the bridge while behind him the citizens of Gelderhaus cowered. Wave after wave of the genetic Warhounds had come charging him, but time and again Iron Mike's unbreakable sword had smashed them down and beaten them back. The gorge far below the bridge was choked with their corpses and the river ran red with their radioactive blood.

Now the Warhounds had fallen back and Prince Viktor himself was striding across the bridge, his sword *Deathpall* in his gauntleted hand. He stopped, just out of sword's reach, his eyes blazing with hatred, his mouth trembling with frustrated rage.

"You shall not pass!" roared Iron Mike Sweeney in a voice that echoed from the walls on both sides of the gorge.

Hissing with fury, Prince Viktor raised his sword and cried—

"—get the fuck out of bed now or do you want me to come up there?"

The roar jolted Mike out of the dream and his body was obeying before his mind could even process what was going on.

"Do you fucking *hear* me?"

Mike was on his feet and he hurried to his bedroom door and pulled it open, crying, "I'm up, I'm up!"

At the foot of the stairs Vic Wingate—Mike's stepfather— stood with a foot on the first step, his hard right hand gripping the banister. "You deaf or something? I have to call you three times before you even bother to acknowledge my existence? What am I—the fucking maid?"

Mike had to head this off at the pass before Vic really got worked up. Though morning beatings weren't usually Vic's thing, it didn't take a whole lot to set him off.

"Sorry, Vic, I was on the toilet with the door closed."

Vic looked up at him for a moment and the anger gradually turned to a nasty smirk. "Yeah, that figures . . . I always figured you were full of shit. Well, get your ass down here and have your breakfast. I don't want to hear about you being late for school."

"Yes, sir."

"You have papers after school?"

"Yes, sir."

"Well, get them done and get home. Don't be late." He leaned on those last three words.

"I won't."

Vic gave him a last perfunctory glare and marched off. Relieved, Mike sagged back against his door frame, exhaling the stale air that was pent up in his chest.

Downstairs he heard Vic yelling something at Mike's mother, and then the door slamming as he left for work. Vic was the chief mechanic at Shanahan's Garage in town and he was never late for work even though it didn't matter what time he got there. Like most people, Shanahan was afraid of Vic and wouldn't have dared risk pissing him off any more than Mike would.

"Eat shit and die," Mike whispered to the closed door down-stairs.

"Honey?" his mother's voice called. It wasn't seven o'clock yet and she already sounded half in the bag. Or maybe she hadn't sobered up from last night. "Breakfast is on the table."

"Yeah, I'm coming." Breakfast would be a box of cereal and some orange juice. Mike went and sat down on the edge of the bed, fingers knotted together, shoulders hunched, staring at the patterns of sunlight on the gray indoor-outdoor carpet on his floor. He tried to remember his dream—something about a bridge—but it was gone. "Just another day," he said aloud. He said it nearly every morning, usually in the same way, with the same total lack of enthusiasm.

This time, however, he was wrong.

(5)

Tow-Truck Eddie always started his day on his knees. As soon as he got out of bed, even if he had to go to the bathroom, he first dropped onto his knees, right on the cold wood floor, and prayed. He had a number of required prayers he had to say before he could start speaking directly to God, and he recited the Lord's Prayer precisely fourteen times, which was twice seven—the number of God that was superior to six, the number of the Beast—and then said a rosary, a dozen Hail Marys. He crossed himself seven times, and then laid his head on the floor, his heavy brow pressed against the floorboards, until he heard the voice of God in his head.

Sometimes it would take an hour or more before God spoke to him, and by then his bladder would be screaming at him, but lately—just in the last few weeks—God spoke to him more quickly. Tow-Truck Eddie knew that this was a very good sign, and he suspected that it meant that God would soon be revealing his Holy Mission to him.

This morning his head had barely touched the cool wood when God's voice thundered in his brain.

Today, my child! it said. The Voice of God was almost too loud to bear and Eddie's head rang with it.

"Yes, my Lord. I am thy instrument. Command me to the holy purpose."

You are my faithful servant, God said, *and you are my holy instrument on earth. Do you know this?*

"Yes, my Lord."

You are the enemy of the Beast. Do you know this?

"Yes, my Lord."

You are the Hand of Righteousness. Do you know this?

"Yes, my Lord."

You are the Sword of God. Do you know this?

"Oh, *yes*, my Lord!"

When the Hand of Righteousness beholds the Beast, what is thy holy purpose?

"To destroy him, my Lord! I am the servant of God!"

And if the Beast should take another form?

"Satan is the Father of Lies. The *Beast* is the Father of Lies. With God as my Lord I shall see through his disguise and know the Beast—and knowing him I will destroy him, for such is the will of God."

And if the Beast were to appear as an ordinary man?

"I would destroy him, for the *Beast* is the Father of Lies. Such is the will of God."

And if the Beast were to appear as a woman?

"I would destroy him, for the *Beast* is the Father of Lies. Such is the will of God."

And if the Beast were to appear as a child?

"I would destroy him, for the *Beast* is the Father of Lies. Such is the will of God." This was an old litany between them, and only once, in the very beginning, had Tow-Truck Eddie hesitated—just for a moment—at this point, but not today. Now his voice was strong, filled with clarity and purpose.

And to this holy purpose do you dedicate yourself?

"I am the instrument of the Lord and his will is as my own. With my body, my heart, and my immortal soul shall I serve the will of the Lord."

In my servant I am well pleased.

Gratitude flooded through Eddie and he wept, his head still pressed to the floor.

See this face. This is the face of the Beast that was.

A man's face appeared in Eddie's mind—a thin black man with blood on his clothes. Eddie knew him at once. This was the face that the Beast had worn thirty years ago—the face he'd worn when he had cut a bloody swath through the town. Eddie knew that face, had confronted him and had given him a chance to confess his evils, but the man had lied again—*the Beast is the Father of Lies*—and Eddie had struck him down. Other men had been there to help, but Eddie had struck the most telling blow. The killing blow.

The Beast has returned and wears a new face.

Eddie jumped. Always before the litany had ended at this point, but this was new and his flush of gratitude changed, becoming an immediate charge of thrilling electricity. God's voice was filled with rage and Eddie trembled.

This then is the new face of the Beast. Look upon the face of the Beast and behold his deceptions.

Tow-Truck Eddie raised his face an inch, two inches, then a foot, and stared into the empty air. Instantly there was an image there—not floating in the air or described in the grain of the boards—but burning in his mind. A figure, slight and shabby, in jeans and a baggy Windbreaker. It was a young person, a boy of no more than thirteen or fourteen, with curly red hair and pale skin and dark blue eyes. He was riding a bicycle along the black wavering length of a road that Eddie knew only too well. A-32.

Behold the Beast! roared the voice of God with such thunder that Eddie's nose began to bleed.

Eddie pawed the blood away, wiping it on his thigh as he stared at the image in his mind.

"I am the Sword of God," he croaked through the agony in his skull. "I am the instrument of the Lord and his will is as my own. With my body, my heart, and my immortal soul shall I serve the will of the Lord."

This is your holy task . . . this is the mission for which you were born unto the earth."

Blood flowed freely now from both nostrils but Eddie didn't care. Through a throat choked with blood and while tears streamed down his face, he said, "I am the Sword of God . . . thy will be done!"

(6)

"How was last night's take?" Crow asked as he gassed up one of the hayride's utility ATVs. Coop was sitting on the top step of the porch out in front of the souvenir shop. "Terry told me they were supposed to bus in some kids from Doylestown."

"Yeah, they brought the whole senior class from the high school," Coop said. He was Terry's brother-in-law and though he was hardly the sharpest nail in the tool kit, Crow liked him. "We were up about eight percent of the daily average, which is what Terry'll like to hear. Though I guess you'd be happy to know that three of the girls came close to getting hysterical from screaming."

Crow grinned as he screwed on the cap. "We aim to please."

"You think Terry's ever gonna come out here and see what you've done to the place?"

The Pine Deep Haunted Hayride was the largest and most profitable such attraction in the country. Terry had a staff of over a hundred teenagers and adults, he charged a frightening fee for tickets, had an amazing concession stand that sold everything from pumpkin-flavored milkshakes to Ghoul Burgers, and he carted the cash to the bank more or less in a wheelbarrow. Every year the place made newspapers all up and down the East Coast, and every year the major TV stations from Philly, Harrisburg, and New York did special segments on it. Yet, he never went to his own hayride, not even to inspect it in daylight hours.

"Not a chance. You know Terry."

Five years ago he'd paid Crow a fat piece of change to design it and had kept him on the payroll as a consultant. Except for counting the receipts and signing the paychecks of the staff,

Terry otherwise ignored the hayride. Weird, Crow mused, then thought with wry amusement that Pine Deep was probably the only town in America where a healthy *dis*-interest in the macabre was considered strange. Very, very weird.

"I was over there for dinner the other night," Coop mused, "and I asked him about it. Want to take a guess at what he said?"

"Shit, I can tell you his exact words." He dropped into an approximation of Terry's voice and said, "That hayride's just a cash cow for me."

"Yep."

"He says that about fifty times a season."

"Yep."

"I'm heading out to the zombie graveyard." Crow said, straddling the ATV. "I wanted to boost the smoke machine a bit and maybe repaint the blood on the crypt walls."

"Well, don't make it too real," Coop said. "You'll be giving these kids heart attacks."

Crow shook his head. "My idea of the absolutely perfect version of this hayride is one where the tourists have to take out insurance beforehand and get CPR afterward. Then I'll be happy." He started the ATV and gunned the engine.

"Hell, you're more'n halfway there now."

"Not good enough!" Crow yelled, and headed out into the vast tract of corn and pumpkin fields that was home to his hayride. As he rode, even though it was drowned out by the roar of the engine, he started humming "Black Ghost Blues" again, totally unaware that he was doing it.

Chapter 2

That year the monsters came to town a whole month before Halloween. The monsters didn't wear costumes. No Shreks or Jedi Knights, no Harry Potters or Orc Warriors, no Aragorns or Captain Jack Sparrows. These monsters weren't white-sheeted ghosts peering hopefully out of eyeholes cut in old percale; they weren't hockey-masked slaughterers of young virgins; they weren't four-foot-high tottering Frankensteins with Kmart plastic faces. They didn't caper from house to house with pumpkin-headed flashlights or ghostly green glow-sticks. None of them carried paper sacks filled with ghoulish gatherings of Snicker's bars, sandwich bags full of pennies, apples, and snack-sized Three Musketeers.

They were monsters all the same.

They blew into town on a Halloween wind, coming into Pine Deep along the black length of Extension Route A-32, whisking over Black Marsh Bridge and through the cornfields. They came in a black car that had bloodstains on the door handles and the single unblinking black eye of a bullet hole on the driver's door. The monsters came rushing into town like a storm wind, pushing cold air before them and dragging darkness behind.

There were three monsters in the car. Two of them sat in the front, a third crouched in the back. They all had their monster faces hunched low into the collars of their coats, hidden by the shadows of their hat brims. They were silently snarling, these three monsters. The monster in the backseat bared his teeth in desperation and fear; the monster behind the wheel bared his teeth in pain and hopelessness; but the monster in the front passenger seat bared his teeth in a grin of pernicious delight.

The black car flew with a raven's speed along the dark road, but it did not fly with a raven's precision: it veered and swayed and staggered from one side of the road to the other as if the monster who drove did not know how to control the machine. Yet it continued to drive fast for all its careening and swerving. In it the three silent, hungry monsters rolled into Pine Deep as night closed around the town like a fist.

But there were other monsters in Pine Deep that night. It was that kind of town.

These others did not need to come to town in a bloodstained black car; they were already there, had always been there. One drove through town every day in his own machine, a monstrous wrecker with a gleaming hook; another one labored all day repairing expensive cars and trucks, and labored all night to destroy precious hearts and souls; one walked around town and smiled at everyone and he never knew that a monster looked out of his laughing blue eyes, waiting, waiting . . .

One monster, the worst of all, waited in darkness under wormy dirt, awake now after a long, long sleep.

There were many other monsters in Pine Deep.

Waiting. All of them, waiting.

(2)

Lightning singed the edges of the dark thunderheads, but no rain fell; thunder rumbled distantly, shaking the trees and shaking thousands of soot-colored night birds into startled flight. They swarmed like locusts and then flew back toward the trees, believing themselves safe when the lightning flashed.

One night bird peeled off from the flock and soared through the raw air until it leveled off just above the tips of the corn, skimming along on the breeze, flapping its dark wings only occasionally. It was a ragged bird, its shape defined more by shadows than substance. The fields whisked along beneath it and when it reached the end of one farmer's lot it veered left, drifting across the knobbed expanse of a pumpkin patch. All of the best pumpkins were already gone, picked and sold to supermarkets in Philadelphia and Doylestown, awaiting the jack-o'-lantern surgeons and the bakers of autumn pies. Only the ugly pumpkins remained, the pumpkins too gnarled and deformed for sale as decorations, too diseased to be welcome on any table.

This year there had been more diseased ones than the good kind; this year all across the township and its outlying farmlands hundreds of tons of pumpkins lay rotting, along with truckloads of fetid corn and wormy apples. It was a blighted year for Pine Deep, what the old folks called a Black Harvest, and they unearthed all the tales—short or tall—about the pestilential harvest of thirty years ago, of bad times come again.

The ugly pumpkins squatted in row after hideous row, or stood in huge mounds like heads piled high after a great battle. The night bird circled the biggest mound once, twice, and then veered off again, rediscovering the black road and following it up and over a series of small hills. More cornfields stretched away on either side of the road, and here and there darkened farmhouses began the ritual of turning on lights to combat the invasion of night shadows. The lights did not make the houses look safe and homey: they made them seem impossibly lonely, as if each house were the only house in the whole world, alone and lost in the eternal sea of dryly whispering corn.

The night bird uttered a strange, high shriek; not a caw, but a sound more like the wail of an abandoned and terrified child. The shrill sound floated through the night air, and the people inside the farmhouses, the ones who allowed themselves to hear it or could not block it out, shivered as if some dark and shambling thing were breathing its damp breath on their naked skin. None of them would forget to lock their doors that night, even if they were unaware of the subliminal dread that wail had sown in the soil of their hearts.

One farmhouse, older than the others, more battered by time and cold winds and disinterest, stood at the edge of a vast cornfield and overlooked a couple of acres of flat ground enclosed by a low stone wall. The ivy-covered stone wall embowered a small and disheveled cemetery in which the rows of shadow-painted tombstones stood in snarls of bracken and pernicious weeds. Wailing again, the night bird flew low over the cracked and wind-sanded headstones, circling and circling. No lights shone in the window of the old house. No lights had shone there in months, nor might ever show there again. Only shadows lived there, stirred now and again by the frigid breath of old ghosts. The night bird wailed yet again and flapped noisily toward a tree where it settled on a twisted and gnarled branch that reached out toward the tombstones. In daylight the fading colors of the leaves would have made the promise of beauty, but by starless night the leaves were a uniform and featureless black, forming nothing more than an amorphous bulk against which the night bird disappeared entirely.

The night bird turned a single black eye toward one headstone that leaned drunkenly just below the tree. It had been pushed off-balance by the roots of the tree but was held fast to the ground by one sunken corner and its own ponderous weight. It was a simple tombstone, blocky and gray and cheap, thirty years old and unkindly worn by each of those thirty winters. Chiseled into its face was a name: OREN MORSE.

Below that, a single word had been cut into the lifeless stone: REST. No date, no other inscription. The wind blew brambles and fallen leaves across the grave and one dry leaf, propelled by the vagaries of the breeze, skittered upward to the top of the gravestone and then tumbled over and off into the shadows beyond. Except for the murmuring wind and the whisper of the cornstalks, there was no sound. Even the night bird held its tongue.

Then a man was there.

He stepped out of a shadow and was abruptly there. The night bird let out a startled cry and fluttered its wings, but did not fly away. The man stood quietly looking down at the headstone, his gray lips moving as he read the name. He was scarecrow thin and dressed in a cheap black suit that was smeared with dirt. He wore no topcoat, no hat. His skin was as gray as the gravestones around him, but there was no moon now to shine on it. Still, that pale skin seemed to cast its own weird light. He held his hands loosely at his sides, and every once in a while those long fingers twitched and clutched as if grasping something, or desiring to.

Then he reached down into the shadows behind the tombstone and when he straightened he held the long neck of a battered old blues guitar in his hand. He looped the strap over his shoulder and drew his slender fingers along the silver strings. The friction made a sound like old door hinges creaking open.

Abruptly the whole graveyard was caught in the harsh white glare of headlights as a car crested one of the small hills and rushed down the other side toward the graveyard. The lights shimmered through the trees and danced along the tips of the corn, casting weird capering shadows. The gray man turned, watching as the car drew near, passed, and drove on. The car was moving very fast and swerving as if the driver was drunk. Three shadowy figures hunched in the car's seats, two in the front, one in the back. Tires squealed as the car careered along the road, sashaying from one lane to the other and back, and then finally settling on a course dead center, as if the grille were devouring the single yellow line. The machine roared past a large billboard that read:

THREE MILES TO PINE DEEP,
THE MOST HAUNTED TOWN IN AMERICA . . .
WE'LL SCARE YOU SILLY!

If the men in the car noticed the sign, they gave no indication. Their shadowed heads didn't turn as they passed the sign, the engine never slowed. The car clawed its way up the far hill, and in a few minutes the taillights were gone, fading first to tiny red dots, like rat's eyes, and then vanishing altogether. A minute later the sound of the engine was gone as well.

The man in the graveyard stared into the distance, his eyes squinting as if he could still distantly see the car, though it was impossible in those deep shadows. His eyes lingered briefly on the billboard and the irony was not lost on him.

Again lightning flickered behind the clouds. In the tree, the night bird shivered its wings and uttered its strange wailing cry.

With a final lingering glance at the tombstone, the thin man tugged on the strap so that the guitar hung behind him, with the neck hanging down low behind his right hip; then he turned and began walking. He walked slowly and without haste, his long legs maintaining a steady, deliberate pace, like that of a pall-bearer. He stepped onto the road and began walking in the direction taken by the car and its three passengers. His shoes made no sound on the blacktop. Lightning flashed again and again, a deception of a storm, but the storm was elsewhere. The lightning cast brief but bold shadows across the road, the wall of the graveyard, the gnarled tree, the night bird . . . everything starkly cast its shadow onto the blacktop. Everything except the man who walked without making a sound.

With slow and measured steps, he climbed the long hill and was soon lost in darkness. The night, and the night bird, followed after.

(3)

"Jesus Christ, Tony!" Boyd yelped, gripping the back of the driver's seat with his one good hand. "Watch it!"

Tony Macchio wrestled the wheel and pulled the car back into the right-hand lane, missing the oncoming milk truck by inches. The car swayed drunkenly on its springs as Tony fought to steady it with clumsy hands. His fingers were caked with dried blood, and they felt cold and weak. He could barely even feel the knobbed arc of the steering wheel.

"What the fuck's wrong with you?" snapped Boyd as the car finally settled into balance and began accelerating again, climbing a long hill.

Tony coughed once but didn't say anything. His stomach felt hot and acidy, and he had too much phlegm in his throat. He just shook his head. Next to him, looking casual in spite of the wild ride, Karl Ruger watched Tony. Ruger's eyes were cold slits, but he was smiling. The smile and the eyes seemed as if they belonged to two different faces: the smile seemed warm and pleasant and affable, but above the smile Ruger looked at Tony with the expressionless eyes of a reptile. Eyes the color of dusty slate, like a blackboard from which all the writing had been forcefully erased. Ruger had a long, thin nose that arced over the mouth like the blade of a very sharp knife, a pointed chin, and a sharp, strong jawline. His cheekbones hung like ledges over the concavity of hollow cheeks, and Ruger's brow was high and clear but cut by the black dagger-point of a widow's peak. He took off his hat and smoothed his greased hair flat against his skull. If he had had a kinder face, he could have looked like a stage magician, and he did have the air of magic about him; but it was a dark magic, and it clung to his soul and to his face, and to his fate. The dark magic was there in his long white fingers and in the shadows of his black, black heart.

Karl Ruger looked at Tony and smiled as he watched the man slowly die.

He found it fascinating to watch as Tony tried to cling to consciousness, tried to deny the coiled snake of pain in his gut where the Jamaican's bullet had capped him. Gut shots were ag-onizing, Ruger knew, and he marveled at the manner in which Tony tried to bull his way through what must be searing pain. Idly, Ruger wondered if the loss of blood was providing Tony with some kind of insulation against the pain. God knows he'd lost a lot of it. Tony was sitting in a lake of it, and more of it was pooled around his feet. The fresh-cut copper smell of blood teased Ruger's senses, and he wondered, not for the first time, why no one had ever made an aftershave that smelled like fresh blood.

The car rolled past a sign that read: WELCOME TO PINE DEEP! Ruger felt a cold wind blow through his chest. It was scary, but he liked it. He mouthed the name of the town, silently tasting it. Pine Deep. Yes. He closed his eyes and for just a moment he thought he heard a voice say: *Ruger, you are my left hand*. But no one had spoken. He opened his eyes and stared at the unfolding black road, feeling the prickle of expectant excitement in his chest, but at a loss to understand why it was there or what it meant.

Boyd asked again what the fuck was wrong with Tony, and Ruger watched as Tony tried to say something but only managed to blow a small bubble of viscous red between his purple lips. Ruger was fascinated by the bubble as it expanded, filled with Tony's ragged breath, and then popped. A mist of tiny droplets dotted the windshield.

"Yo! Tony!" Boyd snapped.

"Shut up, Boyd," whispered Ruger. He always spoke in a whisper. It was all he could manage since a spic in Holmesburg Prison had stabbed him in the throat during a small dispute between Ruger's own Aryan Brotherhood and the brown-skinned critters on the Block. The spic had wanted to kill him so bad he had a hard-on, an actual hard-on, as he drove a sharpened spoon into Karl's throat. Ruger could feel the hard length of the man's dick when he had grabbed the spic's groin and squeezed it. Makeshift knife in the throat or not, Ruger had all but ripped the man's pecker off before one of the other Aryan Brothers had stepped in and cut the spic's throat with a sliver of sheet metal that he'd stolen from the machine shop. The other Brother had taken the rap for the kill, which was fine for Ruger because he didn't get any time added to his stretch. The spoon had not really done him much harm, just a nick on the larynx and a bit of pain. Big deal. Pain didn't mean a goddamn thing to Ruger. Pain was just a "thing" that sometimes happened. And if his voice was now a hoarse and ghostly whisper, well, that was fine. It scared the shit out of a lot of people, and it made them listen closely to whatever he had to say.

"What the hell, Karl? He almost wrapped us around that truck!"

"He's doing fine," Ruger whispered. "Just fine."

Tony turned and looked at Ruger for a moment, his brows knitted together and glistening with cold sweat.

"Fine, my ass!" Boyd said. "He took one back there."

"So did you. So what?"

"Yeah, but I only got clipped and I ain't driving the fucking car. Look at him, man! He's halfway to being dead."

More than halfway, Ruger thought. "He's fine. Aren't you, Tony?"

Tony glanced at him again, his eyes bright with fever but seeing only about half of the things he was looking at. He tried to speak, wanted to actually agree with Boyd, wanted to stop the car so one of them could drive. Boyd had only been shot through the left biceps; he could drive if he had to. Ruger hadn't even been touched, but when he looked in Ruger's eyes, into those icy reptilian eyes, Tony couldn't find the courage to say anything. He felt trapped by that ophidian stare and by the bullet in his belly, completely unable to understand why Ruger was pushing him to drive. It didn't make any sense to him. Ruger was a survivor type, so why would he risk dying in such a stupid and pointless way? Tony had never been able to figure Ruger out, and lately it had been even harder. He knew that Ruger was one evil son of a bitch, but now he thought that he was a little crazy, too.

Maybe more than a little.

Boyd had seen Ruger go crazy on the Jamaicans back at the warehouse. He'd shot nearly all of them himself and then instead of fleeing like anyone halfway sane, the crazy fuck had taken a shovel from the trunk and used the blade to chop them up. Boyd had thrown up watching it and when he'd tried to pull Ruger away, the psychopath had wheeled on him, his face streaked with blood, and had given him a look that made Boyd want to piss his pants. He nearly did.

"Aren't you, Tony?" Ruger asked again, leaning on the question and nudging the driver's shoulder with the tip of a long white finger.

Tony nodded, just once, and then concentrated on the road. For a few minutes he managed to keep the car steady, but with each mile, each minute, it became harder to do. It was like trying to hold on to something from a dream.

Boyd shook his head disgustedly and sank back against the

cushion. His arm hurt like all hell, but the bleeding had stopped. He had a towel wound around it, and kept it in place with steady pressure from his good hand. Tears burned in his eyes, but he turned his head and looked out at the night, hoping that Ruger hadn't seen them.

Ruger, of course, had. His cold eyes missed very little. He saw Boyd's tears just as clearly as he saw the blood and the life seeping out of Tony's gut. He upped the wattage on his smile and chuckled low in his throat, too low to be heard over the roar of the engine.

Three minutes later, Tony crashed the car.

Chapter 3

"This place is a slaughterhouse."

Detective Sergeant Frank Ferro nodded but said nothing. He and Detective Vince LaMastra stood shoulder to shoulder in the doorway of the warehouse. Ferro was tall, his younger partner much taller, and their shadows stretched far across the bloody floor. There were corpses and spent shell casings everywhere. The stink of cordite hung like a pall in the close air of the warehouse, but beneath the gunpowder reek they could smell the blood.

Ferro tapped the shoulder of a uniformed officer who was busily sketching the scene in his notebook. "Al, who's been called?"

The officer looked up. "Hey, Sarge. Some mess, huh?"

"Yeah. OK Corral. Who's been called?" he asked again.

"M.E.'s on his way, and the photographer's already around back taking some shots. A BOLO's been sent out already for Ruger's car."

"You're sure it was Ruger?" LaMastra asked, brightening.

"Yeah, the surveillance team got a positive on him and was about to make the call to you guys when this shit storm went down."

"Where are they?"

"Northeastern Hospital. Ruger must have sniffed them 'cause he fired a clip into the van when he and the others took off."

"Jim and Nelly hurt bad?"

Al snorted. "They're lucky as shit. Cuts from glass and debris, but they hit the deck on the first shot and all the other rounds just tore up the can. Missed them completely."

"What about Johnston?"

The officer shook his head. "He's around back."

Ferro's lugubrious brown face tightened and he flicked a quick glance at LaMastra. A muscle was bunching and flexing in the younger man's clamped jaw.

Al led them around back to where Johnston lay in a limp sprawl, arms flung out and legs wide in a red pool. The photographer moved around him and LaMastra as if they weren't there, taking shot after shot.

"You almost done?" Ferro asked, and the photographer took another shot before answering.

"Yeah," he said as let his camera hang from its strap. "I'm ready to do the inside now."

Alone, Ferro and LaMastra looked down at the corpse.

"Jesus H. Christ," LaMastra breathed.

They said nothing for a couple of minutes, letting time pass, sorting things out, keeping their cop faces intact despite what was going on behind their eyes.

"Ruger," LaMastra said, needlessly.

"Yeah."

"Bastard."

"Yeah."

"Now he's killed a cop."

"Yeah," Ferro said in a dead voice.

LaMastra's jaw muscles kept clenching.

A moment later a uniformed officer came sprinting around the corner of the warehouse. "Sarge!"

Ferro and LaMastra turned. "What is it?"

"It's Ruger . . . he's been spotted!"

(2)

Vic Wingate fell asleep in his Barcalounger in front of the TV, his feet up and ankles crossed, one hand closed limply around a long-necked bottle of beer that had gone tepid, the other lying palm down on his crotch. He wore a pair of faded blue boxers and a Pine Deep Softball T-shirt. He'd never played softball in his life; the shirt was a leftover from Lois's first husband, Big John Sweeney.

Vic slept and dreamed and his faced was bathed with a greasy sheen of cool sweat. Behind his eyelids his eyes jumped and twitched and every once in a while his hand closed around his balls. . . .

Vic stood in the forest, deep in the shadows in the bowels of Dark Hollow, the toes of his work boots sinking into the muddy fringe at the edge of the swamp as he leaned forward and whispered.

"It's almost ready," he hissed. "Everything's just about in place." There was silence except for the incessant drone of the mosquitoes and the hoot of a scraggly old owl in the branches of a blighted sycamore.

Vic knelt, almost losing his balance, and for a moment he windmilled his arms as he fought for balance. Much as he loved that which lay beneath the mud and muck, he did not want to touch it. It was not time for that kind of embrace.

"I've done everything you wanted," Vic said as he crept farther back up the bank and onto firmer ground. He licked his lips and then smiled. "Everything . . . and a few more things. Stuff I thought up."

A crow cawed loudly and flapped down through the branches and landed on the far side of the swamp. It cocked its head and fixed him with an eye that was as black and expressionless as a bead of polished onyx.

Vic stared at it for a moment and then dropped his eyes to the leaf-strewn surface of the swamp. He reached out a hand and just glided his fingers along the surface debris. "The world's changed a lot," he said. "There's stuff I had to do that we hadn't thought of before."

The bird rustled its feathers and he looked hard at it, squinting in the gloom.

"A lot of things have changed."

The bird stared back.

Vic looked back down at the mud. "I've taken care of everything." He paused and a slow, cold smile wriggled onto his thin lips. "Everything."

In his sleep, Vic shifted, a faint smile on his mouth. Beneath his hand he grew hard.

(3)

Ruger saw it happen just in time to save his own life. That he saved the others, too, was inconsequential to him. He saw it because he was waiting for it, because he wanted it to happen. He needed it to happen, knew it *would* happen. He'd know that ever since he'd seen the name of the town and heard the voice speaking in his head. He didn't know exactly what *would* happen, in fact could never have predicted the exact event that caused the wreck, but he knew the wreck—or something like it—was inevitable.

For weeks now he had felt that Death was dogging his heels and that sooner or later it was going to jump him. That, or maybe he'd find some way to turn it around and spit in Death's eye. He found himself taking outrageous risks lately, risks like letting a dying man drive his getaway car. Instead of dreading the nearness of death, Ruger had started to groove on it, getting an almost erotic high from the nearness to total blackness. It jazzed him higher than a spike in the vein, and he'd been running on that high for days now, first planning the drug scam with the Jamaican posse, then forcing the deal to go sour by mouthing off to the chief of the Jamaican crew, then the shoot-out at the warehouse, and now this doomed flight.

It had all been good, all been a wild high. He knew that it would somehow end in a fireball of some kind, and he was perched on the edge of his perception, waiting to take control of it, to force the events to bend to his will, as so many other events in his life had been twisted to his will. There was no rush like it. When Tony lost it, it would be up to Ruger to take Lady Death by the tits and give her a tweak. That's how he saw it. Give Lady Death's tits a good tweak. *No*, he thought in the split second before the car went out of control. *Not fuck me, you cold bitch—fuck you.*

If he lived through the wreck, it was because his will was strong enough, and that, he knew, would mean that he'd been right all along about something a Gypsy lady had told him: that he was "special," that he was protected from ordinary death. Maybe even immortal, a concept he did not consider either outlandish or absurd. If he died . . . well then, he'd just go rushing into that great big blackness with a hard-on and a curse on his laughing lips and see if the darkness could hold him.

This is how the wreck happened. The black car rounded a bend in the road, leaving the canal behind, and zoomed onto a long stretch of straight highway that clove through seemingly endless cornfields. The ranks of dry corn stood at attention on either side of the car as it whisked along the blacktop, and the car's slipstream made them sway and whisper. Tony's hands gripped the wheel so tightly that his knuckles were bone white in the places where they weren't stained with blood. He kept trying to grip harder just to be able to feel something, but the hands at the ends of his wrists were merely dead lumps abruptly ending in coldness. He could not feel any of his fingers or even his palms. He kept looking at the wheel just to make sure he was actually holding it.

They approached a crossroads where a farm road cut the highway and Tony was looking at his hands when the man walked out of the right-hand cornfield and stopped in the middle of the road. Tony looked up just in time to see the man stop dead in the spray of the headlights. Maybe it was a trick of the light, or maybe it was his own failing vision, but Tony thought the man—a tall, pale man with blond hair and heavy features—seemed only as substantial as mist, that the burning light of the headlights cut right through him and that he cast no shadow on the ground.

The man grinned nastily at the onrushing car. His skin was

white as snow. Not merely pale, not even the white pink of an albino, but as white as the cocaine in the trunk, as white as Tony's knuckles, as white as Ruger's teeth when he smiled. The white man stood there, his blond hair fluttering in the storm breeze, his lips curled into a grin as evil and hungry as Ruger's own.

Tony screamed, and then Ruger swiveled around from looking at the driver and saw the man loom in the headlights and just for a moment he felt a flash of recognition punch through his brain like a bullet.

"Ruger," he thought he heard the man say in a heavily accented voice, but it was impossible at that distance and at that speed to have heard anything. "Ruger, you are my left hand."

Time instantly *slowed down*.

The car seemed to almost freeze around him and Tony and Boyd were like mannequins, their mouths opened in comical parodies of screams. Only the man in the road seemed to exist in real time. He raised a hand and beckoned to Ruger.

Ruger's mouth moved to form the name "Griswold" and the shape of it felt familiar on his lips and tongue.

The ghostly figure spoke. "Vic Wingate has been my John the Baptist . . . he has paved the way. But you, Karl . . . you will be my Peter, my rock, and on this rock I will build my church." The voice echoing in Ruger's head was heavy with mockery, but he liked the sound of it.

All at once time caught up to Ruger and the car hurtled at the man too fast to stop or even veer. Tony screamed again and the instant of contact (or had it been a hallucination brought on by stress?) was gone. Tony's hands were moving all over the wheel and instantly Ruger knew what was about to happen. Tony swung the wheel to the right, trying to swerve around the apparition, but he was ham-fisted with blood loss and overdid the turn. The car lurched away from the man, missing him by less than a foot, and rocketed off the road out of all control. Ruger grabbed the wheel with both hands, shoving Tony against the door. He fought the wild turn, swerving into it with a gentle angularity, preventing it from becoming a tumble. The car jolted as the front wheels hit the edge of the drainage ditch forming a border between road and field. The car almost nose-dived into the ditch, but Ruger jerked hard on the wheel to correct the angle, and a microsecond later the back wheels slammed into the edge of the ditch. The impact slackened some of the car's momentum, but Tony's foot was still on the accelerator and the sedan plowed into the cornfield like a runaway train. Cornstalks whipped at the windows and died beneath the wheels in sharp crunches of agony.

"Get your fucking foot off the pedal!" Ruger hissed. When Tony didn't, or couldn't, Ruger cocked his arm and drove his elbow into Tony's nose once, twice. The brittle cartilage in Tony's nose crunched and blood exploded from his lacerated skin, pouring down over his mouth. Tony sagged against the door and his foot slid from the pedal. Thoroughly enjoying himself, Ruger grinned, shifted his hips, then reached over with his own left foot and stamped on the brakes. The car jerked and jolted, throwing Ruger against the dashboard and Boyd against the back of Tony's seat. Tony's seat buckled forward, and Tony's right temple struck the steering wheel with a sharp crack.

A moment later there was a much louder *crack*! and then the car swayed drunkenly to the right, slowed abruptly, then stopped altogether.

The engine growled in confusion as it wound itself down.

Pushing himself away from the dashboard, Ruger reached over and shoved the automatic transmission into park, then switched off the engine. A tarpaulin of silence dropped over the car, broken only by small tinkling sounds from the now still engine and the far-off rumble of thunder.

Chapter 4

Long black lines of burned rubber marked where the car had gone off the road into the corn. The tall man with the blond hair stood at the outer curve of the skid mark and stared into the field for a long time, his mouth cut into a cruel smile of triumph. Despite the total cloud cover his skin and blond hair seemed to glimmer with a luminescence like cold moonlight.

He reached out his left hand, fingers splayed so that from his perspective his hand encompassed the whole of the car; then he closed his hand slowly, forming a knotted fist. A wind seemed to blow past him and into the cornfield.

Then his smile changed as he felt a presence behind him. He slowly lowered his arm and turned, his eyes both bright and dark in the strange light. Across the road, standing just at the edge of the forest, was a second man. His skin was gray as dust and he wore a black suit smeared with dirt The blond man's face twisted into a sneer.

The man in the black suit opened his mouth to speak, but though his lips formed words, there was no sound. His face registered alarm and then frustration. He tried again and the strain of his effort was clear on his face.

The blond man shook his head and laughed. "Pathetic," he said in a voice that was the sound of icy wind blowing through the limbs of blighted trees.

Straining, the other man forced out two words—". . . stop . . .

you . . ."—but the effort drained him and his shoulders slumped. He mouthed *bastard*, but it had no sound and carried no force.

"You thought you had won, didn't you?"

The other man could not make himself heard, his lips writhed without sound. Finally he stopped trying to talk and just stood there looking stricken.

"You have no idea what you did. You have no concept of how powerful you've made me." He took another step closer and was now only a few feet away from the gray man. "So now . . . every drop of blood that falls will be on your head. Every. Single. Drop."

Then his eyes flared from pale blue to a fiery red as hot and intense as the furnaces of hell.

In terror, the man in the dark suit fled into the shadows and was gone.

Lightning flashed in the sky, bathing the road with harsh white light; when the shadows returned, the road was empty.

(2)

Malcolm Crow held the severed arm in both of his hands and wondered what to do with it. Put it with the others? Or maybe hang it in the window.

He opted for the window.

Tossing it playfully up and down as he walked, he went to the long counter that formed the floor of the display window and peered at the tangle of skulls, rats, spiderwebs, tombstones, and necrobilia that lay strewn with artistic abandon in front of the thick plate glass. He pursed his lips, made a thoughtful decision, and then bent down to lay the severed arm in front of the largest tombstone, the one that read:

COUNT DRACULA
Born 1472
Died 1865
Died 1900

Died 1923
Died 1988
Died 2007

He checked to make sure the price tag was showing.

Whistling "Cemetery Blues" along with the CD player, he strolled back to his worktable and began opening a second box of gruesome goodies. Both cartons were stamped with the distinctive death's-head label of *Yorick's Skull: Repulsive Replicas, Inc.* He removed four more identical severed arms, tagged them with his price gun, and set them on a shelf next to the severed hands, human hearts, and glow-in-the-dark skulls. When the bell above the door tinkled he glanced over his shoulder to see a familiar burly, bearded figure amble in.

"Hey! Wolfman!" Crow said playfully, waving a rubber arm.

Terry Wolfe smiled back, his grin splitting the red beard with a flash of white. He was a big man, nearly six-five, with logger's forearms and a huge barrel chest, but dressed with expensive good taste in a Giampaolo Desanti suit in dark blue wool with faint pinstripes, a pale blue shirt, and a tie that matched his suit. His shoes were buffed to a polished-coal sheen, and his red beard and curly hair were clipped short, though Crow noticed that Terry needed a haircut—he usually got one every week—and that his beard was a little uneven. Pretending not to look, Crow saw that Terry's smile went no deeper than the surface of his face and that his eyes were bloodshot.

"Whatcha got there?" Terry asked as he stepped up and peered into the box. "Oh, yuck!" He reached in and fished out a huge black rat that lay crushed and sprawled in a congealed puddle of blood and gore.

"Cute, huh?" Crow said with a happy grin.

"Good God, what on earth are you going to do with this?"

"With 'these,' " Crow corrected. "I have six of them."

"Why, for God's sake?"

"To sell 'em."

"To *whom*?"

"Kids. I already sold out of the first lot. Roadkill Ratz are this year's 'thing.' When you step on them they squeal. Kids snap them right up. And split skulls, severed limbs, popped-out eyes, eviscerated dogs, and even bug-eyed monster babies with bloody fangs."

"When we were kids we used to have rubber chickens."

"Dude, we grew up with Freddy, Jason, and Michael Myers."

"Sounds like a law firm in hell."

"The difference is that you never went to monster movies when we were kids, Wolfman, so you don't remember all the good horror stuff from the seventies and eighties. Zombie flicks and slasher pics and the kids loved it all. But all that changed and now every couple of years they have to amp it up to keep kids interested. It's harder to spook them, harder to gross them out. They want to push the envelope of nastiness."

"To reiterate," Terry sniffed with disdain, " 'yuck!' " He rubbed his tired eyes.

"Rough day at the office? Tired from sitting up all night counting all your millions?"

Terry yawned. "Don't I wish? Do you want me to tell you what kind of week I've had so far?"

"Not really—"

"Since you ask—mostly it's this bloody crop blight that is very likely going to put ten or fifteen farms out of business, and most of the rest of them will be mortgaged to the eyebrows to Pinelands Farm Bank. Gil Sanders told me just yesterday that his entire corn crop was diseased, all of it. They're calling it Scandinavian leaf blight because they don't know what else to call it. That's twenty tons of corn that'll have to be burned. He's already talking of selling his farm to developers and getting out. A few others, too."

"Like thirty years ago," Crow murmured. "Like the Black Harvest."

"God, don't even say that!" Terry rubbed his face with both hands. "Hopefully this won't be anywhere near as bad. We have two EPA guys here and the guy who teaches agriculture science at Pinelands College is taking samples all over. Maybe they'll come up with something. And—" Terry began, then waved it off.

"What?"

Terry gave him a bleak smile. "I know it's just stress and all that," he said, "but I haven't been able to sleep much. Can't get to sleep for hours, and then when I do I have the weirdest dreams. I dunno, I guess you could even call them nightmares—if guys my age actually get nightmares."

I sure as hell do, Crow thought, and was about to say it when a customer came in and Terry watched as Crow sold the kid a pair of vampire teeth and two tubes of fake blood. He gave the kid some advice on how to make the blood trickles on either side of his mouth look real rather than fake and the kid left happy. The intrusion broke the stream of their conversation.

Terry shook his red head sadly. "You are a sick little man, Malcolm Crow."

"Hey, just call me 'Mr. Halloween.' "

"Other names occur to me. What does Valerie think of all this . . ." He waved his hand around, at a loss for an adjective that precisely described the Crow's Nest. ". . . stuff?"

Crow shrugged. "She thinks I'm a fruit ball."

"Why am I not surprised?"

"But," Crow said, holding up a finger, "a lovable fruit ball and dead sexy."

"Oh, I'm *quite* sure." Terry snorted. "You're way too far into this stuff, man. I mean, do you even get mail from the real world?"

"Not often."

Most of the year, the Crow's Nest Craft Shoppe was a respectable, upscale arts and crafts store that sold everything from make-your-own birdhouse kits to Elmer's School Glue, but with the advent of cooler weather a darkness crept over the store, or at least so it seemed to Terry. The basic craft supplies were exiled to the racks in the back room, while the large main showroom of the shop became a place where monsters ruled. Row upon row of rubber horror masks lined the walls, and Terry was always amazed at the horrific detail of these masks. He would have expected the witches and werewolves and ghouls, but these were overshadowed by grinning freaks with bulging eyes and insanely smiling mouths; demons with flaring red eyes and open, running sores; sadomasochistic cenobites that sprouted grids of pins or exposed gray matter; serial killers with thin, loveless mouths and chiseled features; distorted ghost faces from the *Scream* trilogy; alien invaders with multifaceted bug eyes and whiplike antennae; huge dragon heads with horns and saurian scales and plates; leprous fiends with leering faces; undead zombies riddled with bullets holes; mummies whose bandages slipped to reveal monstrously deformed verminous eyes; and many more, each more horrific than the last.

Then there were the monster model kits, stacks and stacks of them, and apple barrels filled with nasty little trinkets: eyeball key chains and human thumb erasers, plastic vampire teeth and stick-on bullet holes, and scores of assorted insects and vermin. Costumes hung on hangers by a makeshift dressing room and accessories were lined up neatly on Peg-Boards. For a few dollars the local kids could walk away with plastic butcher knives, meat cleavers, Freddy Kruger gloves, Jason hockey masks, pitchforks, witches' brooms, ball-and-chains, pirate hooks, headbands that made it look as if there were an arrow through their skull, and a variety of makeup in black and orange tubes, guaranteed to transform any ten-year-old into a demon from the outer darkness or a newly risen corpse. Crow loved it. The kids in town loved it. Terry Wolfe, however, hated all of it.

One small counter—Terry's only haven in the store—was incongruously stocked with rows of beepers and cell phones. Being the local Cingular distributor paid the bills the rest of the year, Crow insisted. The business had its frustrations, though, because the cellular relay tower was on the blink as often as it was working, and no one could understand why; plus more than half the places around town were cell phone dead zones.

"Hey, that reminds me," Terry said, drumming his fingers on a case of colorful cell phone covers, "while I'm here can I recharge?" He pulled his cell from its belt holster. "I've been on this thing all day and it's dead as a doornail." Crow took it and plugged it into a charger behind the counter and then went back to stocking the shelves, glancing covertly at Terry as he did so. He didn't like the way Terry looked and wondered if he was having troubles with Sarah. That, on top of the town's crop and financial problems, would be almost too much.

That, and the coming of Halloween. Terry never liked Halloween, as Crow knew all too well. It had always scared him dry-mouthed and spitless ever since he was ten. Back in the autumn of the Black Harvest when Terry had been so cruelly injured. That had been the worst time for all of them. Crow's own brother, Billy, had been murdered by the same man who had killed Terry's sister, Mandy, and had nearly killed Terry.

Terry and Crow were the only ones in town who had seen the face of the killer and survived—and both of them knew for damn sure it hadn't been that migrant worker, Oren Morse. The one they'd nicknamed the Bone Man. The bluesman that the town had accused of committing the murders, and had killed.

Terry and Crow knew different, but not once in thirty years had they spoken to each other—or to anyone for that matter—about it, and that had been Terry's choice. He'd taken his memories of that autumn and had boxed them up and stored them in a back closet of his mind, never to be opened. Crow, on the other hand, thought about that autumn almost every day of his life, and he'd taken the other routes to defuse the ticking time bombs of memories. First he tried to pickle the memories in bourbon, but that hadn't really done the job, and had nearly ruined his life. Then he went the other route and made a joke out of them. He indulged them, made them a farce by selling monster masks and designing spooky traps for the hayride. Crow thought that doing that had more or less exorcised the demons of memory, but he couldn't bring himself to talk it over with a shrink to find out.

The upshot was that Terry was afraid of the dark, and Crow was afraid of the light. If they could have compared notes, it might have been both funny and comforting to them.

Yet, despite their private terror, both Crow and Terry took a wry amusement at Terry's being afraid of Halloween and at the same time being mayor of the town *Time* magazine had once dubbed "the Most Haunted Town in America." Pine Deep was one of those peculiar little towns that seemed to foster a common belief in ghosts and ghostly happenings; not just among the town's eccentrics, but in everyone from crossing guards to town selectmen. The haunted history stretched back to Colonial times, when ghosts of slaughtered Lenni-Lenape were said to haunt the new European settlements, and the legends hadn't dwindled with time but seemed to gather steam with each passing year. It was on this rather spooky foundation that the entire financial structure of the town was built.

Ever since the Black Harvest of thirty years ago when blight destroyed half the farms in the region, the town had begun to change. Developers had bought up the farms and built expensive houses and estates. Money moved in, as the town saying went, and with it came artists, writers, and craftspeople who bought stores and began shoveling in the tourist dollars. The writers wrote horror or gothic novels that made the best-seller lists, the artists painted moody pieces that became popular spooky posters, and the craftspeople made everything from miniature hand-sewn scarecrows to fabulously expensive jewelry like the Vampire's Tears, a pair of bloodred ruby earrings that Anne Rice wore on the cover of *Publishers Weekly*. The mood and the history of the town seemed to inspire the darker thoughts of the artists, and the tourists loved everything they made.

Terry, always business smart, joined in with the group that capitalized on the haunted history of the town, and used that as gimmicks for advertising. Soon everyone up and down the eastern seaboard came to Pine Deep for the scary fun and games: the Halloween Parade, the Monster Mash dance-concert—once, years ago featuring, appropriately enough, The Smashing Pumpkins—and the seasonal shopping that attracted the most astute and discerning antiquarians. The whole town came totally alive at Halloween and the accounting ledgers of nearly every store went quickly and happily from red to black between September and Christmas, with the definite peak being the weeks leading up to trick-or-treat. Chills and shivers helped

Pine Deep prosper as an increasingly upscale community. The fact that Terry Wolfe, with his secret fears, was mayor of "Spooksville," as the *Philadelphia Daily News* recently called it, was truly ironic.

The topper of the whole strange pie was that, despite everything, Terry owned the Haunted Hayride.

Crow's reverie was broken by the ringing of the phone and he leaned across the counter and picked it up. "Yeah . . . sure, he's right here." Smiling, he tossed the portable handset to Terry. "For you. Chief's office."

"Uh–oh!" Terry said in mock alarm as he reached out a hand to take the phone. Crow strolled a few paces away and began idly poking in his box of rubber vermin and body parts.

"Yeah, Gus, what is it?" Terry listened for a moment, then said, "No, my cell's out of energy. What's the hurry?" He listened for a while and then started saying "Jeez!" every couple of seconds. Terry was a man incapable of profanity and "Jeez" was about as close as he ever got to an expletive. Crow gave Terry an inquisitive look, but the mayor held up a finger and mouthed the word *wait*. Terry listened for over a minute, then said, "Jeez!" again. "Okay . . . what about the three gunmen?"

Crow arched his eyebrows and silently mouthed the word *gunmen*, and again Terry held up his hand. "Jeez-oh-man!" Terry said with feeling, and that was him at his most profane. "Okay, Gus, I'll be there in a minute. Yeah. Bye." He punched the Off button on the portable and stood there, chewing his lower lip and tapping the phone against his thigh. Crow cleared his throat; Terry looked sharply at him. "Man, the manure has really hit the fan now."

"Why? What's up?"

"You are not going to believe this one, man, but Gus got a call from the Philadelphia Police Department. They red-flagged all the jurisdictions from Philly to the state line because apparently three psychos shot a bunch of holes in some Jamaican druggies and made off with a bunch of drugs and money."

"Cool!" Crow grinned in spite of himself.

"Yeah, well, the kicker is that they've been spotted a few times and for some reason I cannot even fathom, they've been heading this way. According to what Gus told me, they probably came through here half an hour ago. There were roadblocks set up. Gus had already been working with Crestville and Black Marsh since late this afternoon. Philly is sending a bunch of their 'advisers' up here to take over from Gus. He said he tried to beep me to let me know, but he couldn't reach me and figured I'd wind up here. Anyway, Gus and the other chiefs arranged some sort of road-check system, some kind of observation-post setup, I don't know. Anyway, there was supposed to be no way the psychos could get through it without at least being stopped."

"Stopped?"

Terry snorted. "Yeah, supposedly Gus Bernhardt and his posse are going to try and apprehend a real criminal."

"Be better to have the Marx Brothers try and arrest them. Gus is pretty good at parking tickets, though."

"And not much else." Terry rubbed his eyes.

Crow could see the pressure mounting in his friend's face, which had gone from a haggard white to a dangerous red.

"So, basically all that the local boys were supposed to do was stop and detain and then turn the bad guys over to the Philly cops. Problem is . . . a good hour ago, the psychos blew past the Black Marsh checkpoint and crossed the bridge. Now here's the fun part. The suspects never made it to the roadblock in Crestville."

Crow said, "Oh," in a very expressive voice. The town of Pine Deep was a comfortably wide spot in the road, a triangular wedge made up of upscale shops and lush farmland and bisected by Interstate Alternate Extension Route A-32, lying hard against the Delaware River that separated Pennsylvania from New Jersey and framed on all sides by streams and canals. A-32 wavered back and forth between the two states, across old iron bridges and up through farm country, and then plowed right through the town. Black Marsh was an even smaller burg just to the southeast, and miniscule Crestville was the next town heading north. A-32 was the only road that cut all the way through those three towns; the other roads were all small farm roads that led nowhere but to someone's back forty or to the asymmetrical tangle of cobblestoned streets in Pine Deep's trendy shopping and dining district. Any car heading to Crestville had to pass through Pine Deep.

"Are they sure they were on the route?"

"Yeah, a Black Marsh cycle cop spotted them. Everyone expected them to run into the roadblock in Crestville. There was a reception committee with eight or nine cars, barricades and shotguns . . . but they never made it."

"Shit."

"As you say. So, now we apparently have to stage a manhunt."

Crow laughed. "You're kidding, right? An actual manhunt? Like in the movies?"

"Just like in the movies. Richard Kimble and all that—though Gus Bernhardt is certainly no Lieutenant Gerard. I only hope the cops from Philly are." Terry cocked his head and peered at Crow. "I wish you'd stop grinning. This is serious."

But Crow just shook his head. "I doubt it, I really do. This is just Gus getting hysterical. Everyone's going to run around like Chicken Little and then we're going to hear that these three clowns are somewhere northwest of Scranton. Sorry, dude, but I just can't take this seriously."

"Well, I do," Terry said, and there was enough asperity in his tone to dial down even Crow's humor. "This isn't just Gus this time. There really are detectives from Philadelphia here and they, at least, seem to be taking this seriously."

"Jeez, Terry," Crow said, holding his hands up. "Lighten up. Don't get mad at me. I just know Gus a little better than you do, and until I see actual bad guys rolling down Corn Hill I'm going to find this hard to buy. That's all."

A nervous twitch had started at the corner of Terry's right eye and he was starting to perspire. He mopped his face on his expensive sleeve, hesitated for a moment, and pasted on a bad attempt at an amiable smile, saying, "Okay, okay. Look, I gotta go but I need you to do a favor for me?"

"Sure, call it."

"Go out to the hayride and let Coop know what's going down. Maybe even shut it down for the night. No, don't give me that look. I think it's the smart thing to do with all this stuff going on. The hayride's on Old Mill, just off A-32, and with all the kids out there . . . well, you know what I mean." Terry was attempting to sound offhand, but his words were coming out in nervous rapid-fire. "Try to call Coop first, but you know he won't answer. He never does. He just lets the tape get it. Coop is a pain in my behind."

"He's Sarah's cousin."

"Nepotism is the only thing keeping him on the payroll. The man's an idiot."

Crow found nothing to contest in that statement. "Okay, I'll button up the shop and head out there. I'm supposed to go over to Val's anyway, and that's more or less on the way."

Terry looked a little relieved. "Thanks for playing errand boy. Oh, and, Crow?"

"Yes, darling?"

"Be extra careful. Don't grin at me like that, you idiot, I'm serious."

Crow smiled regardless and dropped into a Festus drawl. "Gee, Mayor Wolfe, does that mean I can bring along my trusty six-gun?"

With no trace of humor in his voice, Terry said, "Yes, it does."

Crow blinked at him, waiting for the punch line. He said, "You serious?"

"As a heart attack." Terry cleared his throat. "Look, Crow, all of the cops—local and otherwise—are going to be mustering at the station to coordinate this thing. If I could, I'd send one of them, not that any of them are worth the cost of a pack of Juicy-Fruit. Besides, you used to be a cop. . . ."

"Christ, Terry, in this town nearly everyone except my grand-mother has been a cop at one time or other. And she'd have taken the job if she hadn't had the rheumatiz."

"Yeah, well. Consider yourself temporarily reinstated."

"As a cop? You can do that?"

"I'm the mayor, I can do anything."

"That's not what Sarah says."

"That's where you're wrong. My wife thinks I'm Superman." He mopped more sweat and then looked at his friend for a moment. "Look, Crow, just do this for me quick and safe, okay?"

Crow smiled but he could see that this matter really was troubling Terry, so he didn't make another joke. "Sure, Terry. Whatever you want. And about this whole fugitive thing—don't get too wired about it, 'cause about the last place three wanted criminals are going to want to go is to a haunted hayride packed with every teenager from the tristate area. Y'know, they got this whole thing about witnesses and such."

Terry walked behind the counter and retrieved his cell phone, which was only partially recharged. "Yeah, well, just be careful anyway."

"I promise that I will be very careful. The best man for this job is a smart coward, and damn it, Terry, I'm your man." He sketched a salute.

Terry Wolfe shook his head, but then he stepped forward and thrust out his hand. "Thanks."

Crow picked up a rubber severed arm and extended it to shake Terry's hand. Terry batted it lightly aside and shook his head again, sadly this time. "You are very weird," he said with a harried grin, and then left.

For a full minute, Crow just looked out through the broad glass window at the darkness, a lopsided smile on his face. He scratched his cheek with the rubber hand.

"Well, hell," he said aloud. Then went into the back room and fetched his gun.

(3)

Seconds crawled over the car like army ants. Finally Boyd found his voice and croaked, "Tony? Ruger?"

Ruger just grunted at him. He quivered as adrenaline coursed through him. He could feel the hair standing up all over his body. His fingertips shook as he probed his cheek and forehead, which were puffing up and beginning to throb. There was no pain yet, but a growing tingle that forewarned him of it. It felt wonderful. Running his tongue over his gums, he could taste the hot, salty blood, and he drank it down hungrily.

"Is Tony okay?"

Annoyed by the fact that Boyd seemed to be relatively unhurt, Ruger looked at the driver, slumped motionlessly against the steering wheel. "Who cares?" Ruger said.

"What the hell happened?"

"Tony drove us over a ditch and into this fucking cornfield, whaddya think happened?"

"Shit!" Boyd said. "That's just . . . shit."

"Uh-huh." Ruger was trying to recapture the image of the man in his mind, certain that he knew the man, but the harder he tried to grab at the memory, the more elusive it became until finally it was gone for good. He felt a pang at the loss.

Ruger, you are my left hand.

He jerked the passenger door handle, shoved the door open, and eased himself out of the car, listening to his body for signs of damage and finding nothing but a few blossoming bruises. He stood by the side of the car for a moment and then grabbed it as the cornfield swirled sickeningly around him. Closing his eyes, he fought for balance. It came reluctantly and slowly. He opened his eyes and looked around. The cornfield was still swaying, but now it was because of the wind. He wondered if he had a concussion. The last time he'd had one, it had felt like being buzzed on really good sour mash; a very nice feeling.

"Is the car okay?" Boyd asked as he popped open his door and crawled out.

Ruger studied it, lips pursed. "Nope."

Boyd came unsteadily around the car and stood by Ruger. They looked down at the right front wheel, which lay almost flat under the weight of the car. The tire was intact, but the ball joint connecting the wheel to the axle had snapped and the whole wheel had just folded under the car.

"Well, shit," Boyd said again.

"Yeah."

"Never gonna fix that."

"No kidding."

"What're we gonna do?"

Ruger barely glanced at him. "Your legs work, don't they?"

Boyd gave him an incredulous stare and then flapped his good arm. "Oh, shit. Man, this is just the fucking top. Walk? Yeah, Ruger, that's just great. Walk where? Back to Philly? Walk to New Hope? Maybe you want to take a country stroll to Lambertville, I hear they have a good brunch at the inn." He shook his head. "Where the hell we gonna walk to?"

"Anywhere but here."

"Yeah? Well, we're in the middle of East Bumfuck, Pennsylvania. There ain't nowhere around here to walk to!"

"Sure there is, Boyd," Ruger said. "There's always somewhere."

"What are you, a freaking tour guide? Do you know where we're gonna go? There ain't *nothing* around here, man!"

"Hey, shit for brains . . . you think this corn planted itself? If there's corn, there's a farmhouse. Farmers own cars, even in East Bumfuck. Maybe if we ask real nice they'll let us borrow one." He grinned.

"Your mouth is bleeding."

Ruger licked his teeth. "I know," he said softly, smiling.

Boyd opened his mouth to speak and then snapped it shut again. He turned, bent, and peered into the car to look at Tony.

"Is he dead?" he asked.

"Ought to be, the stupid fuck."

"Then why'd you let him drive?"

Ruger shrugged. "He got behind the wheel."

"Yeah, but *you* said he was fine to drive."

Ruger shrugged again.

"Maybe we should see if he's, you know, still alive." Boyd leaned farther into Karl's side of the car. He reached out and nudged Tony's sleeve. "Yo! Tony! You in there, man?"

No response.

"Let it go," Ruger suggested.

Boyd tried again, shaking Tony by the sleeve. Nothing. He

tried one last time, and this time Tony lifted his head and shook it slowly, trying to clear his eyes and his muzzy brain. The lower half of his face was smeared with blood and snot, and his nose was disgustingly askew.

"Yo, Tony! We thought we lost you, man?"

"B . . . Boyd?"

"Yeah, man."

"Boyd?" Tony barely had a voice left, his words croaking out in a whisper not half as loud as Ruger's slithery rasp, and lacking any trace of vitality. A voice muffled and warped by sinuses flooded with blood. "You gotta help me, man. I'm all fucked up."

"Well, yeah, you got shot and then you wrecked the car. You ought to be fucked up," Boyd said, and then his face softened. "Can you walk?"

"I don't . . . know. I can't feel my legs, man."

Boyd looked over his shoulder at Ruger, who was lighting a Pall Mall. Thunder rumbled overhead, deep and sullen, and in the distance lightning flashed continuously.

"We might have to carry him, man," Boyd said.

Ruger took a long drag on his cigarette and looked thoughtfully at Boyd, his cold eyes narrowed. "Tell me, Boyd," he asked mildly, "do you really see either one of us carrying his sorry ass anywhere?"

"Huh?"

"What I said. Can you see us hauling his sorry ass out of that car and carrying it anywhere? Is that how you see things? 'Cause I sure as hell don't. I see us taking the money and the coke and making ourselves scarce as shit, is what I see. I see us having enough troubles getting ourselves to someplace safe without having to cart around a man that's mostly dead anyway."

Boyd straightened and faced Ruger, half smiling. "You're out of your fucking mind, Karl. We can't just leave him here!"

"Why not?"

"It ain't right, man."

Ruger took another long and thoughtful drag on his cigarette. Blue smoke leaked from his mouth and nostrils as he said,

" 'Ain't right'? Is that what you said, Boyd? It ain't right'? That's precious, man. Now, why don't you tell me what 'right' has to do with anything?"

"Hey, we're a team, Ruger. We set this up together and we pulled it off together and we gotta stick together no matter what happens."

"Is that right? Then I suppose we should have stayed behind to fetch Nicky and Lester just so we could give them a decent Christian burial. Wouldn't that have been the 'right' thing to do?"

"Boyd . . . ?" Tony asked weakly, but when Boyd looked inside the car, Tony's eyes had drifted shut again. Boyd straightened and looked hard at Ruger.

"Tony's still alive."

"Not much, he ain't."

"He ain't dead yet, Ruger, and we just can't leave him."

"What do you want to do? Wait here until he kicks? You know as well as I do he ain't going to make it. He's gut shot and busted up. It's not like we can take him to a hospital or anything. There ain't a hospital from here to Harrisburg that won't be on the alert for us. Not that anybody'd keep shut about treating a gunshot wound anyway. So what do you suggest we do? Do *you* know how to treat a bullet wound? Since when are you Marcus-fucking-Welby?"

"We have to do *something!*"

"We have to save our own asses, Boyd, that's all we have to do. Tony knew the risks, and if he hadn't had his head stuck up his own ass he wouldn't have taken one in the belly. But that's too damned bad. I for one am not going to stand around here just to keep him comfortable till he dies. This is capital crime, my man, not male bonding, and Tony sure as hell ain't family to either one of us."

Boyd shook his head stubbornly. "We'll find a doctor somewhere, force him to fix Tony. Or bribe him. Hell, we got enough dough."

"If you think I'm going to waste any of my money on a dead man, then you are actually dumber than you look. I'm getting my money and my share of the coke and I'm getting the hell out of Dodge right now."

Ruger began to turn away but stopped as Boyd opened his coat, revealing the mother-of-pearl grip of his old Colt Commander. Ruger looked at the gun for just a moment, then slowly raised his eyes to meet Boyd's. There was no trace of fear in Ruger's eyes. His flat reptilian stare burned into Boyd's, and Ruger's smile slowly blossomed.

"We have to do something about Tony," Boyd said in a voice that betrayed far more emotion than he wanted.

Ruger nodded slowly. "Uh-huh. Okay, Boyd, we'll play it that way." He took a last slow drag on his cigarette and flicked the butt into the corn, then brushed past Boyd and bent down into the open passenger side of the car.

"Yo . . . Tony?" he asked.

Tony's eyelids fluttered for a moment and then opened.

"Ruger? You gotta help me, Ruger. I'm hurt bad. You gotta help me."

"Sure, Tony. Boyd and me, we'll take good care of you." Ruger drew his .32 snub-nose and buried the barrel against Tony's blood-soaked gut, right next to the bullet wound. "Nice knowing you, Tony, but you're a lousy fucking driver." He fired a single shot.

The blast folded Tony in half. He caved over and crunched his face once more, smashing against the steering wheel.

"Jesus!" Boyd howled and grabbed Ruger's shoulder with his good arm and wrenched him back and spun him, then released his jacket and raised a balled fist; but Ruger went with the turn and stepped into Boyd, jamming the barrel of his gun hard under Boyd's chin.

"Throw the punch or put it away," Ruger said with his wicked grin.

Boyd froze.

"If you're feeling froggy, then jump. Otherwise put that fist away. I'm not in the mood for this shit, Boyd, and we do not have all fucking night." His voice didn't rise above a slithery whisper.

Slowly, gingerly, Boyd lowered his fist, letting it drop limply at his side.

"Good. Now step off."

Boyd moved back a few paces, and then turned and walked ten feet away. He stood facing the swaying corn, chest heaving, fighting for control. Into the waving rows of stalks he yelled, "Fuck!" at the top of his voice.

"See how considerate I am? Now we don't have to carry his sorry ass anywhere," Ruger said. "Well, now the split is two ways. Not five, not four, not three. Just the two of us. That's half a mil each, Boyd, and enough dope to pretty much double that. That'll buy a lot of sympathy cards for Tony's wife and kids. It'll sure as hell take the sting out of feeling like you're feeling now. So, let's just drop this Mother Teresa bullshit and get a move on."

Boyd turned slowly to face Ruger. Boyd's face was washed clean of any emotion, though something moved behind his eyes.

"You're a total piece of shit, Ruger."

Ruger shrugged. "And that's a news flash to whom?"

Boyd spat on the ground between them and walked heavily to the car.

It took them five minutes to split the bundles of bloodstained money and the plastic bags of half-cut cocaine into two over-sized backpacks. It was a very tight fit. Boyd tried to wipe away the blood that soaked the tightly wrapped bundles of used bills, but Ruger told him not to bother. "We don't have time. It's all stained. We'll find a washing machine somewhere. I hear cold water'll take the stains out."

Boyd looked at him in amazement. Karl's voice was so calm, so offhand that it chilled him.

Ruger winked. "Let's do it."

Ruger helped Boyd strap on one pack, buckling it carefully around the limp and useless arm; then he shrugged himself into his own pack and adjusted the straps. Without a single backward glance at the car or Tony's slumped form, Ruger set off into the cornfield. Boyd tarried a moment longer, staring at the silent shape huddled over the steering wheel.

"Sorry, man," he said softly, and then turned to follow Ruger. The tall stalks of corn closed around them.

(4)

Long minutes passed with no sound except the dry rustle of the corn. Then softly, faintly, "Boyd . . . help me . . ."

Then silence.

Chapter 5

After Terry left, Crow stood looking at the closed door for several long minutes, processing everything that had just happened. In the space of a few minutes he'd been faced with the outrageous idea of armed gunmen in Pine Deep, been reinstated as a cop—although a very temporary one—and been assigned the job of closing down the hayride.

None of this exactly fit the way he'd planned to spend the rest of the evening. It was seven-thirty and he'd intended to close at eight, catch the AA meeting at the Methodist church—tonight was a fifth-step night—and then drive out to Val's, sample her cooking—hoping that it wasn't as bad as Mark and Henry predicted—and then at the earliest possible convenience bundle Val off to bed. Then he was going to spring the idea of a weekend at a New Hope bed-and-breakfast on her, which would in turn lead up to his master plan of finally proposing. He'd been working out the details of this plan for about five years and so far it involved a ring, dinner, and a hotel stay. He was hoping for some last-minute inspiration to make the event really memorable. It didn't help any that everyone in town already assumed they would get married, so the proposal wouldn't be much of a surprise. More than once, when he'd stopped by to take Val out to dinner somewhere particularly nice her father and brother had grinned and winked at him, assuming that he was going to propose. Even Mark's wife, Connie, who was as dim as Coop, knew that Crow was going to ask her, which meant Val definitely knew.

So how to make it a surprise? That was the real puzzle, and so far he'd come up with exactly nothing; though a nice cozy dinner with her at her place, and an early bedtime, would give him time to probe for hints of what she would really like. Crow had already bought a ring—a 1.8-carat Asscher-cut diamond with smaller diamonds filling in a channel-cut platinum band. Crow knew that people considered him an affable goof, but no one could accuse him of being cheap. The question was how to present it. Val was not a flowers and candy sort of woman, and traditionally romantic gestures were somewhat lost on her. Crow needed something unique and very, very smart.

Instead . . . he now had to go fetch his gun and play cops and robbers again. Val would just *love* that.

Crow locked up the shop and switched off the lights, then went into the storeroom and through the doorway that led to his apartment. Like him the place was small and messy and filled with a lot of strange things. The front end of a 1966 Volkswagen Beetle (Crow's very first car) had been converted into a jukebox and was parked in one corner of the living room. His coffee table was a snowboard on cinder blocks. His clock was a replica of Dalí's melted timepieces. Every inch of the walls was covered with head shots of Crow's actor friends, interspersed with some very badly painted watercolors Val had done during one of her infrequent artistic phases.

His three cats, Pinetop, Muddy Whiskers, and Koko, flocked around him, rubbing against his legs and mewing for their supper.

"Hi, kids. Miss me?"

Pinetop made his usual, weird little ak-ak-ak-ak sound and walked significantly in the direction of the kitchen. Crow followed dutifully and popped open two cans of aromatic glop, divided it into three equal portions, and laid out their plates. The trio promptly ignored him and set to their feast.

Humming to himself, he wandered into the kitchen, drank a Yoo-Hoo by the open refrigerator door, peering pointlessly at the various Tupperware containers of mystery meat, mystery pasta, and mystery sauce that lurked on each shelf. One vaguely tumescent shape lay swaddled in Saran Wrap. Crow thought it might have been a zucchini, but he just wasn't sure. He was afraid of it and didn't want to touch it. He found a piece of celery that didn't look too hideous and took it over to a large glass aquarium where a rather absurd-looking guinea pig named Professor Longhair sat meditating on a rock. Crow lifted the top and set the celery down next to the guinea pig, who opened one eye, regarded the limp celery with obvious disdain, and returned to his contemplations. Crow went back to the fridge and had another bottle of the chocolate drink, staring once more at the scientific wonders evolving in there among his bottles of Yoo-Hoo, Red Bull, and Gatorade. He shut the door and was wondering why he was stalling rather than getting his ass in gear when the phone rang.

Scooping up the receiver he said, "I'd like to order a large pizza, mushrooms and extra cheese, and an order of fries."

"For God's sake," said a voice, soft, laughing.

"I'm sorry, ma'am, the person you have reached is not a normal person. Please hang up and try your call again."

"Okay, fine. Bye."

"No! Wait! Hey, baby."

"Hello, idiot."

"You always say the nicest things."

"True," Val agreed, "but not to you."

"Mm. So . . . what's cooking?"

"Me."

"Don't I know it?"

"No, I mean food. Supper. Turkey soup, to be precise. You are still coming over, aren't you?" There was a brief moment of silence. "Don't tell me you aren't coming over, Malcolm Crow."

"Well—"

"Damn it, Crow . . ."

"Hey, babe, duty calls."

"Duty? What duty? Do you have a rush order for rubber vomit? Is there a desperate need for glow-in-the-dark dog poop?"

"No, nothing nearly as important as that. Just three psychos on a killing spree."

"Seriously, why can't you make it? I've been cooking since five o'clock. I have actually worked up a sweat."

"Are you covered in turkey blood and gristle?"

"No, but I do have a spot of gravy on my good blue shirt."

"You have to learn to control these domestic urges before they become an obsession."

"Ha," she said dryly, "ha, ha."

Crow had a powerful visceral image of her standing in the bathroom that morning, naked and glorious.

"Actually, sweetie, I actually do have some important civic duties to perform." Briefly, he told her about the manhunt and what Terry had asked of him. There was a considerable silence on the far end of the line. After a while Crow said, "Uh . . . Val?"

The silence positively oozed out of the phone. Finally, Val muttered, "So, you agreed to go gunslinging for Gus Bernhardt. Isn't that special?"

"Well, not for Gus. Terry asked me, but it's not like I'm actually going back on the department. Terry wouldn't ask me to do anything like that. He just wants me to go close down the hayride for the night."

"Carrying a gun."

"Would you rather I went out there *without* a gun?"

"I'd rather you didn't go out there at all."

"Someone has to."

"You know, there's this marvelous new invention, maybe you've heard of it? Called a telephone?"

"We already tried calling Coop. No answer. He must be out with the kids, or walking the grounds, or maybe he really is too stupid to use a phone . . . and anyway I don't want to leave that kind of a message on his answering machine. Can you imagine Coop trying to organize things all by himself?"

Val had to concede that point. George Cooper was pretty good at running the Haunted Hayride, but when it came time for any real decisive action, he was as useful as a freshly beheaded chicken. Terry had once said that Coop was the only guy who could cause a panic in an empty room. "Okay, so maybe someone does have to go. Why you, though?"

"I'm the only guy around. All the local blues are busy being actual cops for a change. Terry needed a gofer who didn't have his head up his ass."

"Again I ask, why you?"

"Oh, we're just a laugh riot, aren't we, Miss Guthrie?"

There was another silence, briefer, less bitter. "Okay, okay," Val said softly, "but please be careful for a change?"

"Me? Careful? Hey, careful is my middle name."

"I'm serious, Crow."

He sobered. "Okay, okay, baby, I promise. No screwing around, and no heroics. And why? 'Cause there won't be any need for heroics. Just there and back, lickety-split."

"Good."

"Okay."

"Then you'll come over here?"

"For leftovers?"

"No one has ever called me 'leftovers,' pal."

"I was thinking of my belly, woman."

"I was thinking of something just south of there."

"Ah," he said. "I see. Well then, I guess I had better get my ass in gear. Sooner I get those kids out of there—"

". . . The sooner you get to come over here and taste my goodies."

"Gad, woman, you are in a bold and licentious mood this evening!"

"Call it an incentive program to make sure you get here as safe and as soon as possible."

"Whoosh. If you count to three and turn around I'll probably be already there."

She called him a nitwit and hung up on him. He looked at the phone for a moment, leaned over and lightly banged his head on the wall a couple of times, then slowly set the receiver down.

"Yes, well," he said aloud as if to counter a return of his desire to stall rather than do what Terry wanted, "let us get a move on, then."

He went into his bedroom, jerked open the closet door, and fished around on the top shelf until he found a heavy object wrapped in a towel. This he carried over to the bed and carefully unrolled it. Inside the towel was a second cloth smelling faintly of gun oil, and inside this was a Beretta 92F 9mm automatic pistol and several clips. Crow sat down on the side of the bed for a few moments, holding the gun in his right hand, turning it over, weighing it, considering it. He hadn't worn the gun since he'd quit the department, and even though he'd gotten off the sauce long before he'd turned in his badge, just the sight of the pistol was a link to unhappier times. His drinking had been so bad that Val had broken up with him for two years and wouldn't start dating him again until after he'd been well into his first year of sobriety. Crow wasn't one to take a lot of pride in being sober—instead he remembered what it felt like to be a pathetic figure in the eyes of the town, and in Val's eyes. He never wanted to let her down again, not in any way big or small, no matter how much he really wanted a drink.

Sighing, he hefted the gun and worked the slide, making sure the breech was clear. He located his box of shells in the closet and methodically loaded the clip. He never kept the clips loaded as the constant stress on the clip's springs could fatigue the metal, and it had been a long time since he'd fired the thing. He slapped the clip into the grip and double-checked to make sure the safety was on.

"Yippee-yi-yo," he said out loud as he stood and jammed the pistol into his waistband, then danced a little jig as the cold steel burned his skin like a block of ice. "Yikes!"

He pulled off his shirt, put on a T-shirt with an R. Crumb painting of Son House on it and tucked it in, then put the gun back into the waistband of his pants and pulled his flannel shirt over it.

At the door he paused and glanced at the three cats that were now performing their post-dinner ablutions, licking their paws and using them to wash their faces.

"Don't stay up too late . . . and no more cable porn." He wagged a finger.

Pinetop was the only one who looked at him, and his expression was pitying. Crow pulled the door closed and locked it.

(2)

Terry hurried up Corn Hill toward the chief's office, which shared the first floor of the township building with the county court. As he walked briskly through each patch of brightness his shadow seemed to lunge and pounce, springing with lupine speed at his own heels and then vanishing as he moved into a different alignment of light and reflection.

Cars swept up and down the hill, gleaming with polished chrome and tinted glass, complicated antennae sprouting expensively as the cars braked and swept along the immaculate street. Terry glanced at a few of them, once or twice giving the driver a curt wave and nodding to others. He was usually expansive, ready to stop and talk, to shake hands and swap familiar jokes and discuss the day's business, doing his mayor shtick with élan and a natural affability, but lately his good mood had begun to slip and any trace of good humor seen on his face was put there by effort and held in place by sheer will.

He felt as though the walls of his life were starting to crack and he was terrified of what would pour through once the cracks split wide enough. His depression and stress had begun at the end of summer, when the first traces of the crop blight had turned the summer wheat into rancid weeds that had to be burned. That hadn't been too bad because wheat was not the town's staple crop, and for a week or so everyone breathed sighs of relief when the corn crop had looked pretty healthy. Then the blight struck nine corn farms in two days, and since then more than half of the town's corn crop was infected. The pumpkins were next to go, and they were hit even harder. Cabbages, apples, and berries, too.

That's about when the dreams started.

Terry had always been prone to nightmares—ever since age ten, when he'd been in a coma for weeks following the death of his sister—but these dreams were new and they were maddeningly persistent. They took two forms, though there was one theme that overlapped them both. In the first set of dreams he was wandering through Pine Deep as it burned—moving past heaps of dead bodies, hearing explosions rip the night apart. Everywhere there was death and pain. Everyone he knew and loved lay strewn about, their throats savaged and bloody, their dead eyes staring accusingly at him, and as he staggered along he would occasionally catch glimpses of his own reflection in cracked store windows. The reflections always showed him not as himself—but as something twisted and bestial. When his dreaming self would try and look closer, as the image became clearer, Terry would come yelping out of the dream, sweating and panting and utterly terrified.

The second type of dream—and by far the most persistent— involved Terry lying in bed next to Sarah and feeling his body begin to change, to reshape, into something horrifying, but horrifying in a way that was not clear to Terry, and no matter how hard he tried he just couldn't get any sense of what the dreams meant.

Sometimes he had the dreams two or three times a night, and he was feeling the drain on his system. He had told his psychiatrist about them, but the doctor had passed them off as stress dreams inspired by the local ambience of spookiness and exacerbated by the growing financial troubles of the farmers. The psychiatrist also told Terry that, as mayor, he was taking on too much responsibility for things over which he had no control. Added to it were the constant demands on him by the business owners as the town geared up for its annual Halloween celebration, the biggest event in the year for Pine Deep. Terry was averaging fourteen-hour days at work, and cruising on about four or five good hours of sleep a night. Terry had listened to what the doctor had to say, and all the advice to find some way of calming down—meditation, yoga, anything—nodded his understanding, and then held his hand out for his prescriptions: antipsychotics and antidepressants and anxiolytics. The three staples of his current diet.

And now there was the phone call from Gus Bernhardt. That call had jolted him into an entirely different frame of mind.

Criminals?

In Pine Deep?

Half of him wanted to laugh out loud at the very thought, and the other half of him was already feeling moths fluttering in his stomach. Halloween less than a month away. Already a third of the stores in town had their windows done up for the coming season, and all of the plans for the costume parade had long ago been finalized. There were still a million details to see to. Terry had managed a magnificent coup of signing David Boreanez and James Marsters to be co–grand marshals of the parade for a lot less money than he was prepared to pay, and *Good Morning America* was going to do a Halloween morning broadcast from Town Hall. He was talking with Regis Philbin's people about doing a spot at the hayride. School buses were bringing hundreds of kids to the farms each week to visit with the pumpkin growers (though some of the farmers had actually had to import clean and nondiseased pumpkins from Crestville and Black Marsh to keep up appearances), and the Pine Deep Authentic Candy Corn was going to be dropped in half the trick-or-treaters' bags from New York to Baltimore.

Despite the crop blight it was a busier year than most, and Terry was already feeling the pressure weighing him down as he balanced the financial crisis of the farmers with the amazing boom for the in-town businesses. Now this: a carload of big-city criminals with guns was something Terry Wolfe and his haunted little town did not need, thank you very much. The very thought of how this craziness might affect business had Terry grinding his teeth and sweating bullets at the same time. The more he thought about it, the faster he walked. His big fists were white-knuckled tight as he climbed the hill.

He crossed Wolfe Lane, glancing by reflex down the winding path to where his family had lived since Colonial times. Nearly one hundred and twenty years ago, Mordechai Wolfowitz had laid the cobbles on which the heels of Terry's expensive Italian shoes clicked as he hurried to the chief's office. Mordechai's great-grandson, Aaron—the one who changed the family name to Wolfe—had planted the long line of brooding oaks that stood like dour sentinels along the south side of the street. As he stepped up on the far curb, Terry slowed his pace just a fraction, imagining as he often did that he could see his little sister, Mandy, running up the lane to meet him, her red curls bouncing as she ran, her green eyes alive with humor and mischief and laughter on her lips.

The memory was brief, as it always was; and it hurt, as it always did.

There were only empty shadows on Wolfe Lane, broken here and there by the glow drooping from antique lampposts and the lights of his house at the far end. Still, he could almost hear the small and gentle sound of Mandy's laughter. . . .

Then the edge of the first store on the next block obscured his vision, and the display window full of the confections of AHHHH—FUDGE! filled his awareness. His frown became a brief smile and then an acknowledging murmur as the owner waved a fudge-smeared spatula at him. Terry moved on up the hill, whisking through light and shadow, heading for the chief's office. Behind him, the now forgotten darkness at the mouth of Wolfe Lane seemed to swirl and roil, becoming vaguely thicker. Nearby, Terry's marmalade tabby, Party Cat, crouched by the roots of the lane's first towering oak hunkered down over a dead starling; he pawed at the broken wings playfully and bent forward to bite—and abruptly froze, eyes snapping wide, hairs springing up straight along his spine. Party Cat stared at the boiling darkness, arching his back and laying his chest low to the ground as something slowly emerged from the blackness of the shadows. The cat's throat vibrated with a feral growl, half of defiance and half of fear.

The shape seemed to be part of the shadows rather than merely in them, but as it moved it became defined, seeking form and structure as it stepped into the spill of pale streetlight. Party Cat hissed, baring his fangs, glaring up at the form with intense yellow eyes. The shape turned toward him, eyes meeting eyes. The cat's wrinkled and snarling lips trembled, the intensity of the challenge ebbing, mouth becoming gradually relaxed, the furry lips sagging down over the fangs slowly and with uncertainty. The shape just stood there, green eyes watching the cat, making no move. Party Cat sniffed the air, searching for a scent, then meowed plaintively at the odor he smelled: staleness, an earthiness mixed with a sharp coppery tang.

The figure stirred, turned away from the cat, and stepped farther out of the shadows into the lamplight. It was a small shape, not even four feet tall. The chilly wind stirred the tatters of dark green cotton that hung vaguely in dress-shape disarray on the tiny form, and the wind teased and tossed the red curls that framed the pale, pale face. Pale except where streaks of dark red cut slashes through the purity of the flesh.

The figure watched Terry's broad back retreating up the hill.

After a moment, it followed.

(3)

Iron Mike Sweeney was the Enemy of Evil.

It was an awesome responsibility for one his age, but it was his special secret that within that shell of a teenage human male dwelled the mind of a thousand warriors from all times and dimensions, drawn together and focused through him, through his perfectly developed muscles and sinews. He was the perfect weapon, the ultimate warrior.

He rode through the streets of Pine Deep on the War Machine, a device of such cunning design that to mortal eyes it appeared to be nothing more than a twelve-speed Huffy mountain bike. The glittering black tubes of its frame were crammed with cutting-edge microtechnology that channeled unbelievable power through the bike and into every cell of Iron Mike's body, filling him with raw power and healing him when he was slashed or cut or burned in his deadly duels with the Agents of Destruction. The handlebars were tightly wrapped with antiradiation insulation simulating black electrical tape, and these power bars threw up crackling energy shields through which no amount of laser fire could ever hope to penetrate. The mother-box of twelve hyperaccelerating gears was fashioned from alien technology Iron Mike had salvaged from the wreck of an old spacecraft. When Iron Mike mounted the War Machine and gripped its handles, he became as one with the machine, and his cyborg system drew energy from it, just as his mind drew knowl-edge from its interface with the InfinityMind uplink he wore on his belt. Disguised as a mere Sony Walkman, the InfinityMind was simply the projection into this reality of an omnidimen-sional supercomputer built by the same race that had made the alien spacecraft. The InfinityMind shared its limitless data with Iron Mike, the Enemy of Evil, giving him specialized knowl-edge that had many times saved his life.

Iron Mike Sweeney was ready for the coming battle. He was more ready than he had ever been. His fighting skills had been refined by a thousand battles, and through the teachings of his Zen master, Shinobi, his mind was cool, detached, receptive.

Upon the War Machine he sat at the top of Corn Hill, watch-ing the town below him. Night had come upon the town, and Iron Mike, Enemy of Evil, was ready. Energy hummed through the War Machine's circuitry. Across Iron Mike's chest was the strap supporting his satchel of fusion bombs. Each was rolled tightly to compress its charge, and bound with a single unbreak-able strand of a rare natural material similar in appearance to rubber bands. Iron Mike had disguised the bombs to look like copies of the *Evening Standard and Times*. He smiled thinly, amused at his own cleverness. None of the Evil Ones would ever suspect that they were under attack. He would ride down among them, heaving fusion bombs onto their very doorsteps, and then he would go to warp drive and soar to a minimum safe distance of one thousand kilometers before he remote-detonated the bombs. The whole of Corn Hill, that wretched hive of scum and villainy, would become one huge mushroom cloud of cleansing nuclear fire. Not even the minions of the Evil One could survive that. Then the rest of Pine Deep could sleep in peace for another night, the lives and souls of all the true humans protected yet again by Iron Mike Sweeney, the Enemy of Evil.

Perched atop the hill like a huge predator bird, he looked at his transtemporal chronometer strapped to his muscular wrist.

It was time.

Very carefully he removed his cerebral interface from his pocket and placed it on his head, adjusting the earpieces so that the data flow would be perfect. Then he touched the keypad of the InfinityMind uplink. Immediately codec data flowed into him. The InfinityMind was in one of its playful moods, Iron Mike noticed with a wry smile; it fed him his battle data in a kind of strange musical encryption that, to anyone else but a cyborg warrior of justice, sounded much like the Beastie Boys.

"Let's do it," Iron Mike said with a cold voice. It was in fact what he always said right before battle.

He touched an invisible button on his handle-grips, releasing the engines from station-keeping. Another button put the battle engines online. They purred like great cats. With his thumb he activated the forward shields. He never used the aft shields. He was Iron Mike Sweeney: his back would never be toward the enemy. They would always see him coming right at them, cramming justice right down their throats!

"Let's do it," he said again, lips curling back into a warrior's smile, revealing gritted teeth.

The War Machine leaped forward, accelerating smoothly as it shot down the steep decline of Corn Hill. As he swooped down toward the first of the Evil Ones' lairs, Iron Mike thrust a hand into his satchel and gripped the first fusion bomb.

"Eat this, alien scum!" he snarled and threw the bomb with perfect precision. It cut through the black shadows and the miserable spray of light from the streetlight and arced over the hedges. Iron Mike knew that they weren't really hedges but holographic projections designed to disguise the front of the alien encampment. He wasn't fooled. The fusion bomb soared past the holograms and struck with a ringing thud on the red-painted front portal. The bomb dropped to the ground and lay there, destruction hidden in Iron Mike's own deceptive covering.

The Evil Ones are going to get a lot of bad news tonight, he thought, and grinned wolfishly.

He sped on, zeroing in on his next target. Target acquired, he delivered his next "special edition" and rode on, laughing with righteous triumph. Above and beyond the town, dark clouds loomed and the gods threw lightning to mark his way.

Iron Mike Sweeney, the Enemy of Evil, rained destruction as he soared down Corn Hill, the warp nacelles on the War Machine channeling limitless power into every atom of the attack craft.

The battle to save mankind had begun!

(4)

"Okay, gentlemen," Terry said as he breezed into the office, "someone want to bring me up to speed?"

A dozen men and women were scattered around, standing, sitting backward on chairs, lounging against filing cabinets; some held cups of coffee in Pine Deep Police Department plastic mugs. A dozen heads turned in his direction; eight of them he recognized, the others were strangers. Of the first batch, Gus Bernhardt dominated the place, not with any sense or aura of command, but with sheer physical size. He was approximately the size of a panel truck, as bald as an egg, and as red as a twenty-dollar lobster. Chief Bernhardt was a massive, sloppy Buddha figure in an ill-fitting gray uniform that was all decked out with whipcord and buttons and polished fittings. His accoutrements were the only neat part of him; the rest of him looked like he'd spent the night in the backseat of his patrol car, which might have been a fair guess. Terry knew that Gus was a lousy chief, but he was related to practically everyone in town and no one else really wanted the job. To be fair, the job rarely entailed anything more capital than ticketing speeders on A-32, citing overtime parking, discouraging kids from shoplifting baseball cards from the drugstore, and rousting the teenagers who went out to Dark Hollow to get drunk and screw. Terry knew that Gus spent much of his shift time eating, reading old dog-eared Louis L'Amour paperbacks, and sleeping.

Gus's crew of officers ranged from subpar to not bad. Jim Polk and Dixie MacVey were longtimers like Gus, career cops in a town that hadn't much use for serious law enforcement. Shirley O'Keefe and Rhoda Thomas were law students from Pinelands State College who took part-time police co-op jobs just to get some vague idea of what the whole cops and robbers thing was all about, though they had quickly discovered there were no robbers, as such, in Pine Deep, and the cops were not exactly *NYPD Blue*. The remaining three officers, Golub, Brayer, and Shanks, were local boys, fresh out of college, who took the job because it was a job and because they hadn't had anything better lined up; but they were decent, intelligent, and conscientious young family men, and they worked their shifts with something approaching dedication if not actual competence. Terry nodded to a couple of them and shook Gus's beefy mitt. The four strangers regarded him with neutral expressions, their faces registering nothing because he wasn't in uniform and that meant that he was a civilian. The wall between the cops and the rest of the world was typically palpable.

Gus made the introductions, waving a hand at the closest of the four, a tall, middle-aged, balding black man with a lugubrious expression wearing a dark blue nylon Windbreaker with PO-LICE stenciled on the breast and back in crisp white letters. Terry thought that he looked like Morgan Freeman without the sense of humor.

"Terry, this is Detective Sergeant Frank Ferro with the Philadelphia Narcotics Division. Detective, this is our mayor, Terry Wolfe."

The narc's eyes registered the information and his attitude softened just a little, accepting the mayor as more or less "one of us." He extended a thin but surprisingly strong hand and they shook.

"A pleasure, sir. This is my partner, Detective Vince La-Mastra." A cheerful-looking and very tan young man with a buzzed head of blond hair extended his hand and gave Terry a wrestler's handshake. He was one of those athletic types who are so superbly muscled that his tanned face looked like a leather bag full of walnuts with each angular muscle in cheek and jaw sharply defined, but the bright blue eyes and the youthful smile offset the effect. Like Ferro, he was wearing a blue Windbreaker over a white shirt and dark tie. Having cast Morgan Freeman as Ferro in his mind, Terry cast Howie Long as LaMastra. Matching everyone he met to actors was a trick Terry had always used to remember people in business. It had long ago become automatic, though oddly he had never been able to figure out which actor could play him.

Gus nodded to the other two, both wearing ordinary police uniforms. "Officer Chremos down from Crestville," Gus said, and Terry shook hands with a Greek-looking man in his mid-forties in starched black and white.

The last man stood and offered his hand before Gus could make the introduction. "Jimmy Castle."

"One of Black Marsh's finest," Gus said wryly.

"Absolutely," said Castle with a grin. He had sandy blond hair and freckles and an instantly engaging manner. The other Pine Deep cops just nodded and kept to the background, clearly intimidated by the big dogs from Philly.

"Okay then," said Terry, looking around at the faces. "Well, ladies and gentlemen, where do we stand?"

Gus opened his mouth to speak, but Sergeant Ferro beat him to it. "If I may? Your Honor, the situation is this—we have three suspects, part of a small team that had worked out a drug buy with your generic Jamaican heavies. Nothing unusual, usually no hitches in an operation like this. A standard midvolume buy staged in an empty warehouse, happens all the time, every day of the week. These things generally don't get messy because that interrupts the regular flow of trade. The product has to flow smoothly in order for everyone to get rich. It's all business."

"Okay, I'm with you so far," Terry said as he settled his muscular rump on the corner of Gus's desk and listened attentively. He composed his face into a stern, slightly superior frown but raised his eyebrows to show that he was ready to hear their report. It was a tactic that worked pretty well on the town council, and seemed to work well enough with Ferro. Inside, Terry's heart was hammering against his chest, beating out a rhythm of excitement and apprehension. He just didn't let it show.

The cop said, "The buy was set up in Philly, which is why Detective LaMastra and I were in on the case. Our narcotics unit is a division of East Detectives, and we sometimes work with state and federal narcotics offices to stop interstate flow of drugs. Now, since there was a shoot-out and one of our officers was killed, we would like to be actively involved in this investigation." His eyes were hard as he said this and the room was very quiet. "I've asked Chief Bernhardt if he would mind if I called in some Philly blues with their units to help with the search. They'll be here within the half hour. If . . . that is acceptable to you, sir."

Terry almost asked if Pine Deep would have to foot the bill for the overtime the Philly cops would be working, but thought the questions would be both in poor taste and poorly timed. "Of course," he said, softening his frown to a helpful smile. "Bring in the National Guard if it'll help. Anything that'll clean this up and get it off my streets."

"Thank you, sir. Anyway, we weren't expecting this to go down . . . it was pure coincidence that our team had this particular band of Jamaicans under surveillance for the last few months. I won't bore you with all the details, but the *Reader's Digest* version is this—we've been tracking a pipeline from the islands to Miami and from there to Philly. Coming up I-95 on what we call Cocaine Alley. They use family cars, you know, station wagons and such, driven by clean-cut regular-looking folks who pony the stuff to Philly, and then use the parking lots of strip malls just off the interstate to off-load."

Detective LaMastra spoke up for the first time. "We were backtracking from the street and thought we could tag a couple of the ponies." He gave a fatalistic wave of his hands. "But that's for shit now."

Ferro nodded. "We had a team, just two guys in a van a block from the site, and another officer outside with a fiber-optic camera and portable recorder. We had audio and video plants in the warehouse where the buy was going down, but we didn't have a full team there because we weren't expecting to make any arrests. We just wanted pictures, data, hoping to tail some of the players back to whomever they worked for, going up the food chain. So our team was unprepared for what went down."

Detective LaMastra snorted. "No shit." Ferro shot him a brief look, which LaMastra appeared to ignore.

"In any case," Ferro continued, "the buyers were a car full of local boys. Five South Philly thugs, low-level tough guys. I had a chance to look over the videotape with a couple of other detectives and we managed to ID all five. The odd thing was that these boys are not part of the drug game. They usually do roughhouse stuff, like collections for loan sharks and that sort of thing. The drug buy was a new career venture for them, and they completely screwed it up. The buy started to go down, business as usual, but then the South Philly boys pulled some guns and suddenly everyone was shooting."

"You should have seen the video," LaMastra said with a twisted smile. "Looked like a Quentin Tarantino film."

"Jesus," breathed one of the law students. Terry glanced at her. At twenty-one and five feet four, she looked like a scared kid dressed up for Halloween in a cop uniform and gun belt. He wondered if she had ever even fired the heavy automatic strapped to her young hip. He wondered if any of Gus's people ever had.

Ferro pulled a notepad out of his pocket and consulted it. "The suspects were identified as follows. One Nicholas Scilini, thirty, and Lenny DiCavellio, twenty-eight, both dead of multiple gunshot wounds. The three that got away included Kenneth Boyd and Tony Macchio, both relatively small fish and barely worth the effort it would take to yank the switch on them."

"And the third? You said there were three?"

Gus Bernhardt looked uneasily at Terry and then at Ferro, and the cop's dour face looked even more mournful and even more like Morgan Freeman's. The grimmer Morgan Freeman, circa *Se7en*, not the older, jollier Freeman from *Bruce Almighty*. "The third gunman is the real problem, Mayor Wolfe. He is one of the reasons we are going to be handling this situation very, very carefully."

Terry grinned. "Who is he? Jack the Ripper?"

No one laughed; no one else so much as smiled.

"We should be so lucky," said Ferro.

"What does that mean?" Terry asked, losing his grin. He didn't like the shifty, scared looks everyone was covertly exchanging, and it wasn't helping his stress level one little bit. The hammering in his chest was turning into an improvisational drum solo. He hoped he wasn't visibly sweating.

"His name," continued Ferro, "is Karl Andermann Ruger." He looked significantly at Terry, but he only shrugged and shook his head.

Gus bent over and said, softly, "Cape May Lighthouse. Last summer."

Terry stared at him and slowly, very slowly he felt the room turn as cold as a meat locker.

Everyone in the room looked either stricken, or scared.

"That's who we think Karl Ruger is," said Ferro quietly.

"Oh my God," Terry whispered.

(5)

Val left the soup on the stove to simmer and went up to her room to take a nap. For the last two weeks she'd been extremely tired. Not just from managing the farm—she had plenty of help for that—but just plain exhausted. And then there was this morning. After Crow had gone downstairs to have breakfast, Val had thrown up.

It was the second time this week she'd done that and she was starting to worry. There was an EPT kit in her purse, but she hadn't yet worked up the nerve to use it. She was on the pill, and she and Crow even used condoms. Surely she couldn't be pregnant with that much birth control running interference.

She took off her jeans and shirt and slid into bed in bra, panties, and socks, pulling the big comforter up to her chin. Val lay there and listened to the wind stir the corn. A storm was coming and the wind had freshened and the illusion of sea surf that the blowing corn made was even more pronounced. The steady rhythm of it lulled her to sleep within minutes.

Her sleep was filled with dreams.

The first dream was sweet and did nothing more than replay what had happened last night when Crow came by. Every delicious detail was there, starting with the long walk they'd taken down the winding lanes of cornstalks, hand in hand, stopping now and then to kiss. About a mile from the house, deep in the fields, they'd stopped at their favorite spot, a small clearing by the rail fence where Val and her brother, Mark, had erected a scarecrow when they were kids. The clearing was the spot where Val and Crow had first kissed, and the spot where they'd first touched each other with trembling and uninitiated hands. Crow had brought a blanket, draping it over one shoulder, and last night, as he had on so many nights over the years, he'd spread it on the ground. Above them the stars painted them with pale silver light as they kissed and undressed each other and then lay down on the blanket. Some nights were slow and tender and patient, and some nights were all about urgency. Last night it was a hammering need in their blood and they dropped their clothes rather than hang them on the fence rails. Crow lay down and pulled her down onto him. She stretched out on him, nearly his match in height and certainly his match in heat and need. Their kisses were hot and breathless and there was no time for words. She reached down to find him hard and familiar and she took him and guided him into her body and they both gasped as he entered and found her very wet and ready.

A few minutes later she cried out as she came—a sound echoed strangely by a startled crow deep in the field—and then a few minutes after her he cried out as he rose to that crest where there is nowhere to go but over, and over he went, sailing into the golden intensity of his orgasm, and Val caught up and she came again.

After that it had been time for tenderness and softness and slow kisses and the dream faded out like a love scene in a movie, dimming to black and then silence, and for a while she just floated in the darkness of sleep.

Then she had *the* dream again.

The other one, the one she had been having for weeks now. In her dreams the pale man was always there. Val had dreamed about him for years, but now he was always there, waiting at the edge of sleep. Sometimes this dream was just a collection of quick flash images like unexpected lightning between longer and less frightening dreams; sometimes the dream was longer and complex, and when it was one of those kinds of dreams she felt panic because she didn't think she would ever find her way out. On nights like that, waking up was like a reprieve from the electric chair.

Now, as evening settled over the farm, she had one of those darker and more complex dreams and its intensity washed away the happiness and tenderness of the previous dream.

First she dreamed of the tall man with black hair and pale skin and no features at all that she could make out, as if his face were a blur, as if someone had tried to take his picture and he'd turned away too fast, but as he moved through her dreams his face remained smeared like that. The only part of his face that she could see clearly was his mouth.

He had a red, smiling mouth and lots of jagged white teeth.

In that first dream she walked through the darkened rooms and hallways of her family's big, rambling farmhouse. She was not fleeing through the rooms—not at first—but there was some indefinable sense of urgency. Every once in a while she'd look behind her and she'd see the tall pale man step back out of sight.

Then suddenly the dream changed and she was running through the cornfields as cold rain hammered down on her. She was naked and streaked with blood and mud and icy rainwater. In one hand she held a sodden fistful of twenty-dollar bills wrapped in bank tape. In her other hand she held a gun. The gun stank of cordite, the barrel still smoking.

She ran through the fields, vulnerable, helpless, and afraid. And the tall pale man followed her.

It was like one of those chase scenes in the old horror movies: she ran fast and ran well and the pale man walked with slow deliberate steps as if in time with a metronome, but somehow he still managed to keep up with her . . . and whenever she cast a terrified look over her shoulder he seemed to be catching up.

She ran and ran.

Once she stopped, spun around, and fired the gun at the man, squeezing the trigger and feeling the shock as the bullet exploded from the gun and her gun hand was jerked into the air. The bullets all hit the pale man.

She might as well have been throwing stones at a statue for all the good they did. The pale smiling man never slowed and he never stopped, and each time a bullet struck him—and passed straight through—his smile grew. It grew and grew until it was an alligator's smile, huge and full of sharp teeth. The smiling mouth was absurd and too big for the rest of the face.

He came on through the rain and Val turned and ran on.

The smiling man kept walking but he got closer and closer and closer, and just as he was reaching out to close his bone-white fingers around her naked shoulder . . .

. . . Val woke up.

She shuddered and shook her head and crawled up until the knobs of her spine were pressed against the wooden headboard. Her face and throat and breasts were wet with sweat and for just a moment the sweat smelled like rainwater.

Chapter 6

"**B**oyd!"

The cry clawed its way out of the car and fled away across the tops of the corn. A few crows stirred and flapped uneasily, casting lifeless black eyes suspiciously around. They sat on the crossbar of a scarecrow perch, but there was no scarecrow here, just the faded old wood of the perch. The birds waited, listening.

There was silence, except for the swaying of the corn.

"Oh . . . Jesus . . ." A whisper now: pale and bloodless, too weak to even rustle the feathers of the crows.

Silence again. Longer this time. The birds fidgeted.

Then a new sound. A creak and then a mild protest of metal. The birds hopped and turned to look. The broken car squatted below them, half buried in toppled stalks of corn. The crumpled metal skin of the car looked like cloth thrown over a pile of rocks; there was no moon and no starlight to give it a metallic sheen. The car simply hunched there on its crippled wheel, abandoned and desolate.

The crows waited. They were hungry crows. They knew.

With ancient black eyes they watched as the door of the car was pushed slowly, heavily open. Its hinges squealed with piglike protest, but the door finally opened.

There was more of the expectant silence again. Nearly ten minutes passed before there were any further movements from within the car. The crows rustled their feathers and tried not to think about their empty bellies. One crow opened its beak as if to utter a loud cry, but closed it again without making a sound.

It was a hand that first appeared. Dark with blood, it reached out of the car and hooked trembling fingers over the frame. The fingers slipped on the smooth metal, but finally the tips caught in the depression of the rain gutter above the door. The hand curled, tensed, tried to be strong. Tendons stood taut on the back of the hand and in the wrist, the forearm muscles swelled with effort as the bloody hand tried to haul its body out of the car. It was a problem in physics, and it should have be an insoluble one; the arm should never have been able to collect enough strength to pull the body from its seat, there wasn't enough blood or life in its veins to carry strength to its muscles. Even adrenaline should not have been enough to allow that engineering feat to come to fruition. But as the crows watched, Tony Macchio pulled himself slowly, carefully, and painfully out of the car.

The nearest crow squawked very quietly as if ironically cheering the performance. The other crows watched with more evident annoyance. Death was sometimes too slow, slowest when the belly was empty.

It took Tony all of five minutes to get himself into a reasonably upright position, but then he sagged into the V formed by the car and the open door. His legs refused to be part of this mad venture and simply buckled, but his arms spread and he hung in bleeding cruciform on the apex of the doorway. He coughed once, sharply, and then again more softly. His ruined nose was swollen and purple. Blood dottled his lips and dripped onto his chest, but each drop was lost against the immensity of the stain that drenched him from sternum to crotch. The two bullet holes in his gut leaked sluggishly, the flow diminishing from a simple lack of hydrostatic pressure. He was bled white and should by all accounts have been dead, but even though his body was dying it lingered at the point of death and life, sustained by a single thread. That thread was the wire of hatred sewn through Tony's soul.

His bloody lips formed a single word.

"Karl!" He said it without sound, but it had all the force of a curse screamed at the top of furious lungs. Just saying the name funneled power into his dying muscles. It wasn't a lot of power, but it was a cold and determined power. It made his legs assume the abandoned duty of supporting him, and with slow deliberation he pushed himself away from the door and stood. More or less. He had to grab the edge of the roof to keep from falling face-forward into the dirt. He couldn't let that happen, he knew. If he fell, he would die. If he could stand, he could find Ruger. If he could find him, then he could kill the evil son of a bitch.

That was the plan and he reviewed it in his jumbled mind. It seemed like a good plan, it seemed like the only plan he would ever need. Simple, direct, and very satisfying. Find Karl Ruger and cut out his black heart. Maybe shoot his way up and down the man, like the Sicilians used to do: put one in each foot, then in each ankle, then through the knees, and keep working up. Firing his gun dry and reloading, making sure not to hit any arteries, keeping Ruger alive for a long time and making it last until Karl was begging and crying for one right through the brain. No . . . maybe Tony wouldn't finish him off at all. Maybe he would just sit there and watch Ruger bleed, maybe have a race, just the two of them, to see which one died first. At that moment, despite the sea of blood that he had lost, Tony believed that he could outlast Ruger. It didn't matter a damned bit if he died a single second later. That was fine. He'd chase Ruger all the way down to hell.

Rotten bastard!

Tony inched his way along the side of the car toward the trunk. He needed something to use as a bandage, something to keep the last little drops of blood within him until he could find Ruger. Maybe there was a towel or something in the trunk. Even a greasy one would be fine; Tony didn't much care about infection. He knew he was going to die, but just needed to stay alive a little while longer. Just a little while longer.

His feet stumbled clumsily over the clods of dirt thrown by

the car's violent entry into the field, but he didn't fall. Once or twice he staggered, but both times his hands had managed to find purchase on the car and pull him back to balance.

The trunk was open, and when Tony finally crept far enough along the side of the car to look inside, he could see that the big bags of coke and cash were gone. Well, what did he expect? Of course they would be gone. That's why Ruger had shot him: to take his cut. Boyd must have been in on it, too.

Tony ground his teeth even as he felt tears well up in his eyes. Boyd was supposed to have been his friend, and yet he hadn't done a fucking thing to stop Ruger. He just went along with it.

Well, Tony thought bitterly, *we'll just have to settle his hash, too. Yes, sir, settle Boyd's fucking hash. Right along with Ruger's. Shoot them both.* Or maybe play Spartacus and give them knives and hold them at gunpoint while he made them fight it out. Fight to the death. That would be a real pisser. *Fucking Spartacus. Thumbs down, fellows, thumbs-fucking-down.*

He leaned on the edge of the trunk and peered in. The trunk light glimmered faintly off the metal edge of a jack handle, a can of Fix-a-Flat, the barrel of a shotgun, and . . .

. . . the edge of a twenty-dollar bill.

Tony grinned. The edge of the bill stuck out from under the cloth cover usually draped over the spare. Tony reached in and pulled away the cover. His grin widened.

Ruger had missed some.

Eight packs of twenties lay in a sprawl. Each pack was banded with paper and initialed by whoever had counted it. Each pack was badly stained with blood, but it was all good money. Well, well . . . what was this? Tony's grin became even broader, stretching his bloodless skin over his yellow teeth. Dusted all around the money was a thick white powder. There was a lot of it, maybe as much as a pound. One of the glassine bags must have ruptured and a fine white snow had fallen in the trunk of the car.

Well, well . . .

Tony reached down into the trunk and lifted out one of the bundles of twenties, looking at it with fascination. If he could

have seen his own eyes just then they would have frightened
him. The lights that flickered in them were not fires so much as
weird neon glowing and blinking and twisting to form bizarre
shapes. Holding the bills up to his nose, he snorted some of the
cocaine off them, drawing the white fire deep into his body. The
anesthetic quality of the coke began to work its magic on him
almost at once.

Continuing to grin, he pulled his sodden shirt open and slid
the money down under his belt as a compress. The crisp bills
brushed across the ragged edges of one of the bullet holes, but
Tony was beyond normal pain. He took another stack of bills and
roughly applied a five-hundred-dollar bandage to the second
entry wound. The cocaine on the money would provide some
mild topical anesthesia as well, should the pain come calling, but
Tony really didn't care. It tickled him to think about his expensive bandages. He adjusted his belt, drawing it tighter to hold the
compresses firmly in place. He had begun to chuckle now,
thinking about Boyd and Ruger slicing each other up as he
watched, each of them hoping that the winner might be allowed to live. The chuckle was low, mean, and wet.

Again Tony reached into the trunk, but this time he pulled up
a loose handful of cocaine. "Finest kind," he said aloud, and then
buried his snout in the snow and inhaled. The rush was incredible.

He coughed a little, gagging on the coke, but then the cough
turned into another nasty chuckle. With a careless flick of his
hand he let the rest of the coke flutter down to blanket the inside of the trunk.

Then he picked up the shotgun. He knew it was loaded, because he was the one who had carried it during the job. One
shell in the pipe and four up the ass. His chuckle bubbled into a
laugh as he pushed himself away from the open trunk and
turned to begin his search for Ruger and Boyd.

"Wait for me, fellas," he said jovially, "I'll be right with you."

He took one decisive step toward the cornfield and fell flat
on his face. The shotgun discharged as his finger spasmodically
jerked the trigger, and the blast swept the crossbar clear of

crows. Black and bloody feathers swirled in the night air and then fluttered down to become lost in the ranks of corn.

Tony lay with mud in his nose and eyes and laughed until he vomited blood into the dirt.

He didn't move at all until the beam of a flashlight suddenly seared into his eyes and he winced and turned away. He heard footsteps approaching slowly, and through the distorted dimness that settled over his brain, Tony thought he could hear the rumble of an engine somewhere off to his left, way over on the road. It took most of his remaining strength to open his eyes, and he could just make out the thick, hulking shape that towered over him. As he watched, the shape moved toward him, following the beam of the flashlight. It was a strange shape: man-shaped, but gnarled and apelike, too much bulk on the shoulders and arms, and a simian gait to the long, bowed legs.

The shape drew near and then squatted down next to him. Tony tried to see past the glare of the flashlight, but the shape held it so close that he couldn't see anything.

"You're hurt," the shape said. The voice was flat. It was a statement, not a question.

"I . . . I've been . . . shot."

The shape reached out one massively muscled arm, grasped Tony's shoulder, and carefully rolled him onto his back; then the shape sat back again. Tony grunted and coughed more blood. He was amazed that he still had any left to lose.

"I've been shot," he said again.

"Uh-huh. I can see that."

"Could you . . . help me?"

The shape said nothing for a few seconds, then murmured, "I could. Sure, I could help you." Still, he did not move. He just squatted there on his hams and appeared to wait.

It was getting very hard for Tony to think. Why did the guy just sit there? he wondered. "I need *help*," he said again, raising a weak hand and trying to grab the man's shirtfront. The strength in his arm failed and the hand fell away.

"Uh-huh."

"Did you . . ." he began and then had to stop until another fierce coughing fit came and slowly passed. When he tried it again his voice was faint, even to his own ears, as if he were listening to it through an old plaster wall. "Did you come . . . to help me?"

"No," said the shape, and reached for him.

(2)

Terry Wolfe stared at Ferro for a long time, trying to work out something to say. The mayor went to the coffee station and poured himself a cup, turning his back to give himself a moment to compose his face. He added sugar and cream, then sipped it to lubricate a throat that had gone completely dry. When he turned back to face the cops his face betrayed nothing, but he stared hard at Ferro for a long time.

Ferro waited it out, used to this kind of reaction, having already gotten it from Chief Bernhardt, his officers, and the two cops from the other towns. Everyone reacted like this: how could they not? The murders at the Cape May Lighthouse had made the papers across the country and throughout much of the world. Two books had already been written about them, and Jonathan Demme was already making a movie based on it starring Don Cheadle and Colin Farrell.

"How much of the story do you know?" asked Ferro, lighting up a Camel with a silver Zippo with the F.O.P. symbol engraved on it.

Terry's throat was as dry as paste as he sipped the coffee. "Just what everyone else in the world knows," he said. "Some madman tore up an entire group of senior citizens who were visiting the lighthouse in Cape May. Forced them all into the observation room of the lighthouse and then cut them to pieces and left bizarre messages on all the walls. Something like eighteen dead, though two were supposed to have actually been tortured to death before being cut to pieces."

"That's the gist of it."

"I thought no one knew who did that. I mean . . . *do* you guys actually know who did that?"

Ferro looked grave and even a little secretive. "This is all South Jersey P.D. and the FBI, but some of it kind of spilled over into my backyard. I know that the investigative team has been looking at Karl Ruger for months now, but it's one of those situations where they know more than they can prove. Most of it comes from hearsay—one ex-con said this and a hooker from Atlantic City said the other—but lately a lot of people seem to know that Ruger did the job. It isn't known if he did it alone, or if he masterminded it, or what. One theory is that someone hired it done with Ruger as the hitter."

Gus was appalled. "Why would anyone pay someone to do something like *that*?"

Ferro exhaled through his nose. "It's complicated. I'm sure you're aware of all the infighting among the families in Philly. The so-called don died of lung cancer nineteen months ago and, since he didn't have any sons, everyone who thinks he has a claim to the title is vying for it. Well, to make a long story short—"

Terry held up a hand. "Detective Ferro, as fascinating as this all would be to another police officer, I personally don't care even a little bit about the dynamics of Philadelphia criminal politics. Just tell me how this is going to impact my town."

Ferro's mouth snapped shut with a click and for the first time he looked off-balance. Terry could see that he was used to always being in charge and probably enjoyed the scope and drama of the ongoing battle between cops and robbers, but right now Terry's head was pounding and listening to what amounted to a recap of the last four seasons of *The Sopranos* was not going to help any.

LaMastra stepped in and summed up: "We think Ruger was hired to do a hit on relatives of one of the crime lords, and he overdid it."

"You don't say," Terry murmured. "So, Ruger gets the Hannibal Lecter award for head case of the decade. And . . . ?"

Ferro pursed his lips, considering. "Well, the degree of rage demonstrated in those killings in Cape May, and what we saw on the surveillance video of the shoot-out earlier today, clearly paint Ruger as both extremely dangerous and completely unstable."

"Mm, I've heard homicidal maniacs can be like that," Terry said dryly.

Ignoring the mayor's tone, Ferro said, "He's on the run and under pressure and he has apparently stopped somewhere in your town. When he did the hit in New Jersey he killed a lot of innocent bystanders as well."

Terry nodded. "I take your point. So why is this guy walking the streets at all?"

"As I said, more is known than can be proved. The killer left no useful clues, and he certainly didn't leave any witnesses. Even so, people talk, and some of the talk has pointed the investigative team in the direction of Karl Ruger. It would be fair to say that an arrest would have been made within a week, two at the outside."

"So, how the heck did a psycho hit man get involved in a drug heist?"

"Philly's getting too hot," said LaMastra. "Word started getting around that Karl was maybe the hitter, and that meant that sooner or later he'd end up in a field somewhere, hands tied behind his back with his cock cut off and stuffed in his—"

"I . . . uh . . . get the basic idea," Terry said, cutting him off and shooting a significant glance at Shirley.

Ferro glared at his partner and LaMastra gave Terry and the officers an apologetic nod. "I think it's a fair guess that not everyone knows it was him, or at least not the right ones. If they did, parts of him would be showing up in fifty different states. More likely it's that no one knew it was him until just recently, probably as recently as last night or this morning. It was all breaking fast. The way we figure it is that when Ruger got wind of the rumors he immediately organized the drug hit to give him some traveling money. The fact that he was working with Boyd seems to bear that out."

"Why's that?"

"Boyd was a kind of small-time fixer. A travel agent," said

LaMastra. When Terry looked perplexed, he explained, "He gets people out of the country when things get hot. Fake IDs, passports, whatever. Because he's good at it everyone leaves him alone."

Sergeant Ferro nodded. "If they were working together, then it's probably a good bet that Boyd was going to arrange to get Ruger out of the States. He stole a lot of money and that buys a lot of plastic surgery and false ID. There are places where a new face and new papers and a million dollars could get you lost in a big hurry."

"So he split," Terry said, "and now he's running around loose in Pine Deep?"

Ferro and LaMastra both looked at him soberly. "Yes," they agreed.

Terry looked at Gus, who shrugged and shook his head. "So, now what?"

Ferro pursed his lips. "Well, Your Honor, the rest of our boys should be here any time now. They have surveillance pictures of Ruger, Boyd, and Macchio that we'll distribute. Since the road posts in Crestville failed to spot them, then we have to assume that they've stopped here and decided to hole up. That means we have to work out a search and detain program that will run them to ground."

"Uh, Sergeant, this is not really the sort of thing that our chief's department is used to handling," said Gus diffidently. "I mean, we don't really *do* manhunts. . . ."

Ferro looked faintly amused. "Don't worry, Chief, you'll be getting a lot of help from my team. We can probably count on the state police and by tomorrow probably the FBI as well, not to mention some pinch hitters from the neighboring towns. We're used to doing this sort of thing. I don't mean to usurp any authority from you, sir, but we have a set way of handing these things, and if you'll let us, we can run the show for you." He glanced at Terry. "If that's acceptable to you, sir?"

"Darn straight!" Terry said. "Like I said, I don't care if you have to call in the National Guard, just do what you have to do. Chief Bernhardt will be more than happy to defer to your greater expertise." He glanced at Gus, who, rather than looking offended at the loss of authority, appeared to be massively relieved. "You tell us what to do," he concluded, "and we'll give it a go."

Ferro nodded. "Thank you, Mr. Mayor, Chief. Okay," he said and clapped his hands, "let's get to work."

(3)

The wrecker was a gleaming, grotesque monstrosity. From the rat-eye red of its running lights to the shroud-black opacity of its tinted windows, it appeared every inch a pernicious and predatory thing, soaring along the road in a hideous silence. The split-rim hubcaps were polished to a spotless chrome finish, as was every cold metal accessory from the twin exhaust stacks to the guardrails that looked as if they had come from some ornate and disinterred coffin. The duel sets of rear wheels pushed the behemoth along the road at a ghastly speed, whipping along past harvested and unharvested fields, past whitewashed telephone poles that looked like old bones, past the bolted doors of night-darkened houses. Aside from the faint whine of the tire rubber on the macadam and the fainter growl of the perfectly tuned engine, the wrecker made no other sound; for all the noise it made it might have been a midnight wind.

In the cabin, Tow-Truck Eddie squatted in a repulsive tangle of ungainly muscularity, unnaturally disfigured by knots of muscles. Muscle upon muscle, tendons like bundles of piano wire, veins like high-pressure hoses. Even his face was hard with bulging muscles, bunching as the driver clenched and un-clenched his jaw. He drove in complete silence, eyes fixed and staring, barely seeing the road as it unrolled itself before his headlights, big hands gripping the nubbed and leather-wrapped wheel with crushing force.

He made no sound, played no radio, listening instead with entranced delight to the voice in his head, the voice that whispered and whispered.

On his massive hands the blood still gleamed bright and

fresh, lit by the dashboard display; in his mouth he could still taste the blood of the man he'd killed. His thick lips twisted and writhed in some semblance of a smile as he drove wildly through the night. The night that was now his.

He savored the taste of blood in his mouth, and he knew that it had made him pure, made him holy. It was the first time he'd ever really paid attention to the taste of blood. It was delicious, and he wondered if he would have more of it. Inside his head the voice of God told him that yes, he would. Soon.

As Tow-Truck Eddie drove, God whispered secrets to him, telling him of the glory that had been, and of the glory that was to come. God reminded him of his own holy purpose—that of finding the Beast and killing him.

You are the Sword of God.

It echoed like thunder in his head.

Somewhere, out there in the darkness, in some unknown spot on the black road, his destiny waited. Destiny in the form of the Beast—a creature of vast cunning and evil power that he must find, must oppose—must *destroy*—because he was the Sword of God, and it was his holy purpose to do God's will here on earth. Now he knew that, after all his waiting, the Beast was out here on the road tonight, waiting for him to find it, to confront it, to begin the battle of Good against Evil, of heaven against hell. That was what the voice of God told him, pounding the words into his brain. Over and over again.

He laughed out loud, and his laugh was an explosion of righteous joy because his holy work was beginning. He had always known that someday God would set him on the right path. He'd prayed for this for years. His destiny had been clear to him since childhood. If he was who he thought he was—who he *knew* he was—then the voice that spoke so powerfully in his mind could belong to no one else but his own father. To God himself.

He laughed again and searched the roadside shadows for the Beast.

The wrecker cut through the night air like a butcher's knife, leaving a screaming darkness behind it.

(4)

"Jesus, Karl, wait for me, will you, for Chrissakes?"

Ruger said nothing and didn't slow his pace a single bit. He plowed on through the corn, moving fast but seemingly not making as much sound as he ought to. He glided through the stalks like a snake.

The corn stood impossibly tall and it stretched outward on all sides in a forever of darkness. Boyd stumbled after Ruger, slapping the stalks aside, feeling the sharp sting of the razor-edged leaves nicking his hand and cheeks. The wind was icy and damp and his exposed skin burned from the raw cold. His lame left arm was tucked into his shirt, and the dead weight of it plus the lumpy burden of the backpack gave him an ungainly pace that consumed energy and cost effort. Despite the chilly air he was bathed in sweat and the backpack felt as if it were filled with rocks.

"Man, do you even know where we're going?"

This time Ruger did stop. He turned and faced Boyd, his face completely in shadows. "Yeah, Boyd, sure I know where I'm going." He jerked a thumb over his shoulder. "I'm going that way. Any more fucking questions?"

Boyd shut his mouth with a click, biting down on all the things he didn't have the balls to say. They burned on his tongue like pepper seeds. With a grunt, a hearty expectoration, and a shadowy sneer, Ruger turned and plunged back into the corn. After a few seconds Boyd followed him. They trudged on in silence for just over a hundred yards before Boyd stepped into a gopher hole and neatly snapped both the tibia and fibula of his right leg.

He never saw the hole, and despite the dropping lunge and the sharp double snap of the bones, he couldn't immediately understand what had happened. All he knew was that the cornfield suddenly rose up in front of him, the stalks seeming to launch themselves into the air, and then his face was rushing at the dirt. He tried to break his fall, but only one hand answered the summons and that was a second off the mark, so he took a cheekful of hard-packed dirt. His eyes jolted painfully in their sockets, he bit his tongue, and his brain felt jellied by the impact. He never even heard the double pop-pop of his leg bones as they broke, and at first all he felt was the pain in his face . . . and then the leg pain hit him. It hit him like a hurricane—blasting through every nerve ending he possessed, boiling up from the torn muscle and severed blood vessels all the way through the top of his head. He howled. He howled as loud as he could, and the shrill sound of it took flight and rose far above the waving corn. He drew in a single ragged breath and then opened his mouth to howl again, but the rough leather of Ruger's glove, backed by bone and gristle and anger, struck him with such shocking force that the howl evaporated on his tongue and he gasped for a shocked breath, tears springing into his eyes. Ruger grabbed a fistful of his hair and jerked his head back and Boyd stared in mute awe at the single black metal eye that glared unwinkingly at him. The hard, cold silver that surrounded that black eye gleamed dully in the bad light.

"If you make one more fucking sound I'm going to blow your face all over this field." The whisper was as cold as the metal of the gun barrel.

"My . . . leg . . ."

"You hear me, Boyd?"

"Jesus, Karl, I broke my fucking leg," Boyd insisted, but in a low hiss, not a howl.

"No shit. Ain't you the genius?"

"My fucking *leg!*"

Ruger pressed the barrel against Boyd's forehead. "Shhhh. You're getting loud again. Shhh, shhh now."

"You gotta help me, Karl," Boyd began, and then his eyes grew suddenly very wide. "Wait . . . Karl . . . don't . . . !"

"Don't what?"

"Don't do me, man. Don't, okay? Don't do me, please, man."

Ruger actually managed to look hurt as he withdrew the gun. "Jeez, Boyd, what kind of guy do you think I am?" He released Boyd's hair and even smoothed it with a caressing hand.

"Don't do me, man. . . ."

Ruger smiled. After a few seconds, he eased the hammer off cock and put his gun away. "Stop shitting your pants, you asshole. I'm not going to do anything to you unless you get loud again. I don't go around killing everyone I meet, you know. I do have some scruples."

Boyd didn't dare make an answer to that. His terror of Ruger was even greater than the searing agony in his leg. With a sigh, Ruger stood and shrugged out of his pack, set it to one side, and then stood there, looking first at Boyd and then around at the rows of corn. A few yards away was the corner of a fence, and nailed to it was a tall wooden support for a scarecrow. The tattered guardian of the corn hung like a hobo Christ, arms outstretched and body slumped. The body was dressed in a cast-off old brown suit, frayed work gloves, and an old blue mechanic's shirt. Instead of a burlap bag for a head, this scarecrow had been topped with a grinning jack-o'-lantern in an early nod to the coming Halloween season. Beyond the figure, the fence trailed away into shadows. Ruger pursed his lips in thought; then he turned back to Boyd.

"I think we're near a farmhouse. See that fence? That looks like some kind of dividing line, maybe between this farm and the next. I'm going to follow it and see what I can see."

"Jesus! You can't just leave me here!" He hissed the words, his face screwed up with the unrelenting pain. Beads of sweat burst from every pore on his face.

"I sure as hell can't carry you. You're too goddamn big. Even if I could, I couldn't lug you and both backpacks. No, m'man, I'll get you set up here and then go get some kind of help."

Boyd was almost weeping. "You're going to run out on me, man. You're gonna do me and take my share and bug the fuck out."

"No, I'm not."

"You're gonna do me and just split—"

Ruger's hand lashed out with appalling speed and slapped Boyd's face hard to the left and then backhanded it to center position. He thrust a warning finger under Boyd's nose, jabbing the air as he spoke. "Shut your fucking mouth, man. Shut it right now, or so help me God . . ." Ruger's whispery voice trailed off, no reason to continue. Boyd shut up, but pain and fear crawled all over his face, twisting his lips and eyes and brows, wrinkling his features into a darkly comical mask. Ruger squatted down next to him, hooked a finger under his chin, and raised his face so that they were nose to nose, only inches apart. "Now you listen to me, Boyd. I said that I wasn't going to hurt you, and I'm not going to. I got no reason to lie to you. If I wanted you dead, I'd cap you now and say-la-vee, but as it happens, I need your sorry ass. I can't carry all that stuff myself, and even if I could, you have better connections for getting us out of the country than I do. I need you, Boyd, and that means you stay alive. You don't have to believe me. In fact, I don't give a rat's ass either way, but there it is. I ain't doing this out of brotherly love, so don't think I've gone all soft on you. Keeping you alive will help keep me alive and out of the slam. Simple as that. No sentiment, no after-school special heartwarming stories, you dig? I need you, and you need me. Case closed. Now, I'm going to lug you over to the fence, right by that scarecrow. That way I'll be able to find you again. I'll set your leg best I can and you can snort all the girl you want to take the edge off the pain, and then I'm going on alone for a little while . . . but I *will* be back." He jerked Boyd's head on the point of his finger. "Do you have all that? Are we clear?"

Boyd searched Ruger's eyes for the lie, for the cruel joke, but he found nothing more than the unemotional determination of a predator looking out for its own hide. He believed him. "Okay . . . okay, man."

Ruger smiled that slithery smile of his.

"That's my man. That's my main man!" He winked and then reached for the buckle of Boyd's pack. "Let's lighten the load a little first." That done, he stood and moved around behind Boyd, crouched, and caught him under the armpits. Before he lifted, he leaned so close that his lips brushed Boyd's ear as he spoke. "I'm going to lift you out of that hole. If you dare scream, man, I'll rip your throat out. Do you think I'm joking?"

"N . . . no . . ." Boyd whispered.

"Good. It's gonna hurt like a motherfucker. Just take it, man. Just take it and screw that pain like you'd screw a little tight-snatch bitch. You hear me? Just screw the hell out of it."

"Okay. . . ."

"Okay. Here we go, buddy-boy."

He hoisted Boyd up out of the hole.

Boyd didn't scream. He almost did . . . Christ knows he wanted to, but instead he bit into his lip so hard that blood burst from it and ran hot and salty down his chin. The world took a sick and dizzying stagger and there was a dull roaring in Boyd's ears as if he were standing too near to a raging waterfall. Nausea punched him in the pit of the stomach and slapped tears from his eyes. Ruger wasn't gentle about it. He lifted the big, heavy Boyd as best he could, arms wrapped like iron bands around his thick chest, and dragged him to the fence. He squatted and lowered Boyd to the ground and more or less shoved him up against the rough wooden slats of the fence. He even tried to position him so that he had a modicum of comfort. The whole process, as Boyd saw it, took about a thousand years.

"Jesus Christ, man, how much do you friggin' *weigh*?" Ruger said, sucking in great gulps of air. He walked around in a small circle, arching his back and stretching his arms over his head. Finally he walked away and returned lugging both backpacks. He crossed his ankles and lowered himself slowly to the ground, sitting Indian fashion in front of Boyd.

"G . . . gimme a cigarette," Boyd wheezed licking the blood from his lips. "Christ, I need a cigarette."

Ruger slapped his pockets until he found his pack of Pall Malls, kissed one out of the pack, lighted it, and handed it to Boyd, who sucked it greedily. Boyd's face was the color of sour milk and it glistened with greasy sweat.

"Ruger, my leg . . ."

"Yeah, yeah, your leg. Wait a minute. Here, toot some of this. Better than Novocain." He held up one of the bulky Ziploc bags and a rolled-up ten-dollar bill. Boyd took the tube and bent toward the proffered coke; his inhalation was long and deep. "Ride 'em, cowboy!" said Ruger in real appreciation as Boyd took a second snort, and then a third.

"Oh man oh man oh man oh man oh man oh man . . ." Boyd sighed, closing his eyes and leaning back against the fence.

Ruger beamed at him like a country doctor watching a kid swallow a spoonful of tonic and honey. "The breakfast of champions, m'man."

"Oh man, that feels so much better."

"Think so? Good, 'cause now I gotta set your leg."

Boyd half shrugged. "With enough of this shit, you could cut the fucker right off."

Grinning, Ruger fished in his pocket for a knife, found it, and flicked it open, a bone-handled Buck with a three-inch locking blade that was always sharp and well oiled. The keen edge sliced almost arrogantly through the tough black fabric of Boyd's double-knits, gliding silently from cuff to midthigh. Ruger cut the pant-leg off and then tore the cloth into long strips, which he then set aside. Using his lighter he inspected the break. Both shinbones had broken a few inches below the knee, and they had broken in an ugly way. There were small mounds where the ends of the broken bones tented the skin, and the whole area was livid and swollen.

"Mm," Ruger said. "Cute."

"How's it look?"

"Like shit."

"Can you fix it?"

"I can set it, but I think you're gonna need a doctor. You broke the hell out of it, Boyd. Man, when you break something, you break the ass off it." He flicked off his lighter.

"I can't feel it too bad. Just hurts a little."

"Not for long. Go on, take another toot," Ruger said, lightly grasping Boyd's shin with both hands and placing his foot against Boyd's chest.

"Gimme a sec . . ." Boyd said, diving nose-first into the bag of coke. Between toots he said, "Just let me know when you're gonna do it, okay?"

Ruger did it right then. He shoved with his foot and threw

all his weight back and away. The leg stretched in its tube of skin and muscle, the bones shifted, the ends scything through meat and muscle, and then he let it snap back into place.

"Now," Ruger said, but Boyd had passed out. His eyes had rolled up in their sockets, his mouth dropped open in the beginnings of a scream, and then he fell over on his side. "You're welcome," Ruger said with a mean smile.

Ruger sat and finished his cigarette, then stubbed it out on the ground, watching with quiet amusement as Boyd slowly drifted back up out of the pool of painless sleep into the real world. He searched for that exact moment when the pain sensors in Boyd's brain came online and connected his muzzy thoughts with all the jumbled stimuli from his leg. When Boyd's eyes suddenly flared wide and he drew in a sharp, high hiss of agony, Ruger closed his eyes for a second, savoring that little moment. Rather tasty.

"Oh . . . *Christ!*" Boyd wailed, clawing at his leg with his good hand. His scrabbling fingers encountered strangeness in the form of wooden slats bound to the leg with strips of torn denim.

"Hi, Boyd," Ruger said, "have a nice nap?"

"My leg . . . ?"

". . . Is set. More or less. Still have to get your ass to a doctor, but it'll do for now, I guess. I splinted it, so you should be okay for a little while. I waited until you woke up before I took off to find Farmer John, or whoever owns all this friggin' corn."

"Man, you can't just leave me—"

"Hey . . . hey! We've been through all that. I'm leaving you here, but I will be back. Just so you see that I'm not shitting you, I'm leaving all the stuff here. Cash, coke—the works. Now, you *know* I'm coming back for that, am I right?"

Boyd gave him a long, uncertain look, but finally he nodded.

Ruger popped a stick of Juicy-Fruit into his mouth and chewed thoughtfully for several seconds, his dark eyes ranging over Boyd's face. "Okay then. End of discussion. You stay here and talk to Mr. Scarecrow, and I'll go see what I can see. Maybe I'll get a wheelbarrow or something. Wheel your ugly butt right the hell out of here. If we're lucky I'll find a nice nondescript set of wheels. Pickup or four-by-four . . . something we can use to go off-road to stay away from our buddies in blue."

"Hurry, man."

Ruger smiled disarmingly, white teeth gleaming. "Back before you even know it." He stood up, stretched his aching muscles, and then did a slow turn, orienting himself. He sketched a little salute to Boyd, told him to be good, and strolled off, ignoring Boyd's pleas to hurry. Within a few seconds he vanished around a bend and was gone.

Boyd stared after him, eyes awash with tears of pain. Above him the scarecrow's loose clothing rustled quietly in the light, cold breeze. Boyd did not see the long scrambling line of beetles and roaches and worms and spiders that swarmed out of the fields, scurried up the fence posts, and scuttled up the pants-legs of the scarecrow. Not all of the rippling of the dummy's clothing was caused by the breeze blowing past, yet all of it was caused by the night itself.

(5)

Iron Mike Sweeney, the Enemy of Evil, looked at his chronometer. Nearly 1930 hours. He had half an hour to get home.

"Oh man," he said in a low, terse whisper, "don't let me be late."

He was all the way out past the Guthrie farm, far down on A-32. Miles to go, and it would be hard enough on flat ground. He kicked the War Machine into action and pedaled like crazy.

"Crap," he said aloud. He hadn't meant to be late, but the papers that should have been dropped off before school was even out had come in an hour after Mike usually picked them up. He'd kicked ass dropping them off, saving the last ones for the long haul down A-32. Home was on the other side of town, and the miles between were mostly hills. No way to get there until sometime after eight.

Yeah, a belting for sure.

He zoomed down one hill and tried to use the momentum to get himself up the next one, but gravity began pulling at him and he had to pump his legs so that sweat popped out on his face and under his clothes. He kept his head down and pumped the pedals, thinking of home that lay one thousand and seven miles away. One million and seven. Where Mom and Vic were waiting for him. Mom sitting by the door with her hand clamped around a collins glass, looking out, waiting for him to come creeping into the yard, steeling herself to try and run some kind of interference for him; and Vic, sitting on the left-hand side of the couch, a Winston burning in one corner of his mouth, the remote-control dwarfed by his hand, clicking through channel after channel. Vic, with his hard mechanic's hands and that little smile of his that he wore only when Mike did something wrong. Which, by Vic's tally, was pretty often. Vic, who demanded to be called "sir" and had enforced his decree with his belt. Vic, who liked how hard his hands were, and how fast. Vic, who liked to use his hands, to hurt with his hands.

Mike looked down the long road and swore to himself that he would not cry. Not this time. Not now, and not after it was all over. No matter how bad it was, he wouldn't let that prick see him cry. Even if it meant that Vic would try all the harder to wring the tears out of him.

After all, he was Iron Mike Sweeney. The Enemy of . . .

He felt the tears begin to well up and he swiped at them with pure anger.

"Damn you!" he suddenly yelled, his voice rising high and loud, bursting out of his troubled chest.

Then, with a snarl of pure rage, he thrust himself over the crest of the hill and plunged down the far side, his legs working furiously, churning around and around as the bike accelerated smoothly; not to get home a moment faster but to channel his fury and fear somewhere. The War Machine became a blur as it shot down the hill.

He saw the glow of the headlights just a split second before the vehicle crested the near hill. It bounded up over the knoll and swept down the other side, moving at incredible speed for so narrow a road. Mike was just beginning his climb up the hill, having taken the last four hills at a rapid clip.

The headlights dazzled him, and with his bright yellow and orange school jacket and white baseball cap, he fairly glowed in their brilliance. The vehicle—Mike still couldn't tell what kind of car or truck it was—swooped straight down the hill at him, never veering to give him space. When he saw the red running lights, he knew it was a truck, and the wide set of the headlights confirmed this, but he couldn't understand why it was driving so fast and why it wasn't giving him any room. Didn't it see him? It hogged the whole side of the road, cramming the shoulder, which was his only lane unless Mike decided to veer over to the other side. The truck sped on, and Mike was sure that the driver didn't see him, despite the brightness of his clothes. In the few seconds he had left, he jagged sharply and quickly to his left and gave the truck as wide a berth as possible.

Those few seconds snapped away like firecrackers and then time seemed to accelerate as the headlights also shifted, and Mike stared in complete horror as he realized the truck was angling toward him. Crossing the yellow line and angling directly toward him!

Mike tried to wave the truck away, but the roar of the engine actually increased, and then suddenly everything in Mike's world seemed to change, to become brighter as if there were spotlights on everything—and somehow he knew that this illumination was not coming from the headlights. It was as if some inner lights had flashed on, and at the same time everything abruptly slowed down. Mike was crouched over his handlebars, his face turned toward the oncoming truck. There was no sound. The truck's wheels were angled and the chrome bumper was so close he could have reached out and touched it. Mike felt his hands jerk the handlebars sharply to one side—and that motion seemed the only thing that happened in real time—and then he threw his weight farther forward, adding his mass to the impetus from the fierce pumping of his legs. In a fragment of a second, as the truck rolled at him—murderously close and yet moving so impossibly slowly—Mike veered his bike at a crazy angle and slipped past the very corner of the big silver bumper.

Immediately he shot back into real time and with a deafening roar the tow truck shot past him, the fenders and wheels inches from him, the slipstream ripping at him. The truck passed in a second and as it ripped past, Mike's bike shot off the highway, crunched across the verge, and flew into black emptiness.

He had no time to scream, and no voice for it anyway. The War Machine hurtled off the edge of the drainage ditch and smashed down in the pumpkin patch that bordered the road. The front wheel hit the twisted vine spiraling out from the top of one large gourd and the bike stopped at all once. Mike kept going.

He passed over the handlebars, turned a neat somersault in the air, and almost—almost—rotated far enough forward for him to land on his feet. It would have been a wonderful accident worthy of a standing ovation, but as he passed over the bars his left sneaker toe caught the rippled rubber of the handgrip and spoiled the rotation. Mike's heels hit first but lacking the right angle of momentum he fell backward instead of forward. His buttocks smashed down on a pumpkin and it burst under him, the stem giving his tailbone a painful jolt; then his back hit a scattering of underdeveloped pumpkins, each the size and approximate hardness of baseballs. He could feel one rib break with a searing detonation of red-hot pain that stole his breath, exploded his nerve endings, and closed a hot fist around his heart. His head flopped back and struck a stone.

Everything stopped. All sound and movement stopped and the only things he was aware of were blackness, searing pain, and the fireflies of head trauma.

Mike's mouth worked like a fish, trying to gasp in air but finding none.

He lay there for thousands of years.

When his mind could function on a rudimentary level his first thought was: *Oh, shit . . . I'm really going to be late now.* Then, *Oh my God, I think I'm dead.*

Turning his head, he could see the receding taillights of the truck, could see that it was a tow truck—lightning seemed to strike sparks from the massive gleaming hook. The engine roared as the truck picked up speed and downshifted to climb the hill.

Mike lay there, dazed, hurting, trying to survive the moment.

Once the truck had crested the hill and vanished, he stared up at the dark and featureless sky. The lightning flickered distantly and underlit the clouds with a dark red glow.

As the engine growl of the tow truck dwindled into silence, Mike tried to make sense of things. He felt smashed and stupid and afraid. Amazed, too. That idiot in the tow truck had actually tried to run him off the road! He had *really* tried, gone out of his way to do it, Mike was sure of it. He simply couldn't understand it.

He tried to move, couldn't, and lay there, focusing on thought rather than feeling.

Sure, he'd seen some people play chicken with cyclists, shifting a little closer just to spook them, but never like this. Never at night on a deserted road and at such high speeds, and with such a clear-cut intention of actually forcing him off the road. Or, he thought, maybe *with* the intention of hitting him. *No, that's dumb.* Mike dismissed the idea as ridiculous.

His lungs started working better, taking in more air.

"Any minute now I'll get up," he said aloud, but he didn't believe it.

I could be dead now, he thought in simple amazement. *If I hadn't moved so fast, I could be dead now.* Just for a second his brain replayed that narrow escape. He recalled the eerie way in which time seemed to have slowed down as he veered his bike out of the way. It was so strange.

It was because of what he'd done that he was alive. He thought about that for a long time, replaying it in his head. Despite the pain, something like a smile formed on his lips. He was alive, he realized, because he had done exactly the right thing at the right time, and done it quickly, efficiently, and without hesitation. No playtime stuff. His own quick thinking had shown him the path and his own reflexes had taken him out of harm's way. *Iron Mike Sweeney, the Enemy of Evil.*

He tried to move again and a fireball the size of North Dakota exploded in his back.

Any minute now, he thought, *I'll get up and get the heck out of here. Any minute now.*

If he'd tried to outrun the wrecker he knew he would have been ground under those big wheels. Mashed into goo. The thought that he'd escaped that fate did nothing to cheer him, because of the very real fact that the driver of that truck had meant to kill him.

The rib was really starting to scream at him. Moreover, time was passing, and Vic would be waiting, belt at the ready, hard hands fondling the remote, waiting for him, pleased with how very late it was. Mike's feeling of pride vanished instantly. His dread of Vic was overwhelming.

Still, he lay a few moments longer, collecting himself, and thinking about that crucial moment when he'd left the road, re-membering what it had felt like. At no time had it ever been panic; no, that particular emotion had not been a part of it at all. Instead, the feeling had been simpler, more profound. He had just done what had to be done, a cool, calculated move, and it had been the right thing. A minor victory, perhaps, on a world scale, but it had been everything to the life of Mike Sweeney.

Slowly and carefully, he made himself sit up. It actually helped the pain, and when he carefully turned to look down he realized that it was the twisted stem of a pumpkin that had been jabbing him in the back. Even though he was sure a rib or two were broken the pain was a lot more bearable sitting up. He took it as a good sign, though he was only partly relived and partly disap-pointed. Getting stabbed in the back by something would have meant a stay in the hospital, and that would have been at least one night away from Vic.

"Oh well," he said, and got slowly and carefully to his feet. It took a lot of doing. Both of his ankles were sore though he didn't think they were sprained, but one rib was definitely cracked. It glowed like a hot ember with every breath.

He limped over to his War Machine. It lay on its side, covered in mud and pumpkin mush. With infinite care, Mike squatted down and raised the bike onto its wheels. Half pulling it, half leaning on it, he walked back up to the road and examined it in the glow from the nearly continual lightning flashes. The frame was undamaged, and when he rolled it back and forth he was delighted to discover that the wheels spun true. How it had come through the crash undamaged was a mystery, but with the way his body was feeling he certainly didn't want to look any gift horses in the mouth.

With a dreadful expectation of the pain, he mounted the bike and began riding away. The pain was exactly as bad as he expected it to be and for a while he thought that fireflies were swarming around him, but it was only more of the fireworks display of sco-toma. It took a long time for his eyes to clear enough for him to ride, but even then there was a fringe of sparks at the edges of his vision and a peculiar tingling in the flesh around both eyes. He plodded on, pedaling slowly and with tremendous care, fearing the exertion of the hills, moving into the night until he had left the site of his calamity far behind, pedaling laboriously up and down the mountains, heading for home to accept his belting.

(6)

State Extension Route A-32 lead up from the center of Pine Deep, curved lazily around the twists in the canal, and then darted off at a right angle through the farmlands. It was the main artery along which the tourists flowed into town, and down which the semis loaded with corn, pumpkins, apples, and pears headed south-east toward Philadelphia. Slow-moving tractors, road graders, and harvesters chugged along it at modest speeds during the day, sometimes causing frustrating backups for the day-trippers from Philly, Doylestown, and Willow Grove who flocked to Pine Deep to shop the antique stores and galleries, dine at the four- and five-star restaurants, and sip expensive wines and rare drams of scotch at the sidewalk cafés. About ten miles out of the town proper was a small dirt road that cut away from A-32 at a sharp right angle. There was no official name for it, being actually a disused farm road, but everyone called it Dark Hollow Road because that's where it led. At night, carloads of teenagers thumped and bumped along its rutted length heading for the Passion Pit, so named in the forties and never changed, where they did some rutting of their own. Nearly every night the pale glow of taillights looked like fireflies through the trees, and here and there some young lover's gasp of climactic delight drifted on the breeze blowing through the pines.

Though the whole area was commonly called Dark Hollow, the true hollow was a deep and narrow valley that wormed between the toes of three substantial hills. Halfway up the tallest hill was the flattened natural shelf that had been commandeered as the Passion Pit, and it was surrounded by snarls of undergrowth that were burned to gnarled skeletons three years ago by a thoughtlessly discarded cigarette butt. The trees were badly charred as well, but few had actually died. Pine trees endured forest fires heroically, though these looked desolate without their needles. Slowly, but surely, the land reclaimed its life and color, and here and there a new green sprig of spruce or Fraser fir could be found.

At night, especially an overcast and moody night like this, Dark Hollow was as dark as a tomb and as inviting as an open, beckoning grave; yet there were worse places in Pine Deep, places where the shadows were darker still and the air hummed with a malevolent tension. But these places were never named and they were never thought about by choice. Dark Hollow, a doorway to those other places, remained as the darkest place known consciously to the people of the town, and in its way, it was dark enough.

The last crickets of the season chanted a weak and dispirited chorus from the withered grass of the hollow, and in a half-burnt old oak, an owl demanded identification of all that moved in the night. All day the spot had been empty and then between one second and the next a man stood by the stump. A moment before he had been standing on the road and now he was here, and he looked as startled as the birds around him as if he didn't understand it, either.

His face looked strained and tense, but also sad. He looked around at the shadows that clung like webs around Dark Hollow, then down at the stump, and then slowly sat down. His pale skin glowed faintly in the darkness, and his deep-set eyes looked like the empty sockets in a skull. A guitar stood nearby, canted back to rest against the trunk of a scrub pine. Before him, on the ground, was the remains of an old campfire left behind months ago by hoboes. The wood was only half burned, but cold and damp.

There was a soft flutter in the air and the gray man looked up as the ragged night bird jumped from one branch to a lower one. It stood there on stick legs, head cocked to one side as it regarded him as if it knew him.

"Yeah, brother blackbird, you know me. And I know you." Though his lips moved to form the words no sound came out. Even so, the bird rustled its wings and edged slightly closer. The man watched it for a long while and thought, *You know the Bone Man*. In his own ears his voice sounded sad. *Yeah . . . everybody know the Bone Man and everybody know that he don't amount to much.*

He pulled his guitar around and strummed the strings. The sound was high and sweet, but distant, like something heard through a closed door.

"Are you cold?" the Bone Man asked the bird. "I'm cold as a motherfucker."

The bird made a faint sound, like the squeak of a rusted hinge.

"I'm always cold." The Bone Man looked back at the old fire logs. He said nothing else, even when the logs suddenly burst into flame. The bird flapped its wings and almost flew away. But didn't. It remained there, watching the man, watching the waxing golden light, feeling the blossoming warmth. The logs caught and settled down into a cheerful, chuckling fire, so strange in that desolate place.

The Bone Man fished in his pocket for the sawed-off and polished neck of an old whiskey bottle. It fit on one finger of his left hand and he rested the fingers of his right hand across the strings, but he didn't play quite yet. Instead he closed his eyes and hung his head as if in prayer and the woods grew still around him. Then slowly, barely touching the strings, he began to play an old blues song. "Black Ghost Blues" by Lightnin' Hopkins. He played it through while the thunder rumbled overhead and the lightning slashed at the sky.

When the song ended he was a quiet for a while, listening to the storm; then he began playing a different tune. It was a sad song, one his grandfather had written a long time ago and called "Ghost Road Blues."

Not far away, close enough for the Bone Man to feel it, down the long hill at the bottom of the hollow, was another place, a place that was far darker even than its name, a place of mold and decay, where seething insectoid life thrived in twisted vitality around a swamp that lay always hidden by shadows. The tall trees were clustered over it like mourners bowed over a coffin, the twisted bracken and shrubs that were tangled along the lumpy ground as thick as moss on a wet stone, bathing it forever in darkness despite the brightest summer sun; and now, with the swelling dark of autumn and the fading of Indian summer's last shreds of warmth, the place was a temple to lightlessness, bitter cold, and a pestilential silence.

The gray man finished his song and for a while he just sat on his log and felt the roiling darkness of that shunned and malevolent place lapping like black waves around him. He remembered that place; remembered it and feared it. In his memories he saw that place splattered with blood and rent by violence. Long ago, the Bone Man had thought—foolishly, naively—that the evil of that place had perished with the evil man who'd used the swamp as a fortress. He'd believed that when the man died his evil would die with him. Now, looking back down the littered corridor of empty years, he finally understood what that cold and evil man had told him. *Evil never dies. It merely waits. And it grows stronger in the dark.* Even now, thirty years later, he could still hear the harsh mockery in that man's voice as he said those words. *Evil never dies. It waits.*

The man with graveyard dirt on his suit and the ragged night bird sat in their silence and watched the fire.

And it grows stronger in the dark.

Chapter 7

The road swept around a tight bend and then settled down into a long stretch of flat, straight highway. Mike pedaled laboriously, trying not to breathe too hard, yet feeling his lungs begging him for more air. The night had grown quiet and close around him, a gelid mass that was hard to move through with any kind of speed. He didn't dare look at his watch. Already it had been nearly an hour since the maniac in the wrecker had driven him off the road, and Vic wasn't going to be pleased at all. Mike wondered if a broken rib would exempt him from the usual belting, and decided that it probably wouldn't. He could almost imagine how Vic would put it: "Your ass ain't broken, boy, just bend over the chair and try for once to take it like a man."

A man, he thought bitterly as he pumped the pedals, *wouldn't take it at all.*

The tears wanted to come again, but he actually snarled out loud to drive them back. He would not—he absolutely would not ever cry because of that bastard Vic. Not ever again! His anger sent energy to his legs and for a while he pedaled on in furious silence, ignoring, even savoring the pain.

If I can take a broken rib, then I can take another belting.

He had gone almost three miles when a series of brilliant and lengthy lightning flashes drenched the road in revealing brilliance. Mike slowed his bike and stared. Just ahead of him, beginning a few inches beyond his front tire, were long black skid marks. They were so dark that Mike knew they were fresh, and they cut away to his right in a very tight arc, ending abruptly at the shoulder of the road. He gingerly got off his bike and walked the length of those skid marks, stopping on the verge with his heels on the blacktop and his sneakered toes hanging out over the deep ruts torn into the near edge of the big drainage ditch. He waited for the next lightning flash, and in its glow he could see where the ruts began again on the other side of the ditch; these ruts were deeper, more smashed in, and huge clods of mud had fallen away into the ditch. As bolt after bolt of lightning danced through the sky, he worked it out in pieces, seeing first the place where all four tires had cut furrows in the dirt as the car must have slewed sideways, then the gap-toothed hole in the other-wise orderly wall of cornstalks. The car must have plowed right into the field and kept on going. Mike crabbed sideways, trying to get a better angle of sight. One final flash of lightning was all he needed to see the gleam of metal many yards into the corn.

"Jeez!" he said aloud. Indecisively he looked back at his bike for a thoughtful second, and then into the corn again. He knew that the car crash must have happened only recently, because there hadn't been any skid marks when he'd come out this way. Say two hours, tops.

The wrecker had come from this direction, he thought, and wondered if that crazy driver had driven this car off the road, too.

A horrible thought occurred to him. *There could still be people in there. Trapped!*

Mike could feel his pulse racing. The thought of people trapped in a wrecked car was one of the truly terrifying images for him. When his own father had fallen asleep at the wheel of his car while driving home from his nighttime job, the ambulance men had told Mike's mom that he had probably been alive for as much as half an hour. Half an hour before the gasoline leaking from the ruptured tank had somehow found a way to ignite. Mike shuddered at the thought of someone else being trapped like that, being alone and afraid. Dying the way his dad had died. That was the stuff of his nightmares.

Before he was even conscious of his decision, he had taken a step off the blacktop and onto the top of the steep slope of the drainage ditch.

Then something truly amazing happened.

A deer stepped quietly out of the woods right in front of him, coming out of the opening that had been smashed in the cornstalks. It stepped out boldly just as a bolt of lightning seared the whole world to whiteness all around him. Mike gasped and jolted to a stop, mindful of the pain in his ribs, but too surprised even to wince.

The deer was a big buck, maybe a twelve-pointer, and normally that alone would have been enough to stop him in his tracks, but that was nothing compared to the color of the thing. It was pure white. Not just pale but an unnatural white, like milk or a freshly whitewashed fence. Hard muscles rippled beneath the smooth hide as it walked slowly out of the cornfield and stood facing him across the few yards of the drainage ditch.

Mike marveled at it, smiling at the majesty of the animal without even being aware of it. For a while he totally forgot about his broken rib and about Vic's hard hands waiting at home, he forgot about the skid marks and the wreck. He was filled with the beauty of the magnificent creature. It was easily the biggest deer he had ever seen, at least two hundred pounds, and stood tall and proud in the road before him; and it stood so close!

The deer looked at him with that quiet nobility and innate wisdom that some animals seem to possess. Not one trace of fear flickered in those large, dark eyes and it kept its eyes on him as the creature turned and paced halfway around him, edging slightly away.

"Wow . . ." Mike breathed, his voice as soft as the light breeze.

The buck's eyes seemed unnaturally expressive and unusually intense. Mike felt as if they projected some kind of force that struck him between his own eyes. He tried to breathe and found that it was difficult to fill his lungs. The buck turned its majestically antlered head and looked at the cornfield behind him, then turned again to face Mike. Mike instantly remembered the wrecked car, and he was torn between his awe of this animal and the thought that someone might need his help. He took a small step toward the edge of the road. The deer lowered its head and shook its massive rack of razor-sharp antlers, then raised its head and stared at him. Mike swallowed something the size of a cantaloupe. He waited for maybe thirty seconds and then dared another step. Through the tangle of smashed corn he could see the gleam of metal shimmering with every new bolt of lightning. He took a third step.

With a flash of white the deer leaped at him.

Mike cried out and staggered back as the front hooves of the deer struck the ground barely a foot from his toes. He fell backward and upward, landing hard with his rump on the blacktop and legs skidding on the mud of the ditch, and the pain from his cracked rib stabbed through him like a spear. Mike cried out and the deer sprang again, and as Mike fell back he looked up in wonder as the deer passed over him, landing with a skittering of hooves on the highway beyond him. The buck wheeled toward him, standing tall and powerful, fire seeming to dance along its antlers as the sky erupted again with white brilliance.

Gasping in shock and pain, Mike sat up, looking carefully over his shoulder, and then cautiously got to his feet. The world took a few dizzying spins but his rib actually hurt less now, as if falling flat on his back had pushed the jagged ends into place. The buck stood there, legs wide and braced, eyes burning black holes into him.

Uncertainly, Mike turned to look across the ditch, made a slight gesture toward it, then glanced back to see how the deer would react. The buck reared up and then slammed down with both front hooves. Perhaps it was only a coincidental crash of thunder, but Mike could have sworn that the earth shook when those hooves struck the ground.

"Damn!" Mike said and reeled back. He lost balance and tottered on the edge of the ditch, arms flailing, but finally caught himself and felt the road settle down under his feet. The exertion made the pain in his rib flare again, and he squeezed his eyes shut and tried to endure the screaming white-hot spears of pain in his side. It took the pain a long while to slide down to a level he could bear. He opened his eyes tentatively. The buck had moved a few feet closer to him. Mike could have reached out and touched its muscular front legs, but he dared not. Their eyes met, locked, held. Mike gasped again as he felt the power of that animal's implacable stare. Something moved in those large, dark eyes. Something old and powerful and wildly beyond Mike's comprehension. Mike was storm-tossed by terror, wonder, and confusion, but something . . .

Something passed between them. Some tiny bit of knowledge, some small breath of understanding.

And for a moment, a frozen fragment of a second, Mike was not on the road, not standing by his bike, not confronting a great white stag. For a splinter of time Mike Sweeney was in a dark swampy hollow. Everywhere he looked there were fires burning. In some places the bushes and trees were blazing, and in others it was bodies that were burning. Bodies that ran and capered and screamed as they burned. Mike looked down and saw that he held a samurai sword in his hands, the length of the blade covered in blood that was almost black in the firelight. Fire danced and flickered in the parts of the steel that weren't smeared with blood.

Mike raised his head and looked around. Malcolm Crow, the guy who owned the hobby shop, lay on the ground near him. He wore a big tank on his back that had a long hose, which was still clutched in his hands. Crow's eyes were closed and he reeked of gasoline. A line of fire was eating its way across the grass toward him. There was blood on Crow's face and his eyes were closed.

Near him were two men—a big white guy and an older black guy—both of them were soaked with blood and stared blankly at the sky.

Mike turned all the way around and he saw Val Guthrie, the woman who ran the big farm outside of town. The one who went out with Crow. She was on her knees, weeping, holding her father in her arms. Her father, Old Man Guthrie, looked dead.

Everywhere Mike looked he saw death, and where there wasn't death there was pain. His mother was there, smiling at him with a mouth that was rimmed with blood. As she looked at him her eyes went from their familiar green to a bloody red and she stepped backward into flame-tinged shadows and disappeared.

A shadow passed over Mike and he turned again to see what had cast it. He turned and looked up . . . and up. It stood there, impossibly huge, monstrous, towering above the flames, laughing in a voice that rumbled like thunder.

"Mine!" the creature hissed, and reached for him.

And time caught up with him so fast and hard it was like a slap across the face. Mike staggered backward against his bike, knocking it over. The stag twitched, shaking its great rack of antlers again.

The image—dream, whatever it was—still burned in his mind, but already it was starting to fade. Mike tried to catch it, to remember it, knowing on a very deep level that it was important—though he couldn't begin to guess why—but it faded almost instantly. Becoming fog and then blowing away, leaving only the faintest memory of fear behind like a bad but indefinable smell.

The deer backed away a few steps. It stood there, eying him, waiting for something; then it turned toward Mike's War Machine and kicked it lightly with a sharp hoof. It kicked it again and looked at Mike. It took Mike a few seconds to understand. He got up very slowly—it was really all he could manage—and stood there, looking from the cornfield to the deer and back again. Another shake of the antlers. Mike advanced toward the bike, and the deer backed away, matching his pace. They never broke eye contact, even as Mike bent down to pick up his bike.

"What are y—" Mike began to ask, but stopped. The deer just looked at him with those wise old eyes, and to Mike it felt wrong to actually say anything. He got back on his bike, confused, amazed, even overwhelmed. *It's just a deer*, he told himself, trying to make himself listen. *Just a deer.*

Yeah, he thought, *right. Just a deer, my ass.*

Slowly, and with great effort, he began to pedal away. He didn't look over his shoulder again until he was at the bend at the far end of the straightaway. He paused and half turned to look back just in time to see the white deer leap gracefully across the ditch and walk slowly and purposefully into the field between the stalks of crushed and trampled corn.

"Man," Mike said. "Man oh man oh man."

He turned to the front again and tried to get his confused mind and battered body to solve the problem of getting home, trying not to think about the deer. Or about the wrecked car. Or about the tow truck that had tried to run him down. Or about his battered body.

Or about Vic's hard hands waiting for him at home.

He did not want to think of any of these things. All he wanted was to get home and go hide in his room. He struggled on, his legs already weary, his breathing forced. Around him, the night loomed with vast black shadows.

(2)

From the edge of the cornfield, hidden by the stalks of corn, the white buck watched Mike go. Then it, too, turned away, moving step by measured step on its four hard hooves. Lightning painted corn-shaped shadows on its white flanks. Between the bursts of light it seemed to vanish, reappearing again as the storm drew closer to Pine Deep and scattered its fireworks across the sky. The deer walked through a space of shadows and then as the next thread of lightning stitched the sky, the creature illuminated was not an albino buck with a massive rack of horns but a gray man in a black suit that was spattered with mud, a guitar slung across his shoulders. He moved just as slowly, along the same angle, and his footsteps began where the marks of the white deer ended.

The Bone Man stopped and looked back the way he'd come.

He wore a crooked smile. "Let's see Tommy Johnson do that," he said in a voice like a faint wind. "Hell, let's see *Robert* Johnson do that."

He went to the top of a rise and watched as Mike labored over the farthest hill. The Bone Man's mind burned with the image he'd seen in Mike's mind. His gray lips formed a single silent word.

"Dhampyr."

Overhead, thunder detonated with apocalyptic fury. The night birds took to the sky and uttered their plaintive ululations, like lost souls on the dark breeze. The moon was climbing into the sky, hiding like a criminal behind the storm clouds.

There were hours and hours until dawn, and the night still had work to do.

(3)

Crow rocketed along the twists and turns of A-32 at unsafe and irresponsible speeds. He found it relaxing. His car was one of those big Impalas from the early seventies: too much engine and about as long as an aircraft carrier. Crow claimed that you could land a plane on the hood and he wasn't far wrong. It was Hershey Kiss brown except for the right front fender, which was an improbable shade of greenish yellow. The interior roof lining sagged down like a windless parachute, constantly tousling Crow's curly hair, and all of the seats had been patched with duct tape of various vintages. There was red reflector tape over some of the rear lights and one headlight shone askew, giving the car a cross-eyed look. Crow had found her squatting dispiritedly in a used car lot, bought her at once, and named her Missy after his first girlfriend, who'd had the same cross-eyed beauty.

He tried never to drive Missy at anything less than a breakneck speed. Terry called Missy Crow's "getaway car" because that's how he drove it.

After Terry had left the store, Crow had been mildly amused at his "mission" and the novelty of having some big-city bad guys fleeing through Pine Deep. It was unreal enough to be funny, and it also tickled his curiosity, though not as much as it would have a few years ago. Back when he was a full-time cop Crow would have relished this kind of scene. Of course, back then there was even some talk about Crow running for Gus Bernhardt's job. It was Terry's opinion that he would have gotten the job if he'd taken even a halfhearted shot at it, and Terry's opinion held enormous sway in town, but Crow had not wanted the job badly enough.

It had been a strange time in his life, full of extreme peaks and valleys. The first couple of years he'd worn the badge were definitely the valleys because he'd also been a drinker, and that had resulted in some bad scenes. He was drunk on the job a couple of times, and once even had a fender bender coming off a long speed trap shift where he'd whiled the hours away with a bottle of Knob Creek and a stack of blues tapes. A guy in a Crossfire had come bucketing down A-32 at ninety and Crow had peeled out after him. The guy saw the lights and heard the sirens and didn't make a game of it, dropping his speed and pulling over onto the shoulder, but Crow was half in the bag and misjudged his own speed and had rear-ended the speeder to the tune of a grand's worth of bodywork on the Crossfire and eight hundred on the cruiser.

Crow would have been fired for that, but Terry had intervened. Gus was purple with suppressed rage when he told Crow that he was only getting two weeks off without pay. During that week Terry had sat Crow down and leveled an ultimatum at him: dry out or lose him as a friend.

Crow's first response was to spend the rest of the night getting totally wasted; and then, after waking up in his own backyard, naked except for socks, and covered in vomit and bird shit, he'd decided that rock bottom was not much fun.

With shaking hands he poured all his booze down the drain and spent the rest of those two weeks developing an addiction to coffee, chain-smoking cigarettes, and bitching about life to anyone who would listen, which was a small community. He also started going to AA meetings, sometimes as often as three times a day. When he returned to the job after his suspension, he was ten pounds lighter, looked ten years older, had yellow skin, red eyes, a case of the shakes, and had been sober for twelve days.

Then his life slipped into low gear and climbed the long road out of the valleys, picking up a little speed as it went higher. Over the next year he picked up two citations for good conduct, never missed a single day of work, and started socking money away for the store he someday wanted to buy. In January of his second year of sobriety he started teaching jujutsu twice a week at the YMCA in Crestville, bought Missy and rehabilitated her, strengthened his friendship with Terry Wolfe and the rest of the world—except, perhaps, for Gus, Jim Polk, and Vic Wingate—and fell in love.

Then eight months before he quit the force he had a run-in with a handful of the Pine Barons, the local bike club that had gradually become a pain in the ass to everyone. That situation was one Crow regretted—not for his actions, which even he felt were warranted, if not as heroic as the press made them out to be, but because the whole Pine Barons thing had been vulgar and gaudy and badly misinterpreted by everyone.

The situation wasn't really that much, as Crow saw it. He and a couple of other units—a total of three officers in three cars— were sent to roust six of the Barons from a truck stop by the canal bridge. It was part of a program to urge the gang to move on to other hunting grounds. Aside from the usual speeding, drinking, drugs, and brawling, a few of them had taken to ha-rassing the girls from Pinelands High School, seducing a few and turning them on to poppers and speed and gang bangs, and pestering a few others in ways that would have shocked con-struction workers. There were several complaints filed and gos-sip of at least one rape that the girl in question refused to talk about, apparently too terrified and ashamed to file charges. The fact that the biker had walked away from any charges both en-raged the townies and fueled the cockiness of the bikers.

The two other officers had arrived first and, despite being told to wait for backup, had gone into the diner, a move that spoke far more of balls than brains. By the time Crow pushed through the door, one cop—Jim Polk—had mouthed off to the bikers and tried to bully them out of there. Crow saw him lying on the floor clutching his balls, his face as red and pinched as a dried tomato. The other cop, Golub, was getting the tar kicked out of him by the whole gang.

Crow yelled to the counterman to call 911 and had just waded in. When he Monday-morning quarterbacked it he realized that he should have drawn his gun and ordered everyone down. Though he didn't care much for Polk, he did like Golub—a part-time cop working on his prelaw degree at Pinelands. Crow jumped in and, as the counterman later described to the reporters, "black-belted the whole sorry bunch of them." Three of the bikers landed in the hospital, two more were treated and released to police custody, and the sixth just ran and hid in the bathroom until the other units came and arrested him.

The newspapers had a field day with the story, and every single article emphasized Crow's shortness and leanness, using all the purple prose superlatives in the dictionary to contrast him with the "monstrous bikers" whose "formidable" size and "animal ferocity" were a "deadly threat" to the safety of all in Pine Deep. The level of journalism in Pine Deep was about that of a high school paper. They made a big thing out of the fact that Crow had a black belt in jujutsu and kept using the term "chopsocky," which irritated Crow to no end. The only moderately mature piece was printed in the *Black Marsh Sentinel*, which included a sidebar on jujutsu (which was spelled wrong) and segued into a short history of biker violence in Pennsylvania.

That incident became the stuff of local legends, and it was around that time that people started talking about Chief Crow as if his election was a foregone conclusion. Gus Bernhardt, who had not been able to do a single visible thing about the Barons during those few times the bikers had previously been in town, was beaten up by the press over and over again for his weak record. Even Crow, who didn't like Gus, thought that was a little unfair. Except for the biker thing, there wasn't enough crime in Pine Deep to allow anyone to establish a reputation. Gus used that same thought as a platform and took credit for the low crime as an example of how he protected "his" town. Crow hadn't even decided to run against him and already Gus was making campaign speeches.

A few months later, when it was getting to the point where he would absolutely have to make a decision whether to run or not, Crow found a bank that liked the idea of an upscale craft store and was willing to front the money. Crow weighed the benefits of being a chief in a town where the usual breed of criminal was a jaywalker and those of being a happy store owner selling, as Val so kindly put it, rubber dog poop. It took him about forty seconds to make his decision. He handed Gus his notice—and tried not to take offense at the chief's beaming smile of pure glee—hung up his uniform, wrapped his gun in oilcloth, and became a businessman.

So, he asked himself, *what the hell am I doing tooling down the highway with a pistol in my belt and bad guys on the loose?*

"I'll be damned if I know," he said aloud. The pistol felt like an anvil in his belt and he was way too aware of it. He drove five more miles trying to pretend it wasn't there. Then, as he sailed past Millie and Gus's big garlic farm, he said, "Oh . . . kiss my ass, Terry!" pulled up his shirt, and yanked out the gun. He bent, thumbed open the glove compartment, and shoved the gun out of sight. As soon as he slammed the little door shut he felt worlds better. He fished around on the passenger seat until he found the CD he wanted, slid it into the player, cranked the volume all the way up, and he and Howlin' Wolf sang about going down Highway 41 as Missy tore through the night.

The twisted length of A-32 was busy with tourist cars heading into town, but was empty in his direction. Crow's cell phone began its hysterical chirping, a sound he thought sounded like R2-D2 being rogered by Jiminy Cricket. He squirmed around as he tugged it out of his pants pocket and saw that it was just a text message. He punched the buttons to bring up the message, which was just two digits: 69. Crow smiled. One of Val's saucy little jokes. Perhaps an incentive. He saved the message and stuffed the phone into his shirt pocket. He'd call Val as soon as he finished at the hayride, which was ten minutes from now if

Coop was in the office, maybe half an hour if he had to take an ATV into the park to find him. An hour tops with getting the kids out of there and shutting the whole thing down.

He conjured an image of Val in his mind, and for dreamy moments he saw her superimposed over the unwinding road. Her lithe body draped in shadows, glistening with passionate sweat, good muscles rippling under a smooth, tawny hide as she lay back on the blanket in the scarecrow clearing. Crow drummed on the steering wheel as he recalled every delicious inch of her. Maybe she'd want to go for another nice late-night stroll through the cornfields, even though there was no moon and a storm coming.

Smiling and drumming on the steering wheel, Crow barreled down A-32 out of town, soaring up hills and swooping down the other sides, taking the curves and bends sometimes on four wheels, sometimes on two. Missy, for all her bulk, was as agile as a circus acrobat.

In a few miles he'd turn off the extension and head west along Old Mill Road to the hayride, and after that he could backtrack and head over to Val's. That made him smile. He began singing very loudly with the music, which had cycled onto the Wolf's jumping version of "I Ain't Superstitious." He was yowling out the lyrics in a powerful and rather unpleasant tenor when he nearly ran over the kid on the bicycle.

(4)

Even with the rib more or less set and holding in place, Mike's side still hurt like hell. It wasn't too bad when the road was flat, but not much of Pine Deep was flat. The long black ribbon of A-32 climbed, dipped, and curved through miles of low hills. Before tonight Mike had always enjoyed the undulating curves of the road, loving the burn in his muscles as he powered up the demanding slopes, but tonight he hated every inch of it. Pedaling in low gear helped a little to ease the pain, but sheer exhaustion was making him pant and panting made his ribs feel as if some little devil were jabbing at him with a red–hot spear. His progress slowed to a crawl. Time had become a paradox: when calculated in terms of how long it would take him to get home at the rate he was going, the night was racing past him; when he tried to climb each new hill every minute was about two weeks long. At his best guess he wouldn't get home until eleven.

Still, he thought with false cheer, that meant Vic's beating would be that much delayed. Cold comfort, he mused, knowing that the longer Vic had to wait the angrier he would get. And like the Incredible Hulk, the madder Vic got the harder he hit.

A few cars passed him, and each time he saw the glow of headlights he tensed . . . but the tow truck did not return and after a while Mike didn't even bother to stop when he heard an engine or the whine of tires on the blacktop.

Mike had given up on his futile attempt of not thinking about everything that had happened to him. It was a stupid thought anyway. How can you not think about someone trying to kill you? Or about a deer that had done the things that big white one had done? So, instead of denial he decided to apply logic to the matter. It gave him something to think about other than the pain in his ribs or Vic's impending fury. Mike was smart, he was very well read for his age, and he knew the rudiments of deduction, and as he labored up another of the long hills he tried to apply what he'd learned from Sherlock Holmes and Hercule Poirot, from Spenser and Elvis Cole. He remembered Holmes's axiom that once you eliminate the impossible, whatever remains, however unlikely, must be the truth. The problem was that he had two inexplicable mysteries to unravel, and in neither case could he simply eliminate the impossible. The thing with the big white deer made no sense at all. He twisted that into all sorts of shapes in his mind and it just stayed as weird and impossible as it had been when it happened. A big deer had jumped out of the woods by the site of the car wreck and when Mike had tried to edge past it the deer had simply chased him off. There was no other way to look at that. The deer had frickin' *growled* at him. Then it had run him off. *Make something of that, Sherlock*, he thought. Mike lived in Pine Deep. He'd seen a zillion deer, from little fawns to big bucks, seen them by ones and twos and seen them by the dozen, but never had he seen a pure white one, and never had he heard of one chasing anyone. It was always the other way around. Sure, he'd heard stories of a buck or doe chasing off a dog that was sniffing after a fawn . . . but this was completely different. This was a buck chasing a person off. From the scene of a car wreck. What the hell did that mean? His inner Sherlock Holmes was at a loss for words.

Then there was the tow truck. That didn't seem to make much sense, either. After all, the driver of the tow truck *had* tried to run him over, had swerved and gone out of his way to do so. Try as he might, Mike just could not see it any other way, but that was ridiculous. *Why* would someone do that? Not even Vic had ever tried to kill him and Vic really hated him.

Suddenly an icy hand closed around Mike's heart and he stopped pedaling for a moment. He leaned over onto one foot, motionless by the side of the road, and stared into the darkness as he reviewed what he'd just thought. Vic really hated him. That was true enough. But how *much* did he hate him? Vic was a mechanic and he worked for Shanahan's Auto. Shanahan probably owned a tow truck. Mike swallowed a lump the size of a fist and turned back the way he'd come, looking at the stretch of road until it vanished into shadows behind him.

Had that been Vic in the tow truck?

The late September wind blew cold across his face, chilling his sweat to ice. *Eliminate the impossible and whatever remains must be the truth.*

Could that have been Vic?

"Jesus Christ . . ." he said, and the wind snatched at his words, pulling them from his mouth like an Inquisitor pulling teeth. Terror welled up in him, and he wasn't sure what scared him more: the thought that Vic might want him dead, or the fact that the concept didn't really shock him. He turned to face the road ahead. Home lay at the end of that road. Home and a belting. Still, if Vic was the driver of that tow truck, would that beating turn into something more? His stomach turned to greasy slush.

Mike licked his lips and got back on his bike, started to pedal slowly up the hill. His heart was hammering now and the sweat on his face turned to ice. The bike wobbled as the first wave of the shakes shuddered through him. Around him the comforting darkness—his longtime friend—seemed suddenly full of invisible threat. He looked at the rustling waves of corn that flanked the road for as far as the eye could see and had the sudden and irrational fear that they were watching him. The stalks swayed hypnotically in the breath of the storm, and when the lightning flashed overhead its white fire danced on the razor-edged leaves of each swaying stalk. He was surrounded by an army of shadowy creatures armed with knives, and panic welled up in him. His legs pumped faster on the pedals and the War Machine gained speed up the hill.

He was nearing Shandy's Curve, one of many hairpin turns on A-32, and he slowed because there was no light to see the road and he didn't want to go sailing off the side down onto the rocks. Shandy's Curve was the one place Mike hated to pass, especially when there was traffic, because the thick brush on either side of the curve hid the glow of oncoming headlights until way too late. If the local legends about ghosts haunting the site of fatal car crashes were true, then the area around the curve was populated by enough specters to fill a graveyard. Mike's own father had died there, though Mike did not know that. John Sweeney had been coming home late from his second job and drowsed at the wheel at just the wrong place. He and his battered old Malibu had gone sailing off the edge and had fallen forty feet down into the gully between the Maplewhites' cornfield and the lower thirty of the Andersens' garlic farm. All Mike knew of his father was that he had died in a car crash.

Yet, even without that unsavory bit of knowledge, Mike still feared the curve, and with his terror already swollen with thoughts of Vic, the hairpin turn looked like the path to hell. He slowed even more, pedaling at little better than walking speed as he entered the far side of the curve, seeing only shadows, hearing nothing but the constant growl of thunder overhead. He thought he heard something behind him and flicked a glance over his shoulder, but the road vanished into total blackness behind him. He swung his head around as he reached the beginning of the sharpest point of the curve and suddenly intense bright whiteness stabbed his eyes and the world was filled with the roar of a big engine as something hurtled around the curve at him.

The tow truck! Mike thought and froze . . . this time there was nowhere to dodge. Harsh light stabbed his eyes as gleaming metal came ripping around the curve right toward him.

(5)

Ruger wasn't gone twenty minutes before Boyd began to shiver. He thought it was just the coolness of the breeze, but when he wiped his fingers absently across his forehead they came away glistening with sweat.

"Oh, shit," he said.

As if on cue, a fresh wave of chills raced right through him, entering through his spine and seeming to wriggle up his neck and out his ears. Gooseflesh pebbled his arms. He didn't know much about shock except that everybody always tried to loosen tight clothing and throw blankets on someone who was in shock. Was that what was happening to him? He didn't know, but the thought scared the hell out of him. The only other thing he knew about shock was that it was dangerous. He didn't know if it could kill, but it was supposed to be really bad for you. He loosened his belt and huddled deeper into his suit coat, which failed utterly to warm him. Boyd sat there, shivering and gradually becoming aware of the immensity of the terror that had built up inside him. He was alone out here . . . alone and abandoned. Ruger had left him for dead.

"Fucking bastard!" he yelled out loud. Then something caught his eye and he closed his mouth. Beside him were the knapsacks of coke and cash and he bit down on that fact. Karl *couldn't* have just abandoned him. Not without the junk and the take. Karl wouldn't double-cross him and leave him alive as a witness. Not

Karl. Not Cape May Karl, who absolutely *had* to skip the country or wind up twenty kinds of dead. That thought made Boyd shiver even worse. Karl didn't know that he knew about Cape May, but Boyd kept his ear pretty close to the ground and he was nearly certain that the rumors were true. He'd always known Karl was a sick bastard, but what had happened in Cape May was right out of a horror movie. If Boyd could have gotten to a phone before Karl had bundled him and the others into the car and headed off to the cluster fuck at the warehouse, Boyd would have made just one call and right now Karl would be screaming as Little Nicky cut pieces off him.

There hadn't been time to make that call, and Karl absolutely had to get out of the country, and only Boyd could swing that for him. *No,* he thought, *he's not going to cap me.*

That fact calmed him a little, but he was still afraid. Afraid of being abandoned. Afraid of what was happening in his own body. The gunshot wound to his left arm wasn't bad, but it was probably a long way to being infected by now. Might have some bits of cloth from his sleeve in the wound. He wondered how long it took for a wounded arm to develop gangrene. It made Boyd physically sick to think about it and he nearly puked in his own lap.

He shivered again, the shudder actually making his body spasm. He felt as if his hair was standing on end, rustling and waving like the stalks of corn that stood tall and black around him.

Flutter.

The sound made Boyd jump, and he craned his head around so violently that it jolted his arm and his leg. The pain that welled up in that one instant didn't give a fuck for the painkilling effects of cocaine; it kicked and clawed at him until he cried aloud. Blinking back tears, Boyd looked up, fully expecting to see Ruger standing there, grinning, and holding his gun out at arm's length.

It took a lot for him to even look.

A ratty-looking crow stood on the fence, inches from his head. It was silhouetted against the corn, just a paleness glinting on its feathers to define its shape. It cawed very softly at him, cocking its head to one side as it stared at him. Boyd looked at the bird for a long time, and then laughed a little. It was a hollow, impotent little laugh, but it was better than the scream that had wanted to come out.

"Fucking bird," Boyd said. The crow cawed again, just as softly as before. "Nevermore," Boyd said mockingly, "never-fucking-more."

The black eyes of the bird just watched him with the infinite patience of its kind.

Boyd felt warmth on his leg and he peered down. Fat droplets of blood hung pendulously from the slats of the splint, and as he watched, one broke loose and splashed onto the dirt.

"Oh, that's just fucking great!" Boyd snarled. He probed the rough bandages Karl had wound around the shattered leg, and his fingers came away black with wetness. Boyd glared at his bloody fingers for a long time, seething one moment, shivering with fear and fever the next. He half turned and swung his good right arm at the crow. "See what you made me do, you worthless piece of shit!"

The crow shuffled sideways just a few inches and the blow missed cleanly. It fluttered its wings noiselessly and again uttered that strange muted cry.

Boyd leaned over as far as his leg would allow him and beat at the bird, but his fiercely scrabbling fingers were inches short of the mark. The bird watched him dispassionately. It was the ugliest bird Boyd had even seen: dirty and disheveled, with greasy wings that shone with oily scum. Boyd grabbed the rail and hoisted himself up, shifting his buttocks to his right just a couple of inches, and then beat once more at the bird. The crow took another delicate sideways step, but this time, as Boyd's fingers clawed at him, the bird darted its head forward and jabbed with its long, sharp beak.

"Ow! Shit!" Boyd howled, whipping his hand away and jamming his finger into his mouth. He could taste the salty blood, and when he held the finger out for inspection, he was appalled to see an inch-long gouge, quite deep and ragged, running from the outside of the nail down past the knuckle. Fresh blood welled from it and ran down between his fingers, onto his palm, and down his wrist.

Boyd turned and glared with naked hatred at the bird. "You motherfucker! I'll fucking kill you, you shit-ass bitch! I'll fucking bite your head off and piss down your neck, you little shit bag!"

Indifferent to the threats, the bird just watched him, swaying slightly with the vagaries of the wind.

A fresh wave of chills swept over Boyd, as if the wind itself had blown its cold breath on him. He shivered so violently that he could hear his teeth actually chatter. Forgetting the bird for the moment, Boyd tried to huddle into himself to keep warm. He yanked his left arm up and stuffed the dead hand into the opening of his jacket and then wrapped himself as best he could with his right. Blood continued to drip slowly and thickly from his torn shin, pooling briefly beneath his leg and then fading as the hungry soil sucked it down into darkness. More blood dripped from his torn finger, dotting his jacket with a decoration of gleaming black red and littering the ground with the salty seeds of his life.

The crow watched him for long minutes, but then slowly raised its head as the clouds overhead were clawed open and the accusing eye of the moon glared down at Boyd and the crow and the endless ranks of silent corn. Boyd became gradually aware of the change in light, and for a while he thought that he was becoming delirious. He remembered hearing someone once say that things got brighter when you were really losing it. Before he could work up a good terror over that thought, he saw the shadow stretched out before him on the ground.

The world once more froze into a microsecond of total terror. Boyd could see his own slumped shadow, etched in the dirt by the fresh moonlight—but above his shadow and spreading out beyond him was a second shape. A man, huge, looming, arms outstretched to seize him.

Boyd screamed and fell over, spinning as he did so to see who was lunging at him, his one arm raised in defense, his good leg curling for a kick.

Of course it was only the scarecrow.

It hung there, arms supported by the crossbar of the post, faded old work clothes fluttering and snapping in the freshening breeze, jack-o'-lantern head smiling emptily as it stared out over the field. The crow cawed ironically at him.

Boyd sprawled there in the dirt, bleeding, shivering, crippled. Laughing.

He felt it rising within his chest, and before he knew it, before he could stop it, the laughter bubbled up out of him. It erupted from his gut and spilled out like vomit, choking him, twisting his gut, and spasming his chest. It boiled quickly to the level of simple hysteria and flew upward from there. He laughed until tears welled from his eyes and snot bubbled in his nostrils and blood splattered the ground as he beat it with his fist. He shook and shivered and rocked from side to side as the blood erupted from his leg and soaked the greedy dirt.

He couldn't stop laughing. He would look at the scarecrow and laugh; he would look at the crow and laugh. He would look at the wide, flat disk of the moon and his lunatic laugh would soar up into the ether. Every once in a while the laughter would be punctuated with a snort, or more often, a sob.

He was laughing even when the scarecrow turned its lumpy head and grinned darkly at him.

Chapter 8

Crow was singing at the top of his lungs as he took the curve on two wheels, feeling Missy lift and tilt and hold in perfect balance, ball joints be damned. The Impala swept gracefully around the curve like a racing sloop rounding a point. Crow was alive with the feel of power and control as he let the steering wheel drift slowly, delicately through his fingers, paying her off into the end of the curve, getting ready for the drop down to all fours.

Which is when the kid on the bike appeared out of nowhere.

"Holy shit!"

The kid was just suddenly there, frozen like a startled deer in the splash of Missy's headlights, and within the split part of a second he seemed to grow from half-sized to a dimension that filled the entire windshield. Screaming out a string of curses, Crow gave the pedal a hard stomp, steered small and fast so that the car heeled to the right just as he reached the boy, and then steered even smaller as he swerved to the left as he passed. The upraised tires swept along about a yard from the kid's handlebars and then lunged down at the ground. Missy landed heavily and sped on for a hundred feet, and Crow was pumping the brakes even before the chassis had stopped bouncing.

Missy skidded to a halt on the verge as dust swept up around her flanks. Crow threw her into park, killed the engine, and leaped out and sprinted toward the kid.

The boy had barely moved, only turning to watch the car soar by.

"Jesus Christ, kid!" Crow yelled as he sprinted up. "That was the stupidest goddamn thing," he bellowed, "that I've ever done!"

The kid blinked at him, half ready to stand up for himself when the words registered. He said, "Huh?"

"Christ, I'm sorry, kid," Crow gasped. "Are you all right? Jesus, that was stupid! Damn, I'm sorry! What the hell was I thinking?"

"You . . . uh, what?" was all the kid could manage to get out.

Crow gripped the kid's upper arms and peered at him. Both of them were shadows in the darkness, featureless in the blackness. "Jesus, Mary, and Joseph, kid, tell me you're all right."

"Uh, yeah," the kid said. "Sure."

"Oh, thank God!" Relief flooded up through Crow, nearly matching the towering level of his complete embarrassment and shame. He gave the kid a kind of reassuring shake and froze as the kid winced in real and obvious pain.

"Jeez . . . what's wrong? Did I hurt you? Did the car—"

"No," the kid hissed, gritting his teeth. "It wasn't you. It was the tow truck."

Crow just looked at the boy's shadow-shrouded face, trying to understand why the kid's statement didn't make any sense. Crow blinked a couple of times. "The, um . . . tow truck?"

"Uh-huh."

"Ah . . . and which tow truck might that be, son?" Crow said, looking around briefly, assuring himself that no tow truck loomed nearby.

"The one that tried to kill me," said the boy.

"Oh," Crow said with a vague smile, "that one. I see." *Kid's in shock*, he thought. *Poor bugger.*

They looked at each other's silhouette for a moment, the conversation stalled by the complete lack of understanding on both parts. Above them, the moon peered out from behind a fence of clouds, bathing the kid's face in a clear, revealing brightness.

"Mike!" Crow said with real astonishment.

"Crow . . . ?"

"Well . . . shit!" Crow said, half smiling.

"Yeah," agreed Iron Mike Sweeney.

(2)

The Bone Man walked out of Dark Hollow and stepped onto a hill on A-32, not three miles from where Crow and Mike stood. Walking slowly with a lanky gait that made his body look as if it were all bones and rags with no meat at all, he strolled to the center of the road and then stopped, turning to lift his face to the brilliant moonlight. Moonlight glittered on the strings and keys of his guitar. A cloud of bats whirled and danced above him, their tiny bodies looking like torn scraps of shadow in the flickering light from the distant storm. The Bone Man stood and watched them, absently reaching up a thin hand as if anxious to join their carefree gavotte. The bats knew him and did not fly away; all the things that moved in the night knew him, knew the pale shadow of a man who cast no shadow of his own.

All of them knew the Bone Man, the sad-eyed wanderer, the boneyard refugee. After a while the bats flitted off into the night and he stood alone in a cold wind.

Then a night bird with a bloody beak came flapping out of the east and circled him once, twice, three times before wheeling and flapping off into the west, where a lonely farmhouse stood amid a sea of corn. From where he stood on the hill, the Bone Man could see the tiny squares of yellow light dotting two sides of the distant house.

He considered the house, looking far and long and into it, reading its fortune in the call of the crickets and the rustle of the corn. He smelled blood on the wind, and some of it, he knew, was not yet spilled. There was still so much of this night left.

The Bone Man turned his rake-handle-thin body to the east and listened to the wind. There were sounds on it. Laughter, the cries and gasps of young lovers, the screech of tires, the lonely and distant drone of a tractor trailer whining along the back stretch of the highway, the call of owls, the deep barking of a dog. The high, sharp wail of a man in absolute terror and unbearable pain, a sound that faded and then abruptly stopped with a wet, guttural gurgle.

Long and dark blew the night wind around and past and through the Bone Man.

His eyes glistened with anger and fear and frustration. The tide of the night was already strong, moving the flotsam around faster than he could keep up. The gray man felt a hopeless surge of sickness in his empty stomach as he sensed the *thing* in the swamp, the evil presence that he had slaughtered with his own hands and buried thirty years ago, stir and flex its power.

Such power . . .

The Bone Man stood for a long time in indecision. The calls of the night birds told him much that he needed to know, told him too much. Now he didn't know which way to turn. Whose life mattered more? Which of the innocent ones needed him more than the others? Which innocent ones would he have to sacrifice to save the rest?

Thunder sniggered in the east.

The Bone Man turned north and began walking toward Pine Deep, his stick legs swishing, his stick arms swinging, and his white face gleaming like polished marble. In his eyes, cold storms raged.

(3)

"I thought you were making supper for Crow."

Val didn't look up from her crossword puzzle. Her father lifted the lid and stuck his whole face into the aromatic vapors and took a deep breath. "Smells pretty good."

"Don't sound so surprised. I can cook, you know."

Guthrie didn't choose to reply to that; instead he sniffed the soup again, amazed that it really smelled like soup and not sewage.

Val's previous attempts at cooking were spectacular disasters. Maybe she'd had a culinary epiphany. He found his mouth watering despite all of the warning klaxons ringing in his head.

"Leave it be," Val said. "You had your dinner."

"What is it?"

"Turkey soup and get your nose out of it, thank you very much."

Henry Guthrie sighed and set the lid back on the pot. "There seems to be an awful lot of it for one skinny little fella like Crow."

"I made enough for his lunch tomorrow." Val finished a clue and then looked up. Her father was still loitering by the pot, trying to look earnest and hungry. She shook her head but she was smiling. "Pop, if you're really that hungry, just take some. You go wandering all around a thing hoping it'll jump at you."

"Well," Guthrie said with a smile, his curiosity getting the better of him, "maybe just a little. I wouldn't want to steal food out of Crow's mouth, you understand."

"Uh-huh."

He fetched a dish and a ladle and scooped a brimming bowlful, an amount that scarcely dipped the level in the heavy spotted black pot.

"There's crackers in the cupboard."

"No dumplings?"

"Pop . . ."

"Crackers it is, then." Guthrie took down a box of saltines, rummaged in the fridge for a bottle of spring water, and sat down at the table across from his daughter. A discerning eye could see the kinship between them. She had his strong bones and dark hair, but her coloring and her laughing mouth were from her mother's Irish stock, not her father's brooding Scottish blood. The elder Guthrie had heavier features and his once jet-black hair had gone silver since Val's mother had died two years before. His nose was hawked and beaky and he had a thick mustache that dipped into his spoonful of soup as he blew on it and sipped.

"How is it then?"

"Just like your mama's."

Val smiled. "Her recipe."

Guthrie's eyes crinkled into a warm grin that softened his dour face into an expression of great love and humor. Val loved him and he knew it, even if she sometimes nagged at him to eat right and take better care of himself. He had slipped a little after Margie had passed, but Val had hounded him until he had begun to take regular meals and even cut down on his drinking. Now she was trying to get him to switch to decaf, but she was going to have a damned hard fight of that. Unleaded coffee was obscene.

He ate the soup, which was thick with fresh turkey, corn, celery, potatoes, and green beans. He didn't dare put salt in it: Val would never let him do it without a familiar and long-winded lecture on high blood pressure. Besides, the soup was good enough not to need it.

Val sat and watched her father eat, enjoying it. Playing the domestic role was new and somewhat out of character for her, but she did it now for her father with no regrets. Left to his own devices, her father would live on pizza and Glenlivet, black coffee and Big Macs. She couldn't bear the sound of his arteries squeaking shut. Still, she was no kitchen girl, not like her sister-in-law, Connie, who seemed blissfully happy to cook, clean, and beam vapidly at her husband, Mark, Val's only brother. Val worked on the farm, out in the field, driving the tractor, harvesting the corn, bartering with wholesalers, doing valve jobs on the Bronco. Connie had her little herb garden and made adorable little needlepoints with poignant scenes of kittens with balls of yarn that made Val want to vomit. Connie always wore a dress, even when weeding her prim little garden. Crow often whispered to Val that Connie was a Desperate Housewife waiting to pop, and that she had some deep dark secret; but after knowing her for years, Val still couldn't see any trace of depth in her sister-in-law, just as she was totally unable to see what Mark saw in her beyond a purely superficial prettiness.

Watching her father eat his soup, Val felt a little wave of acceptable domesticity waft over her. Lately she'd been trying out that domestic angle on Crow, and she found she liked that, too.

Of course, she planned to teach him how to cook because hausfrau was definitely not how she viewed herself. A dash of domesticity here and there was fine.

Guthrie dabbed a cracker in his soup and watched his daughter watching him. "Something on your mind, pumpkin?"

Val shrugged. "Not really."

"Meaning there is." Guthrie stifled a grin. "Not really" meant the same thing to Val as it had to her mother.

"Oh, it's nothing . . ."

"Something with Crow? So . . . you guys have a fight? He seemed pretty chipper when he bounced out of here this morning. Whistling and grinning, and I won't ask why."

"Oh no, nothing like that. I'm just concerned about him, that's all."

He lowered his spoon. "In what way?"

She drummed her fingers on top of the crossword puzzle for a moment, looking down, then glanced up at her father. "He's doing something that might be very dangerous."

"Oh? He's not . . . ?" Guthrie made a gesture as if he were knocking back a shot.

"Dad!"

"Just asking."

"Crow doesn't drink anymore."

"Hey, don't get me wrong—I care a lot for Crow, but alcoholism isn't something you just grow out of."

"Well, it's not that," she said with just a touch of frost. "It's something he's doing for Terry." She explained what was happening and about Crow's mission to shut down the hayride.

Guthrie ate a cracker, dry, munching thoughtfully. "Are you afraid he's going to go back on the cops? Is that it?"

"Oh no . . . no, he would never do that."

"Well then, don't let it worry you. Terry has always had an annoying way of putting people on the spot, getting them to do things they don't really want to do."

"I know."

"He and Crow have always been pretty tight, and you know how persuasive our dear mayor can be."

"Mm." Terry and Crow had been best friends since preschool, which meant that they'd known each other even longer than Val had known Crow. The boys had met Val in second grade, when they were all eight, and by the time of the Black Harvest two years later they were thick as thieves. Five of them—Val, Crow and his older brother, Billy, and Terry and his little sister, Mandy. By the end of that autumn two of them were dead—Billy and Mandy—victims of the Reaper, Terry was in a coma, and Crow and Val were clinging to each other, their worlds shattered.

The memory of that time flickered in Val's eyes, and Guthrie could see it. He smoothly but quickly changed the subject. "Besides, you know Terry," he said. "He likes to make everything seem dramatic. I think he imagines that being the mayor of a town this size actually means something."

"Yeah, him and Rudy Giuliani."

"Like that. He builds things up to be something they ain't. Hell, he's the kind that calls going over to Crestville for pizza and a movie a Regional Fine Dining and Cultural Arts Junket."

Val smiled. "Yeah, I guess."

"If there really is something going on around here, Terry's not going to be doing much about it. You said that Crow told you there were some Philly cops coming in?"

"Uh-huh."

"So Terry is going to be standing around looking important but not actually doing anything, and he'll have Gus Bernhardt hustling around getting them coffee and asking to polish their badges. Terry's one of those guys who needs to be in charge in some visible way, and he loves to give orders—and Crow happened to be there, and your boy can't hardly say no to anybody."

"Except me."

Guthrie gave a comical snort. "Not so's I noticed. He'll be by here, you watch."

"I shouldn't have let him go at all."

"Not yours to say, pumpkin. No more than it's his to speak for you. This is the twenty-first century, my lass." Guthrie took another mouthful of soup, winking at her as he did so. "Soup's really good."

"Don't say it like you're shocked." Val crossed her arms. "Well, I just wish he wouldn't jump whenever Terry says to."

"You think it's really that bad?"

She shook her head. "It's just that he spends so much time with Terry, and Terry is such a pain in the ass."

"You think he should stop hanging around with our fair mayor?"

"Mm."

"Why is it you don't like Terry? You never really have. Even as kids you two were always at each other's throats."

"I don't know. Bad chemistry, I guess. There was just always something . . . off about him. I don't know how to describe it. I just wish Crow wouldn't hang out with him so much, that's all."

"Now, now, darlin', don't be trying to tell your young man who his friends should be."

"Mm."

"Just like your mom. One grunt is worth a thousand words."

"Mm," she said again, but smiled.

"Crow can take care of himself. Hell, we've all seen that."

"I know, Daddy, but you know what it did to him. He probably wouldn't have even started drinking if it hadn't been for that job."

"Yep, and I also know that he pulled himself up by his own bootstraps and put his life back together—*while* he was still in that job. Not a lot of men could do that. He fixed himself, as my pappy would say. He saw that his life was broken, and he fixed himself."

"Mm."

"Will you stop that?"

"Mm-hm."

He threw a cracker at her, which she surprised herself by catching. She ate the cracker and stuck a crumb-covered tongue out at him.

Connie Guthrie whisked into the room, all fresh and cute in her floral-print dress, sensible pumps, bouncing blond curls, and brilliant smile. She favored them with an airy wave of her hand and then made a beeline for the stove.

"Ooo! We have soup!"

"It's for Crow," Guthrie said quickly as if he didn't have a spoon halfway to his mouth.

"Well, you have some. Maybe I'll just try a little." She looked quickly at Val, as if for approval, but neither wanting nor expecting any. Without another word she took a bowl from the cupboard and began ladling soup into it. Guthrie gave Val an apologetic look, but she waved it off. "I didn't even know you could cook."

Connie had just finished arranging her side of the table with a frilly place mat, precisely folded napkin, soupspoon set just so, the soup bowl positioned perfectly in the center of the plate with five crackers laid out overlapping each other around the rim, when the doorbell rang.

"Ooo, there's the door!" Connie said, as if that were a hilarious joke. "Just when I was sitting down." Then she actually sat down. Val exchanged an amazed and exasperated look with her father.

"Shall I get that, then?" she asked dryly.

"Oh, would you, dear?" cooed Connie. "I wouldn't want this fabulous soup of yours to get all cold and nasty."

"Heaven forbid." Val stood up, waving to her father to remain seated just as he began to rise. "I'm up, I'll get it."

She moved toward the door, crossing behind Connie, who was delicately blowing across the surface of her first spoonful. Val paused and mimed strangling Connie. Connie saw none of it, and Guthrie had to pretend to cough to hide his laughter. Sighing audibly, Val walked out of the kitchen, down the long hall, and into the living room. The visitor knocked again. A hard, insistent rap.

"I'm coming!" Val called as she reached for the knob, turned it, and opened the door.

A man stood there, tall and thin and pale of face. He had dark hair greased back from a widow's peak, black eyes, and a wide, friendly smile. In his right hand he held a small, almost delicate-looking pistol. The barrel was pointed at Val's stomach.

"Trick-or-treat," whispered Karl Ruger, and pushed his way into the house.

PART II

Mr. Devil Blues

Gypsy woman told me
I've got to walk the night
Like a fallen angel,
I'm blinded by the light.
—Whitesnake, "Nighthawk (Vampire Blues)"

There's a darkness deep
In my soul
I still got a purpose to serve.
—Santana, "Put Your Lights On"

Well, I ain't superstitious, black cat just cross my trail
Well, I ain't superstitious, oh the black cat just cross my trail.
—Willie Dixon, "I Ain't Superstitious"

Chapter 9

Tow-Truck Eddie made no move to get out of the cab. For fifteen minutes he just sat there, looking at the blood on his hands, amazed. Doubt had plagued him for most of the drive home, but as he sat there and stared at the blood, he could feel his fears fragment and fall away, leaving only a clean, shining belief.

"Thank you, God," he whispered. The gratitude welled up so suddenly and fiercely in his breast that tears sprang from his eyes. "Thank you, my sweet Lord God!"

Finding that man back there by the wrecked car, deep in the corn . . . how wonderful it had been. He marveled at the subtlety of God's intricate design, and how he—humble Eddie, the Sword of God—was guided in such sure but secret ways so that hints and clues of the great plan opened up to him bit by bit.

It had been years since his first epiphany, since that day years ago when God had first whispered to him. An actual voice in his head, not just words on the pages of a Bible. A real voice. *The voice of God.*

Eddie had been twenty when it happened. It was only days after Eddie's first encounter with the Beast. Back then the Beast had taken a different form—*Satan is the Father of Lies*—and Eddie and a few men from the town—Vic Wingate, Jim Polk, Gus Bernhardt, and others—had tracked the monster down and killed him, ending the string of murders that had been destroying the town.

After that night the voice of God started speaking to him during his prayers. Not often, at least not at first, and there were long stretches of months when no matter how fervently Eddie prayed there was no response from heaven. Then a few weeks ago God had begun speaking to him almost daily, sometimes several times a day. Then this morning he had been shown the new face that the Beast wore, and Eddie was filled with such holy purpose and glory that he felt he would burst. He kept looking in the rearview mirror to see if light was coming from his eyes and nostrils and mouth. Not yet. Not yet.

He had been cruising A-32 looking for the Beast, unsure if he had actually been killed or not back there. When Eddie had gotten out of the cab to look, there was no sign at all of either boy or bike. Was that how it was when the Beast, in this guise, was killed? Would he just simply dissolve, returning to the corruption from which he was formed? Eddie wasn't sure and God had not spoken to him to tell him. So, he was prowling the road just in case when either some instinct or perhaps the subtle nudging of God's hand directed him to the spot near the Guthrie farm where a car had gone off the road. Eddie had immediately pulled over and gone to investigate. Was the Beast here? Had the car struck the Beast and then both of them gone off the road? That thought gave him a pang because he wanted to kill the Beast. He—not anyone else—was the Sword of God.

He checked the scene and could find no traces of a broken bicycle, no debris left from even a minor impact. Just skid marks sliding off the road and into the cornfield.

Eddie moved quietly down the lane of smashed-down cornstalks, his big hands held defensively. Though Eddie was now fifty, he was still in perfect health and his body—the temple of the Lord—was packed with muscle and finely toned from relentless exercise with free weights, jump rope, heavy bag, and speed bag. He kept his body a perfect offering to the Lord. He had begun to bathe three and even four times a day now, and he was constantly washing his hands at work, especially if he had touched a customer or one of the other mechanics. Those impure oils had to be cleansed from his flesh as quickly as possible, but he had had to do it in secret. The guys had started to notice his fetish for cleanliness, had begun to rib him about it, saying that Tow-Truck Eddie had a new lady friend who didn't like grubby fingers on her tender flesh. He had laughed along with the jokes, choking down the rage and shame he felt at such suggestions. A lady friend indeed! As if he could allow himself to be distracted with carnal desires at a time like this. What a pack of dim-witted, shortsighted, unenlightened mud heads he worked with. Might as well be working with pigs. They had no idea, no clue, as to why he was preparing himself.

I am God's predator, he thought, then chastised himself for the vanity of that concept. He rephrased it, *I am the Sword of God*, and left it at that.

The beam of the flash sparkled on the black metal of the open trunk of the car, and he walked calmly toward it, surveying the scene. The car was smashed, the ball joint broken; he could see that from fifteen feet away. Eddie swept his flashlight over everything, seeing the carnage, examining the pitiful leavings of some kind of adventure that had ended recently and badly. He paused briefly to shine the light in the trunk, saw the scattering of blood-soaked bills, the small mounds of white powder. He wrinkled his nose in disgust; if there was one thing Tow-Truck Eddie despised it was pollution of the body. Beer and the like were bad enough, but drugs were downright unholy. He clucked his tongue in disapproval and began scouting the rest of the car. He had approached from the driver's side of the car, and everything looked deserted. Shining the light in through the open driver's door revealed nothing but blood. Quite a lot of it, which sent a thrill of excitement coursing through him. The keys were still in the ignition. Tow-Truck Eddie frowned. Straightening from his inspection of the car, he swept his light over the rows of corn, seeing no one. Then he walked carefully around to the other side of the car, and there lay a man sprawled in the bloody mud. If he had shone his light down when he was peering into the trunk he might have seen him, but the man had fallen down by the passenger side of the car and lay entirely in shadow. The harsh white light of his flash made the scene look like a black-and-white photo: black for the man's suit and tie, white for his face, black for the huge stain of blood that had entirely soaked his shirt.

Eddie had squatted down next to the man and looked him over, from death-pale face to bloodstained shoes. Odd how life-like the dead can sometimes look, he thought, and then actually gasped as the man moved his mouth in an attempt to speak, though he made no actual sounds.

Tow-Truck Eddie was amazed that the man was still alive. He examined the man in the light, seeing that the dark stain of blood still glistened wetly. There were two ragged holes in the man's shirt. He'd been gut-shot and was bled as white as the co-caine that had spilled all around him. What a mess, thought Eddie, who couldn't stand disorder of any kind.

The smell of blood was thick in the air: blood from the man, blood from the birds. The smell was appealing, almost intoxicat-ing, and for a moment Eddie just closed his eyes and let the smell wash over him and through him. He felt a little dizzy from it and had to blink his eyes clear for a few seconds.

He bent closer to peer at the man. Never in his life had he seen a man so close to death. He had seen sick people, sure, even badly wounded ones dragged from wrecks, and he'd seen corpses, but never a man hovering on that delicate point between life and death, his life essence fluttering like a lightning bug trying to work free from a child's cupped hands. It was incredible to see. Beautiful and delicate and quite moving, and it did something to him. At first he wasn't aware of it, of what was happening within him, but the realization crept into his consciousness as he watched the man continue his task of dying.

The man looked up at Eddie with pleading in his eyes; eyes that were aswirl with pain and fear, hatred and desperation. Tow-Truck Eddie crouched there, tasting the emotions overflowing from the man's eyes. The flow of pain was exquisite. He licked his lips and sniffed in the scent of blood through both nostrils.

"You're hurt," he said, savoring the intense rush of blood scent and pain, of truly perfect suffering right here in front of him.

"I . . . I've been . . . shot."

Tow-Truck Eddie pushed the man over onto his back so he could see the bullet holes more clearly. Fresh blood bubbled weakly from the wounds. He had a sudden and powerful urge to bend forward and drink from the wounds, but he knew that it wasn't the time for that kind of thing, for that kind of . . .

He sought the right word.

Sacrament? Was that it? Yes, he thought dreamily. Sacrament. It wasn't yet time for that kind of sacrament. Not yet. Everything had to be in its time and place, as it said in the Bible. He took the scent again and nearly cried out as the thick coppery smell of fresh blood shot through his nerves like a white-hot current of electricity. His eyes snapped wide and he rocked back on his heels as door after door blew open in his mind. Suddenly he understood! Suddenly—all at once—this all made sense. Everything made sense. Everything that he had thought about and dreamed about for the last few years made absolutely crystal-clear sense. He laughed out loud for the sheer joy of it.

He looked down at the man, staring at him with eyes that were still wide with amazement, seeing the man for who he was . . . for what he was! He laughed again, and he felt tears gathering in the corners of his eyes. Of course! This was no ordinary accident. How could it be? How could he even have thought that it was? How could anyone be so blind as to think that? It wasn't even an ordinary crime scene. No, no, this was something far removed from all of that, and Tow-Truck Eddie could suddenly see it. This was something special, something meant only for him, something orchestrated solely for him, and yet something immensely powerful.

He touched the wounds and then looked at the blood on his fingers, glistening black in the light of his flash.

Tow-Truck Eddie's mind went *click!* as that thought passed through him.

He was right. This was not the Sacrament in which the Lord

had told him he would one day partake. This was . . . his *baptism*.

In his mind the voice of God very faintly whispered, *Yesssssss.*

Tears burned in Eddie's eyes and he bent his head in humble thanks. All at once, here in this lonely place, amid all this carnage, he fully understood what he was and *who* he was. God, mysterious and subtle, had brought this man, this baptizer here. Just as surely as he had directed Eddie to come here. Amid all this violence and evil.

And did not God direct Jesus to the waters where John was baptizing the penitent? Was that not amid the oppression and violence of Rome's crushing occupation of Judea? Not exactly the same, surely, but the pattern was there, clear as sunlight to Eddie.

This man . . . this dying man . . . the baptizer, and his blood was the purifying waters of salvation. A child could see it.

The man gasped and blood leaked from his mouth, dribbling down his chin. He would be dead soon, but Eddie wasn't sure exactly what he was supposed to do. Was he supposed to care for this man? Was he supposed to rescue him?

No, that didn't feel right to him. This man—baptizer or not—had been manifested to him in the form of a criminal, and Eddie could not believe that God would want his Sword to rescue the wicked. The time for that sort of thing had passed.

What then? Was he supposed to watch him die? Was there a message in that?

That felt closer to the mark, but Eddie still didn't feel right about it. Letting the man's life just slip away—an event that was imminent—seemed like a waste of some kind of opportunity.

He frowned for a moment, his triumph dimming instantly as doubt chewed at him. What if he interpreted it wrong? What if he misread the holy signs? So much hinged on his reading it right that he felt a wave of sickening uncertainty crash down on him. His smile faded and fell away and he looked from the man to the wreck to the dead birds and back again. What if the act of reading the signs was itself a test? A puzzle or a riddle of some kind? He wasn't sure what would happen if he failed to solve the riddle. For a full minute he worried over that as the dying man passed in and out of a haze of delirium.

"No," he said softly to himself, steeling himself. Doubt was a tool of the Beast, not of the Almighty.

In a ragged whisper, the dying man repeated what he had said: "I've been shot."

"Uh-huh. I can see that," Tow-Truck Eddie said softly, reveling in it. The pain in the man's eyes was so finely tuned that it flickered like electricity; he could barely look at it without crying out for the sheer joy of it. His mouth was dry and he could feel his palms grow slick with sweat.

"Could you . . . help me?"

Oh my, how exciting this moment was! The man was actually begging him for help and that fast the answer came to him. It was not rescue, nor the passivity of standing by and doing nothing. This was a direct command from God presented in the form of a test.

"Who am I?" Eddie asked himself with the droning intonation of a litany, and he responded: "I am the Sword of God!"

His purpose was clear to him. A sword was forged for a single purpose, its nature clear to even the meanest intelligence.

"I am the Sword of God!" Eddie yelled and his declaration sent the lurking night birds screaming into the troubled sky.

He smiled, joy flooding his heart and swelling his massive chest.

"Did you come . . . to help me?" And the dying baptizer's words became part of the holy litany, and Tow-Truck Eddie heard the laughter of the Beast buried deep beneath the human pain. This was the key to everything. Compassion and restraint were tools of the Beast and Eddie was being tested on that point right now. Everything hinged on this moment and how he would answer.

In his mind he kept repeating: *I am the Sword of God.*

Then another voice overlay his own, booming in his brain like heavenly thunder as God said, *Do this for me and open the way to paradise!*

Did you come to help me?

Tow-Truck Eddie smiled, tears brimming in his eyes. "No," he said and with great reverence reached for the man. He took the man's face in both of his hands, lifted it, kissed the sacred forehead, kissed the bleeding mouth, and then held the face close, almost nose to nose, as he looked deeply into those eyes, trying to reach down through the barriers of evil to the trapped human soul within. The man struggled feebly, a last attempt to deceive him, a last ruse to really test his faith, his resolve, but Tow-Truck Eddie was steadfast. He looked into those eyes, searching, searching. The demon resisted him, keeping the man alive, denying Tow-Truck Eddie that brief glimpse into the infinite, but he was not to be denied this most sacred of all rewards. Holding the man's head with one hand, Tow-Truck Eddie reached down with his other hand and placed his fingertips over the ragged holes torn by bullets. The man felt the touch and his eyes flared with the dread, but Tow-Truck Eddie smiled mildly at him and then thrust his fingers as deeply as he could into the man's body.

The man screamed with all the agony of man and all the rage of a demon as Tow-Truck Eddie tore out his bowels. Then, the screaming mouth shouted only silence, though the jaws still gaped wide and the throat worked and the chest heaved.

"Bless me," Tow-Truck Eddie murmured softly, gently. "Bathe me in the waters of salvation so that I may be purified, for I am the Sword of God!"

He stayed with the man, creating with his body the rituals of the New Covenant. The new bond of blood and flesh that would be the cornerstone of the world to come.

Now, hours later, sitting there in the cab of his wrecker, staring at the dried blood, he thought about all that he had seen and experienced. The man's death had been so exquisite, so enlightening, and afterward when he had done all that was required and ordained to the man, he had learned so much. He felt glutted with knowledge, and yet much of that knowledge had yet to be processed, to be held up to the light of his new insight and examined. He knew that even now, with his mind so profoundly expanded, it would still take him some time to understand what he had seen, and what it all might ultimately mean.

He mumbled his own name over and over again as he sat there.

He had killed the Beast and been baptized in blood all in one night. He was sure that he would meet other demons in the days to come, now that his own nature had been discovered and declared. Well, that was fine, just fine with him. He grinned and flexed his powerful hands, feeling the muscles ripple on his forearms. Let them come, he thought. He would be ready.

He smiled grimly, still muttering his own name over and over again.

"Jesus. Jesus. Jesus. Jesus. Jesus. Jesus. Jesus. Jesus. Jesus. Jesus. Jesus. Jesus."

(2)

"The mayor is in a meeting right now, may I take a message?"

"Ginny, it's me. Crow."

"Oh, hi, how are you?"

"I'm fine, I . . ."

"My God, do you know about all the stuff that's happening around here?" Ginny asked in a low and conspiratorial voice.

"Some of it. Look, I'm calling from my cell and I don't have much time. Reception sucks out here. I need to speak to Terry."

"Oh, gee, Crow, like I said he's in a meeting." For effect she added, "With Philadelphia narcotics detectives," as if they were something akin to angels with burning swords.

"I know that. It's about that stuff that I'm calling. Or might be, anyway. Can you tell him I'm on the phone?"

"Oh, I don't know—"

"Ginny, Terry deputized me tonight, so you can consider this official business."

"You're back with the department?"

"More or less. Look, Ginny, just get him for me, will you?"

Ginny thought about it for another exasperating few seconds, and then said, "Okay, Crow. I'll just do that."

"Thanks," Crow said, and as soon as she put him on hold, he said, "Hallelujah." Crow had never liked Ginny Welsh, though she never knew it. Ginny acted as if being the receptionist-cum-dispatcher-cum-secretary put her at the very heart of regional law enforcement.

While he waited, Crow looked over at Mike Sweeney, who sat in the passenger seat of his car. The boy's bike was stowed in the trunk, the trunk's hood held down with bungee cords. The kid looked very small and young as he sat there, and it made Crow feel really bad for him. Mike Sweeney, or Iron Mike as Crow had nicknamed him last year, was one of those bright but lonely kids with so much imagination that it almost, but not quite, made up for the fact that he had few friends. It was easy to see that the kid was on a totally different intellectual plane than his age-group peers, and whereas intellectuality would probably see him in good stead among the adult community of Pine Deep in later years, it was quickly turning him into an embittered loner as a teenager. Crow also knew that Mike's home life was a little rough, and that was something he could relate to.

Mike saw him looking and offered a smile.

Iron Mike was a regular customer at the Crow's Nest, converting his hard-earned newspaper route money into model kits, comics, and copies of *Fangoria*. The kid knew almost as much about classic horror films as Crow did, but was the master by far when it came to science fiction. Crow was introspective enough to know that the nature of his own store, as well as his extensive readings of horror fiction and folklore, was part of his personal escape route. To make a monster look less scary, shine a bright light on him—you get to see the zippers and spirit gum and latex. That—and the bottle—had been Crow's way of not dealing with the events of the Black Harvest, and he was fully aware of that fact. His dissociation was entirely deliberate.

It appeared to him, though, that Mike, on the other hand,

walked a very fine line between reality and fantasy and was far less aware of it. Crow knew that Mike called his bike the War Machine, and that he often drifted away in thought, visiting who knew what kind of interior landscape. Crow wondered if he would grow out of the fantasies, or would grow strong enough to confront them. Therapy rather than sour mash.

Crow knew Vic Wingate very well. Vic was older than Crow and had been a legend in Pine Deep for decades. He was known as a hitter. Totally fearless in a bar fight and just as tough as he thought he was, but a world-class asshole nonetheless. More than once Crow had seen Mike walking with that stiffness that only comes from a leather belt wielded with enthusiasm. It made Crow sick and furious, but also frustrated because there wasn't anything he could do about it, as he knew from personal experience. His own dad had a hard hand and used it way too often. In his heart, Crow would love to invite Vic to step behind the proverbial woodshed and dance him a bit. Crow wasn't entirely sure he could take Vic, but he would love to try. The problem there was that Vic was tight with Gus Bernhardt and Jim Polk, and he was too smart to accept a private challenge. Anyone who went up against Vic, or tried to sucker punch him, wound up first in the hospital and then in jail, or in court. Vic was as cunning as he was vicious.

So, not being able to do anything about the problem, Crow tried to tackle at least one of the symptoms and had befriended Mike, treating him like a real person, which was the case anyway, and once in a while trying to work into conversation some of the values Crow himself found useful in life. He had even shown Mike a few jujutsu moves, hoping the kid would get hooked on martial arts the way he had. It had helped Crow stand up to his own abusive father—maybe it would help Mike do the same. Predators generally don't like prey that shows its own claws and teeth.

The kid was looking at him through the window, no longer smiling. Crow shrugged elaborately and pointed at the phone. Mike nodded. Crow had stepped out of the car to make the call, not wanting the boy to hear about the manhunt. The kid looked like he'd been through enough already.

"Crow?" Terry's voice came over the phone with no warning, making Crow jump.

"Terry? Yeah."

"Oh man, Crow, tell me nothing happened at the hayride."

"Huh? Oh no, I haven't gotten there yet."

There was a brief silence on the line; then in a controlled voice, Terry said, "You, ah, haven't even gotten there yet? I see."

"No, you don't. I'm not dodging it, it's just that something else came up."

Another silence. "Something 'else' came up? Crow," Terry said, "you do remember we have a crisis going on around here?"

Crow walked another couple of paces from the car. "I have Mike Sweeney with me."

"Who, may I ask, is Mike Sweeney?"

"Kid who delivers the paper."

"Okay. And you're what—learning his route?"

"No. Actually I almost ran him over. Don't panic, it was just by accident, though . . . I wasn't aiming for him."

"I should hope not."

"But someone else tried to do it intentionally." Silence. Crow said, "Terry?"

There was a sigh at the other end of the line. "Tell me that again. Someone else tried to . . ."

". . . Run him over, yeah. The kid was pedaling along A-32 when this tow truck comes zooming down the road and tries to run him over."

"Oh, for Pete's sake, Crow, the guy probably didn't see him. Kid on a bike out on the highway. Like I said, the trucker probably never saw him. You just said you almost did the same thing."

"Kid says that the tow truck went out of its way to chase him down. The kid was in the oncoming lane, crowding the shoulder, and the truck swerved into the lane and accelerated toward him."

"Oh, come on."

"I believe he's telling the truth, Terry." For just a moment Crow thought about the incident from a different perspective. Mike's stepfather was Vic Wingate, who was widely believed to be physically abusive to the kid; and Vic worked for Shanahan's Garage, and Shanahan owned a tow truck. Could it have been Vic behind the wheel? He thought about that for a second and then dismissed it as fanciful.

"Crow, we really do have more important fish to fry than some trucker, probably drunk, who may or may not have even seen the kid. I mean, really."

"Kid got hurt."

A pause. "Hurt? How bad? Do you need an ambulance?"

"No, nothing like that. Busted rib or two, some bruises. Got a bit of a knock on the head, though. I think he should go to the emergency room. At least have a doctor look at the rib and his head."

"Where are you now?"

"On A-32, on the service pull-off near Shandy's Curve. I can't lug the kid all the way to the hayride with me, though, and if I take him over to the hospital, I won't get to the hayride until well after eleven."

"That's too late."

"Uh-huh."

"Can't you call his folks? Have them pick him up at the hayride?"

"Mm. I guess so. . . ."

"Try it."

"Maybe. Guess who is stepdad is? Vic Wingate."

There was a thick silence on the line. "Oh. Great."

"Uh-huh." Everyone in town knew Vic Wingate. Those who weren't downright afraid of him merely loathed him. "Because of the accident, the kid's really late. Vic has this thing about being home on time. . . ."

"Vic'll probably give the kid a hiding for having the temerity to have his ribs broken."

"That would be my call," Crow agreed.

"So, what do you want me to do?"

"I want you to call him, actually. Tell him that Mike was run down by a reckless driver and is going to be needed as a material witness."

"You know I can't do that."

"Sure you can."

"We'll never find whoever tried to run him down. The kid'll never be called as a witness, you know that."

"Sure. I know it, and you know it, but Vic Wingate doesn't know it. But if he thinks that the cops are going to want to talk to Mike occasionally, he might be a little less likely to slap the kid around. At least for a little while."

"I just don't know. . . ."

"Oh, come on, Terry. You're a politician, *lie* to the man. It's no skin off your nose, and it might keep the kid from having some of his skin belted off."

"Oh . . . okay, okay. Whatever. Darn it, Crow, one of these days all that spillage from your bleeding heart is going to drown you."

"Yeah, yeah, yeah. You'll make the call or not?"

"Yeah, I'll make the call, but listen, Crow, you get your behind out to that hayride. We've got to get those kids out of there. The smelly stuff is really flying around here tonight."

"They still haven't caught the psychos yet?"

"No, and I'm hip-deep in Philly cops. It seems," Terry said, dropping his voice, "that these psychos are the real deal. Not just some clowns running from a stickup at a Wawa. These are some serious bad boys, m'man."

"What do you mean?"

Terry's voice dropped even lower. "One of the guys is some madman named Karl Ruger."

"Never heard of him."

"Yes, you have."

"No, I—"

"Ever heard of the Cape May Killer?"

"Yeah. Who hasn't?"

Terry said nothing, letting Crow work it out. It didn't take long. "Oh my God!"

"Uh-huh."

"I mean . . . oh my *God!*"

"Yep."

"Christ, Terry, are you sure?"

"He was ID'd by the Philly cops."

"Oh. My. God."

"Yeah. So," said Terry, "did you remember to bring your gun?"

"Huh? Oh . . . yeah, I got it."

"Is it loaded?"

"Of course it's loaded."

"Then keep it close, my brother, 'cause Halloween's come to town early this year."

"What d'you mean?"

"There are monsters out there tonight," Terry said, but despite his flippant words, there was little humor in his voice.

Crow switched off the phone and frowned into the shadows for a few moments; then he hit speed-dial for Val's cell phone, but it rang through to her voice mail. He left a message for a callback, ended the call, walked back to the car, got in, and sat behind the wheel staring out at the night for a long time. Beside him, Mike sat patiently, waiting in silence. Finally, Crow turned to him and said, "I just spoke with the mayor. He's going to call your mom and, uh, Vic, and have them pick you up out at the Haunted Hayride."

"At the hayride? How come?"

"Well, it's complicated," Crow began, "and I'm trusting you to keep your mouth shut about this. Okay?" Mike nodded and Crow gave him an abridged version of the facts. By the time he was done, Mike's eyes were very large and for the moment he looked more like a kid than ever. He licked his lips nervously.

"Jeez-us!"

"My feelings exactly."

"In *Pine Deep*?" Mike said wonderingly. "Did the mayor really make you a cop again?"

"Seems so."

"Wow."

"Mm."

"Well," said Mike.

"Well," agreed Crow.

They looked at each other for a dark minute, and then Mike said, "Crow . . . there's something else I have to tell you. But . . . I don't want you to think I'm whacked or something."

"Too late," Crow said with a grin; then he caught the look on Mike's face. The kid was serious. "Um, sure, Mike . . . fire away."

So, Mike told him about his encounter with the white stag. He described the animal and how it moved, what it looked like—and how it had growled at him. The only part he forgot to mention were the skid marks, which was unfortunate.

Crow leaned against the car door and looked at him. A variety of thoughts ran through his head, chief among them a concern on whether Mike had hit his head hard enough to have caused some kind of hallucinations. The kid seemed pretty lucid, though, and even with his youth coloring the description it had been a pretty straightforward and orderly account.

Mike asked, "Have you ever seen anything like that? I mean . . . isn't that pretty weird?"

This whole flipping night is pretty weird, thought Crow. He said, "Yeah, Mike, that's off the hook."

Mike winced and touched Crow's arm. "Crow—the whole slang thing? Grown-ups never get that kind of thing right."

Crow gave him a look. "Do you know what 'precocious' means?"

"No."

"It's Gaelic for 'pain in the ass.' "

Mike grinned. "So, what do you think?"

"I think I haven't a clue about that whole deer thing. I mean, if we were in the Middle Ages I'd say, okay, white stag or white hart—sign of impending doom. But we're not in the Middle

Ages and this is Pine Deep and I think you just saw an albino deer who was acting pretty funky."

"Are deer supposed to act like that?"

"What am I, *Animal Planet*? I don't know from deer. I sell rubber rats and fright masks. What I'll do, though, is tomorrow I'll call Nate Holland, he's a park ranger, and I'll ask him. Who knows? Maybe the deer is sick or something and that's why it was acting so funny."

"Maybe," Mike said, but it was clear he didn't agree.

Crow looked at his watch. "I really have to get out to the hay-ride, kiddo. You game to go with me, Iron Mike?" he said with a grin.

"Fire up the converters, R2, we're about to make the jump to light speed."

Crow chuckled. "Okay, but you're R2-D2, I'm Luke."

"No way."

"Hey, who's driving?"

"Hunh. Well, if you're Luke Skywalker, where's your light saber?"

Crow's smile dwindled slightly and his eyes took on a strange, distant quality. Then he leaned across the seat, thumbed open the glove compartment, and took out the Beretta. He eyed it to make sure the safety was on and then tucked it in his waistband, where it once again felt like a block of sinister ice against his skin.

"That enough of a light saber for you?"

Mike swallowed the watermelon in his throat. "It'll do," he said.

Crow turned the key and Missy sprang to life. With barely a squeal of tires he pulled the car back onto the road and headed toward the hayride at a sedate eighty-five miles an hour.

(3)

Terry hung up the phone with a sigh, knowing it was going to be a very long night. Around him, the station house was in full furor, with officers coming and going, phones ringing, chatter filling the air. For a stretch of moments, Terry just stood by the desk, fingertips still resting lightly on the curved back of the phone, lost in musings. He thought how odd it was that Crow had encountered Mike Sweeney. It bothered him for some reason that he couldn't quite touch. There was something about that kid that had always bothered Terry. Every time he saw him pedaling down Main Street with his canvas bag of papers it always gave him a weird feeling in his gut. Not something he could put his finger on, just a little flicker of the creeps. *Weird kid*, he thought, then shook his head to clear his thoughts. He had enough things to worry about, primarily the organization of a real honest-to-God manhunt in Pine Deep. *Lord,* he thought, *this is all I need, and Halloween just a month away.*

He went into the men's room, closed the door, and locked it. From an inner pocket he took out his bottle of Xanax and popped one, washing it down with handfuls of water from the tap. His morning dose of clozapine had kicked in, and he could feel his bowels cement shut. Though he didn't get the drowsiness his shrink had warned him of, he hadn't had a good bowel movement since he'd started the antipsychotic. With the Xanax on top of the other drug he felt he might be able to get through the rest of the day.

He washed his face, pressing cupped hands full of cold water to his face for a long moment, patted himself dry, straightened his tie, and went back out to the squad room.

Detective Sergeant Ferro was talking earnestly with Gus Bernhardt, but the chief glanced up and waved him over. "D'you have a minute?"

"Sure," Terry said, but as he began to move he caught sight of himself reflected in the large picture window across from the desk. The darkness without and the bright fluorescents within transformed the glass to a dark and opaque mirror. Terry saw himself reflected in the polished-coal surface, saw his own size and brawn, he saw his red beard and red hair, but the darkened glass distorted things, shaded his hair to black and deepened the wells of his eyes so that his reflection looked like that of a bearded skull without eyes or expression, a scowl devoid of humor or compassion. He stood and stared at the distorted reflection, remembering his dreams of the last few nights. The beast reflected in the store windows of a burning town. Then he made a face of self-disgust at his own ridiculous paranoia and turned away to join the others.

As he left, the mirrored glass surface of the window was wiped clean for a moment, but then another image gradually appeared. It seemed to come forward toward the light, like someone stepping out of deep shadows into pale lamplight. If anyone had been watching, the image might have just seemed like someone stepping out of the darkness beyond the glass to a point of nearness where the glass once more became transparent; but anyone on the other side of the glass would have known this wasn't true: there was no one outside the chief's office, no one in the street at all. Yet the image remained. Not a figure outside, not a reflection of anyone inside, for inside the station there was no little girl with bright red curly hair and bright blue eyes and a dark green dress. That image appeared only in the darkness of the glass. A pretty little girl, with an oval face and a stuffed rabbit clutched in the child's hand. A lovely face, even though streaked with blood; a pretty dress once, but which hung now in blood-soaked tatters.

The little red-haired girl watched the big red-haired man move away, watched with troubled eyes as he went over to the policemen and began to talk. A tear like a single pear-shaped diamond appeared on her cheek. It paused for a moment, and then rolled slowly down her face, tumbling over the streaks of blood, becoming tainted with red, metamorphosing into a tear of blood as it wended its way down to her chin. By the time it reached the point of her chin, the image in the darkened window had faded and was gone.

(4)

Val Guthrie stared into the black eye of the pistol, her face blank except for a small half smile on her lips.

"What?" she asked softly.

Karl Ruger's smile swelled like a hammer-struck thumb; his dark eyes fairly twinkled with wit and gentlemanly charm. He stepped forward and pressed the barrel into Val's stomach and like a storm wind, pushed her backward into the house. Without looking he hooked a heel around the edge of the door and swung it shut. It closed with a mild click.

The absurdity and total shock of this man with the feeble-looking little gun still held Val in a bemused thrall. She looked down past her breasts to where the hard metal of the gun made a soft dent in her midriff.

"What . . . ?" she asked again. Her mouth worked, trying to say more, but her brain possessed no adequate vocabulary for this kind of thing.

"Val? Who is it?" Her father's voice floated from the kitchen with amiable curiosity, but it might have been the howl of a banshee for the effect it had on Val's befuddled mind. As if a strong wind had blown sharply across her brain, her wits cleared and abruptly she was back in her own consciousness. There was a gun pressing against her stomach and the smiling man was pushing her backward into her own house.

"Dad!" she cried out in a sharp, shrill voice, and a moment later something struck her face so hard and fast that her newly returned awareness was swept from the saddle. She reeled away and slammed into the wall, only dimly aware that it was a hand that had struck her, not a bullet. The hand had been so fast that she hadn't seen it even twitch, let alone have time to duck the blow. The whole right side of her face burned as if the man had splashed her with boiling water, and tears sprang into her eyes.

"Val?" she heard her father call. "Jesus Christ! Who the hell are—"

Val couldn't see a thing; stars swirled with firework frenzy before her eyes, and before she could shake her head clear, something clawed at her hair and then wrenched her backward with horrible force. She staggered and fell back against a firm yet yielding surface. A body. She could feel fingers snarled in her hair and then something that was cold-hot pressed into the soft flesh below her right ear. Something very hard, small, and round.

A whispery voice spoke and all around her the world froze.

"Stop right there, old fella, or I'll blow this bitch's brains all over the wallpaper and all over you, too. You want that? No? Then just stand right there."

Val's eyesight cleared and she saw her father standing just inside the hallway, face shocked and pale, body held unnaturally straight. Behind him, farther down the hall, was the silhouetted form of Connie, standing with both hands pressed against her mouth.

"Who the hell are you?" demanded her father, his eyes blazing, fists balled at his sides.

"The bogeyman," said Karl Ruger with his graveyard whisper voice. "Now shut the fuck up."

Guthrie shut up, but he looked desperately at Val. Val's eyes were streaming with tears of pain, and her heart felt as if it were going to kick its way out of her chest.

"Hey, you down there," Ruger snapped. "Yeah, you . . . get in here. Right now."

Connie did not move so much as an eyelash.

"I ain't gonna tell you twice, woman. Get your ass in here right now. Don't make me come and get you."

"D . . . Dad?" Connie asked in a tiny voice.

Guthrie met Ruger's eyes, read them. Understood. "Come on in, Connie. Do as he says."

She still hesitated. Guthrie turned halfway around and hissed at her, "Get in here, for God's sake!" That got her moving, and she scurried down the hall with mincing steps on legs that seemed to move like unbending sticks.

Ruger looked at her, all dolled up with a pearl choker and a full-skirted print dress. He chuckled. "Who the hell are you? Donna Reed?"

In other circumstances, the observation might have been as

funny as it was accurate, but at the moment Ruger was his own audience. Still he gave himself a good chuckle at his bon mot. Giving Val a vicious jab with the gun barrel, he said, "Now, who else is here?"

Guthrie shook his head. "No one. Just us."

"You better not be lying to me, old fella, it's been a trying day, and I'm really not in the mood for fun and games."

"Mister," said Guthrie, "as long as you got that gun to her head, I am going to do whatever you say. I don't want no trouble, and I don't want no harm to come to me or mine. If you want money, I'll give you what I got. Just please don't hurt the girls."

Ruger liked the speech, and said so. Guthrie said nothing, but his eyes were hard and steady. "Tell you what, Mr. . . . ?"

"Guthrie."

"Guthrie. Fine. Tell you what, Mr. Guthrie, why don't you and Donna Reed park your butts on the sofa over there?"

Guthrie nodded, and he guided Connie over with a flat palm on her back. Ruger turned to follow, keeping Val between them, but it was clear that Guthrie was not going to do anything stupid. Ruger relaxed a little. He knew that most people weren't stupid or heroic enough to face down a gun. With all the crime nowadays, everyone handled these things like business transactions. Once Guthrie and Connie were seated, Ruger let go of Val's hair and gave her a shove that propelled her stumbling all the way to the couch, where she collapsed onto her father. Ruger stood with the gun pointed at her while she got herself sorted out. Connie edged away from her to make room, moving as far away as possible as if she feared to touch the woman who had touched the man with the gun. Val settled in between Connie and her father, who wrapped one strong and comforting arm around her shoulders.

"You okay, pumpkin?"

"She's peachy," answered Ruger. "Now shut up." He prowled quickly around the living room, peering down the hall and up the stairs and out the windows. Satisfied, he dragged a Shaker rocking chair over and sat ten feet in front of the couch, resting the gun on his thigh. He drew in a deep breath and let it drain out of him slowly, the way a smoker exhales the first long drag of a cigarette.

Val stared at him, fighting the numbness of shock, still dazed from the blow he had struck. She had never been hit that hard in all her life, but it was more the fact of the blow than the force that made her want to scream and cry. Who was this man? What could he possibly want? This was so far beyond her ordinary experience that she didn't know how to react, except to crouch there in fear on the edge of the couch and wait for whatever was going to happen next to unfold. The moment stretched and the man did nothing for a while except sit and stare at them, jiggling the pistol and occasionally pursing his lips the way people sometimes do when they are thinking.

Val tried to get some measure of the man; she studied him without appearing to do so. He was no local man, that was for sure, and no farmer. He was dressed in a dark city suit that was stained with dried blood, and his shoes were caked with mud. The man was rather handsome in an oily sort of way, with a long thin nose and a strong jaw, but his lips were too thin and looked cruel, and his chin was so pointed that it gave him a saturnine countenance. He had very high, prominent cheekbones and an almost Shakespearean brow, except for the sharp dip of his coal-black widow's peak. His hair was as dark and shiny as a magpie's wing. But it was his eyes that disturbed her most: they were a strange charcoal gray and extraordinarily piercing, and despite the pretense at humor, there was no trace of humanity anywhere in those shadowy depths.

Ruger fished his cigarettes out of his pocket and fired one up one-handed, never relaxing his grip on the pistol, even though it appeared to rest casually on his leg.

"Okay, folks, it's question-and-answer time," he said after he had made them sit and stew in troubled silence for almost a minute. "The rules are simple. I ask questions, and you answer them. You get points for all correct answers, but let me warn you—you could lose some substantial points for wrong answers." He jiggled the gun for emphasis. He fixed his gaze on Guthrie. "Okay, Mr. Guthrie, you are our first contestant tonight."

Guthrie said nothing, but Val could feel him stiffen beside her. This was so outrageous and unreal that he didn't even know how to think about it.

"Now, unless you are some kind of Mormon and these young darlings are your harem, I can assume that these are your daughters. In fact, did I not hear Donna Reed there call you 'Dad'?"

Guthrie hesitated for only a split second. "Yes, they are my daughters."

"Good, you get one point. Now, tell me their names."

"Val and Connie."

"Uh-huh. Which is which? No . . . let me guess. That one looks like a Connie," he said, nodding to Connie. "She looks like every Connie I've ever known. Prissy name, don't you think?"

Guthrie didn't think he was supposed to answer that question, so he kept his jaw clamped shut.

"I guess that means you're Val?" Val nodded. "I'm sorry," Ruger said, cupping a hand to his ear. "Didn't catch that."

"Y . . . yes. My name is Val Guthrie."

"Ah, splendid." Ruger looked as pleased as if Val had just won a spelling bee. "Now, ladies, hold up your hands. Mm-hm. No wedding ring on your hand, Val. Too bad. Shouldn't let fruits like yours spoil on the vine. But . . . ooo, look at that, Connie's got a nice fat gold band. Well, where is Mr. Reed?"

"What?" Connie asked, confused.

"Your husband. Don't you ever watch TV Land? Where is he?"

Connie said nothing, looking too scared to even open her mouth beyond the permanent shocked O in which it was set.

"Connie," Ruger chided, "you're forgetting the rules."

"He's not home," said Guthrie.

Ruger smiled, stood, walked over to the couch, and looked down at Guthrie. With another demonstration of his terrible speed he punched the old man in the face. Guthrie's head rocked back as blood erupted from his torn eyebrow. It poured down his face in a shocking flood of brilliant red. Guthrie clamped his hands to his face, and Val seized him protectively in her arms, trying to stanch the flow of blood. Connie recoiled in horror and squeezed herself farther into the corner of the couch.

Ruger stood over them, looking down at them with all of the reptilian humor momentarily gone from his face. "Listen to me, you old fuck. If I ask you a question, you may answer. If I ask anyone else a question, shut the fuck up. Am I clear?"

Guthrie nodded slowly, his eyes blazing with pain and fury.

"I didn't hear you."

"Yes, goddamn it!" Guthrie snarled, and tensed for another blow. Ruger just let his smile return and backed up until he found the rocker and lowered himself into it.

"Okay then. Let's try this again."

Guthrie's face was painted red and blood ran from between his fingers and down his forearms.

"Now, Connie. Where is your husband?"

Connie glanced at the blood still streaming down Guthrie's face and in a choked, little girl voice said, "Mark went to a meeting after work."

"A meeting of what?"

"Rotary Club."

Ruger burst out laughing. "Oh man! That is just too precious! Fucking Rotary Club, and Donna-frigging-Reed to come home to. Tell me, Miss Perfect, does he drive a station wagon, too?"

"How did you know . . . ?"

Laughter spewed out again. "American made?"

"Yes . . . a Ford."

Ruger actually pounded the butt of the pistol on his thigh as he laughed. Val and her father exchanged a very brief glance; Connie just frowned in uncertain confusion and fear. Eventually Ruger sobered. "Okay, Mr. Guthrie, your turn again. How's the face?"

"It's fine," Guthrie said coldly.

"Looks to me like it hurts like a bitch. Whatever. Okay, now,

does anyone else live here besides Donna Reed and her husband, Val the Spinster, and your own self? Is there a Mrs. Old
Lady Guthrie?"

"It's just us."

"What about farm hands? You can't work this big old place
by yourselves."

"We have a few regular hands, and we have some day labor
come in."

"Wetbacks?"

"Some migrant workers, a few local boys."

"Any of them getting any from Val over there?"

Guthrie ground his teeth and tried to find some kind of answer
that would not result in a beating or a bullet, but Karl waved the
question away. "Forget it. Trick question. What I meant to say, is
there anyone else who's likely to come sniffing around after her
tonight?"

Val tensed, her fingers digging in to her father's skin. "No,"
she heard her dad say.

"What, no boyfriends?" Ruger asked Val.

"He lives in town," said Connie, and then clapped her hands
over her mouth, her eyes growing as wide as saucers as she realized she had spoken out of turn. With a weary sigh, Karl stood
up and walked over to her.

"No, please don't!" Guthrie said.

"Let her alone!" pleaded Val.

Ruger looked at them for a moment, considering. "She broke
the rules. Loss of points. What can I do?"

"She's just scared. She didn't mean anything," Val protested,
half rising.

Ruger swung the gun around so fast it became a silvery blur.
The edge of the barrel caught Val across the forehead just below
the hairline and knocked her back against the armrest. Her father began lunging at Ruger, but the man was so frighteningly
quick; Ruger twisted and drove his gun-hand elbow into
Guthrie's solar plexus as the old man struggled to stand. All the
air and fight went out of Guthrie, and he collapsed against the

dazed and bleeding Val. The two of them huddled in a bloody and motionless heap.

Ruger gave a world-weary sigh. "I can see this is going to be a long night after all, folks. Oh well, shit happens, huh?" As his irrepressible smile crept back onto his lips, he turned to Connie, who was so terrified that she was not even breathing. Both of her hands beat the air in front her, warding off imagined blows. Ruger bent down toward her and batted her hands out of the way. Connie squeezed her eyes shut and turned as far away as she could, her whole face twisted in expectation of the pain. Ruger kept leaning forward until his lips were only a couple of inches away from her face. He did not touch her, not so much as a hair on her head. Instead, he said in a sharp voice: "Boo!"

Connie screamed and fainted.

Chapter 10

Tow-Truck Eddie moved through the rooms of his house as if he were exploring a marvelous new country. Everything he looked at appeared fresh and mysterious and wonderful. He stood for a time in the dining room, listening to the old grandfather clock ticking out the seconds of his new existence, and he realized that with each passing moment new universes were being created and old suns were dying glorious deaths. All for him.

In the kitchen, he took tomatoes and crushed them in his strong fingers, and understood the message that they had always tried to tell him about the truths hidden in living blood; how could he have missed the meaning of this parable for so long? He licked the pulp from his hands and marveled in the taste, so like blood.

Upstairs in his bedroom, he picked up a five-pound plate from his weight set and pressed the flat side of it against his cheek, delighting in the coolness and roughness of the hard black iron.

Down in the laundry room, he stripped out of his soiled clothes and crammed them into his tiny washing machine. He poured a precise capful of Wisk over them and washed them in cold water. Naked, he inspected his body, astounded at the fineness of his skin, at the textural differences between the flesh of his stomach and that on the inside of each wrist; at the difference in sensation between the cool air of the cellar on his thighs and on his face. He inspected his flaccid penis and wondered what kind of seed it would dispense, now that he had become a true son of God. Would his children share his power? Would the act of inseminating a woman likewise bestow grace on her? The thought made his penis jump, begin to swell, but he forced those thoughts away. They were not proper for this moment; they were thoughts from *before*, and he would allow them only at the proper time, and with the proper ceremony, but not in the squalid laundry room of his house.

Still naked, he ran up the stairs, and the exertion felt so good he ran up and down the stairs twenty-five times. Sweat flowed from his pores and coated him with a fine sheen. When he walked into the living room and stood before the mirror, he saw how the sweat helped define each of his muscles. He turned this way and that, flexing his arms and chest, swelling his lats, flexing the bulky quadriceps and abdominals. Even with all the thousands of hours he had spent with weights, he had never fully realized just how perfect his body had become, especially for a man of his age. He looked thirty rather than fifty. His body was more superb than any Greek statue: each muscle rippling like bundles of bridge cable beneath the firm tautness of his skin. From the broad expanse of the *pectoralis major* to the tapering *peroneus brevis* he stood as a model of metahuman perfection, and a whole hour passed before he could tear himself away from his own image. *What a perfect vessel,* he thought. *What a perfect temple for the Holy Spirit.*

He wished that he could somehow clone himself so that he could always be able to look at that body, maybe even to hold it, kiss it, make reverent love to it.

What would it feel like, he wondered, *to make love to one's own body? Surely it must be the most perfect love anyone could ever experience.*

Walking back and forth through the house, he watched the clock tick toward ten o'clock. He had been home for nearly an hour and a half, and still the level of energetic excitement hadn't abated even one iota.

He laughed out loud, full of a pure delight, and turned a graceful pirouette in the middle of the living room.

(2)

Vic Wingate was turning the crank of his antique printing press; yellow handbills zipped out from under the roller and settled down into the tray. A haze of blue cigarette smoke tinted the air of the cellar. It fascinated him to watch the blank sheets of paper go in one end of the roller and pop out of the other a second later filled with words and pictures. Even though it was a lot of work to do it this way, and though he could have done it far easier and much faster on his computer, Vic preferred the ink and the mess and the feel of doing it by hand.

The stack of blank papers dwindled down to nothing and Vic stopped cranking. Stubbing out his cigarette in a dented metal ashtray he'd stolen once from the only good hotel he'd ever stayed in, Vic picked up the top copy of the freshly printed handbills. His thick lips moved as he read his own words: WHY THE WHITE RACE HAS THE RIGHT TO RULE, and below that in smaller type: AND HOW THE JEWS ARE TRYING TO USURP THAT RIGHT.

Usurp. He liked the word. Vic always had a dictionary and thesaurus handy when he wrote up his handbills.

He let the handbill flutter back down atop the others and stretched. His muscles were sore from two really difficult transmission jobs at Shanahan's Service Station, where he worked nine to five, five days a week. It was a hard job, but it paid well and Vic loved it. He loved everything about cars. If he had the money, he'd buy Shanahan out, though he'd still do his time in the pits. Then he smiled when he realized how dumb an idea that was. Come the day after Halloween there would *be* no Shanahan's . . . and from that point on Vic wouldn't be working for *anyone*. Well, except for Griswold. The Man would always be the Man.

He worked on his handbills for a while longer, musing now about how things were working out. It was all starting now, he knew that. The Man had a lot of pieces moving on the board, and though Vic knew most of what was in store, he didn't know everything. He was a general, sure, but not the Man himself. That was okay with him. When the Red Wave hit on Halloween night, Vic would be nearly a king himself.

He bundled the flyers and stacked them, then massaged his neck muscles, which had grown stiff as he'd worked over the press. Then a thought occurred to him and he looked at his wristwatch: 9:30 p.m.

"Well, well," he murmured. A smile wriggled wetly onto his lips. "The little fucker's late again. Oh boy." He fingered his belt, wondering if tonight was a belt night or a hands-on night. Hands, he decided. You could never really get the feel of it with a belt. Kid felt it, sure as hell, but Vic wanted to feel it himself. He liked his hands to sting. It was no good if your hands didn't sting, he mused, and you never got that with a belt. All you got with the belt was a jolt up the arm and the sound. The sound was good, but that sting was outstanding. With the thickness of the calluses on Vic's hands, it took a lot of speed, a lot of impact for there to be any sting at all, and Vic always liked to challenge himself to see how many hits it would take until the sting was there, and there at just the right tingling level.

Vic figured that maybe it was time to amp up on the kid. If the Man's other plan for getting rid of the little pussy didn't work out, then it was up to Vic to accomplish his goal. If he upped the ante on Mike, made the beatings a bit worse—but not so bad that those cops that weren't in his pocket would be forced to step in—then maybe the kid would finally get the fucking message and realize that, yes, life is hell so maybe it'd be better to jump off a fucking bridge. Or something. Vic had left razor blades on the side of the tub several times, but the little bastard was too damn dense to take a hint.

Not for the first time Vic wished he could just strangle the little fucker. That would feel so good! But the Man was very, very specific on that point. If Mike were to die from a corrupt or evil hand, then the Man's whole plan would be in deep shit. Which sucked, because Vic ached to feel Mike's throat collapse in his hands. Then he'd be free of Mike, and would be finally able to cut loose of that drunken whore, Lois. What a goddamn waste of human tissue she was. Couldn't cook, lousy in the sack unless Vic beat the shit out of her first, and nowadays she was drunk all the time.

The things I do for the Man, Vic thought, feeling peevish.

Upstairs he could hear the phone ringing. He listened, counting the rings. Three. Four. Five. Five? Christ, how many times had he told that cow to get the phone by three rings at the most? Fucking five rings?

Vic closed his eyes and smiled with the first real pleasure of the day. If both Mike and Lois were going to defy him like this, then it might turn out to be a really interesting evening. Really interesting.

He was already heading toward the stairs when he heard Lois's tentative knock on the door. In a hesitant, quavering voice she called, "Vic? Vic, honey?"

"What?" he growled, mounting the stairs two at a time.

"Phone call for you, honey."

He jerked the door open. "So I heard. Now, correct me if I'm wrong, but did I not hear the phone ring, what, five times?"

Lois stood there, her blue cotton bathrobe pulled tight around her body, the belt cinched and knotted around her slim waist. Her brown hair was tousled from sleep and her eyes were red and rheumy from vodka. Fear reeled drunkenly in her eyes.

"I'm sorry, honey. I was asleep. I didn't hear . . . I mean . . . I got it as fast as I . . ."

He held up a warning finger and she shut up. "You go into the living room and wait for me. Don't you dare sit down, either, Lois. When I'm done with my call, we'll go over the phone rules again. Okay? Go on now."

Lois shrank back, her mouth opening to form words of protest, to voice some kind of plea, but she did not dare make a sound. It would always be much worse if she tried to plead for tolerance, and horribly worse if she begged. She clutched the folds of her robe to her throat and cowered out of the room.

Vic waited until she was out of the kitchen until he let the smile form on his lips. He liked that color blue on her. He reached for the phone.

"This is Vic."

"Mr. Wingate? This is Terry Wolfe."

Vic tensed, instantly on the defensive. Why the hell would the mayor be calling him? "Yeah?" he asked cautiously.

"Mr. Wingate, I'm calling on behalf of your stepson, Mike?"

"Christ, what's the little shit done now?"

"Oh, nothing like that. No, he was involved in an accident, Mr. Wingate."

Equal amounts of hope and fear surged up in Vic's heart. "Yeah? What kind of accident?"

"He was riding his bike on A-32 when someone, a trucker, ran him off the road near where Old Mill Road cuts over to the hayride. Now, he's not badly hurt, but he is banged up a bit. A passing motorist took him to the Haunted Hayride, and the manager there called me and asked if I would notify you."

"The hayride? That's all the way the hell out—"

The mayor's voice cut him off smoothly. "I know it's a bit of a haul, Mr. Wingate, but as the boy's health and welfare are involved, I'm sure you would want to go pick him up."

Vic's eyes were narrowed. The phone call had a weird, fishy smell to it, but there was nowhere to go with it except to agree. "Yeah. Sure. Whatever. I'll go fetch him."

"Thank you, Mr. Win—"

Vic hung up on him and stood for a moment, arms folded, lips pursed, staring at the phone. *A trucker,* he thought. *A trucker running the kid off the road.* He wondered if that driver had been at the wheel of a tow truck.

He smiled slowly, believing his guess to be right. If the little punk had been run down by a tow truck, then that would be perfect. That was what the Man had been trying to orchestrate for a while now, but Vic hadn't known the plan was in full swing already.

He nodded and chuckled. "That's cool."

Then he remembered Lois waiting for him in the living room.

Definitely a hands-on kind of night, he thought as he strolled out of the kitchen.

(3)

"Does the mayor want you to arrest him?" Mike asked as Missy took curve after curve.

"Who—our guest psycho? Two words best express it. Hell no!" Crow shook his head. "I'm just an errand boy, and that's all. I'm gonna go out, close down the hayride, wait for your folks to pick you up, and then I'm done with it."

"But you're a cop, aren't you?"

"Kind of . . . well, not really. I've been reinstated just for tonight. Can't have civilians doing official work."

"You used to be one, though?"

Crow said nothing, his eyes watching the road.

"Crow? Didn't you used to be a cop?"

"Once upon a time, young Jedi."

"Why'd you quit?"

They drove on for almost half a mile before Crow answered that. He gave Mike a brief, searching look and then refocused on the road.

"Sometimes things don't work out," he said simply, then smiled. "Besides, if I was a cop, whom would you buy your comics from?"

"Probably Nick's Comic Cave in Crestville. Or maybe at Waldenbooks in—"

"Mike . . . ?"

"Yeah?"

"Shut up when grown folks are talking."

Mike grinned. Outside the windows the black fields whipped by, beards of corn glowing with the cold moonlight. "Do you think the chief will catch him?"

Crow was about to suggest that Gus Bernhardt couldn't catch the clap in a whorehouse, but thought better of it. He said, "I guess he might. He has a lot of help from Philly cops. By morning there'll be more cops in town than tourists."

"Won't the tourists be scared off anyway 'cause of what's happening?"

Crow snorted. "Hardly. We'll probably have a banner day, once this gets out. People love blood and guts as much as they do a good five-alarm fire. Draws 'em like flies to sh . . . uh, garbage."

"You were going to say 'like flies to shit.' "

"Yes, but I didn't, and you shouldn't, either."

"Jeez, Crow, I'm fourteen!"

"Yeah, well, there's some that think being fourteen is the same as being a kid. Kind of a popular notion, I hear tell."

"Yeah, well. What do you think?"

Crow looked at him, looked past the smile at the Mike Sweeney whose father was dead, whose mother was a drunk, and whose stepfather was known to beat him so bad that he missed a dozen days from school a year.

He sighed. "Not everybody grows up at the same speed, I guess."

Mike grunted.

"I still don't want to hear you use bad language regardless."

Mike smiled. "Okay, boss."

"Okay then." They looked at each other and grinned. Crow said, "How're the ribs?"

"They hurt like a son of a bitch," Mike said. Crow goggled at him, and then they both burst out laughing. Mike laughed, winced, and kept on laughing, clapping a hand to his aching side.

"You juvenile delinquent!" Crow gasped.

A half mile later they passed a massive billboard painted with witches and goblins and leering black cats. Written in dripping black and red letters it proclaimed:

PINE DEEP HAUNTED HAYRIDE
Biggest in the East Coast
5 MILES
WE'LL SCARE YOU SILLY!

They drove on.

Chapter 11

Terry drank the last of the reheated coffee, oblivious of its appalling taste, and set the cup down on Ginny's desk. The Xanax was kicking in and he felt a little of the tension seep out of his muscles. Ginny quickly picked up the cup, put a pink Post-it sheet under it as a coaster, and set it down again. The mayor folded his arms, hiked one half of his rump onto the edge of her desk, and looked hard and long at Gus Bernhardt. "So, here we are."

"Yeah," Gus said. "Fine kettle of frigging fish."

"Language, language," Ginny said sotto voce.

"Frigging's not a curse, you silly bitch," Gus muttered under his breath as he went back to staring at the huge aerial-survey map of the town and its close neighbors covering the entire wall above Ginny's desk.

Across the room Sergeant Ferro and Detective LaMastra were standing, heads together in conversation with officers from the first wave of Philadelphia cops. Every once in a while, LaMastra would look over at Terry and raise his eyebrows by way of sympathetic acknowledgment.

Terry glanced at the clock. It was just past ten, two and a half hours since he'd gotten the call at Crow's shop. Most of that time had been spent laboriously trying to explain the peculiar geography of Pine Deep to the pinch-hitting cops. Geographically speaking, Pine Deep was an island, bordered completely by running streams of water: Pine River along the west and its estuary,

Black Creek to the south, and then the thin and wandering
northern line of the Crescent Canal and the broad Delaware
River to the east. Between Black Marsh and the outlying houses
of Pine Deep, A-32 rose up into a series of foothills and
wannabe-mountains, taking gymnastic turns around sheer cliffs
and doing roller-coaster rises and dips past the vast Pine Deep
State Forest from which the town borrowed its name. The forest
surrounded the farmlands and thrust tentative fingers back toward A-32 every few miles so that the long protrusions formed
borders between some of the larger farms. The main body of the
forest lay solidly westward, and sprawled as far over as Newton's
Reach, a tourist attraction town preserved intact from Colonial
times, right down to the working blacksmith's shop and the
tours conducted by high school seniors wearing tricorns and
three-button breeches.

Looking at the map, with the surrounding expanse of green-
ery from the forestland and the farms, the town of Pine Deep
seemed small and remote. Certainly it was no metropolis. The
population of the town, counting farmers from the most distant
spreads, was just a little under twenty-five hundred, but considering how much square mileage the town covered, the people
were pretty thin on the ground. Most of them lived in the town
proper, on a handful of quaint cobblestoned streets. Downtown,
as it was apocryphally known, was actually situated on a high
saddle between two higher peaks, and though the peaks made
the town look like it was in a valley, it was nearly a thousand feet
higher than some of the farms.

Downtown was where all the "action" was. That was where
the tourists flocked in the thousands from the first moderately
tolerable day in late March until after the Christmas sales. Antique buyers came from as far west as Ohio and as far north as
Boston; rug merchants drove all the way up from Florida to sell
truckloads of Seminole quilts, or mock Navajo blankets. Every
fifth store sold Pennsylvania Dutch woodcrafts, from plain and
sturdy tables to elaborate porch swings with amazingly delicate
scrollwork. Amish baked goods from Lancaster scented the air by
six o'clock each morning, and in the evening, the breeze blowing

past Winifred's Incense gave the place an aroma of magic. Almost everywhere were the delicate tinkles of wind chimes, the rattle of rain sticks, the clack-clickety-clack of hand-carved weather vanes. Windows were filled with rare books, exotic music from faraway places, crystals for healing, and crystal balls for seeing into any reality of choice, improbable varieties of cheeses, and the largest selection of family chateau wines in the region. One tiny store sold nothing but Pine Deep souvenirs and oddities such as the Fireballs, a kind of bright red pinecone unique to the area; countless books detailing, either in lurid prose or scholarly wordiness, the ghost stories of the region; calendars with twelve months' worth of magnificent photos bursting with the incredible colors of Pine Deep in autumn, the wild freshness of spring, the deep green of the summer forests, or the stark and ancient beauty of the snow-swept winters; and the fifty-odd varieties of locally put-by jellies, jams, and preserves, including a famous spicy cinnamon-pumpkin butter that had been touted by the Frugal Gourmet one year and had caused a run on the local supply.

In all that vastness of land, with the millions of tall, full-leafed plants, the hedgerows and groves of fruit trees, the undeveloped forest land and the fields left fallow, the estates overgrown and gone wild, the cliffs and caves and hollows, there were three men and one car hiding from the eyes of the law.

Terry stared at the map and sighed, rubbing at his eyes and half smiling at the enormity of it all, wishing the three psycho bastards had chosen somewhere else to ensconce themselves. He drew in a long breath, held it, and then sighed again. It was going to be a very, very long night.

Terry looked away from the map to see Sergeant Ferro and Detective LaMastra standing at his elbow. "Where do we stand?" Terry asked.

"Well," the detective said, "with all of your people, sir, and with the officers loaned to this jurisdiction from the surrounding townships, we were able to put more than twenty cars on the road, each with two officers apiece. I split the teams up so that most of the cars that are actually patrolling within the town boundaries have at least one Philly officer. I felt that it would be unduly risky to require the local officers to try and apprehend Ruger and his buddies without experienced help."

Terry nodded. He could tell from Ferro's expression that he was trying hard not to give offense, but at the same time make clear the point that the local cops were rubes and this was work for real professional law enforcement. Had Terry lived in any other town in Bucks County he might have been offended, but in Pine Deep Ferro's estimation was right on target. Gus Bernhardt *was* a rube, and because of him the police department was little better than the Keystone Cops. Terry loved his town, but he really had no opinion of the department Gus had built. Look at who Gus had hired. Shirley O'Keefe, who looked like a skinny twenty-two-year-old Meryl Streep, got sick to her stomach every time she had to help with a bad traffic accident. Officer Golub was smart but had no balls. Jim Polk was an alcoholic and was as likely to arrest pink elephants as criminals, and his crony, Dixie MacVey, was on the force just so he could pull traffic duty outside the high school, giving him a legal reason for watching all the teenage girls bounce along. The rest were just as useless.

Until now there hadn't really been any desperate need to change that, which gave Gus his comfortable stranglehold on the job, but this whole thing had Terry thinking about initiating some changes around here. It wasn't the first time he'd thought about putting up some money to try and attract one of these Philly officers to try their hand at rural law enforcement.

"So I think we're as well deployed as we can be," Ferro said. "Unfortunately for those of us here in the office it's kind of a hurry up and wait situation. Until we have more to go on, there's not a whole lot more we can do."

"Fine, fine. That's excellent, Sergeant." Terry picked up the coffee cup, looked into its emptiness, sighed again, and set it down. "Is there any more of this, Ginny?"

"Well . . ." she said doubtfully. "I could make a new pot." She made no move to do so.

Terry favored her with a smile. "Would you mind?"

"We do have some instant. . . ."

"Why don't you get the big urn and make enough for everyone?"

"The instant would be easier."

"Yeah, but I think the officers would appreciate brewed coffee, what do you say?"

"Tastes the same to me."

"Please?" Terry implored, manfully resisting the impulse to strangle her.

Gus tapped her chair with a thick toe. "Shift your ass, Gin. Make some coffee."

Ginny stood up, and with all the self-sacrificing grandeur of Sydney Carton mounting the guillotine steps, she turned and headed for the kitchen.

The four men watched her go. When she was out of earshot, Terry said to Gus, "I'm telling you, Gus, one of these days I'm going to shoot her."

"I'll load your gun for you."

"She's a royal pain in my butt."

"Mine too, but we're stuck with her. Who else could do her job?"

"A trained monkey?"

"Maybe, but where you gonna find one that'll work for what we pay her?"

LaMastra cracked up but, catching sight of Ferro's unsmiling face, turned the laugh into a cough and then busied himself with adjusting his tie.

Reaching up, Ferro tapped the map with a knuckle. "The main idea is to go up and down A-32 in a kind of squeeze pattern, checking both sides of the roads for any place where they might have pulled off the main drag. You know, fire access road, farm road, that sort of thing."

"Uh-huh."

"Chief," the sergeant asked, "how many officers are scheduled for the next shift?"

Gus looked at him with bovine blankness. "Well—" he began, but Terry cut him off.

"Sergeant, every officer we have is on the clock right now. Gus called in all the off-duty people before you guys even got here."

Ferro's face became wooden.

Gus nodded. "That's right, sir. We only keep a couple of one-person cars rolling at a time." He shrugged. "Don't need more."

"Haven't until now," Terry amended.

"Yikes," said LaMastra quietly.

"Do you have any reserves?" Ferro asked.

"Not as such, no," hedged Gus. "A lot of men in town, and a handful of women, have been local officers at one time or another, especially those who did co-op work while they were in law classes at Pinelands. Plus there was a town watch for a while, so a few of those guys had a basic course. Sometimes we'll hire them on during the week of Halloween and all during the Christmas season, you know, to cut down on shoplifting and stuff like that, and make some extra pay."

"More of a presence, you understand," said Terry. "It helps everybody to see a warm body in a uniform. Shoot, I've even worn a badge a couple of times—back before I became mayor, of course."

"I see," said Ferro. He pursed his lips. "Any chance we could reactivate some of these people?"

" 'Reactivate'?" Gus echoed.

"Yes. If this manhunt goes on longer than twelve hours, the officers on shift now are going to get tired. We'll need replacements for them so we can keep the net as tight as possible. If we slacken at all, then Ruger and company will slip right through."

That would suit me, thought Terry. Aloud, he said, "Well, I more or less reinstated one fellow tonight. Malcolm Crow."

Gus wheeled on him. "Crow? Now why'n hell'd you do that?"

Ferro and LaMastra exchanged a brief look. "Who's he?" asked LaMastra.

"A local shopkeeper," Terry said.

"He's a drunken—" Gus began and Terry withered him with a glare.

"Crow has been sober for years, Gus, and you bloody well know it."

"Once a drunk, always a drunk."

"Maybe, but he isn't drinking now. Come on, Gus, even you have to admit he was a darned good officer." Terry almost said, *Crow was the only good cop this town ever had*, but didn't want to appear unkind in front of the Philly cops.

Gus grunted.

Ferro did not want to involve himself in the matter, but LaMastra asked, "What's the beef? Did he drink himself off the force or something?"

"No," said Terry, still glaring at Gus. "He quit drinking before he ever even put on a badge."

"So what's the problem?"

Gus opened his mouth to answer that, but Terry cut him off. "There is no problem," he said slowly, putting firm emphasis on each word. Then he looked at Ferro. "Malcolm Crow was a superb cop. He might even have run for chief," he said, intending the barb to hook itself in Gus's flesh. "He had some issues from when he was a kid and got into the bottle for a while and, all right, he made a fool of himself for a year or two, but he also got himself sober. Started going to meetings and really turned things around. Became a decorated officer. Gus was opposed to a drunk working as a cop, but I vouched for Crow then and I vouch for him now. He's been sober for years, as I said, and nowadays he's a well-respected businessman, a cornerstone of our community, and"—again he focused his eyes on Gus—"a close personal friend of mine."

In truth Terry did have doubts about reinstating Crow and halfway regretted having done it on the spur of the moment. Had he been less overwhelmingly exhausted and less off-kilter he might not have done so. Crow had been a very good cop, and had been sober and going to AA meetings without a break for years, but it had also been a long time since he'd worn a badge and—as much as Terry hated to admit it to himself—Crow was so much of a goofball that it was hard to imagine him even taking what was happening right now with the proper seriousness.

But he didn't see what good admitting it would do now. Especially not in front of Gus and these other officers.

Turning back to Ferro, he went on, "I reinstated him just temporarily so that he could go shut down our Haunted Hayride. It gives him double authority as a contract employee for the hayride and a law officer. That way he'll have the clout to handle any arguments or protests that result. Tourists can get touchy, you know."

"Mm. We saw the signs on the way into town. Chief Bernhardt tells me that you own it."

"Yes, and I'm proud to say that it's the biggest in the East Coast," Terry said with one of his few genuine smiles of the day, "but it's full of kids, and I felt it was best to shut it up for the night and send the kids home."

"Very smart thinking, sir," said Ferro. "Is this Mr. Crow the man for the job?"

"Crow," said Terry firmly, "is the man for any job. Believe me."

Gus, it was clear, did not, but Ferro and LaMastra saw the look in Terry's eyes, and they both nodded. "Fine," Ferro said, "can we keep him on after he's done that job? Help us out until this thing is over?"

"I think he can be persuaded."

"Good, good, anyone else?"

Gus cleared his throat. "I suppose we could make some calls. I don't think we have enough uniforms and sidearms to go around, but we could issue badges and shotguns. Or have the replacements borrow the sidearms of the team going off-duty."

"Well, sir," said Ferro, "I'll leave you to work that part of it out for yourself. For my own part, if we don't get some action in the next few hours, I'm going to call in a request for additional officers from Philly, and we may be hearing from the FBI soon."

"Why would the FBI bother with this?" asked Terry.

"Well, sir, according to your map there, A-32 cuts back and forth over the Delaware River just here, and again here."

"Yeah? So?"

"Well, that side of the river is New Jersey, this side is Pennsylvania."

"Again . . . so?"

"Ah," said Gus. "Something about interstate flight?"

"Uh-huh," said LaMastra. "Interstate flight is a federal rap, and that means the FBI can be asked to step in. But we probably won't ask." He directed this last comment to Ferro, who nodded.

"Federal involvement is seldom a good thing. But that doesn't matter right now. My captain has promised us at least a dozen officers."

"Get all the help you need," Terry said. "I said it twice already, and I'm not joking, call in the National Guard if it'll help. Let me be clear, Sergeant, I surely do not need Jack the Ripper slicing people up in Pine Deep. It's bad for business, and it's bad for me personally because I am friends with darn near everybody who lives around here. Please, do whatever—and I mean *whatever*—it takes to nail these three guys and get them the heck out of my backyard."

Ferro smiled a tiny smile, and gave Terry a curt nod. "We will do our very best, Mr. Mayor."

Terry nodded. Turning to Gus, he said, "C'mon, let's get on the phone and see if we can't raise some kind of posse."

"Hi-yo, Silver," Gus muttered sourly and followed his boss over to the desks.

Ferro and LaMastra stood looking at them, and then turned to stare up at the map, at the immensity of area that had to be covered in order to run Karl Ruger to ground. It was staggering.

"What d'you think, Sarge?"

Ferro shrugged. "Honestly?"

"Uh-huh."

"I think this town is hip deep in shit."

"Yep. Pretty much how I would have put it."

(2)

"Christ, you three look like a hockey team in the penalty box." It was true enough. Val sat with a dish towel full of ice cubes pressed to her forehead; her father sat next to her with a similar compress on his torn eyebrow, still flushed and slightly goggle-eyed from the blow to his solar plexus; and Connie was dabbing at her face with an antimacassar from the couch, sopping up the water Ruger had dashed in her face to wake her up.

Across from them, Ruger sipped a tall glass of Early Times.

"You do realize," he said in his cold whisper, "that all of this was unnecessary. If you would just follow the rules of my little Q and A, we'd all get along. Can't we all just get along?" he said, and laughed. The joke was lost on them, but he gave a fatalistic shrug and kept his own good humor. "So, I think by now the rules should be clear. I will ask each one of you a question, or perhaps questions, and that person will answer. No committees, no debating societies. Just questions and answers. That's pretty simple, isn't it?"

They stared at him, hating him, willing him death.

He said, "Isn't it?" leaning into the words.

"Yes," they each said.

"Nice." He sipped the sour mash and hissed with pleasure at the burn. "Okay. Now, Miss Val, I believe you were about to tell me about your various boyfriends."

Val swallowed what felt like a cantaloupe in her throat. "I . . . don't have any boyfriends."

"What? None at all? What about the one that lives in town?"

"No. That's been over for weeks. There's no one."

Ruger smiled a slithery smile. "I find that kinda hard to believe, nice-looking piece like you. What's the deal? Didn't you give him enough?"

Val just looked at him.

"C'mon, I'm interested. Why'd you break up?"

She managed what she hoped was a casual and dismissive shrug. "Just didn't work out."

"Uh-huh." Ruger's dark eyes glittered like the glass eyes of a stuffed shark. "So nobody new, huh?"

"No."

Val tensed, almost as afraid of more questions as she was of Connie blurting out the truth and screwing them all. She wasn't entirely sure why she denied Crow's existence, but some instinct had triggered her words when she had spoken. No boyfriend, no husband, no attachments that could somehow be used against her, or who could be hurt if she were to be used against them. Keep the man's thoughts away from that kind of thinking. It was bad enough that Connie had mentioned Mark, Val's brother, who was due home sometime soon.

"Okay, you get two points for answering all your questions." He winked at her. "Okay, Pop. Your turn. What kind of car do you have?"

"A Bronco."

"Oh yeah? What year?"

"Ninety-six."

"Any good?"

For some reason, Guthrie felt a brief flash of cockiness. He said, "It gets lousy gas mileage in the city, the clutch sticks, and it has a shimmy when you get it above sixty."

Ruger blinked, and then he laughed. "Well, well." He raised his glass to toast Guthrie and took a heavy knock of the whiskey. "Where are the keys?"

"On a hook by the back door."

"Where is it parked?"

"Right out back. Just outside the door."

"What color?"

"Dark green."

"Any vanity plates?"

Guthrie looked at him for a moment, uncomprehending.

"I mean do you have one of those stupid plates that say 2-FAST or BIG BUX or any of that shit?"

"No . . . no, just regular tags."

"Registration and inspection up to date?"

"Of course."

" 'Of course,' " Ruger repeated, shaking his head. "I break into your house, kick your ass, and am planning to steal your car, and you sound offended when I ask if your inspection is up to date."

"The car's fine. Why don't you take it and go?"

"I will, I will, but not yet. There's just a few things I got to do yet."

The phone rang, but Ruger made no move to answer it. He merely let it ring itself out. He finished the drink and set the glass down primly on the side table. Val was amazed: he must have poured five fingers' worth into the tall milk glass and he'd downed it all in six or eight gulps. How much whiskey was that? A quarter pint? What would he be like when the whiskey hit his system?

"Okay, next question, Mr. Guthrie," Ruger said with no trace of a slur in his voice. "Do you have a stretcher?"

"A stretcher?"

"Yeah."

"No. A stretcher? Why would I have a stretcher?"

"You got anything I could use as one?"

Guthrie frowned. "I guess you could take a door off its hinges and use that. Who's hurt?"

"Hey, hey, now, I didn't say you could ask any questions."

"Okay," Guthrie said in a soft, placating voice. "Sorry."

"Okay then. How 'bout a wheelbarrow?"

"Sure. We have a couple of those."

"Where?"

"In the shed. Small yellow building next to the barn."

"Is it locked?"

"No."

"No?" Ruger chuckled. "Aren't you afraid of thieves?"

Guthrie looked at him coldly. "Not usually much of an issue way out here."

Ruger just shook his head. "Okay, and how about rope? Or that gray tape, whaddya call it?"

"Duct tape?"

"Yeah, duck tape. You got any duck tape?"

Guthrie nodded. "Couple rolls."

"Where?"

"In the cellar."

"Rope?"

"Some in the barn. Washing line, baling twine in the cellar."

"Good, good."

Ruger rocked in his rocker for a little while, again pursing his lips, the smile coming and going, and his reptile eyes staring blackly at them. "Okay, then," he said at length, "here's the plan. Val, you are going to go fetch me some rope and some of that duck tape. You go fetch it and come right back."

Val's heart hammered in her chest as she thought about all the things in the cellar. She stood up quickly and turned to go, but immediately Ruger was on his feet, too. He grabbed her shoulder, spun her around, and looked into her eyes. She didn't know what he was seeing there, but his face seemed angry at first, and then his smile crawled back. He slowly shook his head. "Uh-uh, honey. You sit your pretty ass back down. I was born at night, darlin', but it wasn't last night. Sit down."

She let her gaze fall away and slowly crept back to the couch and sat down. Her father handed her the ice pack she had dropped and she pressed it back it place. Connie was staring at her with a total lack of understanding.

"I think," said Ruger, reaching out with the toe of his shoe and nudging Connie's knee, "that I'll let the Stepford Wife go."

"M . . . me?"

"Y . . . yes," Ruger mocked, "y . . . you."

"Down the cellar?"

"No, I want you to run down to the drugstore and fetch me a bottle of baby aspirin. Yes, the fucking cellar. Don't you pay any attention?"

"For rope?" Connie said in a five-year-old's voice.

"And tape. You get them and then hustle your white-bread ass right back up here. No tricks, no stalling. Just get the stuff and come right back."

"By myself?" Connie seemed to be having a hard time grasping the specifics of her mission.

Ruger rolled his eyes. "Jeez, can you really be this fucking dumb?" He looked at Val and Guthrie, who were studying the pattern of the rug on the floor. He sighed. "Okay, so you probably are this fucking dumb. Whatever. Just go and get the stuff and come right back."

Connie backed away from him, nodding numbly. She reached
the entrance to the hallway, bumped against the door frame, half
spun, and then fled down the corridor. Ruger saw her open the
door at the far end and listened to her feet clattering on the
wooden steps. He leaned against the door frame and called out,
"Remember, darlin', no games. Just find the stuff and hustle back."
Turning to Guthrie, he said, "She isn't too bright, is she?"
  "She's just scared."
  "What about you?" he said to Val. "Are you scared?"
  "Of course I am," she said bitterly.
  "Maybe, but you aren't scared stupid like your sister."
  "I'm scared enough, mister." The image of the EPT test kit
upstairs in the medicine cabinet flashed into her brain, unbid-
den and immediate. Her eyes wavered and fell away, down to her
hands twisting in her lap.
  Ruger looked at her, measuring her. "Good," he said after a
slow moment.

  In the cellar, Connie tramped down the last steps, walked
blindly past the gun cabinet, past the workbench with its collections of awls and screwdrivers and utility knives, past the wall
phone, and made a hectic beeline for the closet where the
clothesline was kept. She snatched up two plastic-wrapped fifty-
foot lengths, and from a lower shelf she took a huge roll of dark
gray duct tape. For some reason she clutched them to her chest
as if they were sacred objects, spun on her heel, and fled back
upstairs. She turned off the light and bathed all of the actual objects of salvation in useless darkness.

  "Good girl, now go sit down."
  Connie went obediently to the couch, turned, and sat down,
smoothing her skirt around her. She sat with her hands folded in
her lap, ankles together, eyes downcast. Ruger looked at her as if
she were something from another planet, which, in a way, she
was, if he was typical of the world that he came from. The bundles of rope lay on the coffee table, but Ruger held the roll of
tape, tossing it lightly into the air and catching it one-handed.

Val glanced at Connie, feeling sorry for her sister-in-law. It was apparent to Val that Connie had retreated—fled—into herself. Beyond the last name she'd taken in marriage she shared absolutely nothing in common with Val. Connie had grown up wealthy, soft, and sheltered. She was middling intelligent, good-hearted, truly loved Mark, aspired to no heights beyond maintaining a household, and apparently spent very little time in her own thoughts. Generally her chatter was borderline inane and Val routinely tuned it out when she could, and for the most part didn't really like Connie very much. Now, though, she loved her and wanted to hug her and shelter her.

She was also assessing Connie, wondering if maybe she had placed a 911 call downstairs, or had secreted a knife somewhere in her clothes, but as wonderful as that would be, Val doubted if it was true. Connie just wasn't like that. As far as Val could see, if Connie had strength of any kind—either wit or courage—it was so deeply submerged that she was unaware of it.

"Now," said Ruger, pouring another finger of bourbon, "anyone want to guess why I had Miss Polly Purebred fetch this stuff?" He took a sip, then knocked it back. "No guesses? Well, I can see it in your eyes. If you think that I'm gonna tie you up, that's right. That should tell you something, shouldn't it?"

Val shook her head.

"I think he means," said her father, "that he wouldn't bother tying us up if he meant to kill us."

Val looked expectantly at Ruger. "You father's on the ball, and he's right, too. I didn't come here to waste your sorry hillbilly asses. If I wanted to do that, I'd have done it already. So, maybe I'm not as much a bad guy as I seem, huh?"

Val almost let loose a derisive snort, but caught herself.

"I can't have you running around loose, either. So, it's hog-tying time on the old farmstead."

"What if we have to go to the ladies' room?" asked Connie, in what appeared to be a reasonable voice. It was such a reasonable and conversational voice that it chilled Val.

"Uh-oh," said Ruger, showing mock horror, "I think Donna Reed is no longer with us. Wonder if I could wake her up some."

"Leave her alone."

Ruger wheeled on Val, his hand raised, but she quickly added, "Please."

He considered her for a moment and then lowered his hand. "Yeah, whatever. Too much shit to do anyway."

Guthrie said, "Is someone hurt?" When Ruger just looked at him, he added, "You wanted a stretcher. Is someone hurt?"

"As a matter of fact, yes. My—how should I put it?—my . . . 'associate' is a trifle banged up. He's out in the cornfield and I think he'd like to come in now."

Val stared at him. "You left an injured man out in the field?"

"Yes, isn't it shocking? On the other hand, what the fuck do you care?"

"He's hurt. . . ."

"So what? If I was hurt, would you give a shit?"

"Of course I would."

Ruger laughed. "Oh, I'm sure!"

Val's dark eyes glittered. "I'd help any animal that was hurt. Even a skunk or a rabid dog."

Ruger shook his head ruefully. "Man oh man, you are something!" For a moment, it seemed as if he were about to say something more, but then the front door opened.

Nobody had even heard the car drive up, which was not surprising with the wind and the soft moist dirt of the road, but they all heard the click as the knob turned and the lock sprang open.

Val turned and screamed: "Crow! No! *Run!*"

Anything else she might have said was drowned out by the ear-shattering blast of the pistol as Ruger spun around and fired two shots through the door.

Chapter 12

The man in the road had a huge butcher's knife driven into his chest and his white T-shirt was a mass of blood that bloomed a bright crimson in the glare of the headlights. Crow slowed to a halt and leaned out of the window.

"How's tricks, Barney?"

Grinning through bloody teeth, the impaled man leaned his forearms on the open window frame of the Chevy and peered inside. "There's a game tonight at the college, so it's been kinda slow. How's with you? Hey, is that Mike?"

"What's up, Barney?"

"How's it hanging, Mike?"

"I'm cool."

Barney Murphy scratched his chest where the adhesive bound the fake knife to his skin. The handle wobbled. "Whatcha doing out here, man?" he asked Crow.

"Look, Barney, there's some stuff going on in town, and we have to shut the place down."

"Shut it down? You mean . . . for good?"

"No, just for the night. Where's Coop?"

"He's out with a bunch of customers in number four." The hayride had four tractors that pulled stake-bed trailers full of tourists. Number two was at Shanahan's for a cracked axle. The other three rotated, each pulling out with a load of kids about every twenty minutes.

"How many and how long?"

Barney considered. "Maybe thirty people. Been gone 'bout twenty minutes."

"Shit . . . er, I mean shoot." He cocked an eye at Mike, who was grinning. "You didn't hear that, right?"

"Shit no."

"Good," Crow said, and in a mock under-his-voice tone he added, "Juvenile delinquent."

"He'll be done in another twenty, twenty-five," said Barney. "Number one just came in five, ten minutes ago. Three'll be out another ten."

"I'm gonna take one of the ATVs and go fetch Coop. Anyone else shows up, turn 'em away. Except for Mike's folks, they're going to pick him up. His bike's in my trunk." Barney looked confused, and Crow elaborated. "He got run off the road by some dumb-ass trucker. Got banged up a bit."

"I'm okay," Mike said bravely.

Crow said, "Busted a rib or two and cracked his head on a rock. No, don't look like that, he's not going to die on you. His folks are going to take him over to the hospital for some X-rays."

"That sucks," he said, but Mike just shrugged. Carefully.

Crow said, "Look, Barney, there's something serious going on. There are three assholes from Philly, bank robbers or something, who may be hiding out somewhere around here. The mayor wants everybody who belongs in town back in town, and all the kids at home."

"What? That's it?"

"That's it, as far as I know."

"Well, that's not so much."

"Yeah, but you know how Terry Wolfe is."

"Yeah. He's scared of his own shadow. I mean he never even comes out here, not even during the day."

"Mr. Wolfe's okay, Barney. He's just a busy guy. He owns a lot of things. He's always busy. That's why he pays me to manage this joint." There was just the faintest edge to Crow's voice, and Barney caught it.

"Cool, man."

"Anyway, if you see anyone you don't know—any adults I mean—or if anything weird happens, call me on my cell."

"Weird? Dude . . . this is a *haunted* hayride, you know."

Crow smiled and winked at him and put the car into gear. "You know," he said thoughtfully, nodding to the knife handle, "you ought to have that looked at."

"Yeah," said Barney, "this thing is killing me."

(2)

The night was stretching forward into darkness, racing toward the dead hours that are forgotten by the light. All across Pine Deep, hearts were beginning to beat just a bit faster, minute by minute; lungs were gulping in air and gasping it out. In just a few hours the pitch and pulse of the night had changed, accelerated, jumped toward haste and action and frenzy.

There was the scent of blood on the dark winds, and the promise of much, much more; a perfume of destruction and pain carried to every part of the town, even to the darkest and most remote of places. The scent seemed to sink into the rich earth of the town, seeking out those who craved that aroma.

Deep in the darkness, someone became aware of that perfume; someone laid bare his senses and absorbed the scent of death, the energy of fear, the electricity of hate. He filled himself with the essence of hurt and dread, and he smiled. Teeth long caked with wormy soil and lips withered to dry tautness peeled into a grin that betrayed the pernicious delight of the smiler. Above and around him the black tons of earth trembled as he laughed.

(3)

Ruger's tiny automatic made lightning flashes and thunderstorm booms that crashed off the living room walls. Two black holes appeared high on the top panel of the door and cordite burned the air. Val screamed and lunged frantically for the door-knob, but Ruger sprang to his feet, knocking the rocking chair over, and with a ferocious sweep of his arm he sent her reeling back into her father's arms. Guthrie fell back onto the couch with Val sitting down hard on top of him; he grunted in pain and the breath whooshed out of him for the second time. Connie screamed, too, but she made no move at Ruger: she just sat there on the couch covering her face with both hands and screaming shrilly through her fingers.

Ruger grabbed the knob and with a violent jerk whipped the door open, bringing his gun up high and steady as he did so. Outside, on the wide plank porch, Mark Guthrie stood in a frozen posture of absolute and uncomprehending shock: half crouched, stock-still, wide-eyed, and staring with dinner-plate eyes at the gun in the hand of a man he didn't know. The bullets must have missed his face by inches and there were tiny splinters on his cheek, standing up like needles in a pincushion.

"Welcome home," hissed Ruger and grabbed a handful of Mark's shirt, pulled him close, and kneed him savagely in the crotch. Mark let loose with a high whistling shriek and folded in half at the waist. Connie and Val screamed, but Ruger ignored them and dragged the man into the house and flung him the length of the living room. Mark was a knotted cannonball of agony and he caromed off the wall and collapsed onto an occa-sional table that splintered under him. Mark, table, a vase of dried flowers, and some small picture frames collapsed onto the floor.

Val lunged up again and Ruger backhanded her down onto the couch; again she sprawled across her father's lap and he caught her as she started to roll off onto the floor. Ruger turned to Val's brother and kicked him viciously in the thigh and as Mark opened his mouth to scream, Ruger jammed the barrel of his pistol under his nose. "Just fucking lie there." The scream died in his throat.

Connie, however, had started screaming as soon as Ruger had

fired his gun and was still screaming, yelling, "Mark!" over and over again. Ruger spun and leveled the gun at her. "Shut your mouth, you stupid cunt!"

Like her husband's, Connie's screams turned to ice in her throat, but as if the desperate forces in her needed to escape in some way her body snapped into action and she hurled herself off the couch and flew like a bird to Mark, who was shaking his head stupidly, brushing at dried roses and baby's breath and bits of broken crockery. Ruger stepped back and let her go, allowing her to flutter around her husband like a flight of nervous sparrows, touching and probing and kissing and stroking with darting nervous hands. All of it amused Ruger, who smiled. In as loud a voice as his mangled larynx could manage, he said, "Now, everyone just shut the fuck up!" He spaced the words out to give them maximum weight and effect.

The Guthrie house became as quiet as a tomb in less than one second, and Ruger actually sighed with pleasure. He looked at Val, who was gripping the armrest of the sofa with white-knuckled fingers. She had managed to disentangle herself from her father, who looked gray and sweaty. "Who's the geek?" he asked, jerking his head in the direction of the young man. "Your brother-in-law?"

Val frowned in confusion. "What? Uh . . . no, he's my brother. Mark."

Ruger also looked confused. "Brother? Hey, I know this is the sticks and all, but I didn't think brothers and sisters actually married out here."

Val shook her head, not getting the point.

"Isn't Donna Reed there your sister?"

"Huh? Oh! Oh, no," said Val, understanding now, "she's my sister-in-law. She's married to Mark, my brother."

"Ah," Ruger said again.

By this time, Connie had helped Mark sit up and had brushed all the debris off him while constantly whispering, "He's got a gun, he's got a gun. Are you hurt? Don't do anything, he's got a gun."

Mark looked up at Ruger, his face lined with pain and glistening with a patina of new sweat. "What the hell's going on here?"

Mark demanded, but with the pain the question carried no authority and came out as a wheeze.

"Are you okay?" Guthrie asked tightly.

"I . . ." Mark began, and then stopped, frowning deeply and looking quizzically at Ruger. "Who the hell are you? And . . . did you shoot at me?" he asked in a voice that betrayed his total amazement at such a possibility.

"No," whispered Ruger. "If I had you'd been fucking well dead." He smiled. "I shot at the door."

Val saw the moment when Mark's shock was overtaken by the first moment of clarity and then she saw the fear take hold. His eyes were wide and he stared at Ruger and at the gun.

Mark snapped his head around to where his father sprawled half on and half off the couch. He saw the blood on his father's face and Mark's own face went white. "Dad? What's going on?"

"Be still, Mark . . . don't do anything. Just do what he says."

Ruger kicked the foot on one of Mark's outstretched legs. "You're Mr. Rotary Club, am I right?"

"I'm . . . who did you say?" He was not following any of this. "What the hell is—"

"It's okay, Mark," said Val. "Just listen."

Staring at her and then back at his father, Mark said, "My God! Val? Dad? What happened to you? What happened to your faces? Did he do this?"

"They're fine," said Ruger. "Everybody's fine."

"Did you do that to them?"

Ruger shrugged as if to say *these things sometimes happen.*

"Do you want to tell me what the hell this is all about?" His words promised a demand that his tone of voice could not back up. It came out somewhere between a growl and a squeak, like a teenage boy whose voice was breaking.

"Sure," Ruger said affably, "but first, why don't you and your little wifey just go and join everyone else on the couch?"

Mark looked about to say more, but the black eye of the pistol stopped him, and the black eyes of the gunman withered his will. He let Connie help him up and they moved slowly, and very carefully, over to the couch, hissing occasionally at the pain in his groin. With the four of them it was a very tight fit. Val sat on the left end next to her father, and Connie did her best to try and vanish between the elder and younger Guthrie men. Mark examined his father's face. "That's a pretty bad cut, Dad."

"Leave it be," Guthrie murmured.

"But, Dad—"

"Leave it be."

To Ruger, Mark said, "Who the hell are you? Some kind of tough guy? Beating up on women and old men."

"Blow me," Ruger said. He set the rocker back on its runners, turned it to face them, and sat down. "Now . . . the only reason I'm going to bother to recap tonight's game is because if you understand the rules, then I probably won't have to shoot you. *Capiche?*"

Mark stared for a long moment, then slowly nodded.

"Good, good." Ruger lit himself a cigarette. "Here's the deal, Marky-boy. I am not here exactly by choice—God knows. My car broke down and I need a new one. Renting one ain't an option right now. Also, I got a friend out there in the cornfield with a busted leg. You bozos are going to help me get him back here so we can patch him up, and then he and I are going to get the fuck out of this episode of *Green Acres* in your pop's Bronco, which, I must admit, I am going to steal."

Mark blinked several times in rapid succession.

"As I see it, Marky, this can go one of a couple of ways. The ideal way would, of course, involve you four helping me and then putting up no fuss as I tie you up and drive off in the car. I think I speak for all of us when I say that that's the way we'd all like it to go. On the other hand, if you folks don't want to cooperate, then I can just simply pop all four of you, take the car anyway, and still be on my merry way. You see, it really doesn't matter all that much to me except that it would be more work for me if I had to do it alone, and work always makes me kind of cranky."

" 'Pop' us? You mean you'd shoot us? You'd actually shoot us?"

"Deader'n shit," Ruger agreed.

"Holy Jesus."

"Mm-hm. So what's it gonna be?"

"I can't believe you'd actually just . . . shoot us. I mean, what have we ever done to you?"

"Mark . . ." Val whispered.

"To me?" said Ruger. "You folks have never done anything to me. If my car hadn't crashed, you'd have never even known I existed, and vice versa. Just luck of the draw, Marky."

"But—shoot us?"

Ruger rolled his eyes. "Yes! What part of 'shoot you' don't you understand, farm boy?"

"Why?"

"Mark, be still," Guthrie said in a quiet but very firm voice.

"No . . . Dad, he's talking about murdering all of us."

Guthrie reached over and clamped a strong hand on his son's wrist. "Yes, and if you don't shut your mouth he just might! Now be still!"

Mark shut his mouth.

Ruger nodded in appreciation. "Your old man is sharp, Marky-boy. You're the kind of fella that could let his mouth get his ass in trouble."

"I'm just trying to understand this," Mark muttered.

"What's not to understand? Don't you ever watch TV? I'm a bad guy on the run, and you all are the innocent saps who get tied up and robbed. End of scene. There's nothing to understand. There's no meaning to it."

"What is it you want us to do?" asked Val, trying to steer the conversation back to a straightforward business negotiation. She eyed Ruger carefully as he took a long drag on his cigarette, wondering why he was stretching this whole thing out. What was he really waiting for? He could have tied them up, taken the Bronco, and been gone half an hour ago, but instead he was dragging this out for some reason she could not work out. More than once she saw him tilt his head to one side as if listening to a voice outside, or perhaps inside his head.

Ruger licked his lips and said, "Well, two of you are going to be stretcher bearers for my buddy. He's out in the field waiting on us."

"Where in the field?" asked Guthrie.

"By a big post with a scarecrow. Good half mile from here."

Guthrie nodded, and to Val he said, "By the new section of fence."

Her stomach turned at the thought of monsters like Ruger and his friend polluting the spot where she and Crow had made love just last night. Her mouth was a thin line as she asked, "And then?"

"Then we try to patch him up."

"You said he broke his leg?" Guthrie asked.

Ruger laughed. "Oh yeah. Stepped in a hole and broke the living shit out of it. He has one of those . . . whaddya call it when the bones are sticking out?"

"Compound fracture," murmured Val.

"Uh-huh. A real motherfucker of a compound fracture. I set it, more or less, and splinted it up, but he needs someone else to check it out. I don't suppose any of you are doctors?"

"I know some first aid," said Val.

"Well, well. That's handy."

"Just some basic stuff, though."

"Well, beggars can't be choosers."

Mark held up a finger and in his formal, pedantic voice said, "Let me get this straight. If we help you, that is, if we bring your friend back here, patch him up as best we can, and let you take the car, then you'll just go away and not hurt us? Is that it?"

"In a nutshell."

"How do we know that we can trust you?"

"I guess you just have to," Ruger said, and then he smiled his serpent's smile, white teeth gleaming, eyes twinkling like cold and distant stars. "Besides, why would I lie?"

(4)

"Hey, what's that?"

Officer Rhoda Thomas slowed the cruiser and rolled to a stop. She flicked on the searchlight and directed it where Offi-

cer Head was pointing. The black stretch of A-32 glowed a dark
charcoal in the harsh white light, and the yellow lane divider
gleamed, but cutting right through the dividing line and across
the road itself were long black smears, intensely black even in
the light's glow. "Just skid marks," observed Rhoda. "Nothing."

"No, wait, they look pretty fresh."

"So?"

"So, let's check 'em out." Head jerked the door handle and
stepped out. Puzzled and reluctant, Rhoda followed suit. They
walked over to where the skid marks began and stood looking at
the road. With a totally reflexive action, Head unsnapped his pistol and jiggled the butt to loosen it in its leather holster. Rhoda
watched and copied the movement. It was the first time she had
ever performed that particular ritual, but she didn't want to appear as raw as she knew she was. She was fascinated by him. She
thought he looked like Samuel L. Jackson with more muscles
and a shaved head.

They were an incongruous pair: the petite Rhoda in her pale
gray uniform with the six-pointed star gleaming as brightly as
all her buttons and fittings; and Head, older, bigger, heavier,
though not at all fat, in his blue Philadelphia Police Department rig, numbered shield on his breast and all of his equipment
showing signs of eleven long years of hard use on big-city
streets. Rhoda looked like an extra in a cheap movie, and Head
looked unpretentiously real. He had hard eyes that had seen it
all, a harder mouth that was drawn tight, and the posture of a
predator. Beside him, Rhoda looked like a child. It wasn't a sex
thing: Head's partner, Maddie, was as serious and seasoned a
cop as he was, and she was buddied up with Officer Jim Polk
farther up A-32. No, this was a reality check for Rhoda, and she
knew it.

"These are from tonight," he said, squatting down and running his fingertips along the smear of burned rubber. "Take a
look. They veer right off the road." He clicked on his own long-
handled flash and swept the beam along the path of the skid
marks. "See? Right there, they leave the road and go off into the
field." He moved to the very edge of the verge and shone his light

into the corn. The light showed them the smashed-down corridor of stalks. "Bingo."

Rhoda came up behind him. "You think they had an accident?"

"Be nice if it was that easy," he said, then smiled thinly and added, "Be really nice if they totaled the car and themselves."

"You think that's likely?"

His smile became a grin and he shook his head. "Nah. Accident, maybe, but if they wrecked their ride, then they probably hightailed their asses out of here hours ago." He stood and rubbed the skid mark with the toe of his shoe. "Could have been a blowout, who knows?" He turned and shone the light up and down the road, reading the scene. "Looks like a big car traveling in one hell of a hurry went off the road here and right into that field."

She looked from the tracks to his face and then into the cornfield. The flash struck small splinters off chrome and glass way back in the field. "Oh, shit."

"Yeah," he agreed and drew his sidearm, laying his gun arm across the wrist of the hand holding the flash so that the beam and the barrel tracked together.

"You think they're still in the car?" Rhoda whispered.

"I doubt it." He listened to the night. Distant rumbling thunder, the caw of a night bird, traffic on the highway miles away. Head sucked his teeth.

"What do you want to do? Should we go check it out?"

"Uh-uh, honey. I'm not going anywhere near that car until we get some backup." He nodded at her sidearm. "You any good with that?"

"I suck," she said.

"Swell."

"I'm better with a shotgun," she said hopefully. "Can't miss with a shotgun."

"Yeah. Got one in the unit?"

"In the trunk."

"Get it." Together they backed up to their unit. Rhoda popped the trunk and Head kept the barrel of the pistol trained on the smashed corridor of cornstalks.

Rhoda removed the pump-action shotgun from the clips that fastened it to the underside of the hood. It was a Mossberg Bullpup 12 with a pistol grip and thirty-inch barrel. With a hand that even in the darkness was visibly shaking, she worked the pump and blew out a puff of air that had soured in her lungs.

Head glanced at it out of the corner of his eye and his eyebrows went up. "That's a lot of shotgun for a small town."

"The chief likes 'em."

"How about you?"

She shrugged. "As long as it doesn't knock me on my behind, I don't much care one way or another."

Nodding, Head indicated the crash site with his pistol. "Point that cannon right there. I'm going to call for backup." He reached into the unit and lifted the handset. "What's your call number?"

"Unit Two."

"What's the call-in protocol?"

"Just ask for Ginny."

Head smiled and shook his head. Gotta love small-town America. Clicking on the mike, he said, "Unit Two to, um, Ginny. Unit Two to Ginny. Over."

"Who's this?" a woman's voice demanded sharply.

"Officer Jerry Head. I'm in Unit Two with Officer Thomas."

"Oh, okay. What can I do for you?"

"Is Detective Sergeant Ferro there?"

"Yes. He's having coffee."

"Can you put him on the line, please?"

"He's in the conference room with . . . oh, well, really, Mr. Wolfe, I didn't say that. . . . I was just about to . . . no, I . . ." The conversation on the other end suddenly became agitated as Ginny and at least two other voices lapsed into an argument. Then a new voice came on the line. "Unit Two, this is Ferro. Over."

"Sergeant, this is Jerry Head. Officer Thomas and I are on

A–32, approximately fourteen miles from the center of town, on the eastern stretch."

"Copy that."

"We're Code Six investigating skid marks indicating a vehicle recently gone off the road and into some cornfields. It looks like a single-vehicle accident, possibly a blowout, though the tracks are clean with no rubber debris."

"Have you located the vehicle itself?"

"Negative. Request backup so we can check it out."

"That's affirmative. Hold for backup en route."

"Copy that."

"Ferro out."

"Out." Head tossed the mike onto the seat and turned to Rhoda. "You heard that?"

"Uh-huh."

"We'll wait. You know who we're after. I didn't wake up this morning as John Wayne and you probably aren't Annie Oakley."

"I have no idea who Annie Oakley is, but I get the point." She grinned. "Waiting here is good."

They stood on the far side of their unit, using it as cover. Head took a foil pack of Orbit gum out of his pocket and popped a piece through the blister; he offered the pack to Rhoda but she shook her head. His dark brown eyes had a gunslinger squint to them that Rhoda found intimidating.

She said, "You must think we're a bunch of backwoods dumb-asses."

He chuckled as he chewed the gum. "Actually, no. Just be happy you don't deal with this kind of freak every day. It juices you for about the first year on the job but it damn sure gets old after a while."

She nodded, cradling the shotgun in her arms.

Head grinned. "Tell you the truth, I'd switch jobs with you in a heartbeat. I love this town. I bring my kids up to the hayride every year. We were up here two weeks ago, and I'm probably going to bring my youngest and his Cub Scout pack up here closer to Halloween. My wife, Tracy, and I come up here Christmas shopping every year. Kind of a ritual. We always have breakfast in that place on Salem Street, what's the name . . . ? Auntie Ems?"

"Yeah, that's a great place. I waitressed there some when I was still in high school."

"Yeah? Be funny if maybe one of those times you waited our table."

"Could have. The place is always packed."

"Yeah, but man, they make the best breakfasts. I love that one they do, the omelet with Granny Smith apples and cheddar cheese? With a little cinnamon on top."

"The Scarecrow."

"Right, right. Man, I love that one. And Tracy really likes the Irish oatmeal with honey and milk."

"Yeah, all their stuff's good."

He blew a stream of blue smoke into the night.

In the far distance they could see red and blue lights racing along A-32.

"That's them," he said.

They stood in silence, their guns still pointing at the darkened field, but their eyes flicking toward the approaching lights.

"Officer Head?"

"Jerry."

"Jerry. Does this stuff—everything they're saying about the suspect, about Ruger—doesn't that scare you?"

"Me? Naw. He chopped up some defenseless old folks. I've faced down his kind before."

"So . . . you're not scared? Really?"

"Hell no!" Head laughed. "This guy scares the living piss out of me."

Relief flooded her face. "God! Me too. You know, we only have a couple of full-time officers here in town. Most of us are law students doing this part-time as a kind of co-op thing. I mean, we get some academy training, but they know that we're not career, so they don't really drum it into us And stuff like this *never* happens."

"So that's why we are going to do this just exactly the way

Sergeant Ferro said, by the numbers and very tight, like professional law enforcement officers. No John Wayne shit. If that is Ruger's car back there, and if he's there, we are going to handle him as if he is armed, dangerous, and every bit as crazy as they say he is."

"Jeez," she said softly.

Head thought, *If it is Ruger and he so much as farts too loud I'm going to send his evil ass home to Jesus quick as think about it.*

The second unit pulled up to a fast stop as both doors popped open at the same time and two officers stepped out. Jimmy Castle, tall and slim, with straw-colored hair and smiling eyes, stepped out from behind the wheel, and from the shotgun sidestepped Coralita Toombes. She was a stocky black woman with a face as harsh and unsmiling as Jimmy's was lighthearted. She wore a Philadelphia P.D. uniform and had a Glock in her strong right fist, barrel pointed to the sky.

"Where do we stand, Jerry?" she asked as the four officers drew together in a huddle by flashlight.

Head filled them in and together the four officers moved to the shoulder. "Toombes, you and me'll take point. One of you two can watch our asses."

Toombes said, "Jimmy here used to be on the job in Pittsburgh."

"Street or clerical?"

"Street," said Castle. "Four years. Then my wife's company transferred her out here, so—"

Head cut him off. "Cool. Okay, let's do it this way. Rhoda, you stay back here by the unit. I want you actually holding the mike the whole time. Give Sergeant Ferro regular reports, even if it's to say that there's nothing to report. Okay with you?"

"Fine with me," she said meaningfully.

"Keep that shotgun handy," he said, then added, "But be careful where you point it." He turned to Castle. "You have a vest?"

"Yeah. First time I've worn it since Pittsburgh, though." He rapped his knuckles on his chest.

"Let's do it like a dark-house search," murmured Toombes. "Check, call, and clear."

Head nodded. "Everyone cool with that?"

"Cool as a Popsicle," said Castle, but he wasn't smiling anymore. His usual open and disingenuous face had taken on that hard cop look as he drew his Glock and slowly worked the slide.

Toombes also drew her weapon. "Let's do it."

They did it.

Chapter 13

It didn't take long for Ruger to get things rolling. He had Val tie Mark and Connie up, overlapping the multiple turns of rope with strips of duct tape to keep them from wriggling the knots loose, and Ruger checked the knots to make damned sure she hadn't pulled any fast ones. The two of them sat side by side on the couch, glaring fear and impotent hatred at Ruger. Meanwhile he had ordered Guthrie to knock the pins out of the hinges on the kitchen door and drag it into the living room. It was a lightweight panel, but sturdy and would serve well enough as a stretcher. Throughout this phase Val made occasional eye contact with her father, trying to see if he was planning something, but the elder Guthrie's face was careworn with concern for his children and when he finally caught Val's look, and her cocked eyebrow, he gave a single terse shake of his head.

Twice since Ruger had arrived she felt her cell phone—always set to vibrate—start shivering in her jeans pocket, but as before she couldn't do anything about it. It had to be Crow calling to say he was on his way, and she prayed that he would hurry.

"Okay, kids," Ruger said as Val and her father stood with him by the front door, "now here's the way it's going to go. First we're going to fetch a wheelbarrow, and then you two are going to come with me and help me fetch my friend and some of our gear from the field, and bring him back here. Then I'll watch as

Val ties you up, Mr. Guthrie. Once that's dcne, you, my little broken-nose chickie, will do your Florence Nightingale on my buddy. Then I'll tie you up and me and my buddy will be out of your lives. Except for fixing your front door and filing an insurance claim for your Bronco, you won't be much the worse for wear. How's that sound? Fair enough? This is a simple one-two-three sort of thing. Anyone gets creative and everyone comes out losers. Everyone but me, that is." He looked at them each in turn. Val nodded first, then her father. Mark and Connie, bound and gagged, could only stare. "Cool. Then let's go. I'm getting a little tired of this Early American decor anyway. Christ."

Guthrie bent and picked up one end of the door, and Val the other, and together they hefted it. Ruger carried his pistol in one hand and a heavy flashlight in the other, with the length of the clothesline slung over his shoulder. They left the house and descended the porch steps.

"Okay, set it down," Ruger said and they laid the door on the ground. "You," he said to Val, "go get the wheelbarrow." Val felt her pulse jump when she thought of all the bladed tools in the barn—and the phone—but Ruger placed the barrel of his pistol against the back of her father's skull. "Just the wheelbarrow, sweet cheeks. You read me?"

"Yes," she said in a voice that was barely above a whisper but well below freezing.

"Okay. Down on your knees, Pops, until our gal Val gets back." Guthrie slowly lowered himself to his knees, and at Ruger's direction, laced his fingers together on top of his head. Ruger closed his strong white hand over Guthrie's gnarled sun-browned fingers and squeezed mildly, but even so the grinding of his fingers made Guthrie wince. Val saw the flicker of pain on her father's face, as Ruger had intended. "Yes, indeed, it hurts," said Ruger. "It'll keep hurting until you get your ass back here with the wheelbarrow. C'mon, bitch, time is money."

Val turned and ran for the utility shed. True to his word, Ruger kept the painful pressure up until Val came running back behind a bright red wheelbarrow that was spattered with mud.

Her father's face was pinched and his lips drawn thin and tight against his teeth.

Nodding with appreciation, Ruger released Guthrie's hands and stepped back.

Guthrie rose, opening and closing his hands to restore blood flow. His fingers rang with pain.

"Pick up the door and let's get rolling." Ruger shone the flashlight on the backs of father and daughter as they walked along the path that ran beside the vast cornfield. The Guthries laid the door sideways across the wheelbarrow and Val hefted the handles while her father steadied the door. Ruger walked three paces behind them, gun in one hand, flashlight in the other.

As they retraced the route he'd taken since leaving Boyd, Ruger watched them with something approaching pleasure. He actually liked the old fart and his daughter. They were both tough and Ruger respected tough. He was on the fence as to whether he would kill them or not. Probably not, he mused. What would be the point? Identifying him to the cops wouldn't exactly be a news flash.

Ruger did wonder how Val would be in the sack, though. Feisty. Probably very feisty, and if things weren't so damned pressing he might have taken the time to get to know her. See if he could tame the filly—not that it would be easy, he thought. Val didn't seem the type to get a case of the vapors. She'd fight him all the way, and he just didn't have that kind of time.

Now the Stepford Wife on the other hand. Yeah, she was a sweet piece. Stacked in a country sort of way, and certainly pretty enough. He might just have the time to show that one a thing or two. Just a quickie, but it would set him up right and ease some of the tension that had been knotting his neck muscles all day. Ruger liked the idea and it made him smile. He didn't believe that Connie was as completely inane or prissy as she appeared— Christ, who *could* be?—and he wondered what kind of fire lay beneath the surface. Maybe all she needed was a little incentive to make her show her true colors. Her stick-up-his-ass husband probably didn't have what it took to get much mileage out of her.

They walked down the lane between the tall walls of ripe corn, the beam of the flashlight keeping the Guthries in a globe of dancing yellow.

Ruger—you are my left hand!

The memory of those words and that voice came again and he missed a step and almost tripped. All the time he was in the house it had kept echoing in his head.

What the hell was it? It was driving him batty because he felt he ought to know that voice—that he *did* know it, but he just couldn't put a name to it.

Yet the voice was compelling, insistent, and somehow . . . comforting.

Ruger—you are my left hand!

He took a deep breath and adjusted his grip on his pistol and focused his attention ahead. It didn't take them very long to re-trace the route Ruger had walked since leaving Boyd with his broken leg. Idly, he wondered how Boyd was doing, not that he cared a whit. If Boyd kicked it, then he'd just find someone else who could get him out of the country; there were enough travel agents in the circles he was used to gliding through. He had enough unmarked cash and enough saleable product to grease the wheels of such bureaucracy. With even moderate luck he'd be in Brazil before the weekend was out; or if things were too hot he could get into Canada for a while, hide out with a woman he knew in Montreal, and use her connections to pick up a new passport and visa and fly to Africa. Maybe pick up some mercenary work.

If Boyd was dead . . . then maybe he would linger here at the ol' homestead for the night. Maybe do a comparison study of both of the gals, and then head north in the morning, blending into the tourist traffic and following the Poconos up into New York State.

Ruger—you are my left hand!

He grinned in the darkness with a wet shark's smile, and recon-sidered whether he would leave anyone here alive when he left.

(2)

The old 9mm Glock 17 felt light and comfortable in Jerry Head's hand. He had a .32 Smith & Wesson strapped to his right ankle, just in case. Not as a throw-down, but as a true backup piece. Twice in the line of duty Head had experienced handgun disasters. The first time his old S&W 439 had jammed, and the other time he'd lost his gun during a chase that required him to jump from a garage roof into a Dumpster. His sidearm had gotten buried in Hefty bags of old pizza, used Pampers, and empty cereal boxes. In both cases the little .32 had saved his ass. Though lacking the stopping power of the heftier 9mm, and carrying far fewer rounds, the little wheel gun had the grace of never jamming, and being there when otherwise he would have had to try and return fire armed only with harsh language. It was a comfortable weight on his ankle. He knew Toombes had a similar backup piece; he doubted Jimmy Castle did. The man may have been big city once upon a time, but why would he have needed a little guardian angel out here in Stickville?

Head moved as quietly as he could down the corridor created by the out-of-control car, but each footfall on the dried corn leaves crackled and crunched. There was no way to move in silence. Behind him and to either side he heard Toombes and Castle making the same noise, and he knew that they would be just as nervous about all the noise as he was. Couldn't sneak up on a dead man making noise like that.

Behind him, Head could hear Rhoda checking in with Detective Sergeant Ferro, heard the squelch of the radio.

They didn't have far to go before all three of them saw the gleam of moonlight and flashlight on metal and glass. It was a big, black four-door sedan and it stood in a small clearing of smashed-down cornstalks. The trunk lid was up and the right front of the car seemed to be pitched unnaturally low. Head turned to the others, and very quietly said, "We go in together. Toombes, you go right, Castle you go left, and I'll go up the pipe. Remember, check and clear."

They nodded and set themselves. Guns poised, fingers sliding into the trigger guards, they stepped into the clearing at the same time, moving quickly but with maximum caution. Castle came up on the driver's side, keeping the muzzle of his revolver focused so that it tracked the light.

"Police officers!" they all shouted. "Freeze!"

Castle shone his flash into the car. "Clear!"

"Clear!" Head called as he checked inside the open trunk and under the car.

He waited for Toombes.

She said nothing.

Rising from a shooter's crouch, Head peered around the end of the car. Toombes was standing just inside the clearing, facing the passenger side of the car, which was still out of sight to both Head and Castle. Toombes stood stock-still, her flashlight trained forward, but her service automatic was pointing limply and forgotten at the dirt by her feet.

"Toombes!" called Head. "Are you clear?"

Toombes didn't even look at him.

"Toombes!"

She opened her mouth to speak, but nothing came out.

Head motioned to Castle to circle around the front of the car, and together they converged fast on the passenger side.

Time seemed to freeze.

Officer Jerry Head stared down at the ground by the side of the car. He stared at the blood-soaked ground. He stared at the blood-splattered corpses of half a dozen crows that had been peppered with buckshot. He stared at the man that lay there.

At least, he thought it was a man.

Had been a man.

Once.

Not anymore, though. Now it was . . . unspeakable.

Head felt his brain go numb and somewhere off to the right of his sanity, he heard Jimmy Castle loudly throwing up.

(3)

Terry stood over Gus Bernhardt as he made the long string of calls to former part-time officers, listening to the chief plead, cajole, entice, and even bully as he tried to press-gang the honest citizenry of the town into some kind of actual police force. In any other circumstance, the whole thing would be kind of funny. At that moment, however, nothing seemed even remotely amusing. Gus was sweating, and Terry could feel his own pores yielding their store of icy perspiration. He turned away and strolled across the office, focusing on Detective Ferro and his beefy sidekick, LaMastra. They were once again in a hushed, intense confabulation.

Terry didn't join them, didn't even linger; instead he moved restlessly around the room. Technically he was the senior official here, a mayor supposedly outranking out-of-town cops, but he felt like a kid who had accompanied an adult to the office. Everyone was busy with their own jobs, saying things he didn't quite understand, doing things he could not help with, trying to accomplish things in which he could not actually participate. It was frustrating, but moreover, it was intimidating.

A phone rang on one of the desks as he passed it, and Terry glanced around to see if anyone was going to pick it up. No one so much as even turned to acknowledge this addition to the cacophony. Shrugging, Terry reached for the handset and picked it up.

"Pine Deep chief's department," he said in an official voice.

A voice said, "Terry?"

The connection was bad, making the voice sound distant and pale. It wasn't a matter of static, for the line was clear, but there was a hollowness to the sound, as if the caller were at the far end of a long tunnel.

"Hello? Who is this, please?"

"Terry?" repeated the voice. "Is that you, Terry?"

It was a female voice, a little girl. Crisply, he said, "This is Mayor Terry Wolfe. Who is calling, please?"

"Terry . . ." the voice said, and for a moment the connection faded almost to nothingness.

"Who is this? We have a very bad connection, so please speak up."

"Terry, he's back!" said the voice, and that was quite clear.

"I'm sorry, who's back? Who is this?"

"Terry. You have to do something."

"Listen to me," he said loudly and clearly, "you've reached the chief's department in Pine Deep. Are you hurt or in trouble?"

Nothing but the hiss of an open line.

"Little girl . . . ? Can you hear me?"

Across the room Detective Sergeant Ferro and his cronies were looking at him.

"Little girl? Are you still there?"

"Terry?" The voice was plaintive, sounding scared, but still distorted as if by a vast distance. "He's back, Terry. He's back and he's going to hurt people again."

"Hurt who? Little girl . . . who's going to be hurt?"

"He's back. . . ."

"Little girl, tell me your name."

Nothing.

"This is the mayor. Please tell me your name and where you're calling from."

Still nothing. Gus Bernhardt was lumbering across the room toward him, a deep frown on his florid face.

"You have to stop him, Terry," whispered the tiny voice.

"Where are you calling from? Little girl? Little girl?" He kept calling for her to answer, but the sound on the phone had changed. Now there was just dead emptiness. Gus reached out for the phone, held it to his own ear for a moment, then set it back on the cradle.

"What gives?" he asked.

"Weird call," said Terry, shaking his head and scratching his red beard. "Some little kid called." He knew that voice, too, but he didn't dare say it, and unconsciously tapped his pocket to make sure the pill case with the antipsychotics and the Xanax was still there.

"You heard a kid on that phone?" Gus asked, half smiling.

"Yeah, and she was going on about—"

"Uh, wait a minute, Terry, let me get this straight . . . you got a phone call on that phone and it was some little kid?"

"A little girl, yeah."

"On that phone?"

"No, on two other phones," snapped Terry viciously. "Yes, of course on this phone. What, are you deaf? You saw me talking to her."

"Well, I'm not deaf, but you must have the greatest set of ears in the Western world if you got a phone call on that line."

"What the heck are you talking about . . . ?"

Still half smiling, Gus bent and snatched up the cord that came out of the back of the receiver. He reeled it up, speaking as he did so. "Since we cut back on staff, we don't use these desks back here much," he said. "These phones have all been disconnected."

"Not this one, for Pete's sake. I was just talk—"

His voice went flat and fell silent as Gus pulled up the end of the cord and presented it with a flourish. The plug stood up between his thick fingers.

Terry looked at it and then bent low and looked under the desk at the wall. He could see no wall jack, and eventually had to shift the desk and move a trash can before he found one. Slowly he straightened and looked at the plug.

Gus said, "No way this was even plugged into the wall. The cord was just coiled up under the desk."

"I'm telling you, Gus . . . I heard that phone ring and I heard that kid talking."

Gus stared at him for a long five count, then shrugged. "What can I say, Terry?"

Terry snatched the plug out of Gus's hand and glared at it. He opened his mouth but couldn't manage to say anything. He *had* heard the voice. Her voice.

Mandy's voice.

The room started spinning around him and he almost turned

and ran when Detective Sergeant Ferro's voice cut through all the chatter in the room.

"It's the officers at the wreck site," he said tersely. "They found something!"

(4)

"Yo! Boyd—shift your ass!" called Ruger as he rounded the bend and followed Val and Guthrie into the clearing.

They stood still, bearing the white kitchen door between them. Val was staring fixedly at the many scattered pools of dark blood that glistened like black pools of oil in the moonlight; Guthrie stood looking up at the scarecrow's post, which was also streaked with clawed finger-trails of blood just below where the straw-filled dummy's shoes stood on their perpetual post.

At the edge of the clearing, Karl Ruger stood with his jaunty smile cracking and flaking away in the freshening night breeze.

"So much blood . . ." Val whispered.

Ruger's face underwent a slow change. The reptilian smile had given way to surprise and confusion, but now his features darkened with all the rage of a storm front moving over a troubled sea. Lightning flashed from his eyes and his lips curled back from white teeth as he ground them in mounting, boiling rage. Like a wolf at the moment of the kill, his nose wrinkled and his eyes were slashed to slits as the rage in him built and then burst forth.

"Boyd!" he bellowed, his voice rising like a roll of heavy thunder. "*Boyd!*"

His voice changed, the words tangling into a steady and inarticulate growl of fury as he tore across the clearing, kicking aside cornstalks, poking into rows of plants, leaning over fences, searching, searching, searching . . .

Boyd, however, was gone. The bags of money and cocaine were gone.

Only the blood remained.

The blood and a single bloodstained fifty-dollar bill stuck fast to the bottom of the scarecrow's shoe, held by the tacky gore, fluttering in the breeze.

Ruger howled in rage and dropped to his knees, beating the ground with the flashlight and the butt of his pistol. The lens of the flashlight shattered and the light flared and then burst into darkness and splintered glass.

"Boyd!" Karl yelled. "Boyd, you rotten motherfucker!"

Val dropped the wheelbarrow handles and shrank against her father's side; they both cringed back from the towering rage and animal ferocity that burst forth from Ruger.

"Boyd! *Where's my goddamned money!*"

Ruger tossed away the broken flashlight, balled his left fist into a mallet of gristle and bone, and punched down at the ground, and again, and again. The shock raced up his arm, flaring with pain as the fragments of the broken lens tore his skin, but the pain only stoked his rage. He kept punching the ground, over and over and over.

"Where's my goddamned money, you spineless piece of shit?" His words were whipped into the sky by the fierce winds of the coming storm.

Guthrie suddenly grabbed Val by the upper arm, pulled her close, and said in a fierce whisper, "Run!"

He didn't allow her the chance to object, but turned and shoved her toward the path that led away from the farmhouse, the access trail that went down to the main road. She staggered for two steps, and almost pitched forward, but then she bent low, dropping her center of gravity like a sprinter, and brought her weight back to the balance point. Off she went like a shot, her toes digging into the soft earth, and she was so fast that fifty yards were unreeling behind her before Karl Ruger was even aware of her flight.

Guthrie didn't waste any time himself. Even as he shoved Val in one direction, he wheeled and made a dash for the house. He was old, but he could run a half mile if the devil was on his heels, which indeed he was.

It took just two seconds for Ruger to understand what was happening, for him to claw himself out of his web of rage and realize that his captive birds had flown.

"Shit!" he growled and leaped to his feet. He started after Val, but before he'd even taken a full step he realized that he'd never catch her. She was already around the farthest bend and running like the wind.

"Bitch!" he growled, and then turned and pointed at the retreating back of old man Guthrie, taking aim with a two-hand grip. Lightning flashed continuously, illuminating the man with enticing clarity, and the ghost of his old smile flickered on his lips as Ruger pulled the trigger.

Chapter 14

Terry Wolfe and the detectives made it to the crime scene in less than ten minutes. Their late-model dark Ford rocketed along, leaving Chief Bernhardt's five-year-old police unit far behind. Terry sat in the back, gripping the door handle with one hand and the back of Ferro's seat with the other. His face was pasty with terror, but most of his dread came from his memory of that phone call. *It couldn't have been Mandy,* he thought, clinging to his denial, needing to be certain that reality was reality and no matter what he thought he'd heard he had been mistaken. *That's impossible.*

The car leaped and skidded and tore like a demon wind along the blacktop and it jolted him back to the moment.

"God!" he whispered as the car took a curve on fewer wheels than Henry Ford had intended, then bounced down onto all fours and swooped hawklike down a long hill. They rounded another, wider curve and saw two revolving dome lights in the distance. LaMastra actually accelerated down the hill and then screeched and slewed the car to a sideways stop that sent up curls of rubber smoke from all four wheels. "Oh my Lord!" Terry gasped, his finger still digging into the upholstery. "Where did you learn to drive like that?"

LaMastra grinned at him in the rearview mirror. "Old Steve McQueen movies."

"My heart stopped beating miles back," Terry complained.

Ferro looked faintly amused. "You'll have to forgive the detective. He lives for this kind of thing. It's what he does in lieu of having an actual life."

LaMastra chuckled and leaped out of the car; Ferro followed, bringing with him a large, heavy briefcase.

Terry slowly unstuck his fingers and reached for the door handle. He stepped out of the car in the same shaky way that novices depart a particularly aggressive roller-coaster ride, placing his feet on the ground as if uncertain that it would hold him.

Officer Rhoda Thomas came jogging over to them, pale and uncertain. She carried a huge shotgun at port arms.

"Okay, Officer, what's going on?" Ferro asked, cutting right to the chase. "The radio reports were, shall we say, a little disjointed?"

Rhoda looked up into Ferro's cold eyes. "The others are still down there by the suspect's vehicle. They wouldn't let me go down and take a look."

"Why's that?" asked LaMastra.

"Well . . . Officer Head said that there was a body down there."

"Uh-huh. And?"

"Well," Rhoda said, licking her lips, "they didn't say for sure, but I got the impression that it was in a pretty bad state. They wouldn't say exactly what condition it was in, but when they first came back, they looked really upset. You know . . . shaken? Then all three of them got sick."

"Oh, come on," said LaMastra, laughing. "Jerry Head and Coralita Toombes getting sick? Get real."

Rhoda just looked at him.

Ferro tapped LaMastra on the shoulder. "Let's go have a look."

"What should I do?" Rhoda asked.

"Just stay here. Stay by the radio. Your chief and additional units are just behind us. Send them on down once they get here."

"Okay."

To Terry, Ferro said, "Do you want to come with us?"

"Not particularly." But he went anyway.

When they were within a dozen yards of the crime scene, Ferro called out, "Coming in!"

"Who is it?" Toombes's voice called tersely.

"Ferro, LaMastra, and Mayor Wolfe."

"It's clear," the woman called. "Kind of."

They entered the clearing and saw the black car squatting there, dottled with dirt and corn pollen and blood. Jimmy Castle sat on the ground, his back against the bumper, smoking a cigarette. He didn't even look up at them, but the three newcomers each exchanged a glance. They moved around the car to where Toombes and Head stood. Both officers held flashlights, but the beams were pointed at the ground to lead the way for the detectives. The side of the car, where the body lay, was in a dark bank of shadows.

Head stepped forward, clearly intending to block the way so they couldn't see past him. His face looked strained, lined, and sick; it had paled from a deep brown to a sickly ashen gray. Beads of perspiration jeweled his forehead. He nodded at them. In a soft funeral parlor voice he said, "Sir, the crime scene is still pristine. Also, gentlemen, you really better hike up your balls before you take a look because this is some sick, sorry shit. I mean . . . I have never seen anything like this." He looked at them, his eyes hard and deep. "Never nothing like this."

"Let's just get on with it," said Ferro sharply, clearly annoyed at Head's melodramatics.

Head just nodded and stepped aside. He turned and lifted his flashlight, training the powerful beam on the side of the car.

"Oh . . ." gasped Ferro.

". . . my . . ." breathed LaMastra.

". . . God," murmured Terry.

Terry wiped the sweat from his face and looked at LaMastra, who had turned an unwholesome green. Ferro's face was set and stony, but there was sweat on his upper lip. Head had joined Castle for a smoke at the back of the car, and Toombes was staring up at the moon as if she'd suddenly discovered a passion for astronomy.

"Get out the camera," Ferro said, and his voice was hoarse. "We don't have time to wait for a forensic unit." He looked up at the sky. Clouds were racing in from all sides and the air smelled like rain and ozone. "It's going to rain soon and we'll lose the entire site."

Nodding mutely, LaMastra knelt and placed the big briefcase on the ground. Opening it, he removed a big digital camera with a powerful flash unit. He checked to make sure it was adjusted for the bad light.

"Take a complete set."

"Balls," LaMastra breathed, but he did what he was told. Approaching cautiously, he came to within ten feet of the scene and raised the camera. He looked at it through the viewfinder, but he didn't . . . couldn't press the Release button. He just stood there, one index finger tapping nervously and unconsciously on top of the camera body.

"Vince," a voice said quietly, and LaMastra turned, lowering the camera. Ferro's eyes were kinder than he had ever seen them. "If you don't want to do this, Vince . . ."

LaMastra inhaled through his nose, then shook his head. "No, Frank. I can do it. It's just that . . ." He let it trail off. The English language didn't really have a proper set of adjectives for describing the scene. Ferro nodded and clapped the younger man reassuringly on the shoulder. LaMastra raised the camera once again, drew in a deep, steadying breath, and began recording horror.

Flash!

Tony Macchio, former felon. Former low-level mob muscle. Former enforcer. Former confederate of Karl Ruger. Tony Macchio, former human being.

Flash!

A mouth thrown wide in the absolute extremity of pain and outrage. Not just the pain of dying, but the pain of violation on an inhuman scale.

Flash!

Eyeless sockets, weeping red-black tears onto bloodless cheeks. Eyeless sockets that saw into the darkness of the soul, a darkness unlighted by any autumn moon or camera flash.

Flash!

A chest raped of its secrets. Heart and lungs and life's breath and soul torn out.

Flash!

A pair of clutching, armless hands, fingers spread out like the legs of dead spiders held fast to the doors of the car with long nails. And a pair of handless arms, folded uselessly across the spill of organs from deep within the invaded stomach.

Flash!

Two legs, broken and rebroken and twisted in puppet directions.

Flash!

Flesh, torn and lacerated, rent and bitten, bruised and gouged so that barely an inch of skin remained unblemished by the leprosy of violence. A destruction so total that it was only by an inventory of all the sundry parts that a puzzle of a man could be made.

Flash!

Flash!

Flash!

The flash kept popping, recording image after hideous image of the charnel house scene, until the film was gone and the Release button refused to yield even one more time to the horror there on the ground.

Once again Ferro laid his hand on LaMastra's shoulder. "Okay, Vince, that's good enough."

LaMastra lowered the camera and looked at it, amazed that so simple and unassuming a machine could record and contain such things. He knelt down and put the camera in the briefcase, squinting up at Ferro. "You know, Frank, I saw the crime scene photos of the lighthouse."

"Uh-huh."

"Same sort of stuff, man. Just ripped apart."

"Uh-huh."

"Like it was a pack of dogs did it rather than a person."

Ferro pulled in a chestful of air through flared nostrils. "Yeah," he said.

LaMastra shifted around and sat down on the ground, only dimly aware of the crushed stalks and smashed ears of corn under his rump. He was also only vaguely aware that Chief Bernhardt had come down from the road, taken a single look, and then rushed past him to throw up into the cornfield. LaMastra turned and watched him with a strange, vague distance.

Ferro stood by silently pulling on thin latex gloves. "If the weather holds we'll get a lab crew in here and see if they can lift prints. If not we have to spread a tarp . . . preserve as much as we can."

LaMastra just sighed and looked up at the lightning. It was going to rain soon, but he knew there wasn't enough rain in heaven to wash away this horror.

After a minute or two, Terry Wolfe joined them. His face was the color of sour milk, and he stood so that his back was to the car. He tried several times to form articulate words, failed each time, and then paused to take in a couple of long, slow breaths. Finally, he managed to say, "Is this one of the men you were looking for?"

Ferro snorted. "Well, that's the car, sure enough. And there is plenty of evidence of cocaine and money in the trunk. As for the identity of the deceased? A pathologist is going to have to make that decision for us. As you can see . . . well, no, don't bother to look, but there isn't enough of a face to make a clean ID, and the fingertips have been, uh, chewed . . . so I don't know if we can get . . ."

But Terry had clamped a hand to his mouth and staggered away to fall to hands and knees beside Bernhardt. They took turns retching and coughing. Ferro tried on an amused and superior smile, but it tasted wrong, so he spat it out.

Terry shambled back, wiping his mouth and looking even paler, if that was possible.

Ferro looked at him. "Are you okay, sir?"

"What do you think?" Terry gulped some air. "You figure that this Karl Ruger did this?"

"Well, I sure as hell hope so."

Terry gave him a quizzical look. "You 'hope so'?"

Nodding, Ferro said, "You should hope so, too, Mr. Mayor. That, or you've got two incredibly dangerous homicidal maniacs running around in your quiet little town."

"Oh no . . ." Terry breathed.

"Relax," said Ferro, "what are the odds of that?"

(2)

Crow closed his cell phone and slid it back into his pocket. He was beginning to get the first tingling of unease. He'd called Val's cell twice and got no answer, and had called the house and gotten nothing. He wanted to get this job done and get over there.

The ATV was a chunky little three-wheeled Kawasaki with puffy low-pressure tires and motorcycle handlebars. Every time Crow used one, he felt as if he were in the jet-speeder chase in *Return of the Jedi.* The ATV growled to life, hinting at more muscle in its belly than one might guess, and as Crow gave her some gas, it kicked out a cloud of dust and leaped forward.

"Hi-yo, Silver," Crow yelled, "away!"

Barney and Mike watched him go, standing side by side: the eighteen-year-old with the fake knife in his chest, and the four-teen-year-old with the broken rib and the marks of a near-fatal en-counter with madness flickering in his eyes. They watched until Crow's taillights vanished around a bend in the road.

"Crow's a friggin' goof," Barney said, scratching at the adhe-sive bandage that held the knife.

Iron Mike considered for a moment. "Yeah, he's just about weird enough."

Just a minute or two after Crow vanished into the night, a pair of headlights cast the parking lot in whiteness. Barney and Mike turned to see a station wagon pull into the lot and crunch across the gravel toward them. Mike hesitated for a moment, then smiled and waved.

The station wagon rolled to a stop and the driver's door opened. Vic Wingate unfolded himself from behind the wheel. He was a big man, just over six feet tall and very muscular, with a military-style blond crew cut and a Marine Corps jawline. That jaw was set as he walked over to meet Mike.

"Hi, Vic!" Mike said, forcing his voice to sound pleased to see the man. "I guess they told you what happened. My bike's in the—"

Vic hit him.

It was a savagely fast, stunningly hard blow. Not a slap, but the full rock-hardness of Vic's fist. It caught Mike in the stomach and seemed to smash back every bit of flesh between shirtfront and backbone. All of the air whooshed out of Mike's mouth along with a strangled cry of surprise; after that Mike had no breath even to scream. The pain was worse than anything he had ever felt. Worse than the broken rib, worse than all the bruises from when he'd gone off the road. Worse than any pain from any punishment Vic had ever given him. It was the first time in his life Mike had ever been punched by an adult. Before that it had been slaps, hard slaps with Vic's hard hands, but just slaps. The punch was so crushingly hard, and so unexpected, that Mike felt as if his entire body had shrunk down into a single twisted knot of white-hot pain. He lay on the gravel in a fetal position and tried to breathe.

"Yo! mister!" Barney called in alarm, stepping forward. Vic wheeled toward him and pointed a finger at the kid's nose. The finger was like a steel dagger and it stopped Barney in his tracks.

"You got something to say, shit bag?"

Barney's stood there, speechless, powerless, shocked, and scared beyond action. He watched in horror as Vic jerked open the rear passenger door, then bent and caught Mike by the belt and the hair, hoisted him off the ground, and literally threw him into the backseat. Mike slid across the seat and thumped against the opposite door.

All the time Mike's mom just sat in the front passenger seat and looked down at the floor. Barney tried to catch her eye, to make some kind of appeal, but she wouldn't look at him. Barney wished Crow was still there, though what Crow could do against a guy like Wingate he didn't know.

"Where's his fucking bike?" Vic demanded, closing on Barney.

All Barney could do was point. Vic stalked over and yanked it out of the back of Crow's trunk. He didn't bother to close the hood. He crammed the bike roughly into the bed of the station wagon, slammed the rear door, and then stalked around to the driver's side. Over the top of the car he again leveled a finger at Barney. "This is a family matter, do you understand me?"

Barney nodded.

"Good, then keep your mouth shut or it won't be a plastic knife you're gonna find sticking out of your chest. Now get the fuck out of the road."

Barney retreated and watched in mute horror as Vic made a screeching turn and left the lot in a spray of kicked-back gravel.

(3)

Crow bounced along the road, following the path he knew so well. The Haunted Hayride covered a huge area, spread out over parts of three different farms, two of which were now owned by Terry Wolfe, one of which leased acreage to the mayor for his attraction. It was wrapped like a horseshoe around the north end of the Pinelands College campus and was itself wrapped in the arms of the vast Pine Deep State Forest. Most of the land was given over to pumpkin patches, cornfields, and wheat fields, but since the harvest had begun in earnest for most of the town, much of the crop had already been cleared. Some of the corn stood unpicked, it having been planted later for a late fall harvest. A lot of the local farmers staggered their harvests so they could keep sending fresh produce to the markets up until the very edge of winter.

Crow loved the place. Even though he had designed every part of it, and knew all of its theatrical ins and outs, he loved the feeling of supernatural dread that he always sensed when he was covering these dark lanes. For a lark, he'd even spent a couple of nights as one of the monsters, scaring the bejesus out of the ten-dollar-a-head tourists.

The hayride was set up so that one main path led through all of the traps. The traps were the spots where costumed staffers waited to leap out and, in their own scripted or improvisational way, go "Boo!" Some of the traps were set scenes, such as a witch trial that showed a poor wretch being crushed beneath planks weighted with rocks, or tied to a chair and dunked into the creek; or where a line of victims were led up to a chopping block where a burly headsman (the defensive lineman for the Pine Deep Scarecrows) waited to shorten them by a head. Some of the traps were shockers, which had either mechanical or human monsters leaping unexpectedly out at the customers during lulls in the ride. There were a few interactive traps as well, such as Leatherface from *The Texas Chainsaw Massacre* rushing at the flatbed with his chainsaw buzzing. The chain on the saw was totally blunt, so when he tried to cut through the planks on the side of the flatbed, he really got nowhere, but Crow had added plastic bags of sawdust taped to the outside of the planks that would burst as soon as the chainsaw was pressed against them. The swirling sawdust and the buzz of the saw made it appear as if Leatherface was really cutting his way through the wood and was actually going to dismember the paying customers.

The nicest touch this season, though, was the Valley of the Living Dead trap. This was a new one, and was Crow's pride and joy. Just past the halfway point of the hayride, the tractor would pull the flatbed through a patch of mud. The mud was only surface muck kept wet by a sprinkler system, but in the darkness it looked real enough to create the illusion that the tractor had become hopelessly mired. Coop, or whoever was driving, would ease the tractor into neutral and just gun the engine, growling and swearing (in a thoroughly PG manner, of course) at the predicament. While all this was going on, dark shapes would begin to move in the bushes near the flatbed. These dark shapes would slowly—very slowly—advance on the flatbed. They were white-faced, decaying corpses, slouching and shuffling with all the gracelessness of reanimated bodies. It would be a race to see if Coop could unmire the tractor and get them on their way before the legions of walking dead could reach the flatbed.

Of course, timing was everything. Coop would get "unstuck," but just a moment too late. The ghouls would manage to reach the flatbed and would, amid a chorus of ungodly screams, drag one poor soul off into the bushes. The screams would be truly terrifying, and as the flatbed was towed away, the stricken survivors would look back and see ghouls staggering away nibbling on an arm or a leg or a string of intestines.

As a set piece, it was a corker. The tourists, especially the ones who had never been to a haunted hayride before, were stunned to a stricken silence. Until, of course, the next monsters leaped out at them. The "victim" was a staffer posing as a tourist, and the victim was changed almost every day so that repeat customers could never tell who was going to fall prey to the living dead.

There were other traps as well, but the Valley of the Living Dead was the star attraction on the Hayride, and had even been written up in *Sci-Fi Universe* and *Fangoria* magazines, as well as every newspaper on the East Coast. When it came to producing genuine horrible thrills, Crow was a genius, albeit a twisted one with a penchant for very dark humor.

Now that twisted genius was skimming along on his ATV. He stopped periodically to tell the staffers that the ride was closing down. He told the Creature from the Black Lagoon to cut across the swamp and let the Pod People know. He sent the Wolfman and the Brainiac down through the gully to bring in the Mole People, the Headsman, and the Flying Monkeys. He had Jack the Ripper go back to the shed for another ATV and sent him heading backward along the path of the ride to tell the Vampire Children and the Bog Beasts to stand down.

Ten minutes later he caught up with the tractor just as Henry Pitts was being dragged into the bushes by the ghouls. Crow honked his horn and flashed his headlights off and on. The ghouls straightened from their bloody feast, and Henry sat up, too, amaz-

ingly unhurt despite the entrails dripping from the mouths of the
zombies.

Coop killed the engine of the tractor and the Valley of the
Living Dead grew quiet except for a faint buzz of inquiring
voices.

Dismounting, Crow walked over to the tractor and looked up
at Coop.

"Hey . . . what's going on?" Coop asked. He was a middle-
aged man with a paunch, loose jowls, and a look of almost total
stupidity.

Crow turned to face the mass of confused and semifright-
ened tourists. "Folks, I have some bad news. Because of severe
technical difficulties beyond our control, we are going to have
to close down the Haunted Hayride for tonight." He had to
raise his voice to be heard over the chorus of groans. "Everyone
will receive a full refund, plus a free coupon good for any night
you wish to return. Mr. Wolfe regrets having to do this, but as I
said, it is beyond our control."

"What's the deal, man?" someone asked.

Relying on the speech he'd rehearsed all the way over, Crow
said, "There is a bridge just a half mile ahead. It has buckled and
won't take the weight of the tractor. We are going to have to turn
around and go back. There's just no way that the tractor can go
any farther forward in safety. I'm sure you all understand."

From the moans, groans, and curses, it seemed they not only
didn't understand, they damned well didn't like it, but they were
also resigned. Crow had affected the attitude of "someone in
charge" and it really left no room for argument.

Thunder rumbled overhead and lightning danced through
the clouds. A few wet raindrops fell, not many, but enough to
dampen any further arguments.

Crow called Coop down from the tractor seat and climbed
up himself, and with very little to-do, he pulled the tractor free
from the "mud," angled over onto the clearing near the road,
and turned around. The tourists, some of them still standing in
postures of indignation or disappointment, continued to grum-

ble, but said nothing directly to Crow. The Ghouls, and the late Henry Pitts, stood to one side and waited, then climbed up onto the flatbed as it passed. Coop, looking disconsolate, followed on the ATV.

Crow gave the tractor some gas and picked up speed. Usually the ride through the dark farmlands and forest was done at little more than a walking pace, slow enough for the spooky shadows under the trees to get the customers in the proper frame of mind for the beasties to scare the hell out of them every couple hundred yards. Crow tooled along at a respectable thirty miles an hour, slowing only to embark a few wandering creatures of the night.

The job, the great and important mission assigned to him by Terry Wolfe, had been accomplished so quickly and easily that Crow almost felt a twinge of disappointment. Not that he wanted any kind of trouble, but the thought of real-life monsters out there had pumped him full of adrenaline, and now he was fidgety.

Back in the office, he supervised the return of the cash and the handing out of rain checks. He also found a moment to take Coop and some of the older monsters aside and tell them about what was happening in town. They were all suitably impressed.

"Okay," he summed up, "here's what I want to happen. Rigger, you and Bailey make sure all of the customers get to their cars. Give the usual spiel about keeping windows and doors locked, not picking up strangers, and driving with headlights and seat belts on. Tom and Del, you two work the road with flashlights and make sure everybody gets onto the right side of the road. Not like last October. We don't want any fender benders tonight. Okay? The rest of you, close down the buildings, lock everything up, and report back to Coop. Coop, I want you to do a roll call. No, don't look at me like that. I want everyone accounted for before you leave. Everyone goes on the buddy system. Even if you have to take a leak, bring your buddy to shake it for you. No one, and I mean no one, works alone or drives home alone. If you came in separate cars, then follow your buddy home. These are really bad guys out there, kids, so let's not get stupid. Let's shut 'er down and go home."

Which is exactly what they did.

While all of this was happening, Crow strolled over to the main office, where Barney was helping count the cash.

"Hey, where's Mike Sweeney?"

Barney looked up and Crow could see the residual shock in the young man's eyes. "His, um, folks came and got him right after you left."

Crow searched his face. "What happened?"

Barney looked around to make sure no one else was close enough to hear, then in a hushed voice told Crow what had happened.

Crow stared at him, eyes hard and angry, mouth a tight line. He said nothing.

Barney shook his head. "And people come *here* to see monsters."

Chapter 15

Vic pulled into the driveway in front of his house and then killed the station wagon's engine. Inside the car the only sound was Vic's steady breathing, in and out through his nose like a bull. Lois Wingate had her hand over her mouth and her face turned away, ostensibly staring out the side window but actually looking at nothing. She hadn't said a single word since Vic had pulled into the hayride.

In the back, Mike was sprawled in a heap just staring at the roof of the car, nearly lost in a world composed entirely of pain.

Never in his life had he been hit so hard. Mike would remember those moments at the Haunted Hayride for as long as he lived. It was the very first time Vic had ever punched him, and the fact of it, far more than the force, had numbed his brain. It had come out of nowhere and exploded a big white bell in Mike's head, then darkened his skies and his thoughts for a long moment. He had been beaten before, but it had always been an open hand or a belt. Never a fist. Vic had just taken him down one level to a lower place of darkness. From now on the beatings would be different. Vic had crossed a line, and Mike knew that there was never any way to go back. Lying there in the back of the car, Mike knew it with a dreadful clarity.

Vic got out, slammed his door, and jerked open the back door.

"Get out." His voice sounded incongruously mild, and for a

moment Mike's optimism flared. Maybe that punch was all there would be. Maybe it was enough.

Moving as if his stomach and ribs were made out of fragile glass, Mike peeled himself up off the seat and got out of the car. He flinched away from Vic as his stepfather swung the door shut.

"Get in the house."

Mike fled into the house and was starting up the stairs when just behind him Vic said, "Where do you think you're going?"

The moment froze in time, and if Mike had a button somewhere that he could push and end his life right there, he'd have pushed it. He had one hand on the banister and one hand on the wall, his left leg raised to step up. His stomach was a fiery ball of pain greater by far than the steady ache in his ribs.

Then there was his mother's voice, thin and wavering, but still there in the doorway. "C'mon, Vic, don't you think that's enough?"

It was the longest moment of Mike's young life as he waited for what Vic would say. He turned and looked down at Vic, who stood halfway between where Mike's mother was framed in the open doorway and the foot of the steps. Vic raised his finger and pointed to her the same way he had pointed to Barney at the hayride. "If you open your fucking mouth one more time—just once more—so help me God, I'll beat you so hard you'll shit blood for a month. You *know* I'll do it, too, Lois."

Mike's mother had paled at the threat and snapped her mouth shut. She came in, closed the door, edged past Vic, and fled into the living room, snatching the bottle of Tanqueray off the wet bar as she went. A second later Mike heard the TV come on.

Mike's gaze drifted across the wasteland of his optimism to where Vic stood smiling. A powerful and implacable figure at the foot of the stairs.

"Come down here," Vic said. "Right now."

Mike debated his chances. He might be able to make it up the stairs and into his room before Vic caught him, but what then? Vic could easily kick down the door, and an open act of defiance would be like throwing gasoline on a fire.

His legs moved before his mind was aware that he'd surrendered, and he came down into the living room.

Vic never stopped smiling as he beat Mike from one end of the house to the other.

Mike didn't remember all of it; maybe he passed out once or twice, or maybe the mind can only contain just so much, but large parts of it were gone, just vague blurs of hard hands and harder words and Vic's smile as Mike recoiled from each punch, peering down at Mike as he waited for flesh to puff.

When the beating had started Mike had pleaded, and begged . . . and wept. Usually the tears stopped the beatings, as if it was a prize Vic sought and was satisfied with. This time there was no stopping, and if anything the tears made Vic hit harder.

The beating had started in the foyer but when Mike's mind was able to take some sort of stock of what was happening he found that he was crammed into the corner of the kitchen with no clear memory of having crawled there, squeezed as far back as he could into the narrow slot between refrigerator and cabinet, his forearms crossed over his face. Vic stood over him, chest heaving from his exertions, sweat running down his face.

"You little piece of shit. Do you have any fucking idea how much trouble you put me to? Do you have any fucking idea how embarrassing it was to have to come out and fetch you like that? Do you have any fucking idea how embarrassing it was to have the fucking mayor of the fucking town call us up to tell us to go get you? It makes your mom and me look like bad parents. Letting you out till all fucking hours of the night. Do you know how much fucking trouble you are, you pissant little turd?"

"Please . . ." Mike whimpered. Tears streamed from his eyes.

"What the hell are you crying for, you little pussy? I ain't begun to hit you yet!"

It began anew. Vic dragged Mike out of the corner and rained down punches and kicks and slaps until that was all that existed in Mike's world.

But then something *happened*.

One minute his mind was filled with pain and terror and shock, and as if some hand had punched a button on a remote control everything *switched*. All at once Mike's mind stepped out of itself. It was the weirdest feeling in his life, and he was fully aware of it. He could feel an actual physical shift as his consciousness just lifted and moved to another place. Not far off, but not in the body that was being beaten. It was like the out-of-body experiences Mike had read about in articles on people who had died and were later revived. He could see Vic standing there, straddling the body that Mike's consciousness knew was his own, but he was just not in that body. Somehow—impossibly—he'd left. Just got up and left.

He didn't know how, and he didn't know why, but without meaning to his thinking mind had stepped out of the body. None of the blows that rained down mattered now. He didn't feel them—at least he didn't care about them. He was aware of a kind of sensation, almost like a vibration, or an echo, as if when each blow landed it sent a tremor through his flesh that only vibrated against his separate self, but it was just that. A vibration without the corresponding pain. Like the tremble from the TV speakers when something in a movie blew up. Only that and nothing more.

Mike had one brief moment of panic when he thought that this meant that he was dead, that one of Vic's punches had done something to him. Burst something, knocked something loose, and that his body was dying as he floated there watching. Was he having a near-death experience? If so, there was no team of doctors waiting to zap him with a defibrillator unit.

The fear faded, though, as if his spirit could not hold such an intense emotion for very long. Or, perhaps, emotion was merely chemical, as his science teacher said it was. Out of the body there were no chemicals to mix to provoke or sustain emotions.

Mike felt the panic quickly replaced with a kind of bland peacefulness. Or, perhaps, a lack of caring.

He watched Vic and saw the man's muscles bunch and roll, saw his hands move up and down, saw him shift to put power behind each blow. It was fascinating, like watching a machine,

and he could study it with a total lack of emotional involvement. The hands rose and snapped down, sometimes as slaps,
sometimes as punches.

As he watched, Mike saw something else, too. He saw Vic's
face grow steadily more red, saw sweat burst from his pores, saw
his hands redden with tissue damage each time a blow struck
one of Mike's elbows or his forehead, saw the labored heave of
his chest as the beating took its toll of Vic.

That was very, very interesting. It was a revelation that focused his mind like a laser passing through crystal. In that moment he was able to think more clearly, reason more incisively
that his mind burst open with new possibilities. He could look
at Vic and see him more clearly and more completely than he
ever had before. In that moment, for the very first time, he was
seeing the *man* Vic Wingate. The man. It was something that
Mike, for all his intelligence, had never once really considered,
and it was something that was of immeasurable importance.
Even without a body or muscles or lips, Mike smiled. His spirit
smiled.

Vic, it turned out, was human.

He was flesh, and blood, and breath. He was meat and bone
and muscle. He could be hurt, he could tire. He was merely
human and because of that it was not possible for him to be either invincible or invulnerable.

Mike had always believed that Vic was both, but Vic was really
only human.

Despite the lack of chemical triggers Mike's spirit was becoming supercharged by this amazing knowledge. It was the most
important thing that Mike had ever learned, so obvious and yet
Mike had never seen it. Never even suspected it.

Vic was *human*.

Mike considered this. Vic was forty-seven years old. Vic was
middle-aged. No matter how strong he was, no matter how
much he worked out, he was middle-aged and every day forward
would take him a day further from his youth and peak strength.
Mike was fourteen. In ten years Mike would be twenty-four and
Vic would be fifty-seven.

Unless Vic actually killed Mike—and even Mike did not believe that Vic would go that far—then one day Mike would be a fully grown adult man and Vic would be—*old.*

All Mike had to do was endure.

Vic was human.

Mike felt pain. Instant and overwhelming. It was everywhere in his body, and in that flash of awareness he realized that he was back in his body. He was no longer a hovering spirit, no longer detached from the bruised flesh and violated nerve endings. No longer a bystander witnessing horror but the subject of it. His mouth and nose were bleeding. One eye was puffed nearly shut—the other peered through a red haze of blood. Mike's broken ribs were worse now, and every muscle felt mashed and ruined. He tasted blood on his thick tongue.

Vic stood above him, impossibly tall and powerful, his arms knotted with muscle, his hands clenched in fists. Gasping for air from his exertions he stared down at Mike, a smile of triumph half formed on his mouth.

But only half formed.

Above the crooked smile Vic's eyes were slowly clouding with doubt, and double vertical lines deepened between his brows.

"You had enough, you little shit?"

On the floor Mike lay like a smashed bug, his limbs sprawled, his skin bloody and bruised, his face a ruin. The pain was everywhere, in every cell of his body, and Vic was there, ready to give him more of it.

And Mike Sweeney did not care.

He lifted his battered head, opened his puffed eyes, parted his split lips . . . and smiled up at Vic.

There must have been something in that smile beyond Mike's joy in knowing that he could outlast this man. That he had taken the worst beating of his life and had endured it. There must have been something there, flickering in his bloodshot eyes or trembling in his mashed lips, that Vic read differently, or read wrong—or read correctly—because he took a single involuntary step backward and Mike saw something in Vic's face that he had never expected to see. Something he didn't believe he could see in Vic's face.

He saw a flicker of fear.

Not much, just a touch, but it was there.

Vic was human after all.

Vic was just a human being, and Mike—well, Mike would endure him. And Iron Mike Sweeney, the Enemy of Evil, would outlast him.

The fear that had flickered in Vic's eyes for the briefest of moments was gone and his usual dark intensity returned. He held his ground, but he lowered his hands.

"Now get up and get your sorry ass to bed. Go on—get out of my sight!"

It took Mike a while to get his arms and legs to work well enough to turn his aching body over onto hands and knees, and then to fingertips and toes, and then, swaying, to his feet. He took a couple of wandering sideways steps before orienting himself.

At the doorway to the kitchen he stopped, holding on to the frame, and turned for a moment to look back at Vic, and once more he gave his stepfather a bloody-toothed smile.

Vic didn't say another word as Mike tottered away and then slowly clawed his way upstairs.

(2)

Standing in the parking lot, Crow watched the last of the tourists and staff go and then heaved out a long sigh of mingled relief and weariness. He was tired, and what he really wanted was to go home and crawl into bed, but—he smiled as the thought sprang into his mind—someone was waiting with a late dinner for him.

He walked back into the office to switch off the lights, but before he did he reached for the phone.

★ ★ ★

Mark Guthrie heard two sounds almost at once.

The first was the first ring of the telephone, and there was a split fraction of a second in which he realized that whoever was calling could send help if only he could manage to get over to the phone, to knock it off its cradle, to make some kind of sound that would let the caller know that there was trouble, but in the second part of that fractured second of time he heard a single sharp report. A gunshot.

Through the gag and through his fear, Mark tried to scream his father's name, his sister's name, and the name of God.

The phone kept ringing.

Crow set the phone down in disappointment, but at the very last moment, just as the handset was touching the plunger, there was a sound. It was just a muffled and inarticulate sound, and Crow tried to catch himself in time, but when he whipped the handset away from the cradle, the connection had already been broken.

"Shit!"

He pushed down on the plunger to clear the connection, got a dial tone, and punched in Val's number again. Busy.

He tried again. Busy.

Once more. Still busy. Crow made a rude sound and hung up the phone. He stood there and looked around, assessing the place. Everything was locked up and dark.

"Okay then," he said to nobody in particular, and started for the door. Just as he touched the knob he stopped, turned, and walked back to the phone, murmuring, "Once more for luck."

He punched in the numbers. Busy. "Shit balls," he observed. He called Val's cell. No answer except voice mail.

"This is bullshit," he said aloud and left the office, locking it up nice and tight, crunched across the gravel to where Missy waited for him, and climbed in. He turned on the motor and then tugged the pistol out of his waistband and crammed it back into the glove compartment. Then he put the car into drive and in a spray of gravel, he spun wheels in the direction of the Guthrie farm.

(3)

Val ran as if all the evil things in the dark were at her heels.

Except for moments of crackling white light from the heavens, the darkness was absolute. Cornstalks stood up to whip at her, slapping her face, biting at her legs, tugging at her wrists. She fought them away as she ran, battering her way through the fields, running nowhere and anywhere.

She ran and ran and ran.

Her strong legs propelled her with great force, and her muscular arms crushed a path for her slim body as she surged forward. Then her sneakered foot came down on something wet and slippery and suddenly she was flying forward, hands coming up to meet the ground that rushed at her in the darkness. Her palms hit hard, sooner than she had expected, and the jolt raced up her arms and into her shoulders and something hot and white and loud seemed to detonate in her left arm just below the deltoid. The arm buckled, refusing to bear even an ounce of weight, and she twisted as she fell, landing with all her weight on the white-hot shoulder.

She didn't want to scream, but she couldn't help it. The pain was a storm of knives whirling around inside her. She had no idea how long she lay there, stunned to breathlessness by the sheer weight of the pain. She tried to roll off the arm, but the pain came with her. Her left arm absolutely refused to work. She could feel the fingers opening and closing, but from the elbow to the shoulder blade everything felt as if boiling oil had been poured over it.

"Crow!" she cried out into the swirling darkness. "Help me!"

But Crow wasn't there. Only the darkness and the pain and the madman with the gun were in her part of the universe. The deep voice of the thunder mocked her pain. Val knew that she had to—absolutely had to—get up.

Get up and run or lie there and wait to be slaughtered.

That was when she heard the single sharp, cold gunshot. It was a small sound, almost lost in the moan of the wind.

It took half a second for her to process the sound, and then she screamed, "Dad!"

That got her up. How, she could never explain, but somehow she was on her feet. Her shoes were wet and sticky from the ears of corn she had slipped on, but she stayed steady on her feet, as steady as waves of nausea and vertigo would allow her to be.

"Dad . . ." she said, looking back into the utter blackness the way she had come.

She didn't know what to do. Indecision born of terror polluted her resolve.

If she kept running, then the maniac might kill her father. Might *already* have killed him!

If she went back, she might be killed, too. What would happen to Mark and Connie?

Seconds burst around her like firecrackers and she didn't know what to do.

She felt something brush against her cheek and she used her only living hand to try and brush it away. Her fingertips touched lips, a nose, a cheek.

Val screamed and spun, backpedaling and almost falling, flailing out with her good hand.

"*Valerie* . . ." said a soft voice.

Val froze. She had a vague impression of a shape, black against the blacker shadows of the field.

"*Go back*," whispered the voice.

"Wh . . . what?"

Lightning flashed overhead, and Val had the briefest glimpse of a tall man, gaunt and sad, stooped beneath some terrible weight, dressed in dirty black clothes, gray face streaked with mud. A guitar was slung down his back, the strap crossing his chest.

"Go back," he whispered.

She *knew* this man . . . but she couldn't place where from.

The lightning flashed again and for just a second the small silver cross that she wore around her neck burned as if it somehow had suddenly flared with inner heat. Then as quickly as the sensation had come, it was gone.

Val was alone.

She stood there, head swimming with pain and shock and terror, her fingers touching the cross, the skin over her heart still tingling from the burn.

"Go back . . ." she murmured to herself.

Then she turned. Limping, her damaged arm swinging painfully, tears streaking her face, she started back toward the house.

(4)

At that same moment, eight miles away, Crow was tooling along the upper reaches of A-32. Jed Davenport was singing "Mr. Devil Blues" from a mix CD, and Crow was singing along, his voice leaping at the note but never quite grabbing it.

A state police car came rocketing up behind, lights flashing, siren tearing holes in the night. Crow sighed and slowed down to something near the speed limit as the unit changed lanes and pulled abreast. The officer riding shotgun dazzled him with a flashlight for a moment, then clicked it off. The patrol car accelerated and passed, taking charge of the lane and barreling way ahead.

Crow was impressed with the speed of the unit. He felt he could top it with Missy, but getting into a pissing match with the state police held little attraction for him. He let them zoom out of sight before he let the speedometer climb back up into the low eighties.

Muddy Waters was now "Screaming and Crying," and Crow sang along.

He only slowed long enough to turn onto Johnson Wells Road, the old farm track that led around the huge cornfields and would take him right to Val's back door. The road was badly rutted and bumpy and not even Missy could safely take it at anything like her best speed. Crow slowed to fifty and grimaced with the teeth-rattling jolts.

The racing cop car stayed in Crow's mind. Where was it going? What the hell else was out here this far down on A-32?

If a thousand volts of electricity had shot up through the seat into his spine he could not have more instantly snapped to a straighter position.

There was only one thing this far down on A-32.

"Val!" He shouted her name and kicked down on the gas. Bumps and ruts be damned. Missy hurtled forward. No answer to any of his calls. *What a fucking fool!* he thought.

The car shot along the old farm road, high beams plowing a path before him. Thunder rumbled again, way over beyond the Guthrie farm.

In the back of his mind he kept hearing one word over and over again: *Hurry!*

"Oh my God!" he said out loud. "Val . . ."

Chapter 16

Ferro carefully unwrapped a stick of Beechnut and laid it on his tongue until the surface sugar melted, then chewed it very slowly. He folded the wrapper neatly and stuffed it in his shirt pocket. For long minutes he had just stood there staring at the devastation, letting the horror burn into him and then burn out, letting the fires burn away all of the sensationalism and emotion until all that was left was a crime scene. Facts, data, evidence, and leads: nothing more.

Ferro looked up, not surprised to see that the moon had vanished behind featureless black storm clouds. "Yeah, Vince, we're going to lose the scene before the lab crew can get here from Philly. I'm going to run through the preliminaries. You up to helping?"

LaMastra hoisted himself up off the ground, slapped dirt and crushed corn from the seat of his pants, and gave Ferro a vague nod.

"Good," said Ferro. "Chief?" Bernhardt, who by now was standing on the far side of the car, well out of sight of the body, looked up. "Chief, can you arrange to get some kind of tarp? We need to protect the site as much as possible."

Bernhardt made an inarticulate sound that Ferro took as an assent and set off back to the road in a wobbling Clydesdale canter.

Ferro knelt down by the opened briefcase and set to work. First he removed a folded sheet of white plastic, opened and spread it out to form a kind of pristine picnic blanket, weighing it down with ears of corn. On top of this he quickly and deftly lined up several items from the case: a small stack of clear plastic bags of various size, from those only large enough to hold a few pennies to some as large as lunch bags; clear glass vials and disposable eyedroppers in sterile plastic sleeves; paper bags; a gunpowder trace kit; tweezers; scissors; evidence tags; and a small battery-powered tape recorder with a voice-activated microphone.

Ferro took one of the eyedroppers and one of the vials and walked toward one of the pools of blood. Over his shoulder, he said to LaMastra, "I'll collect, you catalog and tag."

"Yeah, okay."

Terry left them to it. He walked away from the scene and climbed back up to the road. Chief Bernhardt was chain-smoking Camels as he talked into the handset of Rhoda's unit; he looked like he was a short step away from a stroke. His bald head was bright red and beaded with sweat and he kept mopping it out of his eyes with the back of his chubby paw. The effect made it look as if he were a sniffling kid wiping tears from his eyes.

Gus finished with the radio and came over to stand with Terry. "This is some shit, huh?"

Terry nodded mutely.

"What I don't get is why on earth this Ruger guy would do that to one of his buddies."

"A difference of opinion over the division of spoils perhaps? Who knows? Ruger is supposed to be a super-freakazoid, as Crow would say. Me, I'm amazed at the guy's chutzpah. He has every cop on the East Coast after him, and he stops and takes the time to do something like this. He must be totally whacked out."

"Jesus." Gus finished his cigarette and crushed it out under his toe.

"You think they're still around here, Gus?"

"Christ, I hope not."

"They can't have gone far without the car, and they can't have been gone long if Ruger stopped to do all that. Two men on foot, hauling all the drugs and money Ferro was talking about— they have to still be somewhere close. We have some serious hills around here, not to mention some very thick fields that aren't easy to wade through. I can't see how they could have gotten more than a few miles away."

"Ain't much around here," Gus said thoughtfully. "The road to Dark Hollow's not far, but there's nothing back there. And what else? A couple of back roads. Farm roads."

"Whose farm is this?"

Gus frowned and peered up and down the road, assessing. "You know, I can't quite tell if this is the north end of Henry Guthrie's place, or the south end of Hobie Devlin's." He cupped a hand around his mouth. "Rhoda! Whose farm is this?"

"I think it belongs to Mr. Guthrie."

"Yeah, I thought so."

Terry tensed. "Guthrie . . . You're right. This must be their big field, the one Henry calls the far field, 'cause it's furthest from the house." His eyes snapped wide. "Gus . . . can you get a unit out to Henry's house? I mean *right now!*"

Gus blinked in surprise for a second; then he got it. "Oh, Jesus, you're right! It's the only place they could have gone." Gus spun around and waddled quickly over to Rhoda and the other officers.

Watching him, Terry felt icy fingers close around his heart. Guthrie's farm. Val Guthrie was Crow's ladylove. And Crow was supposed to be going over there after his job at the hayride.

"Dear Jesus . . ." he breathed.

(2)

The thunder growled loud enough to wake the storm. Lightning flashed along its belly, burning the sky, burning the lands below, bursting trees and searing lines into the firmament. The rains came weeping in, angry tears spilled by troubled clouds.

Val Guthrie staggered out of the cornfield amid a crash of thunder that actually shook the dirt beneath her feet. Lightning danced and spun in the air above her, an almost continuous curtain of bright blue white.

She clutched her sprained arm to her body with all her strength, trying to keep it from swinging, but with each step the injured muscles and tendons twitched and spasmed, sending new and sharper spikes of pain. She didn't know how much more of it she could bear. Nausea washed over her in waves, bubbling up in the back of her throat, dimming her tear-streaked eyes, stoking the shock-induced fever burning in her veins.

"Dad!" she cried as she stumbled through a curtain of rain and into the clearing.

The kitchen door lay where she'd dropped it, and the wheel-barrow stood empty, the red paint washed to brightness by the rain.

The madman with the gun was nowhere to be seen.

Val stood there, swaying, uncertain, not ever remotely sure of what to do next.

Thunder broke above her so loudly she screamed, thinking the man had crept up behind her and shot her. She spun—but there was no one there.

Then in the flash of lightning, she saw the ragged form that lay crumpled in the lane only a few dozen yards away. The wind fluttered the sodden work clothes as it blew over outstretched legs and arms.

"Dad!"

She ran, shoving the pain down inside her mind, seeing nothing but the battered figure. Skidding, slipping in the mud, she tripped and landed on her knees in the mud and with her one good hand, she reached for her father's shoulder. He lay on his stomach, his face pressed into the muck. One hand lay stretched out in front of him. In the brightness of the lightning, Val could see the neat round hole burned high in his back, nearly between the shoulder blades, the cloth washed clean of blood by the downpour.

"No!" she screamed and pulled at him.

His big old body resisted her, fighting her with limpness and weight and sopping clothes, but eventually Val found the strength to turn him onto his back. She wasn't even sure if it was the right thing to do, or the wrong thing, or if she should do any-thing at all. She was beyond ordinary thinking.

There was no exit wound on his chest, she saw that right away, and in some dim part of her mind, she remembered how small a gun the man had carried.

Oh, please, God! she prayed and she bent her face to her fa-ther's.

"Daddy . . . Daddy . . . ?"

His face was totally slack, streaked with mud that clumped on his mustache and caught in his bushy eyebrows.

Val wiped the mud off his face and shook him very gently.

"Daddy . . . please . . ."

Henry Guthrie raised his hand just a few inches, all he could manage, and touched her arm.

"Daddy!" Val's heart leaped and she felt tears break and spill as her father slowly opened his eyes, squinting against the sting-ing rain.

"Get . . . get me . . . my sweater, pumpkin," he murmured dreamily, "I'm feeling . . . a chill . . ."

"Oh, Daddy . . ."

Guthrie's eyes opened wider and for a moment clearer lights burned within them. "Val?"

"I'm here, Daddy. I'm here. It's going to be okay. I'm here."

In a whisper, he asked, "Where is he?"

Val shook her head. "I think he's gone. I don't see him any-where."

Guthrie closed his eyes for a moment, then opened them again. The lights had already dimmed perceptibly. "Val . . ."

"Yes, Daddy?"

"You've got to warn . . ." he began, but suddenly a terrible coughing fit made him leap and jerk. Blood bubbled out of his nose and he gagged. It took a long time, and a lot of his dwin-dling supply of strength to speak, and even then it was in a faint whisper, barely audible beneath the roar of the storm. "Val . . . you've got to warn . . . Mark and . . . Con. . . ."

Then his mouth lost the words and he slumped limply against Val's lap. His hand fell away and slapped bonelessly into the mud.

Val screamed. She bent her head to his chest and listened, listened . . .

It was there, the faintest of beats, a feeble fist beating on the window of a burning building. It beat once, paused long . . . too long, beat again.

It grew fainter, and she felt her own heart slowing with it, but it kept on beating. Trying to live. Trying.

Val tried to pull him, to drag him to the house, but she was a battered and exhausted woman with a torn shoulder all alone out in a storm. Half a mile from the house. The enormity of it broke her, and she collapsed back down onto her knees.

She held her father for a brief moment—almost more time than she could spare—and then laid his head down, kissing his forehead and cheeks before climbing to her feet. She turned toward the house and as she did so her lips curled back into a snarl of feral hate that had no trace of humanity left in it. Clutching her bad arm to her body, she set out toward the house at a tearing run.

(3)

Mark Guthrie lay on the floor and strained with every muscle in his body. Sweat burst from his pores and blood was singing in his ears as he fought against the ropes and tape that held him.

As soon as he had heard that single awful gunshot, he'd thrown himself off the couch and had wormed his way across to the ringing phone. It felt as if the effort took twenty years, but he actually made it on the eighth ring, shoving his shoulder against the low table with a dynamic effort. The table toppled neatly over and the phone crashed to the floor. Mark rolled over to it and pressed his ear to the receiver just in time to hear the click as the call was disconnected from the other end.

He bellowed as well as the duct tape would allow.

Connie sat on the couch, watching him with wide, desperate eyes, and he turned to her, trying his best to convey a look of hopeful confidence. He knew it probably looked pitiful, bound and gagged and sweaty as he was.

Since then, he'd tried to hang the phone up by pushing it with his chin. No luck. He did manage to press the plunger down long enough to get a dial tone, but the phone was an old rotary: no way he was going to dial it, not even 911.

Still, he kept trying, using the tip of his nose to try and turn the dial. The labor seemed to take forever, and by the time he would have the dial start to move, the phone would begin signaling that it was off the hook and he would have to push the plunger down again to get a fresh dial tone. It was tedious, frantic, frustrating work.

Karl Ruger made it a pointless exercise as well.

Mark didn't even know that the man was in the house until he saw the shadow that washed over him. He turned quickly, saw the man standing over him, tall and powerful, soaked from the rain, holding the tiny automatic in one hand.

"Howdy, campers," Ruger whispered. "Are we having fun yet?"

Mark tried to squirm away, twisting violently like an arthritic snake, but Karl laughed and kept pace with him, continuing to straddle him until Mark thumped against the couch and could go no farther.

Ruger leaned over and picked up the phone's handset, weighing it thoughtfully in his hand. "You know, when I got up this morning I had no idea how much of a total fuck job this whole day was going to turn out to be. My team gets shot up, we get chased by the cops, crash our car. Tony buys it. Boyd busts his fucking leg. I get stuck here in Green-fucking-Acres. And now, you know what's happened? Should I tell you?" Ruger's eyes were wide and unblinking, like those of an alligator; Mark's eyes were wide and staring, the eyes of a trapped rabbit. "Well, first," Ruger said, tapping Mark on the chest with the phone, "I go to all the trouble to fetch a stretcher for my friend Boyd, lug it all the way out there, and you know what? *Do you fucking want to know what?*" he demanded, thumping the phone with greater force with each word. "Somehow my busted-leg friend, my own buddy Boyd, splits with my fucking stash! Isn't that just fucking precious?"

Mark stared up at Ruger, afraid to even breathe. Stale air burned in his lungs.

Ruger sighed and considered the phone. "Some days just blow . . ." he murmured. "To top it all off, your shit-head old man decides to get all cute and ballsy. Decides he wants to run out on ol' Karl. Now, don't you think that's rude?"

Mark just stared, dreading what Ruger was saying, remembering the gunshot.

"And your broke-nose sister lit out, too. Fast little bitch. Never could catch her. Pity. I'd have liked to show her some city manners." Ruger smiled and winked. "I'm sure you know what I mean." He squatted on his haunches, still straddling Mark's bound legs, still jiggling the phone lightly in his hand. "But old Dad . . . well, he can't run for shit, can he? No, sirree. Can't run worth shit."

Mark's heart was pounding so loud he wanted to scream.

"So, ol' Karl just reaches out and . . ." Ruger extended the pistol and touched Mark's cheek with it. "Poof! No more dad."

Mark tried to scream. The shriek tore its way up from his gut, ripping the flesh of his soul, rending his hammering heart. Even the muffling gag couldn't stop all of it.

Ruger laughed. His appetite fed on just that kind of exquisite pain; it was a far, far better drug than any cocaine or heroin, and after the way things had been spiraling downward all night, he needed a fix to set his mind, to get back onto the edge.

Mark thrashed and bucked and howled. Tears burned in his eyes and then broke and spilled down his cheeks.

Connie whimpered, and Ruger suddenly glanced at her. His smile changed. Something shifted and squirmed behind his dark eyes and his lips seemed to writhe like wriggling worms.

"Well, well," he said softly, "at least I won't come away empty-handed. Hell, I ought to have something for my troubles. Only right, wouldn't you say? Hardly seems fair else."

Shrieking, Mark rolled back and kicked up with both bound ankles, catching Ruger in the rump, dislodging him, but Ruger twisted and caught his balance and as Mark raised his legs for a second kick, he bent forward and jammed the pistol into Mark's shoulder. Mark froze and the world froze around him.

Ruger just smiled again and shook his head.

"Oh no, m'man. Not that easy. No, I ain't gonna pop you. Not yet, anyway. You, m'man, are going to get a front-row seat for my little R and R with Donna Reed here."

Mark began cocking his legs for the kick, but Ruger was much, much faster. With that terrible speed of his he lashed out with the phone handset and cracked Mark across the cheek. It was a hard blow, but not a killing one, not even a crippling one. He didn't want Mark unconscious. That would spoil the fun. It was just enough of a blow to send Mark reeling and twisting over onto his face so hard he struck his head against the hard-wood. Fresh tears sprang into his eyes and he could taste blood in his mouth, gagging him.

Ruger stood up, tossing the handset onto the floor. He bent down and set his pistol carefully on the coffee table, his black eyes fixing on Connie as his smile grew and grew.

(4)

"Oh, Daddy . . ." Val whispered, but only the wind could hear her.

The rain beat down on her, and as best she could with a use-less arm and a broken heart, she tried to shelter her father from the storm. She had done her best to patch the bullet hole in his back, but there was so much blood pooled between his shirt and coveralls. So much. Too much.

The lightning never stopped, and the thunder bellowed in-sanely. A freak eddy of wind brought a sound to her, rolling in muted echoes across the tops of the corn. The high, lonely wail of a police siren.

Val raised her head, listened to the sound, straining to under-stand it, to locate it, but the wind whipped it away again. Still, she thought she could tell where it was coming from. The farm road. The one that connected A-32 with their front yard.

A police siren. *Cops!* Coming this way. Far away, but definitely coming this way.

"Oh, God, please help us!" she cried and staggered to her feet. She looked down at her father. "Daddy, I have to leave you. Just for a little bit. I'll get help and come back. Please . . . wait for me, Daddy." Her eyes were jumpy with madness. "Don't you dare go away, Daddy. You just wait here."

She turned and ran back toward the house.

(5)

Mark kept screaming, kept trying to break the ropes that no human strength could break, to part the layers of cloth-reinforced tape. His wife's screams drowned his out, and polluted his mind and soul.

Ruger had pulled out his wickedly sharp knife and with quick, deft movements had slashed the ropes on Connie's legs. She had tried to kick him, she had that much sanity left, but he slapped her and punched her and tore at her and left her beaten in spirit as well as body. Then the real horror had begun.

He had torn at her clothing, revealing her in the cruelest way, robbing her of what shreds of dignity still clung to her. The knife either cut at fabric or pressed threateningly into the soft flesh of her throat, but it was always there, a constant ugly extension of Ruger's violent lust.

Mark screamed throughout.

Ruger laughed out loud as he stood over her, slowly unbuckling his belt, blowing kisses at Connie, dragging it out.

There was no warning at all when the thunderbolt slammed into him.

One moment Ruger was reaching for the metal tab of his fly and the next he was bowled off his feet, driven away from Connie, driven into the backrest of the couch by something that screamed in a continuous high-pitched wail of inhuman fury. The knife went flying out of his hand, vanishing behind an overstuffed chair. He almost fell, but his knees hit the seat and it doubled him over. He collapsed awkwardly onto the couch, still bearing the weight of whatever had struck him. Most men would have sat there, stupid and dazed, shaking their heads, disoriented.

But Karl Ruger was not so vulnerable a creature.

Hissing like a cat, he turned, lashing out with his elbow even before he could see his attacker. As the elbow struck, there was a howl of agony and Val Guthrie toppled away, clawing at her left arm. Ruger's elbow had slammed into the already sprained tendons and muscles with terrible force.

"You fucking *bitch*!" he snarled and reached down and grabbed her by the hair, hauling her to her feet. He cuffed her across the face, bruising the spot he'd struck earlier. Val was far beyond the reach of that kind of pain. She lashed out with her foot, aiming for his groin, but Ruger turned and took it on the hip. Still, the kick had enough desperate force to stagger him. He lost his grip on her, backpedaled a step, and came within reach of Mark, who lashed out with his bound feet and knocked Ruger sprawling.

Val spun and ran for the door, hoping to lure Ruger out into the fields, away from the house, away from Connie, to make him chase her long enough for those blessed sirens to arrive.

Ruger was up in an instant. He didn't waste time punishing Mark but set out after Val like a bird dog, growling in pain and fury. He went after her barehanded, forgetting his knife, forgetting his automatic. He wanted to hurt her with his naked hands.

Leaping off the porch, cradling her arm as best she could, Val ran straight up the road. Through the thunder and the rain, she couldn't hear how close he was.

She ran.

Twice he almost caught her, twice she faked and darted and changed direction, drawing away from him while he was skidding in the mud.

"You bitch!" he howled.

Val ran back toward the house, dodged around a tree, past a parked tractor, then ran along the side of the house toward the backyard, where her father's Bronco was parked. There was a shovel in the back. If she could get to it . . .

She screamed when she felt the tips of Ruger's fingers scrabble at her hair.

Dodging, darting left and then right, she rounded the corner of the house and burst into the backyard.

Bright lights dazzled her, stopping her in her tracks with all the power of a force field. She slipped and fell

Ruger caught her by the hair even as he skidded to a halt, startled by the intense brightness of the headlights of Crow's car.

Chapter 17

Karl Ruger closed his hand tightly, knotting it in Val's hair as he stood tall, facing the harsh white lights. He reached down and around her and clamped his viselike left hand on her windpipe as the driver's door clicked and opened.

Through the lights and the driving rain he could only just make out the figure of a man, a small thin man, rising from the car. The car door slammed, but the man didn't move.

"Val . . . ?" the man called. His voice was distorted as he shouted over the wind.

"Cr—" Val started to yell a name but Ruger's fingers squeezed the sound from her throat and allowed nothing more to pass.

"Just move along, sonny-boy," called Ruger. "This is just a little domestic disturbance. You be on your way."

The slim man shifted uncertainly, again calling out, "Val?"

"I said fuck off! And I mean now!"

"I don't know who the hell you are, pal, but I want you to let the lady go. Right now."

"Fuck you," sneered Ruger.

The slim man reached into the car and flicked off the headlights, and then took a long step forward, raising his right arm as he did so. Lightning made flames dance along the barrel of the Beretta.

"No," said Crow, "fuck *you*." He took two more steps forward. "Now let her go!"

Val saw his face, clear in the lightning flashes, and her heart leaped in her chest. She tried to pull away, wanting to run to him, to take that gun and turn it on Ruger, but Ruger held her fast, pressing her knees into the mud and choking her throat completely closed. She scrabbled at his hands with her one remaining hand, but she might as well have been trying to chip away at a rock. Her lungs wanted to breathe, but he allowed her nothing, not even a cupful of air.

Ruger stared at the gun, not believing what he was seeing. He almost smiled. How could so many fucked-up things happen all in one day? With a snarl he yanked Val to her feet and pulled her in front of him. "Go ahead and shoot, sonny-boy, but you better be a good goddamn shot or you're liable to blow a hole in this young lady."

"As it happens," Crow called, "I am a good goddamn shot." He fired the pistol. The bullet burned the air a foot from Ruger's ear. He jumped and jerked out of the way far too late, but the bullet hadn't been aimed to hit flesh, just pride.

"Now let her go."

Ruger's fingers were digging so tightly into Val's throat that she saw sparks dance in her eyes and the world was taking on a drunken, swimmy feel to it. She was vaguely aware that it was Crow there, but her shocked and oxygen-deprived brain was losing its ability to care.

Crow fired another shot, closer to Ruger's head. Ruger didn't even flinch this time; instead he pulled Val's head up level with his, lifting her onto her toes, using her battered, weeping, strangling face to block his own.

Crow took another step forward, steadying the gun with both hands. Now he was no more than ten feet from Val and Ruger. "That was the last warning shot, Bozo. This baby carries fifteen shots. The next one's going to go up your nose." Even with Val as a shield, Crow knew he could clip the man in the arm or leg, but he didn't want to gamble. He read the darkening of her face and saw the horrible tension in the hand that was clamped around her throat and felt fear and fury lash at him from within. Fear churned his gut into a greasy mush and despite the rain his mouth was bone dry. He swallowed, trying to lubricate his throat.

"I said, let her—"

At that moment, Ruger lunged forward and shoved Val right at Crow. He shoved her with all his force and she went flying. Crow barely had time to bring the gun up, to wrench the barrel away from her. He tried to step forward to catch her, but just as forcefully as Ruger had shoved her he had also thrown himself forward. He used her as a ram as well as a shield, and slammed into Crow with freight-train force. Val's released throat opened as the two bigger male bodies caught her in the press and she screamed.

Suddenly Crow had too much to do. He tried to catch Val as she crumpled, screaming, to the mud; he tried to pull her away from the madman; he tried to bring his pistol to bear; he tried to evade the man's rush.

In all of these things, he failed utterly. Fear of hitting Val and fear of the man himself made Crow hesitate a fraction of a second too long.

Ruger was on him with all of his terrible force and speed and rage bursting forth. He trampled Val as he leaped at Crow, fists swinging. Ruger knew he had no time or chance to wrestle the gun out of this man's hand, so he swatted it away, sending it sailing end over end into rain and muddy darkness. It struck the side of the car with a muffled metallic *clunk!* His forward rush sent Crow tumbling backward, and Ruger rode him down like a surfer setting for a wave. Crow landed on his back and slid, and before the slide had spent itself, Ruger was smashing him with rock-hard fists.

Karl Ruger had only lost one fight in his life. He had been eleven at the time and a sixteen-year-old kid had plain whipped the tar and tears out of him. The teenager had beat him so bad that young Ruger had lain in the street, crying, peeing in his pants, trying to stanch the bright red blood that blossomed from his nose. The older kid had laughed at him and kicked him when he was down, and other kids, most of them older, but some of them his own friends, had watched and laughed.

That was the only fight Ruger had ever lost.

A week later he pushed the sixteen-year-old under the iron wheels of the elevated train, watching with bruised eyes as the bully's body was torn and reduced to red rags.

Since then, no one had ever beaten Ruger. No one had ever even stood up to him for very long. It was the ferocity of his attack. He went into a fight at full speed, not building to it like most people do. Every blow was backed with a deep knowledge of how to hit, and where, and how to hit hard and fast and often. He'd learned that in South Philly bars, in a dozen jails, in back alleys, and in a score of fights he himself had started just to test himself, to learn how good he was. It mattered to him that he was good enough to survive anything that came down the pike. *Anything.* If a person stood up to him, no matter how tough, how big, how well armed, Ruger took him down. All the way down. Down to blood and death and closed coffins.

He went after Crow like that, and tonight he had all his frustrations and disappointments boiling inside him, putting more steel in his fists, stoking the fires of his rage.

Crow toppled under him, and Ruger straddled his waist, locking his legs around Crow's hips for balance, and began the work of beating this man to death. Blood burst from Crow's eyebrow and nose, his cheek ruptured and tore, and the fists never stopped. They kept hitting and hitting.

Then suddenly Ruger was falling!

Crow had brought his knees up, planting his shoes flat on the muddy ground, and then with all his strength and speed, had arched his back and twisted. Ruger was lifted like a rodeo rider on a bucking bull, and as Crow twisted, Ruger's weight pitched him sideways. As they fell, Crow balled up his right fist so that the secondary knuckle of his forefinger protruded, and as they landed he punched Ruger once, twice very hard in the very top of his thigh.

The pain was so intense that it made Ruger howl.

Snarling in pain and surprise, Ruger kicked himself free and rolled catlike to his feet, and Crow came up off the ground at him. Crow faked high with both hands as if to tackle Ruger around the middle and then dropped suddenly to one knee and hooked a sharp uppercut into the tender flesh on the inside of Ruger's thigh, missing his groin by half an inch. Ruger's leg buckled and twisted, and he went back down.

Crow leaped at him, but Ruger kicked out as he fell and the thick heel of his boot caught Crow in the chest and using his leg like a strut, he threw Crow over his head.

Crow tucked and rolled and was on his feet first, spinning and crouching to face Ruger.

Ruger staggered to his feet, ignoring the pain in his leg. His hands opened and closed, opened and closed as if he were squeezing something that would scream.

Ruger's eyes narrowed as he moved. Suddenly it had become a different fight. From a murderous attack—the kind of attack that had worked for him so many times in the past—he now found himself in a real fight. Whoever this guy was, he could fight, and in a twisted way Ruger was actually enjoying it.

They circled each other for a few seconds, making tentative half lunges, feinting, dodging half-thrown blows.

It was Ruger who made the move, and he made it as fast as the lightning that lit the sky. He used a variation on Crow's trick and faked high, then dipped and dove for Crow's legs. The move was an old favorite of his: wrap the legs just above the knees and bear forward. The poor sap goes down hard on his coccyx with two sprained knees to boot.

Crow stepped into the rush, and as Ruger's arms closed like a crab's pincers around his legs, he punched downward in as hard and true a vertical line as a drill press, driving the two big knuckles of his right hand between Ruger's shoulder blades, dropping all his body weight with it to try and break the man's back. It was a devastating blow, but the mud was soft and Ruger was hard. Still, the air went out of his lungs for a moment and he tasted mud in his mouth.

Crow stood over him for a moment, chest heaving, heart

hammering from fear as much as from exertion. He had never seen anyone move so fast or hit so hard or fight with such animal ferocity. He risked a glance at Val, who was on her knees, one hand massaging her throat, he face slack with dizziness and nausea. He tried to give her a reassuring smile, and even opened his mouth to say something, but Ruger abruptly reached up and punched him right in the balls.

Crow screamed and staggered back, cupping his testicles, yet backpedaling to give himself room.

Ruger got to his feet, covered in mud like a *golem*, and he smiled with muddy teeth. "I'm going to fuck you up so bad they'll have to bury you in installments."

"Talk is cheap, dickhead," Crow wheezed. His groin felt as if it were on fire.

Ruger hurled a handful of mud at Crow's face, and followed it with another rush.

Crow was not as hurt as he pretended. A strike to the groin, even a hard one, does little actual damage. It's just pain, and it is the pain that stops most people, but some people don't care as much about pain. They know it, they're used to it; it may not be an old friend, but it is an old companion. Crow was long acquainted with pain, even the pain of a hard punch in the balls. It hurt him, but hurt can be dealt with.

He waited in his half crouch, looking done-in, letting Ruger close the distance, letting Ruger provide the force.

Then he slid in between Ruger's reaching arms and turned half away, catching one of his arms with one hand, and cupping the back of his neck with the other and then pivoted his body as fast as he could. Ruger's force, plus the speed and arc of the turn, plucked Ruger right off the ground and sent him flying right into the driver's door of the big brown Impala. The back of Ruger's head slammed into it and he rebounded with a grunt, leaving a deep dent in Missy's door. He slid down to the ground shaking his head, tried to get to his feet, and fell back again against the door, head lolling.

Crow stepped forward and grabbed him by the hair, hauled him ten inches away from the car so he could look at the man's face, snarled in disgust, and then literally threw him backward into the same dented spot on the fender, ringing his skull off the crumpled metal. Ruger sagged bonelessly to the ground by the tire and lay there in the rain, blood running from his scalp.

Crow looked down at him, watching for signs of trickery. Ruger didn't flicker so much as an eyelash. Just to be sure, and because his battered face was really starting to hurt like a bastard—and because the dread of this man still turned an icy knife of terror in Crow's guts—Crow kicked him in the mouth and shattered all of the man's front teeth.

Ruger fell over sideways, face forward into the mud.

Crow stood there, swaying, feeling his knees wanting to buckle. Fireworks were going off at the corners of his vision and there was something wrong with his head—it felt as if it had been badly broken and poorly taped back together. He wanted to vomit, or collapse. Instead, gasping, holding one hand to his streaming nose, he turned and slogged through the rain and the mud to Val. He swooped down on her, gathering her in his arms, aware of her hurt, her dangling arm, her bruised face, but needing to feel her solidity, her realness in his arms. He showered kisses on her mud-streaked face, kissed her hair and her eyes. She was crying with big, painful sobs, and each one stabbed into Crow as surely as a needle.

"Baby, baby, baby," murmured. "What happened here? What did he do to you? My sweet baby . . ."

Her voice was a strained croak, the vocal cords bruised beyond normal speech. She was still half conscious, swimming on the edge of a big waterfall that wanted to take her over and down into the blackness.

Somewhere, half drowned by rain, the wail of police sirens could be heard, coming, coming . . . The sirens made her remember.

"Daddy!" she cried. "Oh my God, Crow . . . Daddy's out there!"

"What? *Where?*"

"In the cornfield. He needs help. I tried to help him, but I couldn't, Crow, I couldn't . . ." she rambled, hysterical, almost

inarticulate with trauma. It was all catching up to her now, overwhelming her. The iron determination that had kept her steady
earlier was crumbling now as grief and injury took hold.

"Val," Crow said sharply, trying to steady her. "What about
your dad? What's wrong with him? Where is he? What the hell
happened here?"

The sirens were louder, closer.

"In the cornfield. We were helping the hurt man. We tried to
run. I heard a shot. Daddy . . . he . . ."

"Jesus Christ! Did that son of a bitch shoot your father? Is
that what you're trying to say?"

"I tried to help him. I did. But I couldn't . . . my arm . . . I
just couldn't."

"Shh, shh," he soothed. "It'll be okay. Just tell me where he is.
I'll go get him. And see? See there? Cops. There are cops coming. They'll help, too."

"Help?" she asked in a little girl voice that broke Crow's
heart.

"Yes, baby, they'll help. Now tell me where your dad is. Tell
me so I can go help him."

The police cars screeched as they slid to a halt outside the
front of the house, sirens dying away, but the lights swirling red
in the storm. Crow could hear doors opening and slamming. He
turned and in as loud a voice as he could manage, he yelled,
"Hey! Back here! We need help!"

The sloshy sound of footsteps drew near, and Crow could see
flashlight beams dancing. Two officers, still silhouetted behind
the lights, came racing toward them, guns drawn.

"Mr. Guthrie?" one of them called.

"No, it's me. Malcolm Crow. And Valerie Guthrie. Call for an
ambulance, she's hurt."

One cop peeled off and ran back to the car, the other came
and shone a light on them. Close up, Crow recognized Rhoda
Thomas, one of the younger officers.

"Oh my God," Rhoda gasped. "What happened?"

Val's eyes were swimmy with growing shock and all she could
do was shake her head. Crow said, "I don't know what all went

on. When I got here, Val was running from some maniac. He caught her and all but strangled her. I think he must have done something to her arm, be careful with it."

"Where is he?"

Crow jerked his head toward Missy.

Rhoda looked at the slumped figure and frowned. "What happened to him?"

"We had words."

"Who is he?"

"How the fuck should I know? I think he might be one of the assholes you people are looking for. Who knows? Look, we got to check something out. Val said that this clown shot her father. At least I think that's what she said. Out in the cornfield somewhere. We have to find out what's happened."

"Rhoda!" a voice called, and she and Crow turned toward the house. A cop Crow didn't know stood by the side of the house, pointing toward it. "There are two people in here. Man and woman. Man's tied up, and I think the woman's been assaulted. I called for an ambulance."

"Jesus," Rhoda breathed.

"Oh my God! Connie!" Crow looked from Val to the house to the cornfield and back to Val, trying to decide what to do. He bent his face close to Val, kissed her, and whispered in her ear, "Val, baby. I need to find your dad. You've got to tell me where he is. C'mon, baby, try to think."

Val's eyelids fluttered and her eyes went in and out of focus, and slowly, slowly came back to focus. The pain came with the clarity, and she hissed through gritted teeth.

"Shh, shh, just breathe, just breathe," Crow soothed. "Now, baby, where's your dad?"

With her strained vocal cords, and wincing with the waves upon waves of pain, Val told him which path to take, but her voice dwindled and finally failed. Her eyelids fluttered shut and she went down into darkness. Crow held her, kissing her eyes, and then carefully laid her down on the muddy ground. Blood dripped from his torn face onto her lips, but he brushed it away.

He raised fierce red eyes to Rhoda. "I'm going to see if I can find Mr. Guthrie. You stay here. Watch over her. And, Rhoda . . ."

"Yes?"

"Don't let anything happen to her, you got me?"

"Yes. I promise."

Crow stood up slowly, hissing and wincing as he rose. Every inch of him hurt abominably. "You'd better cuff that son of a bitch before he wakes up. Be careful, though—he's one tough bastard."

Rhoda looked past him to where Ruger lay. Crow was looking past her at the house, but in his peripheral vision he could see her eyes snap wide.

"Watch out!" she cried and shoved at him with one hand as she fumbled with her gun with the other. The sound of the Beretta was like summer thunder, and as Crow dove to the ground, he could see blood blossom on Rhoda's chest, seeding the air with bright red petals. She pirouetted away from him, her own gun firing uselessly into the mud, but as she spun the gun came up and around in a fast arc and the heavy pistol crunched into the side of Crow's head.

Crow fell hard and the world seemed to be made of white lightning and thunder and all of it was inside his head. He fought to clear his vision, and saw with horrified eyes the muddy gun—his own gun—clutched in Ruger's bloody fists. The madman stood there, covered in blood, pieces of broken teeth sliding from between his pulped lips, holding the familiar gun. Something burned along Crow's left side and half the air was knocked out of him. He couldn't tell if he had been shot or grazed. His mind froze. He felt like he was facing something that just couldn't be whipped. How could the bastard get up after that beating? How could he have found the gun in all that rain and mud? How could he be stopped? The gun exploded again. Firing, firing.

Crow rolled away, trying to dodge the bullets, and as he turned one hand slapped mud and the other slapped down on Rhoda's wrist. He fumbled, felt the fist, felt the slack fingers releasing from the butt of her gun, felt the gun itself. It all happened in a bizarre slow motion as thunder boomed above him and a smaller, deadlier thunder boomed across the rain-swept yard. Crow clawed the gun into his own hand, swept it up as he rose to a crouch, slipped his finger into the trigger guard. Something hit him on the belt line on his right side, punching hard against the hipbone and spinning him all the way around and flinging his arms straight up in the air as if he were surrendering. The pistol almost flew from his grip. Now both sides of his body were on fire. There wasn't enough air in the world and black fireworks burst in the corners of his eyes. Howling with rage and pain, Crow wheeled around and brought the gun down into a two-handed shooter's grip and even as his knees started to buckle he squeezed hard on the trigger and fired, fired, fired. Ruger danced backward in a crooked jerking series of steps as Crow's bullets hammered into him.

But he did not go down.

Then he heard shouts and saw an oblong of light at the front of the house and a silhouette burst out onto the porch, a gun held in both hands. He, too, fired, but Ruger was moving now, fading back out of the spill of light, staggering in a drunken zigzag toward the vast rolling sea of cornstalks. The officer on the porch kept firing and one of the shots blew Missy's windshield into glittering fragments, but if any of the bullets hit Ruger it was impossible to tell.

Crow's head was spinning and he lurched two steps toward the cornfield before his legs gave out and he dropped heavily onto both knees, the gun still in his right hand, the barrel now pointed straight upward. His eyes rolled up white in their sockets and he sagged onto his back, Rhoda's gun firing up into the night sky, firing at the storm, firing itself dry, and then falling from his hands as darkness swarmed over him and smothered all light.

Chapter 18

I ts work completed, the storm ended.
Snickering and sated, the bruise-dark clouds slouched away
into the west, leaving behind wreckage and an awful stillness.
Cold and dispassionate, the moon was merely an observer in the
sky, vaguely amused at the debris of hurt and suffering below;
indifferent to the things that still crept and capered in the deeper
shadows of the cornfields.

The flocks of night birds boiled out in their ragged flocks
from under dripping trees, littering the sky, their ironic calls lost
within the long and desperate wails of the hastening police
sirens.

Cars began skidding to a stop along the big curved driveway
in front of the Guthrie farmhouse. One after another, lights slash-
ing red and blue and white swords through the shadows. Doors
opened and people erupted from the vehicles, swarming in and
clustering around the fallen bodies, shining lights, opening emergency kits, searching for signs of life, trying to fight the blood
that seemed to flow like fountain water from too many wounds.

Sergeant Ferro pushed brusquely past the gathering crowd of
assorted police officers and squatted down by Rhoda, shoulder
to shoulder with Jerry Head, who was pressing his fingers against
her throat. Head held his breath and watched, exchanging a worried glance with Ferro.

"She's alive."

Ferro turned and shouted, "Get a paramedic over here. Now!"

"Right here, sir," someone said briskly, right at his elbow. "Please step back and give me room."

Head touched Ferro's arm. "Ruger was here, Sarge. I saw him and we exchanged some shots. Positive ID. It was him."

"Where?"

"He ran into the corn."

"You hit him?"

"I . . . think so. Not sure, though. Looks like the guy who was driving that Chevy hit him, though. Ruger shot him as well, I think."

Ferro looked at him, searching his face.

The officer shook his head. "It was really confusing out there. The storm and all . . ."

Terry came slogging through the mud, his face stricken by all the blood and bodies. Everyone looked so damned dead. He didn't know where to look, or how to feel. It was like being in a war.

He spotted Crow and ran to his side. "Medic!" he bellowed as he reached for his friend, touching his throat as he had seen Head do with Rhoda.

Finding nothing.

He turned away in despair and saw Val looking at him. She lay on her side, curled into a tight fetal position, her slim body battered almost beyond recognition, but her eyes were open. She looked into Terry's eyes and read his anguish.

And screamed.

(2)

It was bloody work, and bloody awful.

Time shambled along, dropping discarded minutes as it stumbled toward midnight. The storm buried itself in the distant west, but now a cold, sharp wind blew in from due north, a wind with biting teeth and scratching claws. The workers labored on, shivering with the cold.

Three bodies were lifted off that stretch of muddy ground, carried gingerly by police officers and paramedics. A pair of female officers, Coralita Toombes and Melanie White, helped get Connie Guthrie dressed and took her to the hospital in the back of a police unit; the male officers gave them space, knowing that their presence, their *maleness* would do more harm to the sobbing woman than their badges would do to reassure her. Mark and another officer followed the ambulance. He was dazed and in shock, and lacked even the presence of mind to ask about his father and sister. His entire mind—what little was left online— was focused on his wife.

More patrol cars arrived. More ambulances arrived. The population of the Guthrie farm swelled, and a crop of flashing lights grew all along the road.

Terry Wolfe tried to organize it all, tried to be the mayor, but he felt beaten up and so far beyond weary that he couldn't remember feeling anything else. After a while the tide of events seemed to swirl around and eddy away from him, and he just drifted along, watching, letting the professionals do their work. He bummed a cigarette off Jimmy Castle and LaMastra lighted it for him, offering him a tight, meaningless smile before hurrying away to help Sergeant Ferro. Smoking in deep, steadying lungfuls, Terry walked around the house, walked in and out of the house, walked up and down the drive past the vehicles, trying to be noticed in case he was needed, but hoping that no one would need him for anything.

The three stretchers lay side by side near the ambulances as paramedics made fast the straps and officers moved their vehicles out of the way. Terry stood over them, and then watched as each person was lifted carefully into the back of one of the medivac units.

Rhoda went first, her face gray and still, eyes sunken. A ventilator was fitted over her mouth and huge compresses were taped to the bullet wounds in her stomach and chest; medics had started an IV of Ringer's and were giving rapid-fire medical assessments via microphone to a trauma doctor at Pinelands E.R. Looking at her, Terry felt so sad. She looked like a child, no more than fourteen or fifteen. A law student who just wanted to do some routine police work in a quiet arts community, just to get a feel for that side of the law. *Well,* he reflected bitterly, *how does it feel, kid? Like a nightmare, I imagine.*

They loaded her into the ambulance and closed the door.

Valerie Guthrie was next. She was swathed in bandages, her left arm taped firmly to her body, eyes lightly closed. Every once in a while those eyes would twitch as if she were watching some scary movie in there, and the monsters kept jumping out. Terry hadn't been able to get a single coherent word out of her, and from what the paramedics said, it was probably more shock than injury. Terry wondered why. He didn't much care for Val as a person, had always thought her too hard-shelled, too forthright, but knowing that Crow loved her—and she loved him—made his heart soften toward her. She didn't seem too badly injured, so what the hell could have happened out here to have broken her down like this? He drew deeply on his cigarette as they carried her past and handed her into the ambulance.

The last to be moved was Crow.

His face was crisscrossed with gouges and cuts, dark with bruised flesh and as waxy as a mask. Terry felt tears burning in his eyes as he looked at his friend. He would, he thought, forever relive that dreadful moment when he had searched for the pulse and not found it, and heard Val scream. He wondered if maybe that had pushed her over the edge, and if so, then he was partly responsible for her present situation. How was he to know that he was feeling for the pulse in the wrong place? He was a politician, not a paramedic.

When the real medics had come over and dug their fingers into the carotid arteries and reported that Crow was still alive, Terry felt at once massively relieved and abominably stupid. He had pressed the wrong spot on Crow's neck and had, of course, felt no pulse. He tried to tell Val, to explain and apologize for his mistake, but she had passed out. In shock, the medics told him. Comatose. Out of it for now, and better for it. Terry wondered if that was true. Knowing that Crow was still alive would probably do her a power of good.

Terry touched Crow's face, feeling the iciness of the skin, the slickness of sweat.

"Jesus, Crow . . ." he murmured.

"Bullet graze on the left side," paramedic had reported after a quick examination. "And another on the right of him. Looks like it glanced off his belt."

"Is he going to die?" Terry had asked, dreading the sound of his own words.

The paramedic gave a philosophic shrug and said, "Maybe of old age. Two hits and neither of them much of anything. Damn lucky guy. But he has lost some blood and somebody kicked the living piss out of him. Nice gouge on his head, looks like it might have been a pipe or something. Now, sir, if you'll just step back . . ."

Terry had let them get to work, and now here Crow was, all trussed up and ready to be carted away to the hospital and the surgeon.

"Okay, Jack, we're ready for him," called one of the medics from inside the ambulance. The medic that had first diagnosed Crow as being among the living came over and double-checked the buckles on the straps.

"Okay down here."

The two medics squatted, grabbed either end of the stretcher, and as one lifted Crow with great care and practiced ease.

"Take good care of him," Terry said in his mayor's voice. The medics swapped a quick glance. They heard that sort of thing fifty times a week, as if they would take less care if someone didn't tell them to do it in an officious voice.

"Ouch!" said someone in a loud, complaining voice.

Terry stared.

Crow opened his eyes, looked around, then closed them and sighed. "Oh, shit," he said groggily. "Now what?"

Unbelieving, delighted, Terry crowded the stretcher, touching Crow's arm. "You bloody idiot," he said.

"I love you, too," Crow mumbled hoarsely. He blinked a couple of times. "Christ, was I that drunk?"

"No, you numbskull, you were shot."

Crow's eyes snapped wide and his face hardened as everything came rushing back. "Val!" He tried to sit up but he hit a brick wall of pain and collapsed back down, aided by the hands of the paramedics.

"Shh, shh, she's okay," said Terry. "She's in the other ambulance. They're taking good care of her. She'll be fine."

Breathing out a heavy sigh, Crow said, "Oh, thank God." Darkness welled up in Crow's mind, and he could barely form words. After several false starts, he managed to say, "Terry . . . did I . . . do it?"

"Do what? Did you do what?"

"Did I . . . kill the rotten son of a bitch?"

Terry patted Crow's arm. "From what one of Sergeant Ferro's men said, you two were standing there shooting at each other, you fell down, and when the officer joined in and started to shoot, Ruger ran off."

"Ruger?" Crow's eyes widened. "That was really . . . *him*?"

"Yeah . . . are you impressed with yourself?"

"Damn, Terry, but he was one tough bastard. Almost . . . couldn't take him . . ."

"You *fought* him?"

Crow licked his split lips and then quickly—but disjointedly—told Terry everything that had happened. "We beat the living shit out of each other . . . and then he shot me. Shot that poor girl, too. Rhoda." He grabbed Terry's sleeve. "She dead?"

"No, but she's hurt pretty bad. They took her to the hospital."

"You sure Val's okay?"

"She'll be fine," Terry said, though he felt that he was lying.

Crow saw dark shapes materialize out of the confusion and there were two men standing there. One tall and black and middle-aged, the other taller, white, and younger. They had the cop look about them.

"Mr. Crow?" the black man said.

"What's left of him."

"Do you know what happened here tonight? We can't seem to get a clear picture of the events of—"

"I just got here a few minutes ago, man. Drove up, saw some

asshole attacking my girlfriend, and jumped right in. I . . . don't know much of what else happened."

"You didn't go into the house?"

"No," Crow said and then felt a hand clamp around his heart. "Val's family—"

"Her brother and sister-in-law are on their way to the hospital. Nothing serious."

Crow was relieved for a second, and then realized that the cop hadn't said anything about Val's father.

"What about Henry—Val's dad?" His head was pounding as he tried to remember something Val had tried to tell him. "Jesus Christ! I think he's out in the cornfield. I think he's hurt!"

"Are you sure?"

"Yes! No . . . oh, Christ, I don't know . . . send some fucking guys out there!"

The cops looked at him for a moment and then melted away. He heard them shouting orders.

Crow's body felt like a single huge bruise and his head was swimming. As much as he was trying to keep it together he felt himself fading fast.

He still had Terry's sleeve caught in his fist, and he gave it a shake. "Terry—"

Bending close, Terry said, "Yeah . . . ?"

"Find . . . Henry!" And then the darkness wrapped itself completely around him and he passed out.

Terry leaned back and sighed in frustration and disgust. "Okay, fellas, take him away. When you get to the hospital, tell them that the township is picking up the tab for all this. Oh, and tell Dr. Weinstock that I want him to call me the moment—and I do mean the very moment—that Mr. Crow comes out of surgery." He glared at the ambulance driver, looking every inch of his muscular six-four. "You boys got that?"

They nodded curtly.

"Good, now get a move on."

The ambulance left in as much of a hurry as safety would allow, and Terry watched them go. Then he spun on his heel and called for Detective Sergeant Ferro. The detective was speaking in low, fast tones with LaMastra and looked up as Terry hurried over.

"How's your friend?" Ferro asked.

"He passed out and they're taking him in," Terry said.

"He say anything more about what happened?"

"More or less. He and one of your bad guys went toe-to-toe. Crow says he beat the man in a fight, though from what he said and the way he looks, it was a close call."

"Then it must have been Boyd who Jerry Head saw run off into the corn," LaMastra said. "If your buddy had gone up against Ruger we'd be scraping him up with a spatula."

Terry half smiled. "Maybe, and maybe not. Don't underestimate Crow. He may be a little guy, but he's just about as tough as they come."

"Good fighter, is he?" asked LaMastra.

"Very. I could tell you stories—"

"Maybe later," Ferro interrupted. "What else did he say?"

"Oh, he said that he shot the other man. He was surprised when I told him that Ruger—or whoever—had run off into the fields. He thinks the guy was hit four or five times."

Ferro grunted. "Officer Head also fired at the suspect but isn't sure if he hit him at all. He said he gave him a cursory look, and it appeared that the suspect fit the description of Karl Ruger."

"Nah, had to have been Boyd," LaMastra repeated, shaking his head.

"Either way," Ferro said glumly, his face as lugubrious as an undertaker's, "the man left a lot of wreckage and at the moment we're no closer to catching him than we were an hour ago."

"Mr. Crow must have only thought he'd hit him that many times," offered LaMastra. "In the dark, in the rain, and having taken some hits himself, Mr. Crow wouldn't have been able to really tell. And Jerry was firing from the porch . . . that's what, seventy, eighty feet?"

"More likely he was wearing body armor of some kind," Ferro said. "Anyone can get hold of it these days. The shots might had knocked the wind out of him, knocked him down—but he could have gotten up and run off."

Reluctantly, Terry had to agree.

The three men looked at each other for a while and then looked away into the moonlit fields.

"That means both Boyd and Ruger are still out there," Terry said softly. "And so is Henry Guthrie."

Ferro sniffed and pointed his chin at the darkened corn. "We're combing those fields now. If Mr. Guthrie—or anyone else—is out there, we'll find him."

They stood there in silence for a while as the cops and crime scene investigators and paramedics swarmed around them, and neither they nor all of the dozens of cops, techs, or EMTs saw the slim form of a man with pal gray skin, a dark suit, and a blues guitar slung over one shoulder standing by the edge of the cornfield. Every time the lightning flashed, the shadows it cast of the tall corn fell not on him, but through him.

Chapter 19

He lay dying in the dark.

The blood wormed its way out of him, soaking through his clothes, seeking the earth below his back, letting the hungry soil feed on him. Overhead the moon looked down at him with typical cold intensity, and stars littered the fringes of the sky. A night bird cawed plaintively somewhere in the corn; other sounds troubled the darkness: sirens, men shouting, car engines roaring as vehicles came and left.

He knew he was still too close to the house, safe only with the cover of darkness and the fact that they didn't know in which direction he'd gone. He couldn't linger here. Soon they would be finished with those assholes back at the house. Soon they would be after him with flashlights and maybe even with dogs.

"Fuck!" he growled softly.

He had to get up, he knew that.

But lying there was better for now.

It wasn't the pain that kept him from rising: Karl Ruger knew everything there was to know about pain, and he'd kicked pain's sorry ass too many times to sweat that now.

No, it was the hate. Hate had put the steel in his legs that let him stagger away from that mean little bastard he'd gone toe-to-toe with, bullet holes and all. Hate had driven him at least this far away from the cops and all the activity. Hate had kept him awake when the damage and the spigot-flow of blood wanted to lull him down into a drowse that he knew would kill him.

Hate made him patient, too.

The hate wanted him to live, not die. The hate wanted him to find some way of staying awake, staying strong staying alive long enough to get help, to force help. It was only hate that had given him the patience to stuff his torn shirt into the bullet holes, and kept him from screaming while he did so. That hadn't stopped the flow of blood, but it had slowed it.

The hate was wise, too. It knew that if he didn't rest, just for a while, then he would die on his feet and the bastards would win. The bastards would prove that they were stronger than he was. There was no way in hell that Karl Ruger was going to let that happen. His hate was the power that had always kept his black heart beating. It was what kept the vinegar that pumped through his veins cold and fast. It was what made his mouth smile and his tongue water whenever he saw the fear of him that was always there in other people's eyes. The hate was Ruger's secret self, defining him, completing him. Now it protected him, teaching him the secret of how to survive this long and nasty bitch of a night.

More than all of this, his hate was his one and only god. A dark god that nightly listened to his blasphemous prayers, offering not absolution, but permission, encouragement, enticement.

Lying there, dying, bleeding, trying to gather together the power to rise once more and move, he prayed in his own way for strength.

He prayed for the strength to live long enough to find that little bastard and kill him. Slowly, painfully. Artfully. He prayed for the strength to find that broken-nose country bitch and teach her some big-city manners. His own kind of manners. He prayed for the strength to hurt them all. Hurt them so bad and so deep that even if they did somehow live past his revenge, they would beg for no new tomorrows. He prayed for the strength to find Boyd, and his money, and to make Boyd sorry that his father had ever fucked his mother. To make him sorry that the thought of betraying Karl Ruger had ever wormed its way into his tiny brain. To make Boyd sorry that he hadn't been simply killed during the drug buy back in Philly.

He prayed for the strength to be all things in all ways to them that were as dark as the utter darkness in his heart.

Above him the cloud-free sky rumbled with improbable thunder, like an old echo of the storm come rolling round again.

Ruger, you are my left hand.

The words rang suddenly in his head, clear and strong as if someone had spoken them aloud.

Karl Ruger lay there in the cornfield, feeding the soil with his life and his hate and his black prayers.

In the vastness of the night that overhung the cornfields, something stirred. Something that heard Ruger's secret murmurings and the rage-filled screaming of his soul; something that had been given life by the same force that had crash-landed Karl Ruger in Pine Deep. The thing rose from where it had crouched, dragging horror with it, and slouched through the fields toward the place where Ruger lay, a missionary of hell coming in answer to those prayers.

(2)

Where was Val? Hadn't she been there a while ago? Henry thought she had, but now he couldn't remember. Maybe it had been a dream.

Where was Mark? Mark would help him. Mark was strong, he could carry him back to the house, get an ambulance for him.

Mark . . . ? he thought he called out, but the word echoed only in his head and he knew that he hadn't found the power to say his son's name out loud.

Henry Guthrie closed his eyes again, the lids pressing tears out from under the lashes.

Please, God, he prayed. *Please, God . . .*

He wanted to say the words out loud. Maybe they would have more power that way, but he was slipping away from that, or any other, ability, sliding down into a long and formless darkness. He tried to conjure images of Val and Mark and Connie, but his mind was going blank, and it broke his heart.

Please, God, he begged. *Help them.*

Something rustled the corn near where he lay, and Guthrie managed to open his eyes; it was like jacking up a truck. He searched the shadows with his failing vision, hoping, hoping . . .

But it was not Val come back to help him; it wasn't Mark. It was a stranger. The man walked slowly toward him and stopped, standing over him. He had a face as gray as the mist that was starting to form in among the cornstalks. His cheap suit was soaked and rainwater glittered like diamonds in his kinky hair.

Guthrie tried to speak, and found he could manage, just a single word: "Who . . . ?"

The man lowered himself slowly to the ground, sitting cross-legged by Guthrie's side.

"I won't hurt you, Henry," said the gray man.

". . . who?" Guthrie croaked.

"Just an old friend. I just come to wait with you awhile."

". . . need . . . help . . ."

The Bone Man shook his head sadly. "No, Henry, no. It's too late for that. I'm sorry."

Guthrie closed his eyes for a moment, feeling the emptiness overwhelm him.

When he opened his eyes, he expected the man to be gone, a phantom conjured by his dying brain. The gray man sat there still.

"Val . . . ?" Guthrie forced the word out past all weakness. He needed to know, but dreaded the answer.

"She's alive."

"Mark?"

"Mark, too. And Connie. All of them. Alive."

"Thank . . ." Guthrie began, but it took him a long time to finish. ". . . God."

The Bone Man had no response to that, but his face looked so much sadder. He pulled his guitar around and laid it across his thighs.

Guthrie tried to raise a hand, tried to touch this man. Seeing the feeble attempt, the gray man took his hand and held it. His long fingers were even colder than Guthrie's numb and blood-less skin.

"Who . . . are . . . you . . . ?" Guthrie asked. "Do I . . . do I know . . . you?"

A small sad smile drifted across the Bone Man's lips. "You did. A long, long time ago," he said in a distant voice. "You were kind to me once. You were kind to me when no one else was."

"I . . . don't remember . . ."

"Maybe you will. Soon. But right now, just rest, Henry." The gray man's face looked so sad, and a single silver tear gathered in the corner of his eyes. "It's time to sleep now. Just let it all be. You're done with it now. Just go to sleep, Henry. Just go to sleep."

Guthrie's eyes had been drifting shut and his hand sagged loosely in the Bone Man's grip. Guthrie seemed to sigh and then he settled back against the ground, the tension of fighting for words and breath easing.

The Bone Man sat with him for a while, still holding the slack hand. Then he bent forward and kissed Henry Guthrie on the forehead. The tear that had gathered in his eye spilled and a single silvery drop splashed down on Guthrie's face. The Bone Man touched the spot where the tear had landed and then he picked up his guitar and began to play softly.

"Good night, Henry," he whispered as the long, cold wind of the void blew past them both and lifted the sound of the blues up to heaven.

(3)

Karl Ruger felt the darkness closing in, and he cursed it.

But this darkness wasn't to be cursed; it was the answer to the curses his soul and his hate and his rage had invoked.

The darkness was not formless. It shambled out of the shadows and stood over him, looking down on him, immensely powerful against the distant moon.

Ruger gasped as he looked up at the thing, trying to calculate its outline, silhouetted against moon and stars. Arms, legs, the body of a man—but the head was all wrong. The head had night-mare proportions, and as the thing bent toward him, Ruger could see it had a long and crooked mouth, a mouth that smiled and smiled. It was the misshapen head of a jack-o'-lantern, carved with a wicked grin and burning eyes.

Ruger looked into the eyes that he could finally see: eyes that burned like coals, eyes that *knew* things. The creature reached for him, clamping iron fingers around Ruger's arms and lifting him bodily off the ground. Pain shot through him, but Ruger didn't care, didn't even notice. His whole mind was fixed on the face of horror that leered at him out of the darkness, the face of horror that bent close to his own until he could feel the hot breath of hell blown sourly into his own mouth, up his nose. The thing's body seemed to writhe and ripple, the clothes bulging and stirring. As Ruger watched, a few insects crept out from between folds of the old suit, and then scuttled back inside. The hands that held him did not feel like human fingers: they were strong, but something was wrong with them. They also rippled in a way Ruger could not understand, as if what was inside was not skin and bone but was instead composed of thousands of separate parts that writhed and scuttled under the cloth. Even he—dissipated, dying, and evil as he was—shuddered at the creature's touch.

Yet Ruger did not fight against the thing that held him; wouldn't, even if he had the power. This was not something he could fight, his rage told him that, but more importantly, this was not something he *should* fight. Not this thing.

Ruger, you are my left hand. Again he heard those words echo in his brain.

Perhaps it was in that moment that Ruger began to understand why he had delayed leaving the Guthrie farm, and why he had let Tony drive the car. Those choices had worked to bring him to Pine Deep, and to keep him here. As the tide of events had swept along tonight he had sensed that some stronger purpose was having its way with him, that some will—stronger even than his—was putting things in motion.

Ruger, you are my left hand.

Now Ruger thought he understood, and he accepted what was happening. Welcomed it. The thing that held him in the darkness bent to his accepting ear and whispered terrible secrets in his dying ear.

After a long time, the night birds were driven to startled flight by the sound of Karl Ruger's wild laughter.

PART III

Dry Bone Shuffle

Black ghost is a picture, black ghost is a shadow, too.
Black ghost is a picture, black ghost is a shadow, too.
You just see him, but you can't hear him talkin',
Ain't nothing' else a black ghost can do.
—Lightning Hopkins, "Black Ghost Blues"

Tombstone is my pillow,
cold ground is my bed.
—Blind Willie McTell

I got an axe-handled pistol on a graveyard frame
that shoots tombstone bullets, wearin' balls and chain.
I'm drinking TNT, I'm smoking dynamite,
I hope some screwball start a fight.
—Muddy Waters (after Willie Dixon), "I'm Ready"

Chapter 20

Malcolm Crow was deep down in the darkness and for a long time he did not dream at all, not while they brought him into the E.R. and then up to surgery. He did not dream while they pumped him full of drugs and stitched and swabbed and bandaged his body. He did not dream while he lay in post-op, or for the first few hours after they brought him up to his room.

It was only later, as the last of the night was wearing thin and dawn was coloring the edges of the horizon, that his mind finally gave way and he dreamed . . .

. . . he was walking through the town and Pine Deep was burning. Many of the stores were blackened shells with their windows blown outward by the heat. Smoke curled upward from the open doorways. The pavement was littered with a smudged scattering of broken bricks, twisted metal awnings, and millions of shards of broken glass.

Crow walked down the center of Corn Hill. He was dressed in jeans and sneakers and a T-shirt and his clothes were torn and stained with grass and soot and blood. Some of the blood, he knew, was his own; most of it was not. Some of the blood was strangely dark and thick, and it smelled like rotting fish.

He carried a samurai sword in one hand; the blade was smeared with gore and bent in two places. The sword hung limply from his right hand, the blunted tip tracing a twisted line behind him in the ash that covered the street.

Above him the sky was as black and featureless as a tarp thrown across the top of the town, and yet he knew that above the black nothing of the clouds there was a moon as white and grim as a bleached skull.

As he walked down the street, weaving in and out between burning cars, Crow was drawn to the sweet sound of a blues guitar. He strained to hear the song and had to hum a few bars to lock it down. "Hellhound on My Trail." The old Robert Johnson song but played with a different take on the refrain . . . less threatening, more wistful.

No, that wasn't it. The sound wasn't wistful, it was sad, like a lament, and as he walked Crow, sang the words.

> *"Blues falling down like hail, blues falling down like hail.*
> *Mmm, blues falling down like hail, blues falling down like hail.*
> *And the day keeps on remindin' me,*
> *there's a hellhound on my trail.*
> *Hellhound on my trail, hellhound on my trail."*

The music played on and on until the song ended, but then the same song started up again. Crow walked all the way up to the top of Corn Hill and finally stopped at the entrance to the Pinelands College Teaching Hospital. The hospital parking lot was a shambles. Cars were on fire and overturned. An ambulance leaned on two wheels against a police car, crushing the car down onto flat tires. There were hundreds of bodies everywhere.

Crow looked at the bodies and his heart turned to stone in his chest.

He knew them.

He knew every one of them.

Henry Guthrie sat with his back to a crushed Ford Bronco, his chest peppered with red bullet holes. A few feet away Terry Wolfe lay facedown on a massive and ornately framed mirror, its surface cracked and distorted; none of the images reflected in the

shards were of Terry's face. The image the broken mirror fragments showed was the face of some huge dog. Across the en-
tranceway from where he stood, Mike Sweeney, the kid who
delivered his paper, lay with a samurai sword through his chest.
Crow looked down at his hand and saw that the sword he carried was now gone. There were so many others he recognized.
Friends from town . . . other store owners . . . farmers . . . teach-
ers from the college . . . staff from the hospital . . . cops. He
knew them all. Or, almost all. There were four bodies he couldn't
put names to, though he felt he ought to know their names.
One was a short, chubby young guy who lay in cruciform, his
legs straight and arms out to each side. In one hand he held a
tape recorder and in the other he held a gun, but the gun was
fake. Near him was a very tall black woman who must have
once been beautiful but not anymore. She had been savaged by
someone. Something. There was so little of her left. Sickened and
sad, Crow looked away. Two men lay propped against the wheels
of a police car. One was middle-aged and black, the other was
younger and white. Both of them had badges looped around
their necks on cords and both had guns lying near them. The
right hand of the black man and the left hand of the white man
were stretched out toward each other and clasped. To Crow it
didn't look like a romantic grasp, but more like the way soldiers
might grip each other in the last moments of a firefight gone
bad. Crow felt he should know them, and felt sad that they were
dead, but he could find no names for them, and so he moved on
through the debris and through the dead.

He looked around, looking for Val . . . needing to find her,
but needing not to find her like this.

He walked to the entrance of the hospital and peered inside.
There was blood everywhere, and bodies. The slaughter was too
horrible to grasp and so Crow's mind went a little numb and he
stared through it, just needing to find Val.

He was about to step across the threshold when a voice behind him said, "Don't do it, little Scarecrow."

Crow turned, startled by the voice. No one had called him
Scarecrow in years. Not since he'd been a little kid.

There was a man there. He sat on the hood of a burned-out Saab, his bony legs crossed and a guitar lying across his thighs. His face was the color of coffee with just a small drip of milk in it—and Crow knew that this was how the man once described himself—and he wore his hair in a late 1970s style Afro. The man wore brown work pants and a white cotton shirt unbuttoned halfway down his thin chest. There were small pink scars on the man's chest and on his hands. His hands were very large for so thin a man.

Crow looked at him.

"You don't want to go in there, Scarecrow," said the man. He was smiling, but his smile was sad.

"I have to find Val," Crow said.

"Yeah, you do," agreed the man. "But you don't want to go into that hospital. Val ain't in there . . . and you don't want to meet what is in there. Believe me when I tell you." The guitar player had a strong Mississippi drawl, and it was deep and soft and Crow liked the sound of it.

"I know you, don't I?" he said.

"Yeah, boy, you did. An' I'm sorry as all hell to tell you that you're probably gonna have to get to know me again."

"Were we friends?" Crow said. His voice sounded dreamy and on some level he knew that meant that the dream was coming to an end.

"Yeah, little Scarecrow . . . I guess we was at that."

"Do you know where Val is?"

"Yeah, I know, but she ain't here, man. You gonna have to keep looking for her. You gotta find her, man, 'cause these is evil times and she's the heart. You may be the fist, but she's the heart. Do you understand what I'm saying?"

Crow shook his head.

"Do you remember . . . a long time ago I told you something about good and evil?"

"I . . . don't remember."

"Don't worry, you will. Now, listen close, little man," the man said and leaned forward over his guitar, his voice dropping to a whisper, "you gotta know this."

Crow leaned closer, too.

"Evil . . . it don't never die," the bluesman said and looked left and right before adding. "Evil don't die. It just waits."

"I don't understand."

"Yeah, you do, but you don't want to understand." The man leaned back and laughed. "Hell's a-coming, little Scarecrow. Hell's a-coming and we all gotta learn to play the blues. 'Cause you know . . . it's all the blues, man." He grinned and strummed his strings. "Everything's always about the blues."

Crow drifted on into another dreamless place, but the sound of the blues followed him.

(2)

Outside the hospital window the dawn had given way to brilliant sunshine and a warm breeze out of the southeast. The rain had scrubbed the air clean and standing in the window of Crow's room, Terry could see for miles. He hardly remembered seeing a morning so clear. Birds were singing, the nurses who came and went were smiling, and everything had a veneer of freshness and vitality.

Terry loathed it. He personally felt dirty and grubby and old. His clothes were a mess, his hands shook, and when he'd gone into the little bathroom to throw water on his face his reflection looked like a street person. He popped a Xanax and shambled back into Crow's room and sank down into the chair.

Crow had awakened around dawn and Terry had filled him in on most of the night's events, but as he talked Crow's eyes kept drifting shut and Terry had no idea how much of it his friend had absorbed. A nurse came in, woke Crow up, and then gave him a sedative—a hospital policy Terry had never quite grasped the logic of—and Terry sat by the bedside and watched Crow sleep, feeling wretchedly guilty.

He felt that by sending Crow to the hayride he'd somehow been party to Ruger's attack on the Guthries. Maybe if Crow had just gone out to Val's as he'd planned Henry would still be alive and the rest of the Guthrie family—*and* Crow—would not be in various rooms in this hospital. On the surface he knew that such thinking was absurd, that no one could really ascribe any of the blame to him, but his deeper self refused to let go of the notion, and for that reason he could not bring himself to leave Crow's side.

As he sat there he wondered how long he would have to wait before he popped another Xanax. The first one was really not doing him much good and he was using every ounce of his willpower not to scream.

(3)

There was nothing rewarding about waking up, so Crow gave it up and passed out again. He slept for hours and dreamed that someone was sitting by his hospital bed, playing blues to him on a sweet-sounding old slide guitar.

A couple of hours later he gave it another try and opened his eyes. This time the pain in his head wasn't quite so sharp, and the nausea seemed to have ebbed—but every other part of his body hurt like hell, and his entire waist felt constricted and on fire.

He jacked open one eye and peered around until he saw Terry Wolfe sprawled in an orange plastic chair a few feet away. Terry had his ankles crossed and propped up on a small table, thick arms folded across his chest. His tie hung limp, his red hair was badly combed, and he looked like he'd slept in his suit in an alleyway. He had a copy of the *Black Marsh Sentinel* folded on his lap. "Good morning," he said.

"Ug," Crow said with a dry throat. "You're a picture to wake up to."

Terry's smile made him look old and thin and miserable. "How d'you feel?"

"Like shit."

"That's pretty much how you look."

"What time is it?"

"Almost ten," Terry said, then added, "In the morning."

"You been here all night?"

"No," Terry said, gesturing at his clothes, "as you see I went home and changed into my best dinner jacket."

Crow licked his dry lips and Terry took the cup of ice water off the bedside table and held the straw up to him. Crow sipped, sighed, sipped again, and then nodded.

"Don't get used to me waiting on you," Terry said, replacing the cup. As he sat down again he peered assessingly at Crow. "You faded out on me earlier. Don't know what you heard or didn't hear."

"About what happened? I dunno." His faced clouded as he tried to think through the cobwebs. He gave a sad sigh as the pieces fell back into place. "Ah, jeez," he murmured. "I know Henry's dead. And Val, Mark, and Connie are all here in the hospital. Remind me again . . . does Val know about her dad?"

"Yeah," Terry said. "I told her last night, but she was wired to the eyeballs with morphine, so I had to go through it again this morning. She took it as well as somebody can, but that isn't saying much. She's pretty torn up."

"When will they let me in to see her?"

Terry shook his head. "I asked Saul Weinstock earlier, but he said that you shouldn't get out of bed for at least a full day. Besides, they have her pretty heavily sedated. I think letting her rest would be a greater kindness, Crow."

Crow nodded, but he didn't like it. "I can't believe that son of a bitch got away. This is too weird for me, man. I feel like I dreamed all this shit. When I woke up this morning—I think I must have been coming out of the recovery room—I thought I was back in my drinking days and waking up after a bender. I still feel like I'm half in the bag." *And, God, could I use a drink right now!* he thought, aching for a Jack Daniel's neat and an icy schooner of Sam Adams.

"Almost be nice if that's all it was."

"How's that officer? The one who was shot? Rhoda?"

Terry frowned. "She's alive, doing okay. They took a couple of slugs out of her, but she's young and that'll probably count for something."

"What about Val's family?"

Shadows drifted across Terry's face and he rubbed his eyes. "Connie was roughed up pretty badly. Not raped, thank God, but smacked around and terrorized. They admitted her and she's still under sedation. Mark's here, too. He has a broken nose, lost two teeth, and is suffering from shock, but he'll be fine."

"Jesus. No trace at all of Ruger?"

Terry drew in a breath, held it, and then blew it out. He shook his head. "Nope. They didn't find a single trace of him except some footprints that went nowhere and then vanished into some mud puddles and that was that. I mean, Val backed up your story that it was definitely Karl Ruger, which the cops are finding hard to take. They can't wrap their minds around the idea that you were able to fight him, or that you shot him. As far as that goes, by the way, the general consensus is that either you missed, or that he was wearing a vest of some kind and all your shots did was bang him around a little and then drive him off."

"That son of a bitch," he said in a soft hiss. "I should have killed him with my hands. I should have made sure. It's my fault that kid Rhoda got shot, and it's my fault Henry's dead. If I'd killed him, then we might have gotten to Henry in time."

"Oh, give it a rest, Crow," Terry said wearily. He rubbed his red-rimmed eyes. "Last night you did more than anyone else, so skip the what-ifs. Right now you have to focus on getting well and on being there for Val. She's in pretty rocky shape." He tried on a smile but it didn't seem to fit. "Besides, you've survived two gunshots and lived to ride off into the sunset like a real hero."

"Oh, big deal. A graze on one love handle and a bullet graze on my hip. Even the recovery room nurse told me it was nothing. Five measly stitches and a bone bruise."

"For which you should thank your lucky stars. Couple inches over and it would have punched a big hole in your kidney. Plus you look like you've been mugged by a whole platoon of prize-fighters."

Crow gave a rueful smile. "Yeah, there's that. Jeez-zus, but that son of a bitch could hit. Hardest fists I ever felt. Fast, too."

"Don't forget, you have another eight or nine stitches on your ugly mug, not counting those pansy little butterfly stitches. Your face looks like a tropical sunset. You'll look great when the news guys come in to take your picture."

"My picture? What for?"

"Dude, you've become quite the celebrity."

"For what? Standing too close to a coupla bullets?"

"No, for kicking the bejesus out of Karl Ruger."

"As I remember, he kicked some of the bejesus out of me, too."

"Mm-hm, but from what Val told us and the police were able to piece together from the crime scene, you canced Ruger real good."

Crow just grunted. "He was choking Val, and I made the mistake of trying to hold him at gunpoint. He used her as a shield to knock the gun out of my hand. We tussled some, and I came out lucky. In a manner of speaking."

Terry smiled and looked up at the heavens, reciting, " '. . . We tussled some and I came out lucky.' Dear me but those Philly cops are gonna love that." He looked at Crow, his eyes amused but intense. "You have, I believe, the distinction of not only being the first person to kick his butt in a fight, but the only person he's tried to kill who's still sucking air."

"Sucking it through a tube, mind you," Crow said, tapping the line that fed cool oxygen into his nose.

"The point is," Terry said, lacing his hands behind his head, "that you kicked his behind and the cops think you're Superman."

"So, what did I get shot with? A kryptonite bullet?"

"According to Detective Sergeant Ferro, you must have."

"Great, when the nurse comes in I'll check out her bod with my X-ray vision."

"Go ahead, she looks like Steve Buscemi."

"And . . . who is Detective Sergeant Ferrell, or whatever?"

"Philly cop," Terry said and explained the interjurisdictional arrangement.

Crow leaned back and stared up at the ceiling for a long moment, overwhelmed by the enormity of it all. He ached to see

Val, to hold her and do something to try and comfort her. "Jesus. One man did all this?"

"Uh-huh."

"Um . . . weren't there supposed to be three of them?"

Terry sucked his teeth. " 'Were' is the operative word, boyo. One of them—Kenneth Boyd—is unaccounted for. Mark said that Ruger told them he had an injured buddy out in the fields, but he never showed up, and nobody's been able to find him."

"Maybe he took a hike when he heard all the sirens and stuff."

"That's the talk around the shop. Took the money and lit out for parts unknown. He was supposed to have a broken leg, but then we only have Ruger's word for it, so take that for whatever it's worth. Either way, the cops aren't as worried about him as they are about Ruger."

"What about the third guy?"

"He's dead."

"Cops get him?"

Terry hesitated briefly. "No. They think Karl Ruger killed him. Possibly over a dispute about the split, who knows? Point is, Ruger messed him up pretty bad."

"What's 'pretty bad' mean?"

"You don't want to know."

Crow saw the green creeping into Terry complexion, and realized that the mayor had seen the body. He didn't pursue it. "So, then the manhunt is still on."

"Uh-huh, and stronger than ever. We're hip-deep in cops. We even reinstated a dozen local boys."

"Oh? Like who?"

Terry recited a list of names.

"Mm," said Crow doubtfully. "I'd classify them more as 'warm bodies' than cops. Most of them aren't much good for this sort of thing, wouldn't you say?"

"I agree, but they know the turf, and they can drive a police car. A couple aren't too bad. Jack Tunny's okay. Eddie Oswald's a stand-up guy, though."

"For a Bible thumper."

"He was a good officer and stayed by the book. And B.B. Harrison's not too wretched. We've paired each of our locals with one of the cops from Philly, and we have a few loaners from Black Marsh and Crestville. The Philly cops were supposed to be meeting with some FBI types half an hour ago, so pretty soon we'll have everyone but the National Guard on the job."

"Wow. All trying to arrest one man."

"Tell you the truth, I really don't think anyone is really going to try too hard to arrest this Ruger character. I think this has gone all the way over into a 'shoot on sight' kind of thing. Or, rather, shoot to kill."

Crow grunted. "Maybe they should drive a stake through his heart, too."

"Maybe." Terry rubbed his eyes again and sighed.

"You know, man, you look about as bad as I do."

Terry smiled weakly. "Well, aside from the fact that I haven't had a good night's sleep in weeks, the crop blight, Halloween, and Karl Ruger . . . I'm just peachy."

"Yeah." Crow studied Terry's face. "Any troubles with you and Sarah?"

"Hm? Oh, heck no, nothing like that. Sarah's the best. No, it's just that I've been having really bad dreams lately. I told you about it yesterday. Very vivid, very intense."

Crow frowned. "Hunh."

"Whyfore the 'hunh'?"

"I've been having nightmares, too. Real corkers."

They looked at each other for a moment, and just as Terry was about to say something, the door opened and a nurse came in. Crow glanced at her. She did look like Steve Buscemi, but not as pretty. The nurse pointed a finger at Terry and said, "Out."

Terry blinked in surprise. "Me?"

"You. Vamoose."

"You do realize," he said, "that I'm the mayor of this town."

"I'll faint later, but for right now get out." She turned and glared at Crow. "It is time for your vitals."

"But I—"

She gave him a stern glance, fiercer than anything Crow had

seen on Ruger's face. Terry and Crow exchanged a brief, help-less look, and Terry got up. Behind the nurse's back, he raised his right hand and mouthed, "Sieg heil!" and then crept out. When Crow opened his mouth to say good-bye to his friend, the nurse stuck a thermometer in it.

(4)

No one laughed at the joke, so Dixie MacVey tried it again. "I said . . . you guys look like a police lineup." He chuckled for them, hoping it would encourage them. It didn't. The gathered officers just stared at him, unamused and unmoved. They all stood in a relatively straight line, their assorted uniforms a mix of local gray, big-city blue, and state-police black. "Get it? A *police* lineup."

"We get it," Officer Shanks said tiredly.

"Jeez, you guys got no sense of humor."

Officer Jerry Head snorted. "You're right, we all ought to be laughing our asses off. Everything is so carefree and funny."

"Hoo-ha," added Toombes. "I better watch so I don't bust a gut."

"Okay," called Ferro as he rose from behind Gus Bernhardt's desk, "knock it off and listen up." The officers straightened up and MacVey, sulking, joined the line.

"Sorry we don't have enough chairs for everyone," Bernhardt said from where he sat by the door. The uniformed officers stood in their lineup, hands at their sides or clasped behind them in the manner of parade rest. Polk and MacVey sat on folding chairs and LaMastra sat on the ledge of the window bay. Ferro looked down the row, recognizing some of the faces from last night, but seeing plenty of new faces as well, more new ones than old ones.

"Okay, ladies and gentlemen, I want to thank you all for being here. I know some of you are not actively working in the law enforcement field, but the fact that you were willing to be reactivated as part-time officers is commendable. Again, thanks."

The eighteen new recruits nodded. "All right, well, here's the scoop. We were able to borrow some patrol cars from neighboring towns, so that means that most of you will be able to go right out and join in the search. After I take roll, you folks will get your unit assignments. I had a crate of Kevlar vests brought up from Philly, and I think there are enough to go around. Everyone who goes out wears one, is that clear? Good. Every officer is to have his or her sidearm cleaned and loaded. No mistakes, no heroics, and no sloppy police work. We are all professionals, and we don't often have to prove how really good we can be. This, however, is one of those times. This is a very dangerous man. This man has killed without hesitation or remorse. He has gunned down innocent citizens, as well as law officers. Don't take any chances. I don't want you to investigate a cat up a tree without backup. Is that understood? Good. We have one officer down right now, as well as one reactivated officer. We've already seen what Karl Ruger is capable of doing to one of his own gang—imagine what he would be willing to do to one of you."

The speech was more for the locals but Ferro's hard stare ranged slowly over every face in the lineup, meeting each set of eyes in turn. The officers he'd brought with him from Philly each met his gaze; Head even nodded to him. Most of the local officers could only meet that glare for a few seconds before their eyes faltered and found something less intense to look at. One of the reactivated men, a big blond bruiser with a broad, almost simian face and long muscular arms, did meet his eyes, and returned intensity for intensity. Ferro thought he looked tough and clear-headed, and wondered if he'd been military, perhaps even M.P. "Any questions?"

No one moved for a few seconds; then the big blond officer held up his hand. "I have a question, sir."

"Your name?"

"Edward Oswald, reactivated volunteer, sir."

"Okay, what's your question, Officer Oswald?"

"This man, this Karl Ruger . . ."

"Yes?"

"Well, sir, the rumors have been flying all over the station house about him. The others said that this man is supposed to be the Cape May Killer. Is that straight?"

Ferro pursed his lips. "It is a possibility, but no more than that."

Oswald gave him a flat stare. "Sir, I don't mean any disrespect, but if this fellow is the Cape May Killer, shouldn't we know about it? I know we're only temporary cops, but we're still going to be the ones out there, the ones who might have to face him. Shouldn't we know everything about who we might be up against?" There were some faint and discreet murmurs of agreement.

It took Ferro a long five seconds to make his decision. He looked at Gus, who just spread his hands. "Okay, that's fair enough, but let me say this. You people took an oath, however temporary. You are bound by policies of confidentiality, and I want each of you to respect that. For the moment, we can't allow the full facts about this case to come out. There are reasons. Are we clear about that?" They all thought about it, then nodded. "Right, then. Okay, Karl Ruger is wanted for questioning in the Cape May Lighthouse killings. He is not only the prime suspect, he is the *only* suspect. Am I going to come out and say that he is the Cape May Killer? No, but I would be one very surprised cop if it turned out to be anyone else. Does that answer your question, Officer Oswald?"

"Yes, sir, it surely does."

"Okay then? Any further questions? No? Okay then, listen up for your names and patrol assignments," Ferro said loudly. "Officer Burke . . . ?"

(5)

All through the long night and longer day they gave her sedatives and each time she tried to fight the drugs, tried to fight the tentacled pull of sleep; and each time she finally lost the battle and was pulled beneath the surface. Val Guthrie didn't want to be down there in the darkness. Time and again she would swim upward toward the faint and distant light; time and again she would lose her way and sink back into the darkness. It hurt less in the darkness, but she wanted the light.

There in the dark Karl Ruger smiled at her from out of the shadows. He chased her endlessly though the black stalks of corn, his eyes burning with a hellfire red and his wet teeth glistening and sharp. He chased her and reached for her with impossibly long arms, tore at her with improbably sharp fingers. And as she ran, she would stagger past the bleeding and dying body of her father. No matter which route she took, no matter how far she ran, she would always find him again, lying there, broken, bleeding, face streaked with tears and rain and mud and blood. Every time she stumbled past, her father would reach imploringly for her, his voice pleading with her to stop and help him, to save him. He begged her to get him out of the cold rain, called her name with a mouth that bubbled with fresh blood.

Always she ran on, knowing that Karl Ruger was right behind her.

When she managed to get to the light, to come awake for whatever period of time fatigue and morphine would allow, the specter of Karl Ruger lagged behind, losing her in the maze of cornfields. Yet when she felt herself falling away once more in the darkness, Karl Ruger would be waiting.

It was the chime of the distant bell on City Hall Tower that woke her, a sound she shouldn't have been able to hear through the distance and the thickness of walls and windows. With each chime, she came one increment closer to the light, one increment further from the darkness and the pursuing monster.

At the tenth chime she was fully awake. The room around her became a realness of machines beeping, tubes dripping, metal gleaming, flowers scenting the air. The tenth chime seemed to echo in her head, and for a few moments she lay there, extending her senses into her corporeal body, feeling the damage and feeling thankful for its realness and weight up there in the light.

There was a soft knock on the door, and after a few tries she managed to find her voice, still weak and hoarse from the assault on her throat.

"Come in!"

She could barely turn her head with the cervical collar, but out of the corner of her eye she could see the door swing silently open, and on the other side of it she could hear the faint scuffling of footsteps. The dragging footsteps of someone, perhaps injured or sick. Immediately she knew who it was.

"Crow?"

The footsteps paused for just the briefest moment, and then resumed. She waited as Crow shuffled into the room, shuffled around the edge of the open door, shuffled into plain view.

Everything in the world froze into a moment of absolute horror.

It was not Crow.

It was Karl Ruger.

He stood there, grinning with wet teeth that were smeared with black mud and dark red blood, his eyes flickering as red as rat's eyes, his hair in disarray, his skin bled white and crawling with grubs and maggots. He stood swaying at the foot of her bed, his rumpled clothes stained darkly with blood, dotted with bullet holes. With hands that were as white as headstone marble, fingernails that were curiously thick and sharp, Karl Ruger reached for her.

Val felt something heavy in her hand and looked down to see that she was holding Crow's gun. It hadn't been there a second ago but it didn't matter. Fury welled up in her, matching and then overmatching her fear, and she raised the gun, holding it straight out, inches from Ruger's chest.

"You killed my father!" she shrieked as she pulled the trigger. The bullet slammed into Ruger's chest. She fired again and again, punching bullet after bullet through his black heart.

All he did was laugh, and when the gun was empty he lunged at her.

Val's scream burned her damaged throat, and suddenly she was surrounded once again by the damp and swirling darkness.

The darkness owned her, engulfed her, and she realized that she had never left the darkness at all, had never found the light. The darkness had simply learned how to fool her.

In the darkness, she tried to flee, but now the self that was in the darkness was as wounded and weak and helpless as the self who lay up there in the light, lay with tubes and drains and stitches.

(6)

Vic Wingate took an extended lunch break from the shop and was tooling down A-32, smoking a Hav-a-Tampa Jewel and listening to Travis Tritt as sunlight sparkled off the polished skin and chrome of his pickup. Vic felt pretty good. Last night he'd been in a foul mood because of the attention focused his way by the goddamn kid, but that matter was settled now. He had done his public duty and gone and fetched the little fucker from that faggoty hayride thing, and when he'd gotten the kid home Vic had eased his tensions by some recreation with the boy. Vic was pleased with the thought that he had "graduated" the kid from slaps and shoves to some real manly duking. It was about time, he thought. Kid had to learn sometime. But he wasn't pleased about how the beating had ended. Just as he'd worked up a great sweat kicking the living shit out of the punk, something happened that had rattled Vic. The kid had suddenly smiled up at him, bloody lips, black eyes, bloody nose—and there he was smiling at the guy who'd just handed him the worst whipping in his life.

Not only had it taken the real pleasure out of the beating, robbing Vic of a serious high, that smile had been—weird.

He'd never seen the kid give him a look like that. It had damn near cut the legs out from under him because for a moment—just for one really twitchy moment—that smile made the kid look like . . . well, like Griswold. It was the way the Man used to smile after a kill. As a teenager Vic had seen that smile time and again, and he knew it well. He saw it in his dreams all the time.

He really didn't like seeing that smile on Mike's face, and he wanted to ask the Man about it. Frowning he stepped on the gas.

Several police cars whipped past Vic's truck. Jim Polk was driving one and he waved to Vic, who nodded. Vic made a mental note to call Polk later on; there were some things that had to be taken care of, and Polk was a good gofer.

Four miles shy of the spot on the highway where the police had found the wrecked car, Vic made a sharp left along a narrow country lane. It was a farmer's road and it cut through several of the major farms on the east side of town before finally branching off into the State Forest. At that point the macadam faded into gravel and then to dirt. The truck took the changes in stride; it was well used to this route.

Three miles into the woods, the road petered out and died. Vic rolled the truck to a stop and got out. Even though there was no one around, he scanned the dense forest and listened for human sounds, heard none, and nodded. He walked over to a thick clump of brush that stood in a gnarled tangle beside the end of the road. Vic looked around again, then squatted, took hold of a length of knotted rope that was cleverly hidden by weeds, and pulled on it as he stood. He backed up and a whole section of the shrubbery shifted with him, opening outward like a door and swinging on a pair of sturdy hinges. It took a lot of effort for Vic to shift the barrier, and as it moved the deception became obvious. The shrubs were actually seated in a long, low, flat-bottomed trough that was carefully camouflaged; from the outside the facade was perfect, from the inside it was clearly a kind of door. Vic pulled it wide, then got back in the truck and moved it twenty feet down the pathway revealed by the open barrier; then he went back and painstakingly pulled the foliage back into place. Anyone passing by would be fooled unless they knew exactly where to look and knew what they were looking for. Vic made sure that the shrubs were always overgrown and healthy, and he had chosen evergreens for the job because he wanted the deception to remain constant year-round, as it had for many, many years.

Back in the truck he drove a serpentine route that seemed

composed of nothing but hairpin turns. The lane was just barely big enough for the truck to pass, and Vic liked it that way. Any larger and it would be too visible from the main road.

He drove for several miles, singing country along with the radio. Eventually, the tortuous route became wider as the hidden road joined with an actual lane, though one that had been left to grow wild decades ago. Vic kept it just trimmed enough to allow a clear passage for the truck, but that was it. The lane led him deep into the forest, past huge old oaks and maples, and then fed into an area that was populated with much younger trees, most of them less than thirty years old. He threaded his way through these until the lane brought him out into a field beside a deserted stone farmhouse. Vic drove up and parked outside the house.

As he killed the engine he caught movement out of the corner of his eyes.

He tensed for a second and then in the next moment he was out of the truck, a Remington .30-30 held at port arms. He dashed along the front of the house, following the hint of movement he'd seen, and then rounded the corner, bringing the rifle up and looking along the barrel. The figure continued to move away from him but then it seemed to sense him and stopped, turning slowly toward him. Vic studied it, his green eyes narrowed.

He lowered the rifle and looked back at the front porch. There were two dark bundles on the top step. Vic nodded to himself, understanding, then glanced back at the figure.

The figure stood there at the edge of the forest wall, nearly invisible against the tall weeds. Vic knew what it was, though he had never actually seen one before, except in the strange and wild dreams that the Man sometimes sent him. He knew that the thing was alive, in a manner of speaking. A homunculus. It stood in man-shape, but that shape twisted and fought to change, bound into that man-pattern by a will, Vic knew, greater than the sum of its parts. The homunculus wore shabby old clothes, rough canvas gloves, castoff shoes. The clothes were splashed with long streaks and splotches of old, dried blood. Less than a day old, Vic reflected. On its shoulder squatted a huge carved pumpkin—a jack-o'-lantern with a wicked grin. Vic thought it was a nice touch, and he grinned in return. Through all of the openings in the face, Vic could feel himself being watched by a thousand coal-black eyes. The carved smile seemed to Vic to be a reflection not of the things of which it was made, but of the mind that directed all such things in this place. He felt as if he was seeing the Man's real smile this time—not the weird imitation of it he'd seen on Mike's battered face last night—but a real reflection of the Man and his power.

He really missed the Man, missed being with him, running with him the way he had done thirty years ago.

A sound rent the air, and both Vic and the creature turned toward it, knowing the sound. Vic frowned. Dogs. Probably police dogs.

"Shit," he said aloud. Now he wouldn't be able to head down to the swamp and commune with the Man. That really blew.

The barking was a good mile off, but it was coming closer, probably following the blood scent clinging to the creature's clothes. "We can't let them find a scrap of anything around this place."

The homunculus stood there amid the corn for a moment longer as if considering. It nodded its monstrous head just once. Then, as if a switch had been thrown or a door slammed shut, the power of will that held it in its parody of human form was abruptly withdrawn. In an instant it no longer had the strength to maintain that shape, even if it had wanted to. In that instant the body collapsed into tens of thousands of smaller shapes that wrestled and fought and fluttered and scurried to be free of the suffocating press and the closeness of the other shapes. The huge and misshapen jack-o'-lantern it had worn for disguise when it had come for Boyd and had gone in answer to Karl Ruger's dark prayers wobbled and toppled and fell to the ground, exploding on impact into fragments of orange pulp, just as the man-shape exploded into rat-shape and roach-shape and worm-shape and mouse-shape and weevil-shape and beetle-shape, and poured outward among the weeds and tangled undergrowth.

The dogs were getting closer. Vic quickly gathered up the empty suit of clothes, shaking them to dislodge the last few spiders and roaches, then carried the rags to his truck and tossed them carelessly into the bed of the pickup.

Then he went back to the porch and examined the two bundles. They were backpacks, both of them sprinkled with blood, but both of them packed to bursting with bags of white powder and bundle after bundle of bloodstained money. A fortune. Vic's mouth went dry as he looked at it.

"Well, fuck me." He hefted the backpacks; each was a considerable burden, and a great avaricious smile carved itself onto Vic's face as he realized what this unexpected treasure trove was. He had heard the news stories all night. "Well, fuck me blind and move the furniture."

He put the backpacks on the front seat, humming happily to himself. Finding that took the sting out of not being able to visit Dark Hollow. Maybe he'd swing back around later.

Vic lingered at the house just long enough to take a considering look at the forest, the stretch of denser brush that led off into the woods at the foot of Dark Hollow.

"I'll put this to good use," he said to the woods. "Trust me."

Then he got in his truck and left. By the time the first of the bloodhounds reached the spot, there was nothing left to find but a fractured jack-o'-lantern that still wore part of its twisted grin.

(7)

Iron Mike Sweeney lay on his bed and stared at the water stains on the ceiling. There was one stain that looked like a TIE fighter from *Star Wars*. The standard fighter, not the bombers or Darth Vader's personal ship. Mike looked at it and tried to think about that rather than the pain. Sometimes he succeeded. All morning he'd tried most of his old tricks for shoving back the hurt, to force the pain back into its dark little box, to shoo the shame out the window. He'd recited bits of movie dialogue, did the alphabet based on the first letters of the titles of science fiction novels, cast fantasy remakes of classic sci-fi flicks with his favorite current actors. Usually he could get lost in those games, but not today. Today none of it worked. The memory of last night was too fresh, too sharply painful in every way. And too strange.

His revelation about Vic's humanity was still with him, but as the aches and pains asserted themselves more with each hour since the beating, the wonder and delight of the epiphany diminished somewhat in grandeur. Yes, he'd outlast Vic. Sure, but how many beatings would there be between then and now?

Mike wasn't sure how many more beatings like that he could take. There was no part of him that wasn't sore or swollen. He had ice packs pressed against his mouth and cheeks. When he'd gone to the bathroom his pee had been bloody, which really scared him.

He could outlast Vic if he wanted to, but would he want to live through the years between now and then? Mike really wasn't sure.

On the other hand . . .

The one thing that kept Mike from sliding right over the edge was what had happened at the end of the beating. The look in Vic's face. It had only been there for a split second, but it *had* been there. Mike could not understand it, but for that second Vic had looked scared. Of *him*.

But—why? It made no sense. Vic had been in total charge. He'd beaten Mike to a pulp and Mike hadn't been able to do so much as block a punch. It had all been Vic.

So, why had he stepped back like that at the end? What had happened? What had he seen, or had he thought he'd seen? Mike remembered smiling, but it had been involuntary. He had no idea why he had even done it.

And yet . . . it had stopped Vic cold.

Why?

With a hiss of pain he made himself sit up. He needed to get out of the house, to be out in the sunlight, to be away from here. He tottered into the bathroom to pee, and it was still coming out more red than yellow. *Maybe I'll get blood poisoning and die*, he thought, and the idea comforted him. He opened the medicine chest and took down the oversized bottle of Advil. He went through a bottle that size every month. Mike shook four of the blue gelcaps into his palm, slapped them past his bruised lips, and washed them down with two glasses of water.

It took him a long time to put on a sweatshirt, jeans, and sneakers. His ribs hurt, but not nearly as much as his face. When he looked in the mirror to comb his hair, the only thing he recognized were the blue eyes staring hopelessly out of the mask of purple and red. The eye that had puffed up last night had settled down now, thanks to ice packs, but there was a splash of yellow and dark brown bruising ringing both eyes.

He lowered his head. Vic's face swam before his inner eye and he thought some of the blackest thoughts he owned. He wished he had a gun.

The image of Vic's locked gun case popped into his head and he spent several minutes considering his options. Breaking into that case wouldn't be difficult, not as long as it didn't matter if Vic found out. Only stealth was difficult, but to smash the glass and take a hammer to the locks . . . that would be easy. Mike had never shot a gun, but TV was a pretty good teacher, and he figured he could load one, find the safety, point it, and shoot.

The question was—who would he shoot? Would he blow Vic's head off his shoulders, or his own? Both options held a lot of appeal to him.

Real serious appeal.

He walked downstairs carefully and quietly, not wanting to be heard. He was pretty sure Vic was still at work, but he did sometimes come home for lunch. The house was quiet. Mom was asleep in front of the TV in her room, her teacup still smelling of gin and fresh lime even this early in the day. Mike was lucky: Vic was at work, and Mike hoped that a car would fall off the lift and crush him. The thought made him want to smile, but his face hurt too much to make him dare flex those pulped muscles.

As Mike fished in the closet for his nylon Windbreaker, he

heard the TV rattle on about some no-fly zone somewhere in a country he never heard of. He was at the door when he heard the words "Pine Deep." Mike stopped in surprise and listened.

". . . in Bucks County, where authorities are investigating a shoot-out that left at least one person dead and three wounded, including two police officers."

Mike held his breath and strained to hear every word.

"According to Pine Deep Police Chief Gus Bernhardt, at about nine o'clock last night, an unknown assailant broke into the farmhouse of Henry Guthrie, one of the town's most prosperous farmers, and attempted to rob Mr. Guthrie and his family. The police department has not released complete details yet, but what is known is that the intruder physically assaulted several members of the Guthrie household. When local officers arrived, the intruder opened fire. After a short but intense exchange of shots, the intruder fled, leaving behind a scene of devastation. Mr. Henry Guthrie, sixty-four, a well-respected member of the Pine Deep Growers Commission, was shot and killed."

Mike gasped, clapping one hand to his bruised lips.

"Wounded in the exchange of shots were Officers Rhoda Thomas, twenty-six, a law student doing intern work with the Pine Deep Police Department, and Malcolm Crow, forty, a local businessman who had recently been reinstated as an officer. Ms. Thomas sustained two gunshot wounds and is listed in serious condition at County Hospital. Mr. Crow also sustained a pair of gunshot wounds, among other injuries, and is listed in stable condition. Also injured during the break-in were Mark Guthrie, thirty-six, son of Henry Guthrie, his wife, Connie, thirty-one, and Valerie Guthrie, forty. Ms. Guthrie, the daughter of the murdered man, is said to be close to Officer Crow. Mark, Connie, and Valerie Guthrie are all listed in fair condition. Sources in the chief's department claim that the intruder may have been seriously injured himself during the exchange of shots. Chief Gus Bernhardt is conducting a full investigation as well as a manhunt for the intruder who has brought such heartache and pain to the Guthrie family.

"In other news . . ."

"Crow . . ." Mike breathed. "Oh no!" He left the house as fast as his battered body could manage.

(8)

Crow stared up at the ceiling, trying to count the tiny holes in one selected panel of acoustic tile for want of something—anything—to do. He was well into triple digits when there was a tentative knock on the door. "Come in," Crow called. "Please!"

The men who entered the room were total strangers to Crow, but he knew their type. They had the cop look, despite stubble-covered chins, eyes smudged with sleep deprivation, and badly combed hair. One man was tall, balding, and had the dour face of a mortician; his colleague was younger, bigger, brawnier, and looked more cheerful, though that was muted by a mask of weariness. The younger man had a blond buzz cut and a cold cigarette dangling limply from the corner of his mouth. Both men wore rumpled suits that looked as if hoboes had slept in them first.

"Mr. Crow?" asked the balding man with the mournful face.

"What's left of him."

"Do you mind if we ask you a few questions?"

"Since I'm bored out of my mind, I wouldn't mind if you wanted to sell me life insurance."

The younger man grinned at that; the older one did not. They both pulled up orange plastic chairs of the type that had aluminum legs and looked like they had been designed for the sole purpose of making the user uncomfortable. Both men sat down, sighing in unison with obvious weariness.

Crow looked at them, half smiling. "Let me guess," he said, "Philly cops?"

"Right the first time. I'm Vince LaMastra, and this is my partner, Detective Sergeant Frank Ferro."

"Did I meet you guys last night?"

"Yes, sir. We were out at the house."

Crow's hands were bandaged, and one was hooked to an IV, so they just exchanged nods, and Crow was even careful about that. His head still felt as if it had been used in a soccer match.

"Mr. Crow," began Ferro, "first, I want to say that on behalf of myself, my partner, and the other law-enforcement officers, I want to thank you and commend you for your bravery and re-sourcefulness last night."

"Aw, shucks," Crow drawled. " 'Tweren't nothing."

"I'm serious, sir. You managed to save the lives of four people, not to mention yourself, and faced down a man who is widely regarded as extremely dangerous."

"Oh, come on."

"No joke, man," LaMastra agreed, nodding vigorously. "You went up against Karl Ruger and whipped his ass."

"Truth to tell," Crow said, rubbing his jaw with a skinned knuckle, "it was kind of a mutual ass-whipping. And quite frankly—isn't everyone making a bit too much out of that? Okay, so I won a fight. Considering everything else that's going on, what's the big deal?"

"Uh-huh," said Ferro quietly. "Mr. Crow—"

"Look, if you would, just call me Crow. My old man was 'Mr. Crow' and he was kind of an asshole. I'm just Crow to every-one."

"Tell me, Crow," said Ferro, trying it on, "how is it that you are as dirty a fighter as Karl Ruger? You box?"

Crow shook his head. "Martial arts."

"Karate?"

"Jujutsu."

LaMastra brightened. "No kidding? I did some judo in col-lege, and I—"

Ferro looked at him until he stopped talking, and then the detective turned back to Crow. "The mayor and quite a number of the town's officers have been telling us stories of your ex-ploits. Fighting biker gangs, that sort of thing," Ferro said in a tone that suggested he didn't believe much of what he'd heard.

Crow didn't feel like making a case for himself, and besides, half of what the cop had been told probably was a pack of lies. "People love to exaggerate."

"Frequently," Ferro said quietly.

Was the cop baiting him? Crow wondered. "Tell you one thing, though, I never fought anyone tougher. Or faster. Son of a bitch was something else. You can't imagine how cat-quick this guy is. He's every bit as dangerous as everyone thinks he is. Maybe more. No remorse, either. He shot Rhoda Thomas and me without any hesitation."

"He's killed a lot of people," LaMastra said. "It's nothing new to him."

"It's nothing to him at all," Ferro summed up. He tilted his head to one side, appraising Crow. "You know, despite how banged up you are, you're lucky to be alive and in fairly good working condition."

"Gosh, I feel like dancing."

"No, seriously. Ruger has a habit of doing some rather horrible things to the people he doesn't like."

"I heard about the whole Cape May thing."

"Ah. Well, that's just part of it," LaMastra said. "He also did a number on one of his buddies. Spoiled him. Tore him to—"

"I think Mr. Crow gets the point."

"Yeah, Terry Wolfe said something," Crow agreed. "So, why'd he do it?"

Ferro shrugged. "It's possible there was a power struggle over who was going to lead the group and Ruger flipped out on his partner."

"Sounds thin."

"It is thin, and it's just a guess. Another guess is that there was some kind of dispute over the money and drugs, which is an idea I can more easily live with. We're talking about a lot of money, and a very large amount of very expensive cocaine. People have killed each other for just a snort of coke, let alone a fortune in it."

Crow grunted and shook his head. He felt himself losing interest in the criminal aspect of the case. He believed—knew—that he'd shot Ruger and that the bastard was dead or next to it somewhere in the fields or in the forest just beyond the Guthrie farm. Probably the latter, and in that case his bones would turn to dust before anyone found him. The forest around Dark Hollow was dense, largely impassible, and it seldom gave up its dead. Just to be polite, he said, "So what's next on the agenda for you guys?"

Ferro waved a hand. "Oh, the investigation is proceeding. We're pursuing various leads. We have teams out checking all the likely routes of escape. . . ."

"Meaning you have bubkes."

"Meaning," Ferro nodded slowly, "that we have bubkes."

Crow sniffed. "You know you're never going to find him."

"Rest assured, sir," added Ferro, "if Karl Ruger is still in Pine Deep—we will find him."

Crow open his eyes and studied the cop. "There's some bad woods out there, Mr. Ferro. You sure about that?"

LaMastra shifted uncomfortably in his seat, coughed, and brushed a fleck of lint from his mud-spattered cuffs. Ferro smiled thinly at Crow. "I am very damn sure about that, Mr. Crow."

Crow closed his eyes, settled back against the pillow, looked up into his own interior darkness, and thought: *Bullshit. You're never going to find him.*

Chapter 21

D r. Saul Weinstock snapped the cuff of the latex glove against his wrist, adjusted his surgical mask, and strolled into the autopsy suite in the Pinelands Hospital morgue. The CD player was playing John Hammond's "Wicked Grin," which Weinstock always considered good cutting music. Also on the changer were two Elvis Costello albums, Led Zeppelin's *Physical Graffiti*, and the second greatest hits album by the Eagles. It was going to be a long morning.

There were three autopsies stacked. One was a little girl from Crestville, almost certainly a SIDS case, and the other two were tied into what was going on in town. Poor Henry Guthrie, whom Weinstock was going to leave for a colleague to do. His family had been friends with the Guthries since his grandfather's time, and Weinstock didn't very much relish imposing the necessary indignities of an autopsy on a man he greatly admired. It felt ghoulish and rather rude.

The third case was before him on a stainless steel table, still in the dark gray zippered body bag, fresh from the crime scene on A-32.

Weinstock took the clipboard off the hook on the side of the table, switched on the tape recorder by stepping on the treadle positioned under one corner of the table.

"This examination is dated September thirtieth, beginning at 1035 hours. This autopsy is carried out by Saul Weinstock, M.D., deputy chief coroner for Bucks County and senior staff physician for Pinelands College Teaching Hospital, and performed under the authority of Judge Evan Doyle, justice of the peace for the Township of Pine Deep. The name of the decedent is believed to be . . ." He consulted the clipboard, ". . . one Anthony Michael Macchio, age thirty-seven, a resident of Philadelphia, Pennsylvania."

That said, he pulled down the zipper and parted the plastic folds.

Saul Weinstock stood there and stared as the tape rolled on, beholding the handiwork of Tow-Truck Eddie, the Sword of God.

"Holy shit!" he said, and it forever became part of the permanent record of the case.

(2)

When Vic got back to Shanahan's the place was deserted. There should have been five mechanics on shift, including himself. One was down with a cold, one had just not shown up that day, one, Sammy, was out road-testing a car and probably parked somewhere with a sandwich and a cold beer, and the other guy had been called in to the chief's department for some kind of reinstatement bullshit. It pissed Wingate off, because there were four jobs that absolutely had to be done that day, and one was a valve job that was a real prick. Sammy should have been there working on it, not tooling around in Dr. Crenshaw's BMW. *Road test, my ass*, thought Vic. He glanced at the wall clock. Half past two. Shit! There was no way that he was going to get out of there any earlier than six, and maybe not that early.

With the backpacks full of bloodstained cash still locked in his truck, he was uneasy. He wanted to get it home, clean it up, count it, and then start spreading it around where it would do the Man—and himself—the most good, but he couldn't blow off his job because he absolutely did not want to do anything that would give him a high profile. His name had already been on the lips of the mayor and that jerk, Crow—all because of Mike—and he wanted to drop completely off the radar.

Grumbling, he snatched up the worksheet on the pissant little Saturn in bay two and glowered at it. Brake job. Well, that wasn't too bad, time-consuming but easy. He found the keys in the office and moved the car onto the ramps of the lift, put on the emergency brake, and hopped out. The old hydraulics wheezed as they lifted the bright red car six and a half feet off the grease-spattered floor. Vic hooked a droplight on the chassis and set to work with an impact wrench. As he worked, he thought about the kid. Fucking kid. Fucking four-eyed little sissy piece of shit. Vic hated Mike, had hated him ever since he'd first seen him sucking on Lois's tit. Scrawny little shit-heels. Vic found it nearly impossible to believe that Mike was actually the son of . . . well, the offspring of someone so powerful.

He wondered if the kid would have grown up different if he'd known who his dad really was, instead of growing up thinking he was the son of that jackass John Sweeney, the fucking loser Lois had married before. Maybe if the kid had known who his real father was he'd have grown up with some brick in his dick. But no . . . the *Man* didn't want the kid to know. *He* wanted things kept quiet for reasons Vic could certainly understand, but it still rankled him. A kid should be brought up to respect the father. Honor the father. Someone like the Man deserved to be honored, especially by his own son. But no, the Man just wanted the kid raised and protected—at all costs protected. At least, Vic thought with grudging approval, the Man did not require a hands-off policy for the little shit. The Man couldn't care less if Vic pounded the piss out of Mike morning, noon, and night as long as no life-threatening harm ever came to him. Personally Vic thought the Man worried too much about the kid. The no-balls little punk could never be a threat to the Plan. Never. Vic firmly believed that, no matter what the legends said. Kid was only a useless piece of meat. But . . .

He sighed, thinking about it, about the Man, about the Return, about the kid. It really torqued his ass that the kid always had his nose in a goddamn book. Thought he was so smart—but he didn't know squat. Couldn't even *hold* a football let alone throw one. Had posters of superheroes up all over his room. Vic shook his head. When he'd been fourteen, Vic had had posters of Farrah Fawcett and Barbara Carrera all over his room, not Green-fucking-Lantern and that faggy-looking Cyclops. Real women from the real world, not some dorky superjocks. When he'd been fourteen, he'd had a stack of *Penthouse* magazines a yard high in his closet. When he'd been fourteen he was buying a pack of Trojans every week or so. He doubted if that puke kid even knew how to put one on, let alone what to do with it afterward.

Goddamn! Why did the kid have to be such a pain in the ass? Why did he have to push it all the time? Like giving him that spooky smile last night. All it did was make more trouble for him, for Vic, who tried to set some kind of an example of how to grow up to be a man, even if the Man didn't tell him to. The kid pushed it, though. He always pushed it; and when he pushed it, Vic just plain had to slap the kid back into place. How else was the little shit going to learn any damn thing about life? If the little idiot had any kind of brains, then maybe he'd understand that Vic was just trying to set him straight, make him tough, teach him to be strong. After all, he was the Man's only human son. Vic just couldn't stand to see *his* son grow up to be a wimp-ass piece of shit. Did the kid ever get it? Fuck no! All he did was cry like a little girl. Last night, well, that was the topper, wasn't it? Having the fucking mayor call him and tell him to go pick the kid up, at the Haunted Hayride no less. God! Vic wondered if the kid still had any idea of how dangerous that had been. Probably not. How could he? He had no idea what was in the woods out beyond Dark Hollow.

Vic paused in his reflections and allowed himself a smile. Well, it wouldn't be long before the kid did find out. Soon, they'd all find out.

Still smiling, he set about the brake job, pleased with the way the future was spreading out before him. Vic worked in silence, unaware of the bright blue sky beyond the half-closed garage doors, and the golden, enriching sunlight. Unaware, also, of the tall, gray-skinned phantom who stood across the road and watched him from the shadow of a skeletal old maple tree. The stiff breeze whipped at the Bone Man's clothes and carried away flecks of dried graveyard mud.

Then abruptly Vic straightened and looked up—not across the street to where the image of the Bone Man was fading into illusion like a sun dog, but instead he looked inward, his head cocked as he listened.

Vic lowered his wrench and let it dangle from his greasy fingers as he heard the voice speak to him in a soft, secret whisper. Vic smiled a very ugly smile and set down his wrench. Screw the workload. He quickly cleaned his hands, shut off the lights, hung a CLOSED sign in the window, and locked the door on his way out. He climbed into his pickup and for the second time that day headed out of town toward the abandoned farm that bordered Dark Hollow. He never stopped smiling.

(3)

Terry hid in a bathroom stall for half an hour, fighting a case of the shakes that was so bad that he had uncontrollable diarrhea. Trousers down around his ankles, head bowed and held tightly in both hands, he waited it out until the Xanax finally kicked in. Each pill took longer to work and did less, but at least the shakes finally eased up.

When he was sure the bathroom was empty he left the stall, washed in the sink, combed his hair, and straightened his clothes as best he could. Then he went to meet Gus in the doctors' lounge.

"Ah, there you are," Gus Bernhardt said. He was sitting on the couch over by the coffee station.

Shit! Terry thought, the use of the expletive not even hitting a speed bump in his brain. For one crazy second he considered fleeing, but then he spotted Ferro and LaMastra as well, sitting in chairs that flanked the couch. *Son of a bitch.*

"Your Honor," Ferro said mildly. "We were just discussing our options with the media. The chief here wants to go public with the story and my partner and I feel it would be best to keep things low-key. No sense exciting the citizens and drawing rubberneckers."

"Yeah," LaMastra agreed, "a manhunt is worse than a fire for bringing out every idiot with a video camera for fifty miles around."

Still standing half in and half out of the door, Terry looked from one to the other and felt like screaming. Were they all crazy? Who the hell cared what the media thought? Or the tourists? Or any of this? He just wanted to get out—to crawl out of his own skin and just run. His best friend was in the hospital, along with every surviving member of his girlfriend's family. Henry Guthrie, one of the most respected and influential farmers in the area, was dead. Madmen were having their way with the residents, and not twenty-four hours ago Terry's little sister—his *dead* little sister—had called him up on the phone. He couldn't give a rat's ass for what did or did not make the papers.

But old habits die hard, so by reflex his face assumed an approximation of his Mr. Mayor facade and he cleared his throat, entered the room, and sat down in one of the overstuffed chairs.

"Let's play it your way, Sergeant," Terry said curtly. "I don't want to have to go on TV and explain it fifty times. Not now."

"I fully agree" Ferro began but Terry cut him off.

"In fact I don't want to release anything to the press until we have actually accomplished something," he said with a touch of asperity.

LaMastra gave a surreptitious little silent whistle and raised his eyes significantly to Ferro, whose face had become wooden.

"As you say, Your Honor."

Terry rubbed his red-rimmed eyes and sighed. In the back of his mind Mandy's voice was whispering to him over the phone. The force necessary to keep a bland smile on his face was immense.

Ferro opened his mouth and was about to add something else

when the lounge door opened and a very weary-looking doctor came in, his green skullcap and surgical scrubs stained with unpleasant splotches of various colors and viscosities. He sketched a weary wave, lumbered bleary-eyed over to the coffee station, and poured himself a cup of very strong black coffee in a chipped ceramic mug that said: #1 DAD.

Sipping the coffee, he ambled over and sank wearily down onto the couch beside Gus. He crossed his ankles and rested them on the coffee table, and Terry could see that the soft paper scrub booties he wore over his shoes were spattered with dark drops of dried Betadine. The doctor looked bleakly at the gathered faces, sipped his coffee, and sighed.

"Doc, have you met Detective Sergeant Ferro and Detective LaMastra?" Terry said, and the doctor gave them small nods.

"Yeah, but last night things were a little too busy to be social." The doctor toasted them with his mug. "Saul Weinstock." He tugged the green skullcap off, stared for a moment at the sweat stains that darkened the soft papery material, and then tossed it onto the table. Weinstock was thirty-five, looked thirty, and had a face that looked remarkably like a younger, tougher Hal Linden. A *chai* on a gold chain glittered from within the tangle of curly black chest hair.

Terry said, "Dr. Weinstock is the administrator here at Regional, as well as the chief surgeon and county coroner."

"In small towns we wear a lot of hats," Weinstock said with a small grin. "I also double as the mailman and the fire chief."

"Uh . . . really?" LaMastra asked.

"No," said Weinstock.

"Oh."

The doctor glanced at Terry. "Christ, you look like shit."

"Been a long couple of days, Saul," Terry said. "So, where do we stand?"

"Well, that's a loaded question. Which do you want first, the good news, the so-so news, the bad news, or the *really* bad news?"

"How about in that order?"

"Okay, the good news." Weinstock had a clipped but affable voice. "Officer Rhoda Thomas is an exceptionally hardy and fit young lady. We removed two 9-millimeter bullets from her last night, and she is doing very well. She's conscious and aware."

"Prognosis?" asked Ferro.

Weinstock shrugged. "She'll be fine. No truly life-threatening damage, except for the collapsed lung, and we fixed that. She gets the right P.T. and she'll be playing tennis in the spring, no problem. In a couple of months, you'll have to be a damn close friend to even see the scars."

"Good," Terry said. "And Crow?"

"Oh, also good news there. I told him he ought to be ashamed of himself for taking up bed space. Pissant little wounds both of them. If he didn't eat at McDonald's so much he probably wouldn't have had big enough love handles for the bullets to graze. He'll be out of here tomorrow."

"What about his face?"

"Jeez, have you seen it?" Weinstock asked with a malicious grin. "Looks like something out of a Frankenstein movie, but that's just bruising, couple lacerations. Piddling stuff. He'll have a couple of scars, sure, but nothing that will spoil his looks."

"What about his girlfriend?" asked LaMastra.

"Val? Well, that's the so-so news. She has a couple of cracked ribs, some torn cartilage, a helluva lot of facial bruising, and assorted minor lacerations. Her shoulder was wrenched, but that's just a sprain, nothing to worry about. We shot her up with some cortisone, and I had our sports med guy take a look at her and he said she'd be doing cartwheels in a few weeks. In short, the body trauma is in no way debilitating, so all that will heal." He blew across the surface of his cup and then took a careful sip. "The real issue is the emotional and psychological trauma. I mean, she was threatened by a madman, was injured while fighting for her life, she more or less saw her father get gunned down, and saw her boyfriend get shot. That's one hell of a lot to take in one night."

"Val's as tough as iron, Saul," said Terry.

The doctor nodded. "I agree. I've known Val forever. Hell, my uncle David delivered her . . . she used to babysit my sister and me. I know she's *tough*, and I think if anyone could recover from the psychic trauma of this, then she's the one. This morning I had a long talk with her, and she's tearing herself up with guilt."

"Guilt?" asked Gus. "For what?"

"For leaving her father to die out in the field while she went to help her brother and sister-in-law, then for being too traumatized to help him after all the fireworks were over. No, no, don't say it. We all know that that's just grief talking, but grief coupled with this kind of trauma can really do a number on a person. Seen it too many times."

"So," asked Terry slowly, "will she recover? I mean, in your medical opinion?"

Weinstock sipped the steaming coffee, then paused and stared into the middle distance. "It is my considered medical opinion that it beats the hell out of me. She'll need a good therapist, probably."

"Swell," grunted Terry. "What about Connie?"

"Now we come to the bad news. She is physically unharmed. In fact, she is the only one that really went through this relatively unscathed. Some minor bruises from rough handling and from a few hard slaps, but none of the brutal bashing the others experienced. Nevertheless, her trauma is even deeper and more dangerous than that of Val Guthrie. She was nearly raped, but in her own mind she actually *was* raped. Or at least violated beyond her capacity to endure. You have to understand, gentlemen, that this is a very old-fashioned, very modest woman. Probably a little naive, too, one of those people who just isn't prepared for this kind of visit to the real world. Her kind isn't made for a night in the swamps with all the alligators. Will she snap out of it? Probably yes. In most ways, yes, but can she put the event behind her and not let it haunt her and warp her like it does to so many of the innocent ones?" He just shook his head. "I don't know, fellows. I'm a doctor, not a shrink. And she is going to need a *very* good shrink."

"So's her husband," said LaMastra. "I had a talk with him, or tried to, but he just keeps saying that he doesn't want to talk about it. He's on some kind of denial trip, thinks his father's death is his fault somehow. He's tearing himself to pieces because, while Ruger was ripping his wife's clothes off and running his hands all over her, all young Mr. Guthrie could do was sit and watch and scream."

Weinstock nodded. "Yeah, Ruger hurt him by making him watch. If the rape had actually happened, with Mark watching and unable to do anything . . . well, I don't even want to speculate."

LaMastra made a sour face. "I've seen cases like that. Poor bastard's held down by one guy with a knife or gun or whatever, and has to watch the other guys take turns with his wife or girlfriend. What man could take that?"

"I sure as hell couldn't," Weinstock said grimly.

The room grew quiet as the men stared down at the floor and down at the dusty bottoms of their hearts, thinking of loved ones, trying to imagine what Mark Guthrie had felt, putting themselves in his place. It was a terrifying and sickening thought, as was the speculation, however distorted, of what it must have felt like for Connie Guthrie as well. It was harder for these men to relate to her trauma and her pain, but even from a distance, the feelings burned holes in each of them.

Gus blew out his cheeks. "Well, if that is the bad news, I just can't wait to hear what the *really* bad news is."

Weinstock sipped his coffee and considered the darkly rippling liquid for a long five seconds. "I just finished the postmortem on our friend Tony Macchio." He heaved a long sigh. "You know, fellows, I never signed up to do this kind of shit. I'm essentially a country doctor. My patients are upscale suburbanites who get expensive conditions and rare and glamorous diseases. When they die, they die in bed of very old age, or they have heart attacks on the back nine, two under par, and still smiling when they're wheeled into the morgue. But this crap . . . this body you brought me last night . . . ahh, I just don't know. I mean, God knows I've been doing this long enough not to be squeamish from blood. I've pieced together high school kids after the paramedics peeled them out of wrecked Lexuses. That I can deal with, but this . . . man, this is nightmare stuff, you know?"

"We all saw the corpse, Saul," said Terry quietly. "We know."

"No," Weinstock said emphatically, setting down his coffee cup with a thump. "No, you don't know. You don't even know the half of it." He looked at them each for a moment, then said, "For starters, I pulled two slugs out of his abdomen, both of different calibers. One was a nine millimeter and the second bullet wound was a thirty-two caliber—delivered hours later from comparisons of bruising and clotting, but almost in the same spot."

"He was shot at least once during the drug buy, in Philly," said Ferro. "That was probably the nine, and Ruger has a thirty-two caliber belly gun. Raven Arms automatic."

"Okay. The first shot was from a distance, the hole was clean and there were no powder burns, no tattooing, just a clean hole. But the other was a classic near-contact entry wound, possibly even on-contact, fired through clothes. The entry wound had a clear burn-rim, so your boy Ruger must have jammed that thirty-two-caliber pistol into his gut and popped him. Neither, gentlemen, was a fatal wound, and Mr. Macchio would have been far better off if it had been, but no. From the amount of bruising and so on I can make a good guess that he lived another half hour, maybe a little longer, and it's what happened in that half hour that scares the hell out of me."

"We know he was tortured, Dr. Weinstock," said Ferro.

Weinstock tilted his head to one side. "Is torture the right word for it, I wonder? Torture almost seems, I don't know, too *clean* a word for what happened. The perpetrator inserted something into Macchio's two bullet wounds, possibly his own fingers, and literally tore the front of his stomach out. Then he pulled his intestines out, unraveling them like a tangled rope. Next, he . . . uh . . . bit the skin around the wound."

"Bit?" Terry said softly, his face paling, and suddenly he was back thirty years and something big and powerful was clawing at him, biting his shoulder. . . . He had to shake himself to break free of the memory and stay focused.

"Bit. Chewed. Ate! We found clear impressions of teeth marks all around the wound. He bit the fingers, actually chewing off the man's fingertips. He bit his face, tearing off most of the nose, the lips, the eyebrows, the ears . . ."The doctor's eyes were glassy. "You all saw the dismembered hands? Well, at first we thought they had been hacked off crudely, perhaps with a small knife or dull hatchet, but when we examined the edges of the bones, we discovered that the hands had been bitten off, the muscle and bone chewed clean through by very strong, very sharp teeth."

"Holy shit," breathed Gus.

"We were able to lift saliva from the wounds and the lab is doing a workup on it now. There were bite marks on other parts of the body as well. Thighs, groin, neck, and, uh, so on. If you ever catch this guy I can guarantee you a perfect set of dental impressions."

Ferro's face was as drawn, and he mumbled, "Uh, well, thank you for your report."

"There's more," Weinstock said quietly.

"More?"

"Yeah. From the amount of bleeding and the remaining lividity, I've been able to determine that somehow—and don't ask me how—Tony Macchio was alive for almost all of this." They all just stared at him. "So the actual cause of death was when this sick, murderous son of a bitch reached up into Macchio's body and literally tore his heart out of his chest."

The words battered them all into silence. After a while, Ferro asked quietly, "Is that even possible? To tear a man's heart out?"

Weinstock looked at him. "If you had asked me that question this morning, I'd have laughed at you. The heart is pretty securely anchored in the chest. It has to be to do what it does. To actually rip it loose from all that internal structure . . . well, that's a new one on me. Now, here's one last little tidbit for you gentlemen." They tensed, almost cringing, waiting. "Whoever did this . . . took the heart with him."

(4)

The TV in Crow's room didn't work and he'd whiled away some of the interminable evening reading a seven-month-old copy of *Good Housekeeping* that a nurse had given him, it being the only thing on hand. Val was still sedated, they said, and couldn't have visitors. There was a police guard outside his room, and that kept traffic to a crawl, but by ten o'clock he would have been ready to invite Ruger and his cronies in for a few hands of old maid just to keep from screaming. Partly it was the utter boredom—and Crow was never one of those types who could be quiet and alone and still for more than five minutes. He always had to have music playing, preferably very loud blues or some avant-garde stuff, like Tom Waits's later albums, or the punk covers of Leonard Cohen. He loathed the echoes in his head, and the memories they provoked. And partly it was a gnawing need to see Val, to hold her hand, to be there for her the instant she woke up and had to face the towering grief.

On top of all that, he believed that at that moment he would have sold his soul to the devil for a drink. Or, maybe for a whole lot of drinks. He brooded over it for a while, wondering if maybe he should call his AA sponsor tomorrow. The ache for a drink was getting stronger the longer this craziness went on.

Even with those thoughts, the flaccid writing of the article on how to make centerpieces for the Easter dinner table worked on him like a dose of codeine and he drifted off. His eyelids slid down, his chin dropped onto his chest, and he began to snore like a tired bear as the shadows outside the hospital windows grew thicker and the wheel of night turned slowly.

He felt the hand on his shoulder. Light, tentative, gentle. A ghost of a touch, and in his sleep he smiled, knowing that the touch was Val's. Crow was way down in the darkness and he moved upward against the current of his dreams, rising toward the touch, wanting to break the surface of sleep so he could open his eyes and see her. He rose, rose . . .

The hand touching his arm splayed its fingers and wrapped around his biceps. Firm, strong.

Crow, still more asleep than awake, felt a pang. What was wrong? Was Val hurt?

He moved faster through his dreams, upward to where she waited.

Then the grip changed again. The fingers flexed, contracted, tightened.

Pain instantly shot through Crow's bruised arms and he sprang awake, his eyes snapped wide, gasping and calling out: "Val!"

And he stared straight into the black reptilian eyes of Karl Ruger!

The sight of the killer wrenched Crow's mind into disjointed shapes. It was impossible. He *couldn't* be here!

Ruger's face was as white as moonlight and he was smiling a thin-lipped smile. Crow opened his mouth to yell, to call for the cop outside the door, but Ruger's other hand shot out and clamped like an icy vise around Crow's throat.

"Shhhhhh!" he said, leaning close to Crow to whisper. "You make a sound, hero, and I'll rip your fucking throat out. You know I can do it, too . . . don't you?"

The hands on his arm and throat were immensely powerful and as cold as death. Crow gripped the wrist of the hand holding his throat, but it was like clapping onto an iron bar. The cold flesh didn't yield at all and the tendons and muscles beneath were like bridge cables.

Ruger leaned forward and pressed Crow back against his pillow, still leaning close so that his mouth was inches away. When he smiled Crow could see the jagged line of broken teeth—the teeth he'd kicked out after he'd driven Ruger headfirst into Missy's fender. The man's lips were so red they looked painted and his skin was colorless and smeared with drops of black muck. The worst part was Ruger's breath . . . he reeked. Each exhale was like a damp wind blowing from a slaughterhouse. He smelled of spoiled meat and blood and feces.

"Don't worry, stud," Ruger whispered in his slithery voice. "It ain't your time yet. Soon, mind you . . . but not now. I got better plans for you." He chuckled. "No . . . because of you I lost everything. My money, my dope, and those two sweet sluts at that farmhouse. Was that broken-nosed bitch yours? Val? Was she yours?" He shook Crow by the throat, squeezing harder.

Black poppies bloomed in Crow's vision. "Listen to me now. You took everything away from me, so I'm going to return the favor. Everything you care about, every-*one* you love, everything you own . . . I'm going to take it away from you. How's that sound?" He squeezed harder and Crow started beating at the wrist, smashing at it with his balled-up fist—but it was like hammering on a tree limb. "And then . . . when you are stripped down to nothing, when everything you love is either dead or in ashes, *then* I'm going to come for you, motherfucker."

Crow struggled against the grip, but it was like fighting a statue. Ruger squeezed harder.

"And the real fun part is . . . I'm going to fuck that broke-nosed bitch so bad that she'll beg for the bullet." He pumped his choking hand with each word: "She'll . . . fucking . . . beg . . . for . . . it!"

The pressure on Crow's throat was robbing his arms and legs of strength. Blackness painted the edges of his vision and he could feel himself slipping away as the whole world became a huge black nothing.

He felt the hand on his shoulder. Light, tentative, gentle—and he came awake screaming, flailing with hands and legs, tangled in sheets and IV tubes.

Val screamed, too, and nearly fell off the side of the bed trying to avoid his swings.

"Crow!" she cried, and the voice coming from her bruised throat was a horribly feminine approximation of Ruger's icy whisper. "Crow—stop it!"

Crow's eyes snapped wide and sanity came back to him in a rush. This was no dream, no nightmare. It was real . . . and Val was there. Not Ruger . . . not some nightmare image of that murderous bastard . . . but Val. Right here. Warm and real.

He sat up and took her in his arms and held her as tightly as his bruises and hers would allow. "Oh my God!" he sobbed as he gave her hair and face and lips a thousand small quick kisses. "Jesus, baby! I'm sorry!"

Val hugged him back with her one good arm and for a long

minute they just sat there, as connected to each other as will and closeness would allow. She wept against him, her tears hot on the side of his neck, and he wept, too. Her grief and pain were as real to him as if they were his own, and he did have his own. Henry Guthrie had been a far better father to him than his own had ever been and he still could not accept that he was gone. Just . . . gone. The loss of him left a huge hole through his chest.

Finally, slowly, and by degrees, their tears slowed and stopped and they released the dreadful intensity of their embrace. Val sniffed, got tissues for them both from the box on the bedside table, and sat back a bit. She wore a thin pink robe over a hospital gown. Her hair was unwashed and her left arm was in a sling. An IV port was taped to her right hand and Crow suspected that she had removed the tube and slipped out of her room without permission.

Val bent down and kissed Crow lightly on his torn lips and again on the forehead, closing her eyes and holding her soft lips there. He stroked her tangled hair and murmured soft words from their private language.

At length, she sat back again and looked at him with tear-bright eyes. Her face was bruised and scratched and puffy from unearned tears. Fatigue and grief had carved new lines around her mouth, and her beautiful face had a pinched quality that broke Crow's heart.

"Daddy . . ." she began and then her face crumbled into a mask of overwhelming grief and she buried her head into his chest again.

"I know, baby," Crow murmured, "I know." Tears burned in his eyes, crested, and broke, spilling down his face and into her hair.

"Oh . . . Crow . . . why him?" She raised her head. "Why Daddy?"

He just shook his head.

"He never hurt anyone, Crow." She screwed up her face and looked at him. "He made me run, he saved my life."

"I know."

"That man—that bastard!—he killed him because of me."

"Hey . . . hey, now. Let's not start thinking like that. There is no way that any of this was your fault."

"Crow . . . I just ran away. I ran away and he shot Daddy . . . and I . . . and I—"

"Shhhh, shhhh. Listen to me, baby, just listen, okay? Okay? That was an evil man. Not just some ordinary crook, but a truly evil man. You have no idea how terribly evil he was. He would have killed all of you once he got all the things he needed. Your dad probably guessed that, and he did what he felt was the right thing. He chased you off into the corn and he ran to draw Ruger's fire. He died to keep you and Mark and Connie alive. And it worked, baby. Don't blame yourself, because if you do you'll make your dad's death pointless. It wasn't pointless, was it?"

"N . . . no . . ." she said hesitantly.

"Your dad was a great man, and I loved him, too, you know. It took a lot of courage and a lot of love for him to have done what he did. That's what you've got to hang on to. He made a heroic decision. Few men could have taken such a step. Few men would have had the depth of love for their children, or the sheer guts to do it. Are you listening?"

She nodded, eyes wide, tears still streaming, but the look in her eyes had changed. It was a look of innocent childlike wonder that was not in any way childish.

Crow kissed her hand again. "If you hadn't run when you did, and as fast as you did, then Ruger would probably have killed both of you. Then he would have gone back to the house, attacked Connie, and killed her and Mark, too. But your dad screwed all that up. He helped you get away, and that left you free to go back and save Connie, and you kept that bastard busy long enough for me to arrive. Your dad bought us all that precious time." He held her fingers to his lips as he spoke. "Your dad made his own choices, and he died a hero. That's how you've got to think about it. Okay?"

"Oh, Crow . . ." she said, and her voice broke, but this time she didn't descend into sobs or hysterics. This time there was just a hint of her old strength in her eyes and in the line of her jaw. Crow prayed that more of that strength would come back.

He touched the IV port taped to her wrist and smiled at her. "You snuck out of your room, you naughty girl."

"They wouldn't let me see you . . . and I had bad dreams." A wince of disgust flickered over her face. "Horrible dreams."

"Dreams?" he said hollowly, remembering the doozy of a nightmare he'd just had. "About . . . what?" he asked and immediately realized how stupid that question was.

Val shivered. "You know . . . about *him*." Then the sobs came again and she wept quietly, slow tears carving warm trails across the battleground bruises of her cheeks. Crow held her hand to his own cheek, and he wept with her.

(5)

Tow-Truck Eddie lay on his back and looked up at the plain, unbroken expanse of the ceiling above his bed. Sunlight slanted through the windows, bisecting his recumbent nakedness. He had not moved so much as a finger since he'd come home from the orientation for his new part-time job. He'd just walked in, gone right upstairs, stripped, and lay down on the bed. Only his massive chest moved, rising and falling with deep regularity. Lying there felt good. A mild late afternoon breeze was wafting in through the open windows, the cool air murmuring over his bare skin, puckering his flesh into goose bumps that felt vaguely erotic. He felt his nipples harden, and then his . . .

"No!" he snapped, immediately angry with himself. With a grunt of self-disgust he rolled out of bed and went over to the closet, yanked the doors open, and stared inside. The clothes were all neatly folded and precisely stacked. He selected a pair of black sweats and pulled them on, hiding his nakedness, his hands jerking the clothes into place with ferocious shame. After he was dressed, he stood for a while and made himself calm down. The warmth of the cotton sweats changed the tightness of his skin, chasing away the gooseflesh and the shameful erection. He stood with his eyes closed, focusing inward on the events of last night. A smile slowly dawned on his face as the image of the dying man, the Baptizer as Eddie now thought of him, floated with bloody clarity in his mind. It steadied him to think of the Baptizer lying there, covered in blood, broken into all the ritual pieces, arranged in the correct way. Tow-Truck Eddie knew he had done it just right, had gone through the rite in exactly the correct way, and the knowledge of that chased away the baser thoughts of the flesh, of his own flesh.

He turned around and looked at the shrine that stood framed by shafts of rich golden sunlight. It was as if God had cast a spotlight on it, and it lifted Tow-Truck Eddie's heart and made his soul soar with joy.

He crossed the room and knelt in front of the shrine, bowed his head, and prayed for a long time. His prayers were unformed, just random thoughts and images from deep within his being that he offered up to his Father. Outside, birds sang in the dogwood trees and Tow-Truck Eddie thought it was the sweetest thing he had ever heard, like the singing of angels.

He crossed himself and then reached down for the little mallet and struck the tiny Sanctus bell seven times, because seven was God's number. The bell, though small, had a clear, high ring and the reverberations wandered gently around the room. Then he reached forward to the small ambry he'd made late last night. It was made from the knotty pine that had formerly been his entertainment center, but Tow-Truck Eddie's skillful hands— the hands of a carpenter, he reminded himself—had taken that wood and reshaped it from something of pointless value to an object that was most holy. He pulled the doors open, reached inside, and removed the vessels of the Eucharist and placed them on the credence built onto the side of the ambry. He closed the doors and addressed the elements, again crossing himself. He took the paten and placed it on the top of the ambry, which was to be his altar. He had not had time to procure official vessels, and so his paten was a heavy white porcelain dinner plate that he had washed seven times before consecrating it with many prayers. His chalice was a thick pewter boxing trophy he'd won nearly twenty-five years ago. Into it he poured pure water from a bottle of Evian he'd bought at the Wawa for just this purpose;

Tow-Truck Eddie did not believe in alcoholic spirits of any kind, not even wine. Finally he lifted the ciborium. It was only a Tupperware container, but it would have to do until he could obtain the real thing. He pried the lid off and removed the Eucharist, holding it in his hands, feeling its weight. He raised it to his nose and filled his nostrils with the scent. It was extraordinary.

He set it down on the paten and took the knife he had prepared specially for this moment. "When first I came among you," he said aloud, addressing the whole world, "my blood was shed and my body broken by mine enemies. My blood became your wine and my body became your bread and each of you fed upon me to keep alive the New Covenant. Now I make with you a Final Covenant. No longer shall you drink of my blood or eat of my flesh, but of *your* blood shall *I* drink, and of *your* flesh shall *I* eat. In this way, the Son of Glory shall know his place, and in this way shall the righteous know their Lord. Today, in your hearing, I declare myself the Son of man, the Son of Heaven's King, the righteous and unyielding Sword of God. Today, I accept the offering of this man who was beast and man, who was unholy and holy. Today is the first Holy Communion of the Final Covenant. All glory to God the most high!"

Tow-Truck Eddie carved a thin slice of the Eucharist and held it up even as he lowered his eyes in humility before his Father. He prayed for many long minutes, and then he raised his head and put the Eucharist into his mouth and ate it. When he had eaten, he took the cup, and after he had blessed it, he drank.

Instantly the power within him seemed to grow, to swell, to explode with the light of a thousand suns in his brain, and he cried out in sheer joy and wonder. Tears ran down his face and his face crumpled into a mask of sobs. He bent down and beat his head against the floor, thanking God.

It took a long time until he could even raise his head, so great was his joy, so overwhelming was the moment. When he did, he sat for a while and made himself calm down, breathing slowly in and out, sniffing back tears. Then he took a freshly laundered white towel and began cleaning the communion vessels. Last of all, he lifted the Eucharist and returned it to the container. Tow-Truck Eddie was surprised at how large it was, and how heavy, though it was a bit lighter since he had washed all of the Baptizer's blood off it. He sealed the human heart in the container and returned it to the ambry, satisfied that there would be enough of it to last him for many days. He was not worried about it spoiling; if it came to that he would simply find another. There were always sinners out there.

After a while Tow-Truck Eddie got up and dressed for his part-time job.

(6)

The big cop looked mildly down at him, and then frowned when he saw the bruises on Mike's face. "Did you get the number of the truck?"

Mike blinked. "What?"

"The Mack truck that did that to your face, kid."

"Oh," said Mike, and he forced a fake grin. "I, uh, fell off my bike. Rolled down a hill over some rocks."

"And then what? A Mack truck fall on you?"

"It looks a lot worse than it feels," Mike lied. "Hardly feel it."

"Okay," said the cop, a knowing skepticism in his eyes. He wore a glossy black nameplate that read GOLUB. "So what can I do for you?"

Mike nodded at the hospital entrance. "I just want to go in."

"To see whom?"

"Huh?"

"Increased security, kiddo. Haven't you been watching the news?"

"Oh. Yeah. Uh, I'm here to see Mr. Crow. Malcolm Crow."

"What's your name?"

"Mike Sweeney."

Golub consulted a clipboard and then shook his head. "Nope. Not on the list, kiddo."

"List? What list?"

"The list of people who are allowed to see Mr. Crow. You, my battered young friend, are not on the list. So, kindly go buzz off." His smile was pleasant but unyielding.

"This is stupid. I just want to visit him."

"What part of 'nope' was beyond your grasp?"

Mike peered up at him. "Are all cops this weird?"

"So I am reliably informed."

"Shit."

"Hey! Watch your mouth, youngster."

"It's not fair that I can't get to see Crow. Can't you just let me in? I'm not going to bother him or anything."

"Well, Mike Sweeney, do you know how many people today have asked to get in to see Mr. Crow?"

"Uh, no."

"Lots. Do you know how many of them swore that they wouldn't bother Mr. Crow?"

"No."

"All of them. Now, here's the bonus question. Do you know how many of them I have admitted into this Hippocratic establishment?"

"No."

"Exactly none," said Golub. "See that guy over there on the bench? He's a reporter . . . and I didn't let him in, either. Now, you seem like a nice kid, so I want you to continue to be nice and nicely buzz off."

Mike trudged dispiritedly toward his bike and trying not to wince, he gingerly bent down to open the lock and pull the plastic-coated chain through the spokes. He was just coiling it around the frame below the seat when a shadow blocked the sunlight, and he looked up to see the small dumpy man Officer Golub had mentioned standing over him. The man looked a little like George, the bald guy from those *Seinfeld* reruns. A red PRESS card was clipped to his jacket lapel.

"Say, kid, do you mind if I ask you a couple of questions?"

Mike slowly and carefully got to his feet, his defenses rising and snapping instantly into place. "What for?"

"I couldn't help overhearing you talking with that Gestapo agent over there. My name's Willard Fowler Newton, *Black Marsh Sentinel*." He stuck out his hand, and Mike hesitated only for a second or two before accepting it. "I thought I heard you say your name was Mark Sweeney?"

"*Mike* Sweeney."

"Mike, right, right. Well, listen, Mike, is it true that you know Malcolm Crow, the guy who was shot?"

"Sure. He's a friend of mine. I go to his store all the time."

"You mean the Crow's Nest. Place that sells all that Halloween stuff? Well, the thing is, Mar . . . I mean Mike, I'm doing a story—well, I'm trying to do a story—on the shootings, and I need some background on Mr. Crow and the others. Do you think I could ask you a few questions?"

Mike hedged.

"I'll buy dinner."

Mike's eyes narrowed suspiciously and he took a half step backward, flicking a glance over at the cop.

"Look, kid, I'm not a kidnapper or child molester. I really am a reporter."

"Uh-huh."

"If you don't believe me, go and ask Officer Godzilla over there. He'll tell you."

"Look, I got to get home. It's getting late."

"Maybe I could drive you—"

"Yeah, right."

"No! No, nothing like that," Newton said quickly, holding his hands up, palms outward. He drew in a deep breath and tried again. "Look, kid, I need to get this story in by press time. So, whaddya say, Mike? Just fifteen minutes? We can sit right on that bench over there, in full view of the nice officer."

Mike glanced over to the benches, three of which were unoccupied, and on the fourth, the town's only homeless person, Mr. Pockets, was stretched out, asleep under tented newspapers. He still hedged. "I don't know what more I can tell you than what the cops would have said. I mean, you already know who got shot and all that, and I guess that you already know that it was probably the Cape May Killer who did it, and—"

Newton's hand suddenly closed on Mike's bruised wrist with such force that Mike actually cried out in pain and jerked back. Officer Golub looked over at them, but Newton instantly let go and this time he backed up a step. While he was doing this his mouth went through a number of shapes and yet he wasn't able to squeeze out a single word. He stopped, swallowed, licked his lips, and with a glaze in his eyes said, "Wait, wait, go back. What was that you said about the Cape May Killer?"

"Yeah," Mike said, nodding, "I mean, I guess it was him. After what the mayor told Mr. Crow and all. . . ."

Newton looked like he was about to cry. He placed both hands—lightly this time—on Mike's shoulders. "Mike . . . has anyone ever told you that you were the greatest person to have ever walked the earth?"

Chapter 22

There are shunned places in this world where no one should ever go. Black places where the darkness clings to the sides of trees and the undersides of rocks, like lesions from some ancient disease.

These places are not consciously shunned; they don't call enough attention to themselves for that. The oldest and most instinctive parts of our minds avoid them perhaps, just as the hummingbird abhors the dying flower and the bear eschews the diseased fish. Year after year, century after century, they endure. Sometimes they fade away to paleness like the dust on old bones, the malevolent fires banked, almost cold—but never, never going out. Sometimes that dark energy flares, stoked by the deliberately manufactured death of some innocent thing, or by the desire of some hateful heart.

Such a place can be infused with even greater darkness if enough deliberate evil is enacted there: the blood and tears, fear and malfeasance imprinting the soil and stone and trees, the corruption leaving a stain that no rain or hand can sponge away. There have been houses that have endured and witnessed such horrors that they have become like batteries storing up evil; some battlefields are like that, the blood-soaked soil still vibrating with the echoes of dying heartbeats, cold with the last pale breaths of fallen soldiers who lay and bled and begged for salvation and ultimately cursed God as they died. In a kinder world, such places would be locked away behind impenetrable forests, or buried unreachably deep beneath granite mountains, or lost in the sands of the most remote and forbidding desert. In a kinder world, such malignant places would be fewer and weaker and would not possess the power to reach out into the world of men and whisper the doctrine of darkness, to seduce minds hungry for some corrupt purpose, to inspire tainted hearts to apostolic devotion; but in this world the evidence that such things have happened time and again is all too clearly written in the book of human suffering. In a kinder world such places could be eradicated, made pure, washed clean. In a kinder world, but not this world. These shunned places endure, waiting, patient, and always hungry.

Black-hearted men who sense this are drawn to these places, and finding them is like coming home.

The town of Pine Deep lay nestled in the arms of the mountains, overlooking vast forestland and farmland, streams and brooks, the silvery thread of the river, hollows and marshes, and one dark, forgotten, shunned place. It lay southeast of the town, pushed down into the shadows of the three tall hills that stand over the narrow valley known as Dark Hollow.

There is a place, deep within the hollow, where the ground is always marshy with black mud, the air thick with blowflies and mosquitoes. The leaves and pine needles that lie like a blanket over the swampy ground turn black within seconds of landing there and they give off a stink like rotten eggs and spoiled meat. From beneath the carpet of leaves there is a darker ichor that bubbles up every once in a while and stains the banks of the marsh; the ichor smells like fresh blood but tastes like tears.

Thirty years ago there was a murder there at the edge of the swamp. A thin black man from the Mississippi Delta and a big white man from Germany, both of whom had traveled long and strange roads to get to that spot, and fought as night fell and the moon rose, and the black man had killed the white man. He beat him down and stabbed him with a stake made from the shattered neck of a blues guitar. The black man buried the white man in the swamp and an hour later he himself was dead, beaten to death by rednecks who thought he was the devil himself and not the man who had saved the whole town from a monster. It was the kind of thing that should have ended up in a song, maybe even a blues song, but no one ever knew about it and no song was ever written to tell about how the Bone Man killed the devil with a guitar.

For thirty years that swamp lay like a secret, its reality becoming something akin to rumor as the years passed. It was too difficult to get to except by intrepid hikers, and for some reason hikers never went that way. Only one person ever came there, but he came there not as a hiker but as a supplicant, kneeling to worship at the edge of the Dark Hollow swamp.

Vic Wingate's soul and mind were as dark and rancid as the muck beneath the leafy covering of that swamp, and he had appointed himself to be the caretaker of that terrible grave. He knew its secrets—had known them since he'd coerced those other men into beating the Bone Man to death. At first he'd thought killing the Bone Man was just revenge, but now he knew that it was part of a master plan so comprehensive that it rolled forward like destiny. He was caught up in it, and he loved it.

Vic had been part of it even then. Even as a teenager he had belonged heart and soul to the fallen devil at whose graveside he worshiped. When Ubel Griswold had still lived in Pine Deep, Vic had become something between apprentice and lapdog, just as now he had become something between priest and general. As those long years had passed, Vic had labored to keep his secret safe and to prepare the way for those events that were foretold by the dark whispers of the buried dead; and for his labors the ancient voice of shadows told him many secrets, forcing Vic's inner eyes to open wide and behold things that were only possible when love and compassion and restraint were abandoned. It spoke to him of a time when even the dreaming dead would awaken and then the whole world—not just the town of Pine Deep—would drown in a tidal wave of blood. In the unsanctified shadows of Dark Hollow the ghost of Ubel Griswold converted Vic Wingate into a believer in the glory of the Red Wave.

Vic had waited patiently as the years had passed, but over the

last few days his heart beat faster, his breath came in short ex-
cited gasps because he knew that the waiting was almost over. It
was Thursday the thirtieth of September, just one full day since
Karl Ruger had come into town like a bad storm, bringing violence and death. In a few hours it would be October, and that
was *his* month. The month of the sleeper beneath the swamp. By
the end of October, Vic knew, for the people in Pine Deep, perhaps for all the people in the world, the sands of time would
have run out. The first time he'd thought of that it sounded
grandiose, but now he understood how it was going to work,
and he believed—*knew*—that it would work. He would be at the
Man's right hand when it happened, a general with more power
than kings.

During the days Vic worked on his cars in Shanahan's Garage
and he thought about that dark, shadowy place, about *him* who
slept there, but who came awake now every night. He could feel
the calls the Man sent out every night, the call to other darkly
beating hearts, hearts like Vic's own. Like Karl Ruger's. Vic knew
now that Ruger had been drawn to Pine Deep somehow; the
Man had done that by some means that even Vic didn't understand. Probably Boyd, too; after all, the Man had wanted him
and had sent the construct out to fetch him from Guthrie's
farm. Vic knew that every night the dead thing in the swamp
burdened the earth with its prophets, and they went forth through
the forests and the fertile fields, spreading a perverted gospel to
the damned. Vic loved it all, and he loved *him—the Man*—the
sleeper on the threshold of awakening.

Now Vic waited for the Man to awaken him who would be
his left hand. The other general in the army of the Red Wave.
Vic understood some of it, but not all of it. For all of the darkness in his soul, he was still a creature of the light and could not
fully grasp the subtleties of the world of night. He read a lot,
though. He tried to fill himself with knowledge on everything
that might pertain to the Man and his plan, but he was still
human. Boyd no longer was. And Ruger . . . well, the Man had
special plans for him.

Vic squatted at the edge of the swamp. It was getting late. In another hour the sun would be down. Lois was home, probably deep inside a bottle by now. That punk Mike had better be there, too. No matter how much his creepy smile had unnerved Vic last night, if that kid so much as stepped one cunt-hair's width out of line Vic was going to break something this time. Maybe an arm bone. Maybe a collarbone. Something that would hurt so much Mike would not even *think* about giving him any kind of jerk-off smile. Fuck that. Vic would do what he had to do to show everyone who was the big dog.

He'd felt the Man call him to the hollow, and he'd come, but since he'd been there the Man had said nothing. There were whispers in his head; the only thoughts there were his own.

He lingered though, knowing that he wouldn't have been called without a reason. So he hunkered down and watched with growing fascination as thousands of insects—beetles, roaches, ants, praying mantises, caterpillars—crawled out of the woods on all sides of him and threw themselves into the swamp. They vanished beneath the carpet of blackened leaves and there were small popping sounds as the bigger ones were yanked beneath the surface. The smaller ones didn't make a sound as they were sucked beneath the surface. The Man was hungry, Vic thought, and he smiled. He used to love watching the Man eat back in the day. Sometimes he'd bring him tied-up rabbits and toss them into the swamp, watching as the Man's black blood bubbled up around them and dragged them down.

A twig snapped behind him and Vic was instantly up and turned and there was a German Luger in his hand. The gun had once belonged to the Man and Vic had found it years ago, lying in the mud almost where he now stood facing the woods. It had been Vic's most prized possession—the last thing the Man had touched before he died.

His finger had five pounds on an eight-pound trigger and Vic was a twitch away from killing something. His eyes cut back and forth across the wall of evergreens and shrubs. Then a tangle of vines parted and a figure stepped out into the gloom, and Vic lowered his gun, smiling thinly. He slid it back into the shoulder rig he wore beneath his Windbreaker.

" 'Bout fucking time you showed up," he said, squatting down again. "You look like shit."

The figure stared at him with fevered eyes. It stood swaying on dirt-streaked legs, its clothes in rags and showing skin that had been bleached white with blood loss. There was a brightness of sweat on the stranger's face and his mouth hung open, lips slack, teeth clotted with blood and dirt. There were bullet holes in its chest and stomach; some of them still seeped blood and pus.

Vic cocked his head and peered up at him. "If you can hear me, then do what you came here to do. You're on the edge now, and you gotta do this right—and right means right now."

The figure took a single step forward and then fell to his knees. His eyes were demented but pleading as they locked on Vic's, but the mechanic shook his head. "Uh-uh, chief. *You* gotta do it. It's no good if I help you. Spoils the mojo." He took a toothpick out of his pocket, tore off the plastic wrapper, and stuck it between his teeth. Mint. Very nice.

The dying stranger toppled forward onto his chest and lay there. Vic frowned at it for a moment, then relaxed when he saw that there was still a little movement of the chest. Still alive, but definitely on that edge. He idly chewed the toothpick from one side of his mouth to the other.

"Come on, Sparky. You're four feet away. If you want it that bad, crawl."

The dying man did that. Slowly at first, just a faint flexing of white fingers in the dirt and a weak kick of the feet, and then the fingers dug into the mud and the toes of the shoes found purchase on a tangle of root, and the dying man began to crawl, wriggling like a misshapen snake through brown grass and mud.

Vic watched him, fascinated. He'd read about this in some of the books he'd found at the Man's house, and on Web pages he'd prowled on the Net, but he'd never witnessed the process before. It was nothing like in the movies.

The man made it to the edge of the swamp and Vic felt a jolt of excitement shoot through him. This was it, he realized; the shit was really happening!

The dying man was at the end of his strength now, and with his very last effort he pulled himself over the bank and into the swampy mud. Blood still leaked from his wounds and it soaked into the black muck, becoming part of it. Vic could hear how hungrily the mud sucked at the wounds, drinking from them.

"Oh, hell yes," he said softly.

"Yes . . ." This time it was the voice of the dying man. Faint but real, and it was full of joy as the swamp sucked the last blood out of him. "Oh . . . yes!"

Then there was a smell like sulfur and burned meat and gasses erupted from the swamp, curling up on either side of the dying man's head. A moment later something black bubbled up all around him and Vic leaned close to see. It was thick, like blood, but it was the color of ink. Steam rose from it. It splashed all over the dying man and his face was completely covered in it. It pooled on the surface of the swamp and the biggest pool formed around the dying man's head.

Vic waited for a moment to see what would happen next. The man looked dead; Vic could see no movement at all in his chest or back. And then he heard it . . . a faint sound. Like a baby nursing at a breast. A sucking sound.

Vic put his hands on the bank and lowered his head so that he could see the man's mouth. Yeah, there it was. The man was drinking the black ichor of the swamp.

Smiling, Vic sat back on the bank and chewed his toothpick, feeling immensely pleased and powerful. It was a full ten minutes before the man raised his head from the surface of the swamp and sucked in a huge lungful of air. He turned with painful slowness and crawled back to the firm muddy ground and lay there, gasping, his eyes jumping with fever, his fingers twitching.

Vic tossed away the toothpick and took a cigarette out of his pocket and lit it. He smoked it all the way down, smoked another. It took about that long for the man just to sit up, and even then his head drooped down between his knees, muck and black goo dripping from his mouth and nose.

"How do you feel?" Vic asked sarcastically.

Karl Ruger just shook his head. A heavy barking cough spasmed through his chest and he vomited between his splayed legs. It was a mixture of red and black blood.

"I feel strange. . . ."

"You don't say," Vic purred, enjoying this.

"My head . . . all fucked up . . ."

Vic snorted. "Pal, you don't know the half of it."

Ruger looked at him, his rheumy eyes sick but hostile. "Who the hell are you anyway?"

"Well, let me put it in words you might understand. I," he said, "am the right hand of Ubel Griswold."

The dying man's eyes jumped.

Vic saw the words hit home and nodded. "Yeah, baby. Two dogs, one leash." He bent forward, leaning his forearms on his thighs. "So listen close. My name's Vic Wingate and the Man has work for both of us to do."

Frowning, Ruger looked down at his chest, at the bullet holes that were not clogged with black goo.

"Good luck with that," he rasped. "I'm fucking dying here."

Vic shrugged. "Yeah, you are. But you're one of *his* now, so pretty much Griswold will decide when and if you die—and what being dead will mean. It's outta your hands as much as it's outta God's hands. New boss, new rules."

Ruger coughed up a clot of blood. "You're not making any sense. Christ, I've got four bullets in me."

"Five, actually. But, lookee here—you ain't dead yet. How about that?" He cocked his head to one side, considering. "Well . . . you ain't completely dead. And you ain't gonna really ever be dead until the Man wants you dead. Y'see, Ruger, ol' buddy, you've got some work to do. I believe you have some unfinished business to attend to, old hoss."

Some of the fire returned to Ruger's cold eyes. "Fuck you, pal. If I'm going to do anything before I die it's find that son of a bitch who shot me and tear his fucking throat out. And that broke-nose country bitch."

Vic stood up, brushed the dirt off his pants. "I believe we're on the same page here, so I want you to listen to me for a minute. Yeah, you gotta square things with a few people. The asshole that shot you is named Malcolm Crow. He's that Guthrie bitch's boyfriend. It serves what the Man wants that both of them should stop fucking up the works. The Man has an old score to settle with Crow and it would go a long way toward getting with the program if you were to rip that little prick a new one."

Ruger's laugh was cold and wet, but Vic's own face was sober as he added: "Understand something, though, sport. Make sure that however you do it, it makes headlines. Let's give this fucker a Hollywood ending. Big, noisy, and nasty. Go down in a blaze of glory with the sons a' bitches who did this to you. Hell, everybody'd believe that story. And belief, my friend, is what we need."

"Why?"

"Like I said, the Man has his reasons. And then there's one more thing you gotta do, and it has to be tonight."

"What?"

Vic told him. As he spoke, black goo oozed from Ruger's smiling mouth. His tongue flicked past his shattered teeth and over his purple lips, lapping up the ichor. He coughed again, spitting up more blood and pus and mud, but each time his lungs sounded clearer, though his face was still a waxy white from all the blood he'd lost. The fever in his eyes danced brighter and brighter.

Vic smiled, too; he took a long draw and snorted smoke out through his nostrils. "I'll be seeing you later." With that he turned and walked the mile back to his truck. He was still grinning when he slid behind the wheel.

Chapter 23

He didn't even notice her when he stepped into the elevator, a small figure standing silent as a ghost in one corner; all he saw were the images crashing together in his mind. Terry jabbed the button for the fourth floor and was sucking on a kiwi-flavored Life Saver, thinking about Crow and Val, about Mark and Connie, and about Henry Guthrie dying alone out in the rain. He was close to overdosing on the Xanax, but he didn't care. His plan was to go out, buy a bottle of something very strong—maybe bourbon, maybe scotch—bring it back, and sit vigil in the doctors' lounge until they released Crow in the morning. He couldn't make himself go home to Sarah, and he was too terrified to sleep.

Terry felt like he was a short step away from screaming. The effort of keeping a bland, normal expression on his face was driving him up a wall. Every time something else happened with this catastrophe he wanted to shout at everyone, to tell them to leave him alone; he felt constantly poised to run. Everything was starting to spin out of control, or slip like oily snakes between his fingers. Just in the last few weeks—since those awful nightmares had started, since a full night's restorative sleep had become only a memory—it seemed as if each separate element of his life was becoming warped. The town was a mess. The crops were failing, the banks were going to have to foreclose on people Terry had grown up with, people who looked to him for answers because he was the mayor.

On top of that the town had become a battleground. Henry Guthrie was dead; Guthrie's whole family was in the hospital. It was impossible to fit his mind around that. Crow had been shot! Police were swarming all over, taking control away from him. At home it was just as bad. Sarah wanted him to go back into therapy because of his dreams. Normally Terry liked the catharsis of therapy, but not lately—not with the kinds of dreams he'd been having. He did not want to be told that he was going crazy. It made him want to scream, because he thought he truly was losing his mind. Day by day, night by night, nightmare by nightmare. All he wanted from his shrink now was a fresh set of prescriptions. The antipsychotics and the anxiolytics weren't doing their job, so he'd have to lean on Dr. Calder to prescribe something a whole lot stronger. Anything, as long as it took things down a notch and let him sleep without those dreams.

He stood there in the elevator, staring at his reflection in the polished steel of the elevator's inner door; he stood there and looked at his face. No, not *his* face. The *other* face.

The face of . . . *what*? What was it? He didn't even know what to call it.

It was the face of the thing that every night rose up and hunched over Sarah's sleeping body, reaching for her with twisted hands, opening its mouth to reveal those huge . . .

He shuddered and closed his eyes, not even wanting to think about it, because every time his mind tried to put a name on the face reflected in the stainless steel door, his thoughts drifted immediately back in time, drifted thirty years back, revisiting the Pine Deep of his boyhood. The town had been so different then. It was a smaller place, and a darker place; darker without the merchandising and licensing of spooky things that now made the town rich, not the mildly scary darkness of Pine Deep, Bucks County's Haunted Playground. Terry tried not to think about those days. He tried often and he tried hard, but he rarely succeeded, not when he looked in any reflecting surface and saw the daily changes that made his face less and less his own, and more and more the face of the nightmare beast. Those long-ago days had left their mark on him in more ways than one, scaring him body and soul, and snatching away from him the one thing he loved most in all the world. Mandy. Little red-haired Mandy. Three years his junior and more precious to him than most little sisters are to little boys. She was always happy, al-ways smiling—something Terry as a child rarely was—and she always managed to find some way to trick him into laughing. But she was thirty years dead, lost to the darkness of those times.

"Terry?"

Terry Wolfe stiffened as he heard the tiny voice behind him in the elevator. His big body became suddenly rigid and he stared forward, instantly afraid to turn and look.

"Terry . . . ?" asked the voice.

He stared at the closed door of the elevator, too terrified to even move. He knew he was alone in the car. *This is it,* he thought with something like resigned acceptance, *this is the way it happens. First the dreams, then the hallucinations, and finally the voices. This is how people become insane. This is what it feels like when your mind dies. Oh God!*

"Terry, please . . ."

"Go away!" he hissed between gritted teeth. He brushed a hand behind him as if shooing away a cat. "*You're not here!*"

"Terry, please . . . look at me."

"No," he muttered, grinding his teeth. The elevator stopped at his floor, but the doors refused to open. He stabbed the but-tons but they remained cold and dark.

"Just look at me . . . look what happened to me."

Behind him she shifted and now he could see her hazy re-flection in the stainless steel of the closed elevator door. A small, slim figure, girl-high and girl-shaped in a ragged and tattered green dress. Even though the reflection was smeared and dis-torted, he could see her face, see the slashes on it, the blood that welled from it that ran like rainwater down her dress and clung to the matted red curls.

"Oh . . . God . . ." he breathed and pressed his eyes shut against the sight; tears struggled out from under his eyelids and burned their way down his cheeks. "I'm so sorry . . . please . . ."

"Terry, I don't want to make you cry."

"Then go away!"

"I can't, Terry. You know that." The voice was a little girl's voice, but the words and the manner of speech were far older than that.

"For the love of God, why can't you leave me in peace?"

"God?" she echoed with soft mockery in her voice. "God didn't save me, Terry. God didn't save you, either. And God won't save this town. Don't you understand yet? *He's not dead*, Terry."

He almost turned, almost wheeled around to face her. "What? What did you say?"

"He's not dead, Terry," she said quietly, but there were echoes of sadness and of fear in her voice. "He's still there, Terry. Still there after all these years."

"No! That's not true."

"Yes, Terry. It is and you know it. He's still there—still *here!*—and he is going to start it all over again."

"No!"

"Yes. All of it, over again. All the hurting, all the dying. Can't you smell the blood already? He's coming back, Terry, but this time he's *different*. He's a lot stronger now. Being dead has made him so much stronger." Her voice was so old now, ancient with cynical grief. "You thought he was a monster back then, Terry? He's worse now. You know I'm right—you've seen it in your dreams. And you know what he wants from you, what he wants you to *be*. You see that, too. You see that every time you look in the mirror."

"Shut up! Please!"

"You can stop him."

"I can't stop him! How could I ever stop him? I couldn't stop him from . . . from . . ."

"From hurting me?" she offered. "I know, Terry, but you tried. You *did* try, and I love you for it. But he hurt me, and he hurt you, and then the Bone Man came and hurt him."

"Killed him, you mean."

"No, hurt him. Reduced him," she said in her young-old

voice. "Don't you understand? Evil never dies . . . it just waits, and it gets stronger in the dark. He can't die. He isn't like other people. He isn't real."

"Neither are you!"

"I know," she said in a sad whisper of a voice, "I know. That's why it's up to you, Terry. You have to fight him."

"It's you who doesn't understand! How could I fight him, even if he was still alive?" There was a long silence, and then Terry felt her hand slip into his. Her fingers were small and cold and wet, and he almost jerked his own hand away—almost, but he didn't.

"You know how to fight him, Terry."

"Then how?" he suddenly snarled. "How am I supposed to fight someone like him? Fight—some-*thing* like him?"

"By coming with me. By not being like him."

"What are you talking about? I'm not like him!"

Her silence answered him; then after a pause she said, "Terry, the only way to not be like him is to be like me."

Now he did jerk his hand away. "What is that supposed to mean?" He wheeled at last and faced her, but she had vanished completely, leaving only the chill of her touch on his fingers. He looked at his hand, at each finger where she had touched him, and saw the tiny droplets of blood. "Mandy . . ." he whispered. Behind him the elevator doors opened and he spun and blundered out into the empty corridor.

(2)

Officer Jim Polk slipped the little pint bottle of apricot brandy into his hip pocket and tugged his uniform jacket down to cover the bulge. He felt tired, but now with an ass-pocketful of good times, he felt relaxed.

He was not a good-looking man by any stretch. He was average in height, weight, color, and build, but his whole appearance was spoiled by a shiftiness in his eyes that hinted at the avaricious pettiness of his soul. At fifty he looked like a seedy used car salesman in someone's borrowed cop uniform. Out of uniform, no one would ever have guessed him to be a professional law enforcement officer with thirty-one years on the job. Not that he cared. If he had a bottle of something sweet, or maybe a good fifth of Wild Turkey for those really pissy days, then he was sitting pretty. The weight of the brandy bottle in his back pocket was a comfort to him, and it made him want to smile.

Across the street, his new temporary partner sat slumped behind the wheel of his unit, arms folded across her chest, head nodding. Polk grinned as he walked up to her side of the patrol car, and stood there for a moment, watching her sleep. Polk liked having a woman partner. He liked it a whole lot. He had never been paired with Rhoda Thomas or Shirley O'Keefe, and he had always wondered what it would be like to share job time with a chick. A chick with a shield and a gun. A chick who knew guns and could talk rough and act tough.

Polk thought it was just Jim-jumping-Dandy.

He conceded to himself that this one, Melanie White, was no Pamela Lee, but she had a good rack of bombs—he could tell that even with the Kevlar vest she wore. Despite the bagginess of her uniform trousers, she looked to have nice buns, too. Polk was pleased as punch. Her face wasn't much, though, he decided, a little too rough, nose too long and bent, and her lips too thin. What the hell, he reminded himself, they all looked the same in the dark.

Still grinning, he tugged the Jacquins out of his pocket, broke the seal with a twist, and took a warming mouthful of the burning syrup. Licking his lips, he glanced quickly around as he replaced the cap and stowed the bottle once more out of sight. There was no one looking in his direction except the town tramp, Mr. Pockets, who was looking up from a trash can he'd been picking though. He favored Polk with a faint smile and went back to his explorations. Polk ignored him, still smiling, feeling very good.

Polk's smile froze into a mask of semicurious delight. It occurred to him that if he leaned over until his forehead was pressed against the frame of the closed door, he could probably see down Melanie's shirt. Hmm. His tongue searched for more of the brandy residue on his lips, and, once again checking the street, he eased himself forward. The cold metal of the door frame felt nice against his forehead, and as he shifted and squirmed for just the right angle, he could see the top inch of cleavage, caught in shadows cast by the vest and the folds of the shirt, but there sure as hell. Dotted with freckles, too, and Polk thought that was just the cat's ass.

"Still going for the cheap shots, Jimmy?" a voice asked him.

Polk jerked erect and spun around, his heart suddenly hammering in his chest. A pickup truck that he hadn't even heard drive up was idling five feet away. Vic Wingate leaned against the fender by the open door, arms folded across his chest, head cocked to one side, and a mean little smile on his face. Polk stared at him for a moment, flicked a guilty glance back at the quietly snoring Melanie White, then faced Vic again. He shrugged and walked over to Vic's truck, lowering his voice. "My new partner."

"No shit," Vic said blandly. "You fuck her yet?"

"Shh! Christ, she'll hear you!"

Vic chuckled. "Who cares? Ugly bitch anyway. Face like a stone wall." He considered for a moment. "Nice jugs, though."

Polk took an unconsciously covetous step to one side to block Vic's view. "What's going on, Vic? You want something?"

"Can't a guy stop to say hi to one of his buddies?"

Polk made a face. "Yeah, right. You wouldn't piss on me if I was on fire, so don't jerk me off, Vic. I'm on the clock here, so what do you want?"

Unfolding his arms, Vic turned, reached into the truck, fished around on the floor of the passenger side, and then turned back. He had an old grease-stained rag in his hands and he handed it to Polk, who took it with a puzzled frown, then felt the weight and shape of it. Polk almost unwrapped it, but Vic touched his hand and shook his head. Instead, Polk felt the shape of it again, judging it by its thickness. He looked at Vic with a face like an expectant schoolboy's. "This is . . ."

"Yeah," agreed Vic.

"But . . . wha . . . . ?"

Vic leaned close and spoke very quietly. "For services rendered."

"For what? I don't get it. I haven't done anything for you since . . ."

"Let me put it another way. It's for services *about* to be rendered."

"About . . . ?" Clouds formed slowly on Polk's face and he stared through confusion for several minutes as traffic swept past the double-parked truck. Vic let him work it out. Finally, Polk's face cleared of doubt and a mask of shock formed instead; his eyes grew very wide. He could actually feel his knees starting to tremble.

"Don't even fuck around, Vic—"

"It's no joke, Jimmy. You've known all along it was gonna start someday."

"Oh, come on! That's just crazy shit. It was a joke. Stuff we talked about when we got high back in school." Polk was shaking his head back and forth.

"Jimmy . . ." Vic said softly, coaxing. "Don't let's play games. You know what we were talking about, and what it meant. Don't play like it was all LSD trips. You know, man, you *know!*"

Polk looked at him for a minute, still shaking his head. He could feel a burning in the corners of his eyes and a tingling in his nose and realized with horror that he was about to cry. He made a face and started to turn away. "This is bullshit, Vic—"

Vic's hand caught his shoulder in a grip so fast and hard that Polk was jerked back around to face the mechanic. The wrapped bundle of money fell to the ground. "Don't you fucking walk away from me, Jimmy." He leaned close and his voice was a whisper as cold and hard as the edge of a new razor blade. Polk didn't want to look into Vic's eyes, but they bored into him, the intensity compelling and unmanning at the same time. Polk was terrified, but he was trapped, too.

"You took money from me before, Jimmy. Hell, you took money from *him!* You think you can take the Man's dime and not work for it?" He tightened his grip and pulled Polk even closer. Polk could smell cigarettes and something sour on Vic's breath. "You took the man's dime, Polk. You took your thirty pieces of silver, just like me, and that means the Man *owns* us! He owns us. You should be fucking filled with joy that someone like him counts us among his chosen few. That's an honor, you shit bag, and don't you ever forget it. Ever!" He released Polk with a small shove that knocked Polk against the door of Vic's truck.

Polk caught his balance and quickly looked up and down the street to see if anyone had seen him get roughed up. His partner was still asleep in the front seat of their cruiser, and no one but the old tramp Mr. Pockets had seen anything. The hobo stared at him for a moment and then continued rooting in the trash.

"Now," Vic said softly, "pick up that money." His eyes were hard as fists.

Polk didn't even try to stare him down; his eyes dropped and he bent over and picked up the bundle wrapped in the greasy rag.

You took your thirty pieces of silver, just like me.

Vic nodded his approval, and then suddenly smiled. "It's gonna start happening soon. That's your starting salary, man. It's an advance, and there's a shitload more where that came from. I'll call you to tell you how to earn enough of it to let you buy all the broads and scotch whiskey in the world. I'll call you soon." He paused and pointed a hard finger at Polk's face. "You be ready."

With that, Vic turned and climbed back into his truck. He slammed the door, put it in gear, fought his way aggressively through the evening traffic, and vanished around a corner. Polk stood and watched him go, his eyes still wide, his heart hammering in his chest, and his mind reeling with the implications. Melanie slept through it all, waking only when she heard and felt the trunk slam shut. She raised sleepy eyes and looked at Polk as he climbed in beside her.

"Something wrong?" she asked.

You took your thirty pieces of silver, just like me, and that means the Man owns us! He owns us.

Polk dabbed at the sweat on his brow and upper lip. "No," he said huskily. "I . . . uh, I suddenly don't feel all that good."

She shrugged, turned the key in the ignition, and eased the patrol car into the lane of traffic heading south.

(3)

"I gave her a sedative and she'll sleep through," Weinstock said as he settled into the bedside chair.

Crow nodded. About ten minutes after Val had snuck into his room, a tribe of nurses had come hustling in, scolding and clucking and scowling at Crow as if her elopement from her own room had somehow been his idea. They bundled her off to her room, shooting looks of disapproval over their shoulders as they went. A few minutes after that Saul Weinstock had come in.

"She tell you why she slipped out?"

Weinstock nodded. "Bad dreams. Who can blame her? I'm probably going to have my fair share of them tonight, too."

"She only told me that she had a dream about that guy Ruger. No details."

Weinstock sucked his teeth. "She said she saw Karl Ruger in her room. Oh, don't look at me like that. With all that she's been through I'd have been concerned for her sanity if she didn't dream of that prick. But with the stuff we pumped her up with she'll probably be dreaming of nothing more threatening than Santa Claus for the rest of the night."

"Yeah. Maybe."

"Look, Crow, I want to be serious for just a bit, okay? We both know how tough Val is, and believe me, when she's in form I would never want to cross her. But with everything that's happened she's likely to be a little flaky. And you"—he reached over and tapped Crow's knee with a thick finger—"have to be the stabilizing force in her life. You're going to have to represent sense and order so she can get back to herself."

"Sense and order? Me?"

"I know, it's a stretch for you."

"Eat me."

"You're not kosher."

"How do you know?"

"I'm a doctor, I know everything."

"Ah."

"Anyway . . . she's going to need time and a lot of love. And patience. This could take weeks or even months for her to get over. You up for all that?"

Crow laughed. "Can I share something with you, Saul?"

"Of course."

"Last night I was going to ask Val to go away with me for a weekend to a nice bed-and-breakfast in New Hope. Over a nice dinner and a superb bottle of nonalcoholic wine I was going to pop the ol' question."

A great big grin broke out on Weinstock's face. "Then I guess you're all set for the long haul."

"As the routine goes . . . in sickness and in health."

Weinstock patted his leg and stood up. "Good man."

(4)

Saul Weinstock closed the door but lingered for a moment outside Crow's room, staring up the hallway to where Val lay asleep. A police officer paced the hallway between the two rooms, and when he saw Weinstock looking in his direction he blushed and dropped his eyes. The officer—Barry Whitsover—had snuck downstairs for a smoke, leaving both Val and Crow unprotected, and hadn't been on post when Val had gone truant. Weinstock had taken him aside and had reamed him out so long and so hard that the man's ears were still bright red. Weinstock told him that it was only his compassion for the mentally impaired that prevented him from reporting it to Chief Bernhardt. The officer had no defense and had slunk away, relieved but humiliated.

But Weinstock wasn't staring at him at the moment. He was looking at the door to Val's room and thinking about what Crow had just said about proposing to Val. He smiled. The timing couldn't be better. First, it would probably give her something to feel joyful about when everything else around her was dragging her down. Optimism was the best drug in the world. And, more importantly, it was a damn good thing because, based on what Val had said—and the blood and urine tests done when Val was admitted—they were already a fair way to starting a family.

He wandered away to start his rounds, his happy whistle at odds with the pall of dread that hung over the town.

Chapter 24

As a quiet autumn darkness settled over Pine Deep, Vic Wingate pulled his truck right up to the edge of the drop-off at the Passion Pit, his bumper jutting out of the steep drop down to Dark Hollow. He killed the engine, fired up a cigarette, and settled back to wait. No radio, no sound.

He was in a happy mood. Everything was in motion and things were working well, just as the Man had assured him they would. And just as he, himself, had planned. Ruger had come to town, as the Man had foreseen, been stranded here, and had begun the Change. The Man had sicced Tow-Truck Eddie on Mike, which should efficiently take care of that problem—after all, considering what Mike *was* and how soon he might discover his own nature, it was best to get him off the board as soon as possible. Vic just wished that he could kill the little snot himself, but he knew the folklore and shared the Man's dread of what would happen to their plans if Mike died by a corrupt hand. It had to be a clean hand, or the whole plan would fail—and whose hands were cleaner than Tow-Truck Eddie's? The guy was a fucking saint. A major league fruitcake, to be sure, but as clean as a whistle when it came to matters of the spirit. That meant that Mike—and his potential—would be neutralized. With him out of the game the Red Wave could really work, and that jazzed Vic so much he actually got hard.

He smoked and considered the Ruger thing. There was still way too much heat around Ruger. Far too much for comfort. If that psychopath did what he was supposed to do, though, then the heat would be turned off. Vic wondered how Ruger would manage it, and what he'd do. Would he take his suggestion and take Crow and Val Guthrie with him, down in that blaze of glory? If so, that would simplify things, too, because the Man hated Crow. The "one that got away" all those years ago. Griswold had literally been a second away from tearing out Crow's throat when that fucking Oren Morse had stepped in and saved the boy. That's when things had gone wrong thirty years ago. Morse had saved young Crow, and had then managed to kill Griswold.

Vic shook his head in wonder. How that skinny guitar-strumming nigger had managed to kill the Man was beyond him, but then he smiled when he thought about how bad a move that had been for Morse. Not just because it gave Vic a reason to orchestrate his murder—which had been quite a lot of fun—but because it had started the Great Change for Griswold. Not even the Man knew about that. Vic had always thought dead was dead, and though he served Griswold back then, the Man had been more or less mortal. Yeah, a werewolf, but still alive and still mortal. Then he'd been killed and buried in the swamp. Not in hallowed ground; not blessed by clergy or read over; but stuffed down in the swamp just the way he had died: halfway between man and monster.

That's when Vic had learned that evil never dies. It waits, it changes, and it always comes back. Unless its force is blocked by prayers and the proper burial rites, it always comes back—and it comes back far stronger, and in the Man's case, different. Not a werewolf anymore, and certainly nothing human. Now the Man was evolving into something beyond anything the people in this town would understand. Nor was the Man becoming like Boyd or Ruger. Hell, once the Man finished manifesting his new body and rose from his swampy grave, garlic or stakes wouldn't mean dick to him.

Vic broke off in his reverie and thought about that for a second. Garlic and stakes. He realized that he didn't actually know if they would stop Boyd and Ruger, either. He'd have to find out. Not just so that he would always have an edge over them, but because he wanted to make sure they wouldn't be stopped by some asshole who'd just had an Italian dinner and sneezed on them. Stakes he could experiment with to see if the legends held up, but if they did work, he knew that he wouldn't be able to do much about it. Garlic, on the other hand, could be bought locally from growers, which meant that the supply had to be controlled. He made a mental note to work on that tomorrow.

His cigarette was low and he chain-lit another, but just as he rolled down the window to toss away the butt he heard the crack of a twig under a foot. Automatically he pulled the old Mauser C-96 Bolo short-barreled pistol from the shoulder rig he wore. The gun had been made in the 1920s and had belonged to Griswold, which made it sacred to Vic.

He laid the barrel on the frame of the open cab window and waited as someone thrashed his way up the slope toward the parking area. If it was anyone else than the person the Man had sent him here to meet, he'd blow their head off. The Mauser was unregistered and untraceable. Vic had killed five women with it and three vagrants over the last thirty-five years, and every one had been a one-shot kill. You have to love efficiency of that kind.

The bushes at the top of the drop-off trembled, the dry leaves shivering and flickering with silver moonlight, and then a man stepped up onto the flat ground of the Passion Pit. He was covered with mud and blood and his right leg was twisted askew, though he walked with no flicker of pain on his mushroom-white face. The man's eyes were dark, hostile pits and his mouth hung open, revealing teeth that were caked with blood and strings of raw meat. He saw Vic's truck and snarled, baring those filthy teeth in a mask of pure hatred.

Vic relaxed and clicked the safety back on.

"Over here, asshole," he said. "Get the fuck in, we're wasting time."

The snarl lost some of its venom as the man shambled toward the truck. Vic reached over and jerked the handle, pushing the door open so Kenneth Boyd could climb in.

(2)

"Jesus!"Terry's eyes snapped wide as he jerked awake from his doze as if he'd been slapped. The abruptness of waking had thrust him forward and he crouched on the edge of his chair, gripping the armrests with spiked fingers, his big body leaning forward as if to vomit. Thunder boomed in his chest and lightning flashed in his eyes and his pores rained icy sweat. Around him, the doctors' lounge was quiet, softened with evening shadows, and very still.

Terry looked around, trying to understand what had shocked him awake—but there was nothing. For one horrible moment he feared that his sister's bloody ghost had returned to torment him with her desperate pleas. No. Nothing.

Nothing, except the vague and fading feeling that something horrible had just happened. A terrible feeling of dread seemed to be clustered around his heart, like moths around a light. The sensation, or awareness, or fading dream—whatever it was—eased gradually. His heart stopped hammering, the rhythm slowing as minutes passed.

He heard heels clicking along the floor outside, coming closer very quickly, and then the door opened. A nurse leaned into the room, her face wearing a quizzical smile.

"Sorry," she said. "I thought I heard—"

Terry looked at her with his red-rimmed eyes, a false smile nailed to his rigid lips, his fingers clutching the arms of his chair.

"Is everything okay?" the nurse asked.

"Um . . . yes. Everything's fine. I was, um, taking a nap."

"Sorry to bother you, Mr. Wolfe. It's just the strangest thing. I thought the TV was on." She glanced at the dark screen. "Guess I'm hearing things."

"What do you mean?" he asked.

She laughed self-consciously. "You'll think I'm a loony tunes, but I thought—just for a moment—that I heard a . . . well, a roar."

"A roar?" His voice was tight in his throat.

"Isn't that silly? I thought I heard a roar. Like a lion, or a bear. Or something."

"In here?"

"I know, I know . . . I'm too young for Alzheimer's!" She laughed. "Sorry to have bothered you." Her head vanished and she pulled the door shut.

Terry sat stock-still, staring at the door, feeling under his fingers the jagged tears in the leather upholstery. Stiffly, he bent forward and looked down, first at one arm of the chair and then the other. The tough leather was slashed in long lines, as if dull knives had been viciously racked across them. Several sets of tears, four lines to a set.

"God save me!" he whispered, and in the back of his mind he could hear Mandy's voice whisper to him.

God didn't save me, Terry.

"No!"

God didn't save you, either. God won't save this town, Terry.

"Get out of my head!" he cried, beating at his skull with both fists.

And you know what he wants from you. You see that, too. You see that every time you look in the mirror.

He bent forward and put his face in his hands and wept for his sanity—and his soul.

(3)

Officer Jim Polk lay on his back and blew cigarette smoke up at the ceiling. On the radio, Jerry Garcia was insisting that any friend of the devil was a friend of his. Beside him, Donna Karpinsky moaned softly in her sleep and turned away. Polk turned and looked at her back. She was a pretty girl, half his age, with lots of black hair, almost no ass, and eyes that were often pretty but could turn as hard as fists when she was in one of those moods. Polk understood the look. It was the whore look, old as time and as uncompromising as a hammer. She had given him that look when he had flagged her down two hours ago, thinking that he was rousting her or looking for a freebie, but the look had dissolved when he had waved a fistful of long green at her, and after that she got all dewy-eyed and as willing to please as a twice-kicked dog. Polk knew he could have gotten her to do him for free, just by flashing his badge, but it felt good to have her full and unreserved attention, with no resentment to spoil the mood.

He had given her two hundred bucks, which was four times the rate for a half-and-half, and he'd paid for the motel room and the bottle of Napoleon brandy that stood half-empty on the bedside table. Polk would have been happy just to have her be nice to him while they did it, but she must have been really psyched by the extra cash, and for over an hour they had made out like high school kids, kissing and touching and making it feel like something tender for a change. Then it had gotten down to business and she had properly hauled his ashes for him. Even so, he thought, she had been nice about that, too. She had made it seem like two people doing it, not just a half-drunk cop and a motel hooker.

Polk sucked on his cigarette and thought about the money that had bought him that evening's pleasure. Vic's money. Polk felt his insides twitch every time he thought about Vic and his money. In the past Polk had done a lot of things for Vic. Things that sometimes weren't so bad, and sometimes made him sick to his stomach. Only once over those years had Polk ever tried to tell Vic that he wasn't into it anymore. Only once, and then he had been out of work for four weeks because of the way Vic took the rebuff. Four weeks in which he pissed blood and tried not to breathe too deeply and had to eat only soft foods. He told Gus Bernhardt that he'd taken a bad tumble off his motorbike. No way Polk was ever going to tell Gus, or anyone else, that Vic had stomped him nearly unconscious and then stuffed a handful of dog shit in his mouth and held him at gunpoint until he'd swallowed it.

Lying there in bed, Polk thought back to that day, more than eighteen years ago, and the hand holding the cigarette began to shake.

He took three slow pulls on the cigarette to steady himself, and he blinked repeatedly until the tears of shame dried up. Eighteen years ago and it still felt the same. As Vic had stomped him, he had told Polk over and over again that he was getting off light. Polk believed him with a whole heart. Over the years, the little jobs for Vic had dwindled down to a trickle, just something here and there, usually for small change. But now he had a wad of bills so thick they wouldn't even fit into his pants pocket.

What the fuck was Vic going to want him to do to earn that kind of scratch?

He had always been afraid that Vic would one day ask him to kill someone, and after that beating, Polk was not so sure that he wouldn't do it. No devil in hell terrified Polk more than Vic Wingate, and no court or jail came close to intimidating him half as much.

It was a lot of money—a whole lot of money—and Vic always wanted every penny's worth for his buck.

Please, God, Polk silently prayed. He coughed unexpectedly and sat up, his gut tightening as the spasm shook his whole body. He jammed a fist against his mouth to stifle the sound, and all Donna did was turn over and begin snoring. Polk felt a hot wetness on his hand and when he looked at it, he was confused and scared to see a splatter of dark droplets on his skin. It looked like tar, or like the black goo you find under compost heaps, but it smelled like . . .

He frowned, feeling sweat burst from his pores.

It smelled like blood.

Polk stared at it, absolutely unsure of what to do, say, or think next. He blinked a few times, and as he did so the light values in the room seemed to change. He angled his hand to let more light fall on the black goo, and suddenly it wasn't black at all. That must have been the shadows cast by his own face as he bent down over it. No, this was clear, probably just spit, or . . .

He sniffed it again. A frown touched his mouth. He tasted it with his tongue, and his smile broadened. It wasn't spit at all. It was brandy. Napoleon brandy. A short laugh bubbled from his throat as he licked up the brandy.

After a moment, Polk slowly lay back on the bed and stared at the ceiling, a contented smile on his face. When he had coughed, when he had seen the stain on his hand, not as brandy, but as some kind of black goo, the doubts and fears about what Vic was going to ask of him had vanished from his thoughts. Now all he thought about was the last few tasty drags of his cigarette and the sleeping girl next to him who was not going to be getting a full night's sleep. Not with two hundred dollars to earn.

(4)

Iron Mike Sweeney was throwing up. With each spasm of his chest the broken rib exploded with agony, and fresh tears of pain sizzled in his eyes. He knelt by the side of the road, knees on the macadam, hands braced on the curb, head bowed, vomiting pints of a thick, black, viscous liquid into the gutter. It tasted hot and salty, like tears, or blood.

Mike had been halfway home from the hospital after his aborted attempt to visit Crow, and the ensuing lengthy third degree by that shrimpy little reporter, Mr. Newton. He was just crossing Mayfair Street when suddenly his stomach convulsed in such a powerful cramp that his knees had buckled and he'd slumped down over the handlebars of the War Machine and slowed to a stop hard against a curb. He stepped off the bike and let it fall into the street and then sagged against a parking meter, holding it with one hand and pressing his other hand to his stomach. His knees suddenly buckled and he sagged down to the pavement, sitting down onto the curb with a thump. The first spasm faded and for a moment his brain cleared of the greasy mist that had formed as soon as the sick wave of pain had hit, but then a second wave, bigger, darker, far more powerful slammed into him and he fell forward onto hands and knees and vomited into the street over the iron grille of a culvert. It was so sudden, and so unexpected, that it scared him, and when he saw what it was he was throwing up, the fear had blossomed into total terror.

He thought he was hemorrhaging, throwing up blood from some ruptured part of him. The thought that Vic had finally done it, finally beat him so bad that he was dying tumbled through his brain. The vomiting gradually stopped and he coughed and gagged and choked, eyes squeezed shut against the pain that twisted his guts and closed his throat. For almost two minutes he knelt there on the empty street, eyes still pressed shut, waiting for the spasms to start again. Gradually, very gradually, the awful tension in his stomach faded and went away. He could still feel the stricture in his throat and the searing pain of his rib, but his stomach no longer felt like a bubbling cauldron of sewage.

Slowly, afraid to look at the blood he'd puked out, he opened his eyes.

There was nothing in the gutter. Just a drop or two of spit glistening on the bars of the culvert grille. Nothing else.

Mike stared down, trying to understand. He had seen the blood, damn it, black as paint and as searing as raw whiskey. He had felt it as it flooded out of him. It *had* happened. Except—apparently, it hadn't happened.

Mike Sweeney stared down at the gutter and felt a powerful wave of terror of some vast and unidentifiable kind sweep over him.

(5)

Officer Coralita Toombes and her temporary partner, Dixie MacVey, cruised along the winding stretch of A-32 under a haphazard scattering of stars overhead. The edges of the sky were black as a ring of cloud cover was moving in to cover the region again. The road shook itself out in front of them as they swept southeast toward the Pine Deep–Black Marsh border. By now it was a familiar circuit for Toombes and MacVey, one they'd been covering for nearly seven hours. They had a loop that started at the intersection of A-32 and Old Mill Road, dropped south as directly as the winding A-32 would allow, past the Guthrie farm, then down to the bridge that spanned the Delaware to Black Marsh in New Jersey, and there they would jog west on Peddler's Trail, which looped past the rusty stretch of Swallow Hill Bridge and turned northeast again until it once more hit the Extension by Old Mill. The whole loop ate up an even thirty miles, though as a crow might fly it the trip could have been done in just over ten, but there wasn't a straight road to be had anywhere in or around Pine Deep.

Toombes and MacVey drove in silence, partly from tiredness, partly from boredom, and partly because they couldn't stand each other. From MacVey's point of view, Toombes was a know-it-all big-city bitch cop who thought that she had seen it all, done it all, and had it all under control. MacVey saw Toombes as one of those cynical and dismissive types who had no time for small-town cops because they weren't "real cops" and hadn't tangled with "real criminals" and therefore didn't rate much, if at all. MacVey was also clearly intimidated by Toombes for these very same reasons.

As Toombes saw it, MacVey was just another one of those NRA types who collected big guns because they were disappointed by the size of their own dicks, and had wet dreams about real honest-to-gosh shoot-outs with real honest-to-gosh criminals. The kind of small-town rube (though Toombes had to admit that there were plenty of them in the city, too) that had a stack of *Soldier of Fortune* and *American Handgunner* magazines next to his bed, watched every episode of *COPS*, and could recite the specs and stats of every high-caliber gun made since 1950. Toombes, in short, thought MacVey was an adolescent ass wearing a cop's disguise, and having him as a partner made her miss Jerry Head, her own partner from back in the city, and it also made her uneasy, because one thing a cop needs for peace of mind is the knowledge that her backup is a professional and not likely to shoot her instead of the bad guy. Toombes figured that if push ever really came to shove, MacVey would probably shoot his own balls off while trying to remember how to get that monster Blackhawk .44 out of its fancy breakaway holster.

As partnerships went, it was something less than a roaring success.

There is an old cop belief that under the right circumstances, given the proper negative stimulus, even the best law enforcement officer will sink to the level of an incompetent partner. Stupidity, as the saying goes, is catching. So is clumsiness. As they cruised along the road, they were both so caught up in mentally psychoanalyzing each other that they forgot to pay attention to what they were about. They forgot to look for Kenneth Boyd, who was walking alongside the road, knee deep in withered onion grass, heading in a straight line toward the Black Marsh Bridge.

If the officers had been driving more slowly, if they had been shining their spotlights along the side of the road, if they had not been fuming about being partnered with each other, then they would very probably have seen him, but they didn't. Instead, they sped right past him, made the left that put them on Peddler's Trail, and headed east. In minutes the unit was nearly lost in dust and distance, and then swallowed whole as they dropped over a hillock.

From his vantage point twenty yards up a darkened side road, Vic Wingate stared as the cruiser passed Boyd.

"Jesus fucking Christ!" he growled. "How thick can you get?" He fired up the truck and pulled out onto the road until he was just ahead of Boyd and then pulled to a stop in front of him.

"Get the fuck in!"

Boyd stopped and stared at him with intense hatred and naked hunger.

"I said get in! C'mon, we don't have time to waste. And don't get any maggots on the seat this time."

The creature climbed in beside Vic and pulled the door shut.

"So much for getting a couple of trained observers to spot you leaving town. I mean, Jesus, how far up your own ass do you have to be not to spot an ugly fucked-up piece of shit like you right there by the side of the road? Maybe I should have put some neon friggin' lights on you."

Boyd just glared at him.

"Okay, new plan," Vic said, putting the truck in gear. "I'm going to drive you over to Black Marsh and drop you off somewhere. Make sure you're seen by at least two or three people. Make a scene . . . break a window or something—but don't fucking bite anyone and don't get fucking caught! You hear me? You have to be seen—clearly seen—but you have to get away. Do whatever you got to do to make it back across the river. Hide in the fields until you hear from me or the Man." He reached over and smacked Boyd on the forehead. "Hey! You listening to me?"

Boyd's eyes were red torches in the dark pits of his eye sockets. He opened his mouth, his gray tongue flicking over his lips. The hands in his lap twitched and spasmed, wanting to grab, to rend.

Vic pulled onto the bridge and the wooden beams rumbled beneath the wheels. Watching Boyd out of the corner of his eye, Vic said, "You'd just love to rip my throat out, wouldn't you?" He laughed. "Go ahead and try it . . . and see what the Man will do to you. That's providing I don't kick your sorry dead ass first."

The creature's torn and bloodless lips formed a single word, *Griswold*, but there was no sound.

"That's right—Griswold. You know you don't want to fuck with the Man. Don't think being dead would save you if you fucked with him. The Man would eat your *soul!*" Vic's voice was thick and heavy and he leaned into the words, his smile gone now. Boyd's hands gradually stopped their twitching. "Yeah, there are worse things than death, Boyd, and trust me when I say you don't want to find out what they are." There were fires in Vic's eyes now, and Boyd slowly recoiled from them. "You don't want to find out what they are," he repeated softly as the truck rolled off the bridge and he headed southeast to Black Marsh.

(6)

Tow-Truck Eddie sat behind the wheel of his wrecker and felt something in his mouth. Frowning, he raised a huge hand to his lips and then looked at his fingers, surprised to see them glistening wetly, darkly. His frown deepened as he bent to sniff at the wetness. It had the sheared-copper smell of fresh blood. Tow-Truck Eddie touched his tongue-tip carefully to the viscous smear. It didn't taste at all like blood. It tasted like tears. Nodding to himself in sudden understanding, Tow-Truck Eddie licked the black blood from his fingers and savored the taste.

(7)

A murder of night birds stood in a row along the branch of a fire-blackened tree on the edge of Dark Hollow. Seated on his log, the Bone Man stared into his lonely fire and read the secrets of the flames. The wind carried still more secrets to him, and he listened, hearing the echoes of distant, beating hearts. The Bone Man could still feel in his mouth the aftertaste of the black blood that had burned so unexpectedly on his tongue. When he had first tasted it he had cried out in disgust and spat the ichor into the flames. The flames had burned it all up, but the sound it made was more like whispery laughter than the hiss of super-heating moisture.

The north still blew its cold breath across the town, and the Bone Man shivered. He was always cold, even so near to the fire. Always cold. Now, sitting there, the taste of the black blood barely fading, the Bone Man read the winds and the fire and saw the days to come.

And he wept.

Chapter 25

Mike couldn't get into the hospital but he was able to get through on the phone, though he had to claim to be Crow's younger brother to bluff his way past the switchboard operator.

"Hello?"

"Crow?" Mike asked, not sure that the tired old man's voice on the other end of the line was his friend's.

"Yeah. Who's this?"

"It's Mike. Mike Sweeney."

"Hey, Iron Mike . . . how're the ribs?"

In truth the ribs hurt less than the rest of him, so Mike said, "I'm cool. Question is . . . how are you? I mean . . . you got *shot!*"

"Twice. Both bullets right through the brain pan. Killed me deader than a doornail."

Mike laughed. "How are you, or is that a stupid question?"

"I'm fine, bra. Just got caught in a drive-by while I was drinkin' gin and juice with my homies."

"Crow . . . I told you about the slang thing. It's kind of sad when you try to be hip."

"Sorry, kid, lost my head."

"It's okay, but don't let it happen again."

"Seriously, though, I'm okay. I'll probably be getting out tomorrow or the day after."

"Cool," Mike said. "I tried to get in to see you but the cops stopped me. They're not letting anyone in."

Crow was quiet for a moment, then said, "Look, Mike, if I can swing it so they let you past the dragons, would you do me a big favor?"

"Sure. Anything."

Crow told him what he wanted done.

"Oh, man! That's so cool!"

"Will you do it?"

"Of course! I'm on my way right now!"

"Thanks, Mike. I'll owe you a big one for this."

Mike paused, then said, "Crow . . . you don't owe me a thing." And hung up. For the first time that day his bruised face wore a genuinely happy smile.

(2)

Detectives Frank Ferro and Vince LaMastra sat at a deuce in the lounge of the Harvestman Hotel. Ferro was taking thoughtful sips from a mug of Miller Genuine Draft and LaMastra was halfway through his fourth Pumpkin Ale. The storm clouds that had been lumped over the town the night they'd gotten there had blown away into someone else's sky and the temperature had dropped so fast the news was warning of a possible frost. It was already a chilly forty outside and the moon was a sliver of ice in the total blackness of the evening sky.

They'd eaten chicken cheesesteaks and French fries, had listened to jukebox music, had eavesdropped on half a dozen ordinary conversations, but between them barely a half dozen words had passed in the two hours they'd been there. The report Dr. Weinstock had given had shaken them both and their shared frustration over the lack of progress in the case was running them down.

LaMastra looked up at the clock over the bar, watching the hand go from 11:58 to 11:59. He picked up his glass and drained the last of it in two big pulls, set it down, and shook off the bartender. Ferro just took another sip and stared moodily into the unhelpful amber depths of his glass.

Tomorrow they were scheduled to take a quick trip to Black Marsh. An hour ago they'd gotten reports from three separate eyewitnesses, including a USPS letter carrier, that someone closely resembling the posted description of Kenneth Boyd had been spotted. In all three reports, though, the suspect had been running or walking, and there was no visible evidence at all of the broken leg that Ruger had mentioned to the Guthries. Had Boyd been faking it to escape from Ruger? That seemed likely now, and the man was obviously doing everything he could to put as much distance as he could between his former partner and himself. If that was the case, then on one hand their immediate problems were cut in half, and on the other hand the scope of their manhunt just broadened. It was Ferro's contention that Boyd was of so little importance in the scheme of things that going to Black Marsh was almost a waste of time, except for the chance that he might have some idea of where Ruger was or about how he planned to escape Pine Deep.

"Shit," LaMastra said softly.

Ferro glanced at him, eyebrows raised in query.

Vince said, "It doesn't add up. Boyd being seen like that. By three witnesses . . . and then vanishing from the face of the earth as soon as the cruisers show up. It's a little much, don't you think?"

Ferro pursed his lips but said nothing.

"I'm telling you, Frank, this whole fucking situation is wrong."

"Of course it's wrong."

"No, I mean *wrong*. We're not seeing something here, Frank. We're not looking at this the right way."

"How should we be looking at it?"

"Shit, I don't even know anymore," LaMastra said. "I know Crow claims that Ruger was shot . . . but I don't know. This whole thing has me spooked."

Ferro looked at him. "That's an odd way to put it."

LaMastra shrugged. "Yeah, well, I guess 'odd' is pretty much

the best word to describe this whole thing. Pretty fucking odd."
He shook his head. "Screw this, I'm going up to my room to
watch TV."

He got up, tossed some bills on the bar, and shambled out.
Ferro lingered for a while, still staring moodily into the uninfor-
mative depths of his beer.

(3)

Crow called the hospital security and put Mike's name on the
entry list and then made a few calls to friends who had sent
flowers, assuring them that he was not at death's door. They all
asked him to pass along their concerns and condolences to Val,
Mark, and Connie, which he promised to do. When he finished
the obligation calls he then punched in Terry's number. The cell
rang and rang and Terry didn't pick it up.

A small flicker of concern tickled the edges of his awareness.
He asked his nurse if she'd seen him and was told that the mayor
had left for a meeting, though he said he would be back. He didn't
say when.

Crow gave it a half hour and then called again. This time
Terry picked up on the second ring.

"Yes?" His voice was harsh, abrupt.

"Terry . . . Crow. Did I catch you at a bad time?"

Terry gave a short laugh. "Anything after the doctor said 'it's a
boy' and smacked me on the ass would have been a bad time."

"That bad, huh?" Crow was still processing the fact that Terry
had just said "ass." It was the first time he'd ever heard Terry use
even so mild a curse.

"Bad? For the last hour I've been wrangling with the selectmen, trying to convince them that the whole town isn't falling
down around our ears. This after spending all day with the cops
and listening to the autopsy report on one of Ruger's chums.
No sleep in going on forty-five hours now, and I've got a case of
the shakes so bad that if someone gave me a pair of drumsticks
I'd be able to do a jazz improvisation that would make Hal

Roach look like a beginner." Though he tried hard to make a joke, there was no humor in his voice.

"Hey, how about this? Go the hell home and get some sleep. The town will still be here in six or eight hours."

"Yeah," Terry said, "but will I?"

"What do you mean?"

"Oh, nothing. I'm rambling. Look, Crow, I have to go. I'll drop by later and check in on you."

"I'd rather you went home to bed."

"See you later," Terry said and disconnected.

Crow frowned at his cell phone for a while, unhappy with the tension he had heard in his friend's voice. Terry saying "ass." Sure, it was a small thing, but it spoke volumes to Crow about how out of character Terry was acting.

He was mulling this over when Officer Jerry Head walked into his room carrying a paper bag. He paused in the doorway for a second, rapping on the door with a knuckle.

"Mind if I come in?"

It took Crow a second to place him, and then he waved the man in, indicating a chair. The big Philly cop sat down gratefully, looking spent and tired. He still wore his uniform, but his tie was loosened and he had the "off-duty" air about him.

"Mr. Crow—" he began.

"Just Crow."

"Cool. Crow—I only caught the tail end of what happened last night. I didn't see you kick the shit out of Ruger, but I heard the details, and I did see you help that girl, Rhoda. You stood your ground, man, can't nobody say otherwise."

Crow didn't know how to respond to that, so he just shrugged.

"So, I wanted to come in, see how you were doing, and . . ." Here he paused as if a little embarrassed.

"And what?"

"Well . . . I guess I just wanted to shake your hand." He extended his hand to Crow, who stared at it for a second, and then, half smiling with his own embarrassment, he reached out and took it. Out of courtesy for the IV, Head had offered his left, and the cop's hand was like a piece of unsanded wood—hard, dry, and rough. "And I also brought you something." Head opened the paper bag. "I've spent my share of time in hospitals—two car wrecks, a couple of knee surgeries, and a knife wound on the job—so I know you must be climbing the walls by now." Out of the bag he pulled two thick paperbacks—a Keith Ablow mystery and Dean Koontz's latest in paperback—and three magazines. *Sports Illustrated, Entertainment Weekly,* and the latest issue of *Maxim* with a lingerie pictorial featuring the women from Fox TV. Beneath the books there were two cans of cold Coke and a couple of packs of Tastykake chocolate cupcakes.

Crow was touched. "Jesus, man, you are a saint."

"Least I could do," Head said. "Even though it was just for a couple of hours, Rhoda was my partner last night."

Crow nodded. "Sit down—sit down and keep me company. Open these cupcakes for me and let's have a feast."

They lapsed into a conversation about the job, Crow relating some stories about small-town police work and Head talking about the streets of Philadelphia. Their rhythm was almost immediately comfortable and friendly, and Crow found he liked the Philly cop quite a bit. He was touched by the big man's thoughtfulness, and by his loyalty to Rhoda.

"So, where do you guys stand with all this?" Crow asked.

"Shit if I know." He told Crow about Boyd being spotted. "So with Macchio dead, that just leaves Ruger."

"Yeah."

"Which kind of brings me to the other reason I wanted to talk with you."

Crow nodded his encouragement.

Head said, "I was on the porch and just caught the tail end of the firefight between you and Ruger. As you may remember I fired off some rounds myself."

"Vaguely remember something. I was pretty well out of it by then."

"My question is—did you hit Ruger? I mean, are you sure you hit him?"

"Your boss, Ferro, asked me the same thing. So has everyone else, and I'll tell you what I told them."

"Which is?"

"I'm absolutely fucking positive I hit him. At least three times, and maybe as much as five times."

"No doubts?"

"No doubts. I saw the impacts, saw his body jerk with each shot."

"What about a vest? Could he have been wearing body armor?"

"No way in hell. I fought him hand to hand before that, Jerry, and I know damn well I was hitting meat and muscle, not Kevlar."

Head nodded and sat back, sipping his Coke. "Yeah, that was my read on it, too. I saw you shoot him. I'm pretty sure I missed, but I'll go before a judge and swear that I saw at least two or three of your shots nail him."

They looked at each other in silence for a moment.

"You want to ask it, or shall I?" Crow said.

"You mean . . . with a hundred searchers and five teams of dogs, how did a man with five bullets in him disappear?"

"Yep."

"Man, I don't even know. Fucker's painted with magic."

"Yeah."

At that point the door opened again and Mike Sweeney poked his head into the room. He saw the officer and stopped, silent.

"Come on in," Head said, rising. "I'm leaving anyway." He reached out again and shook Crow's hand. "I hope your lady and her family come through this okay."

"Thanks," Crow said. "That means a lot."

Head turned and as he passed Mike he gave the boy a quick appraising glance, taking in the bruises. He turned briefly to Crow, eyebrows raised significantly, and then left without comment.

Mike came over and sat down, dragging the chair closer to the bed.

"Dude!" Mike said. "Look at your face!"

"Yeah, well, look at yours, too. What the hell happened to

you?" And as soon as he asked the question Crow wished he could take it back. He remember Barney's account of how Vic had beaten Mike when he picked him up.

"I, uh . . ."

"Fell off your bike again?" Crow asked, one eyebrow raised.

"Yeah."

"Yeah," Crow said, and then had to leave it there because Mike was clearly not going to go any more distance down that conversational street. He didn't let it show on his face, but he made a mental note to look up Vic one of these days and find some way to kick the living shit out of him and yet not wind up in jail, or in court. That son of a bitch was way overdue for an attitude adjustment.

He sighed. "Thanks for coming, kiddo. Did you get the—"

Mike suddenly grinned and dug into his jacket pocket. "I got the key from the lady at the yarn shop. I fed the cats, too."

"Oh, jeez, I totally forgot about them!"

"They peed on the rug."

"Swell. It's their way of expressing disapproval at my tardiness."

"They peed on your coffee table, too. I had to throw out your magazines and some of the mail was wet. I put that in the sink."

"Little furry bastards."

"Anyway . . . I got the box you wanted." He produced a small box that was an inch and a half square and covered with navy blue velvet. Crow took it carefully and opened it. The engagement ring fairly lit the room with its brilliance. The Asscher-cut stone was huge—nearly two carats—and according to the salesman, it was a nicely cut, G Color, VS1 clarity diamond—and it had put a serious dent in his savings, to which Crow did not even blink.

"Whaddya think?" he asked Mike.

"Is it real?"

"Duh!"

"Wow! Are you going to propose to her? I mean—*here*? In the hospital and all?"

Crow grinned. "Ever heard of distraction therapy?"

"No. But I get the idea."

Crow closed the box and hid it in his bedside table. "Look, Mike, there's something else I wanted to talk to you about."

Mike tensed, and Crow could see it, but he gave the boy an affable smile. "Rumor has it that I've been shot. As a mortally wounded person I can't be expected to manage the daily affairs of a business as critical and cutting edge as mine. I mean—if a kid needs a tube of vampire blood, how is someone in my condition supposed to get it for him? The whole industry would come crashing down."

Grinning, Mike said, "Can't have that."

"So, as the proprietor of the town's most prestigious boutique for the gruesome and horrific I thought it might be time to hire myself an Igor. You appear to have an appropriate hump . . . what do you say?"

Mike's face beamed with happiness. "You're offering me a job?"

"Well, if you can call hours of endless toil and drudgery for little pay and occasional scorn and derision from a heartless taskmaster a job, then yes."

Mike jumped to his feet, then froze, wincing and gasping. "Ouch!" he said, standing hunched over in pain, then immediately followed it with, "I'm in! Oh my God! Thanks!"

Crow held up a cautionary finger. "I will have to call you Igor, though, you understand this?"

"I believe," said Mike, laughing, "that it's pronounced Eye-gor."

(4)

Mayor Terry Wolfe sat in the doctors' lounge drinking Glenkinchie from a Dixie cup, his elbows resting on his knees, the cup held lightly in his big hands. Head low between hunched shoulders, he stared moodily at the irregularities of the wax coating on the cup, breathing through his nose and sighing every eighth or ninth breath.

He had just spent an unproductive hour in a late meeting with the town selectmen, trying to calm them, cajole them, make them believe that everything was under control, when it was quite clear that not one damn thing was under control. Somehow during the last two days, Pine Deep had sunk up to its ass in shit. That's how he thought about it. No more silly euphemisms for it, no more Sunday school expletives like "darn" or "heck." Not today. Nope, not for Terry Wolfe. Not after that little elevator ride. Not after the things he'd seen last night. Not after the nurse hearing a roar coming from this very room while he was sleeping. Not after what happened to the arms of the leather chair.

Not after looking into the bathroom goddamn mirror again not five goddamn minutes ago.

Terry sipped the scotch and winced. He really loved scotch, but right now it tasted like boiled socks. On the way back to the hospital from the meeting he'd stopped in the liquor store and laid down forty-four bucks and change for the bottle and would normally had savored every sip. Now he just drank it and hoped that it would either flush out his brain or knock him blind and senseless. Either one would work. He had even held out the reasonable hope that the drug interaction between the scotch and the Xanax would do the trick, but it didn't. He couldn't even passively kill himself.

He had never felt so powerless in his life.

No. That wasn't true.

Thirty years ago, almost to the day, he'd felt even more helpless, and that was a cold hard fact. That had been the day that Mandy had died and he had been nearly killed. He'd spent weeks in the hospital and even now, after cosmetic surgery and three decades, his chest and shoulder still looked like patchwork.

Thinking about that made drinking more urgent, so he swallowed the whole cup and refilled it. The bottle was down about a third and he could feel the paint peeling on the walls of his brain, but he was still way too sober and he was still alive.

He hefted the bottle and considered it, wondering how much of it he would have to drink before he succumbed to alcohol poisoning, and then wondered if his system would rebel first and throw it up. Probably. His gut felt like an acid wash.

It was all falling apart. Everything. The cops and the feds pretended to defer to him as if he were a person of some actual importance, but he could see in their eyes that he was just a figurehead in a pissant little town where the worst and most typical crime was overtime parking, and the local idea of a crisis was rain on Sidewalk Sale Saturday. His best friend was in the hospital. The town's most prosperous farmer was dead. The selectmen were in a panic. Every night he had those horrible dreams—dreams that were now intruding into his waking life.

And my little sister's ghost wants me to kill myself.

He raised the refilled cup in a toast. "Here ya go, Mandy. Maybe this one will do it." He closed his eyes, tossed back the shot, hissed as the gases burned his throat, and then opened his eyes again. Nope. Still alive, damn it.

Terry closed his eyes for a moment, took in a deep steadying breath, held it for a moment, and then let it out as slowly as he could. Then he took his cell phone from his coat pocket and hit speed dial. It rang four times before a woman answered. "Hello?"

"Hello, sweetheart," Terry said in a softer tone than anything he'd managed for days.

"Terry?" His wife's voice was instantly concerned. "Where *are* you? You haven't called all day and I've left a dozen messages—"

"Sarah . . . things are really bad right now."

She paused, then said, "Yes, I know. Rachel Weinstock called me and told me some of what was going on. She said Saul was pretty rattled about an autopsy he had to perform."

"Pretty bad right now," Terry said again. He could feel his eyes filling with tears.

"Are you okay, honey?"

God didn't save you, either. God won't save this town, Terry.

"I'm . . ."

And you know what he wants from you. You see that, too. You see that every time you look in the mirror.

"Terry?"

Terry, the only way to not be like him is to be like me.

"I'm just tired, Sarah."

"Can you get away? Can you come home?"

Tears were running freely down his face now. He took the full bottle of Xanax from his pocket, popped the lid off with his thumb, and poured the pills out onto the table next to his chair. Twenty-two pills. More than enough.

"Terry," she repeated, "can you get away?"

"I don't know," he answered softly. "Maybe. Maybe there's a way I can get free."

"Please come home, Terry," Sarah begged. "You can't run yourself into the ground like this."

"No," he said.

"Will you try?"

"Yes."

"I'll wait up."

Terry squeezed his eyes shut against a wave of grief and pain. The image of Sarah's face burned in his mind—dark eyes flashing, thick fall of straight black hair just touched by a few strands of gray, a laughing mouth—and he fought not to sob out loud.

Terry, the only way to not be like him is to be like me.

"Call you later, sweetheart," he said, when he could master himself enough to keep everything out of his voice.

"I love you, Terry."

"I love you, Sarah. With all my heart."

He disconnected and dropped the phone on the floor. With a growl of mingled anger and fear and heartbreak he swept all the pills into his hand and held the closed fist above his upturned mouth.

His upraised fist trembled with a palsy born of a dreadful inner conflict and slowly, as if moving against an almost irresistible force, he lowered his hand down to the level of his lips . . . and then down farther, past chin and chest until the clenched fist lay in his lap. Tears ran down his cheeks and his lips trembled with sobs.

"No!" he said in a hoarse and alien voice that was filled with a rage of passion.

Sarah had said, *Please come home, Terry.*

He sat there for many minutes, still holding the Xanax, feeling them grind and crunch in his fist. Beside him the bottle wafted its own perfume of escape.

Please come home.

He struggled to his feet and shoved the fistful of Xanax deep into his jacket pocket. He almost—almost—went to the bathroom to flush their temptation away, but did not. Ultimately could not. In order not to embrace the option he needed to know it was still there. The same with the bottle. He capped it and put it in his briefcase. He did go to the bathroom, though, and there he ran cold water and splashed it on his face by the handful for over a minute, then patted his face dry. It was still clear that he'd been crying, but there was nothing more he could do to repair that.

Turning, he went back into the lounge and stopped still. There, by the chair in which he'd been sitting, stood Mandy. His face was still streaked with blood, but tears now ran down and cut paths through the caked red. She looked at him with a mixture of horror and reproach.

Terry stood there in the bathroom doorway, gripping the sides of the frame with both hands, his nails digging into the wood. What could he say? How could he defend against the accusation in her eyes?

"I can't do it!" he hissed. "I can't! I have Sarah! I have my friends . . . my *town!* You can't ask this of me."

Mandy lifted her eyes to his and the look in them changed from one of horror to a look of total hopeless defeat. She shook her head from side to side, closing her eyes and finally hanging her head.

"It will all be worse now," she said, but her voice was a ghostly whisper that he could barely hear. Between one teary blink of his eyes and the next she was gone.

Terry stood there, unable to move, for a long time as his heart hammered in his chest and icy sweat pooled at the base of his spine. When he could finally make himself let go and walk out of the room and through the hospital hallways he moved with the unnatural stiffness of the condemned walking the ghost road to the chair.

(5)

Mike was nearly dancing with happiness when he left Crow's room. All the way down the hall and in the elevator he kept breaking out into grins. Working for Crow at the Crow's Nest would be the coolest! He could quit his paper route, which was okay money but a real pain in the ass, especially in bad weather. And he'd get his comics at a discount. Crow said that he could start at eight dollars an hour, which was huge! Anything he wanted to buy from the store would be at cost. Crow even said that they could maybe do a little jujutsu when things got slow. If Mike wasn't in so much pain he would have thought he was dreaming.

His face was locked into a broad happy grin as he exited the elevator and headed across the broad hall to the exit doors, passing nurses who saw his smile and returned it automatically. Mike passed two police officers who were heading into the hospital—one medium-sized and skinny and one huge and muscular. The skinny one grinned at him, but the big one gave him a flat, wide-eyed stare and as Mike passed he craned his head all the way around to watch him go. Mike barely noticed the cop's attention as he pushed through the doors and jog-limped over to his bike.

In the lobby, the cops stopped and the bigger officer stood staring with total intensity out through the glass.

His partner said, "What's up? You know that kid?"

Temporary Officer Edward Oswald stared slack-jawed, not even hearing his partner. His heart had suddenly started hammering in his chest.

His partner, Norris Shanks, tapped him on the arm. "Yo! Tow-Truck. What the hell's with you?"

Tow-Truck Eddie Oswald blinked, becoming aware of his partner. He cleared his throat and forced himself to turn away from the sight beyond the glass doors of the Beast—the very much *alive* Beast—unchaining his bike.

"No . . ." he said absently. Then recollecting himself, he said, "No. It's nothing."

Inside his brain the voice of God was telling him: *Wait! Wait until you are alone!*

"Yes," he murmured.

"What?" asked Shanks.

"Nothing," Tow-Truck Eddie said and moved on into the hospital.

(6)

Val was awake when Crow came in and she felt her heart lift when he poked his head through the doorway.

"You order a pizza?"

She held her good arm out to him. "Come here and kiss me this instant, you idiot."

With as much consideration for their mutual injuries as he could manage, Crow gathered her in his arms and showered her face with kisses. Val could feel his heart beating against her chest as he held her close, and she leaned into him, kissing his neck, inhaling the scent of him—sweat, anesthetic, a hint of chocolate—and the reality and familiarity of him, even in so unfortunate a place as this hospital, made her feel more human than she had all day.

Val touched his hand, where the nub of the IV port was still taped to the skin. "You playing copycat?"

"Yep. I waited until they started a new IV bag, popped it out, tied a loop in the plastic thingee, and snuck out. The cop on duty is Norris Shanks and he's an old bud. He played lookout for me while I snuck in. If we get caught, though, we have to say he was on a bathroom break."

He settled himself on the side of the bed and his eyes were searching her face. "I'm okay," she said, forcing a smile. "No more bad dreams."

"Did you sleep much?"

"For a bit. They must have really knocked me out, because I don't remember anything. If I dreamed it wasn't—"

"It wasn't about him?"

She nodded. "No, thank God."

"Me neither. I had just that one about him sneaking into my room. I wonder if everyone who goes through stuff like this has these kinds of dreams." He kissed her forehead. "Well, whether or no, I don't think we'll need to worry about him for real."

He told her about his conversation with Head, and how the officer confirmed that he had seen Ruger take several hits.

"Most likely he's dead out there in the fields, or at best made it across the road to the Passion Pit."

Val's eyes were hot but her voice arctic as he said, "I hope he fell over the edge of the pit all the way down into Dark Hollow and is lying down there in *great* pain, bleeding to death."

The venom in her words did not shock Crow in the least; he couldn't help but agree, but it was a conversation stopper and for a while they held each other and thought ugly thoughts of revenge as the bedside clock ticked closer to midnight. In half an hour it would be October 1. Maybe the season of bad luck would end with September and the Halloween winds would blow their usual good fortune into the town.

"I had a long talk with Saul," Crow said at last. "He said that we could both get out of here tomorrow. Connie and Mark, too."

Val nodded, said nothing. Crow could imagine how little she wanted to go back to that farmhouse now. The whole place would probably have the feel of violation and grief about it. While Val had slept Crow had called her farm foreman and instructed him to replace the front door—the one with the bullet holes was to be turned over to the cops if they wanted it or otherwise burned—and the living room put back to rights. Crow had been very clear when he said that there were to be no signs at all of the events of the night before, including the removal of all of the crime-scene tape and any mess left by the hordes of officers and lab technicians who had been swarming over the place all day. The foreman, a smart and capable fellow, had entirely agreed and said that he would see to everything.

Even so, Crow had no intention of taking Val there when they were released in the morning.

"I have a plan," he said.

"Oh?"

"The cops say we can't go back to the farm yet," he lied. "So instead I've booked a room at the Harvestman for Mark and Connie. It's where the cops are staying, so they'll be safe, and it'll be easier for them to come back here for treatment and, um . . . therapy."

Val just nodded. Saul Weinstock had explained to her the kind of treatment Connie would need. Mark, too, in all probability.

"What about us?"

"We'll be moving into the Pine Manor Inn for the next night or two."

Her eyebrows rose. "Wow!"

"A little elegance won't hurt us, baby. Sunken tub, Jacuzzi to massage away our aches and pains. Great food. A nice bottle of wine for you and an equally nice bottle of Pepsi for me."

She closed her eyes and leaned against him. "God, it sounds wonderful, but—"

"No buts, sweetie. I ran it by Saul and he approved, so this is on the level of doctor's orders."

"But the Pine Manor costs an arm and a leg! That's too much to—"

"Not at all, not at all," he said smoothly. "Nothing's too good for my fiancée."

He felt her stiffen against his chest as she processed the words. Then she opened her eyes and raised her head, staring with puzzled uncertainty into his eyes. "What did you . . . ?"

Then she saw what he had taken out of his bathrobe pocket while her eyes were closed. He held it flat in the palm of his hand. A square blue-velvet box.

Val's eyes were as wide and huge as those in any painting by Keane, and her mouth formed a perfect O.

Since she had only one arm free, Crow opened the box for her and showed her the diamond ring.

"I wanted to do this over dinner at some fancy restaurant in New Hope, but things got a little crazy and . . . well . . . I want this whole thing to end on a happy note. For me it would be the happiest note of my life, Val, if you would agree to be my wife. I love you more than anything in the world and if you say yes I'll be the happiest man who ever walked the planet."

"Oh my God!" she said . . . and she said it several times.

"Can I take that as a yes?" He cleared his throat. "I . . . hope?"

Val's eyes filled with tears and with her one good arm she clung to him with incredible strength, showering his battered faces with kisses by the dozen, saying, "Yes! Yes! Yes!" over and over again.

He steered through the deluge of kisses until he found her lips with his and then kissed her as deeply and as sweetly as he could, feeling his own tears flow and mingle with hers. He came up for air only long enough to slip the ring on her finger, and then pulled her close again.

"I love you!" they both said at the same time, speaking the words into each other's panting mouth.

And at that moment all of the lights went out.

Chapter 26

"**C**row! What's happening?"

He pulled away from her, turning toward the open doorway, but all he could see through the darkness were vague forms hurrying about, sometimes colliding with one another.

"I don't know," he said, rising. "Power failure, maybe." He moved to the window and parted the heavy curtains. "Lights are on in the parking lot." He pulled the curtains back and faint light spilled into the room. "Must be a generator. The emergency lights should come on any second."

A full minute passed and the backup lights did not so much as flicker.

"That's weird," Crow said. He was standing by the doorway looking at the confusion in the hall. He saw the police officer assigned to guard him standing by the nurses' station and called out, "Norris! What's happening?"

Norris Shanks turned around and shone a flashlight beam full in his eyes. "Crow? Go back into your room. We have a power outage."

"Really? Never would have guessed." He went out into the hall.

"Hey, Shanks," he said, batting the flashlight gently to one side. "You sure that's all it is? I mean . . . aren't the backup lights on a different generator or something?"

He couldn't read the cop's face in the dark, but he saw Shanks stiffen for a second and then snatch the microphone from its clip on his shoulder.

"Base, this is Officer Shanks at Pinelands Hospital on guard duty with Crow and Val Guthrie."

"What is it, Norris?" Ginny's bored voice answered.

"We have a total lights-out here at the hospital. Mains and backup generator. Requesting backup."

"All the lights?"

"Yes," he snapped, and Crow could hear that Shanks was actually afraid. "This may not be a technical issue. Please roll all available units. Now."

His tone was such that for once Ginny didn't argue. "All units, this is Base. Officer needs assistance at Pinelands College Teaching Hospital. Hospital lights are out, repeat hospital lights— main and backup—are out. All units respond."

There was a flurry of voices calling in to report their whereabouts and say they were on their way.

"That ought to do it," Shanks said, sounding relieved.

"Yeah," agreed Crow, but he didn't relax. Patients were coming out of their rooms and demanding answers, nurses and orderlies were still colliding into one another, a few doctors were calling out orders that apparently no one was paying attention to.

Crow turned and called to Val's room, "I'll be right in, baby. We're calling for backup."

He started to turn back to Shanks and then paused, having not heard a reply. He took a step toward her room. "Val?"

Nothing.

Crow hurried over to the open door and peered into the gloom. Val was in bed, the sheets pulled up, turned away. Just a series of lumps in the darkness.

"Baby, you okay?" he asked as he entered the room.

She didn't stir and he reached over to touch her shoulder and then he froze. Val was lying on her left side, turned away from him toward the window.

Her *left* side.

The injured side.

With a cry of terror bubbling on his lips he grabbed the sheet and pulled it down.

She turned toward him, her face and body edged with silver from the pale light from outside, and as she turned Crow felt his heart freeze in his chest and his guts turn to icy slush.

It was not Val at all.

The figure in the bed that grinned up at him with a jagged smile of broken teeth was *Karl Ruger!*

(2)

Detective Sergeant Frank Ferro had just finished brushing his teeth, had changed into pajama bottoms, and was about to sit down on the edge of his hotel bed when his cell phone rang. When you're a cop, a call at midnight is never going to be good news. He picked his trousers off the bedside chair and pulled the cell from the belt clip.

"Ferro."

"Frank?" It was his partner, Vince LaMastra, sounding tired but stressed. "Something's happening at the hospital."

"What?"

LaMastra told him.

"Shit," Ferro said. "Lobby. Two minutes."

He snapped the cover of his cell phone shut and reached for his pants.

"Jesus Christ," he said.

(3)

Crow's mind was frozen in a black hell of panic. Ruger lay there in Val's bed—Val was nowhere to be seen—and none of it was possible.

"Surprise, surprise," Ruger said, and then without a flicker of warning cocked his foot and kicked Crow in the chest with shocking force. Crow flew backward against the wall of the bathroom cubicle, striking the back of his head with a heavy thud.

Fireworks exploded everywhere and he felt his knees starting to go.

In a flash Ruger leaped out of the bed and caught him before he could fall, taking two bunched fistfulls of Crow's robe and hauling him back to his feet. He pulled him close and Crow's nose was assaulted by the smell of Ruger's breath—like rot and sewage. It was just the same as it was in the dream he'd had earlier.

"Bet you're wondering where your little bitch is, aren't you, boy?" Ruger banged him back against the wall again and again. Crow was more than half dazed and his mind was spinning with a nauseous vertigo.

"Val . . ." he gasped.

Ruger stopped banging him off the wall long enough to lean close to his ear and whisper, "The bitch is mine, asshole. I'm going to enjoy splitting her right up the middle." He slammed him back again and held him there. "But you . . . I just wanted to introduce myself again before I ripped your fucking heart out." He let go of Crow for a second but before Crow could fall, Ruger closed one hand around his throat and pinned him once again to the bathroom wall. He raised the other hand, holding it flat, and simply slapped Crow across the face.

It was the hardest blow he had ever felt. It was like getting hit by a piece of board or a slab of stone. Ruger's hands were icy cold and immensely powerful. Crow's head shot to one side and his face felt mashed. Ruger backhanded him, catching the corner of his mouth this time, and the blow ground lip against tooth so sharply that blood splashed from Crow's face onto Ruger's.

Ruger stopped hitting him as he opened his mouth and his tongue—gray and dry—quested out like a hungry worm and found the droplets. He licked each one into his mouth, his eyes fluttering half closed for a moment as he savored the taste.

"Oh my God . . ." he breathed and he looked like a man in the throes of an orgasm. "Oh my God . . ."

Crow struggled to make his senses work and he shook his head like a drunkard. Ruger's eyes snapped open again and the look in them—the appearance of them—nearly stopped Crow's heart in his chest. Ruger's eyes had changed. They were no longer a brown so dark that they looked black—now they were as red as the blood he'd just licked off his own lips.

Even with a hand clamped around his throat, Crow screamed.

Ruger's lips were peeled back like a feral dog's as he leaned in toward Crow's throat and they were less than an inch away when Norris Shanks yelled, "What the fuck are you doing?"

Hissing, Ruger turned toward the cop who stood in the doorway. Shanks held his flashlight to one side and was reaching for his handgun when Ruger grabbed Crow with both hands and threw him across the room. Yelling in pain and fear, Crow spun through the air and crashed into Shanks with a teeth-jarring impact that slammed them both against the far wall. Shanks slid to the floor and Crow landed hip-first in the officer's lap, mashing his testicles and tearing loose all the stitches on both sides of his hips. Shanks shrieked with pain and Ruger took two quick strides toward him and kicked him in the forehead, knocking his head back with a crunch that silenced the scream at once.

Crow rolled off Shanks and spun around on his hands and knees. Despite the searing pain in both hips, with the hand removed from his throat Crow's oxygen-deprived brain was working better now and adrenaline was starting to pump through his system.

"Cr . . . Crow . . . ?"

He turned and saw Val's head and shoulder appear from the far side of the bed, silhouetted against the window. She was *alive!*

Ruger reached for him but Crow launched himself forward, surprising the killer and driving his right fist into Ruger's crotch; then as he bent over the pain Crow reached up with both hands, grabbed his hair, and yanked him downward. Ruger hit chest-down on the floor with a crash that sent a shock back up through Crow's arms. Crow lifted his head and slammed it down again—and again. He could hear bones break.

He lifted a third time and Ruger's icy hands shot out and caught his wrists like two vises. After those three blows it was an impossible move, something no man, not even Ruger, could have done. But there was no loss of strength in those hands and Ruger held them, pulling Crow's fists away from his scalp so forcefully that Crow could feel hair and scalp tearing. He still held them as he rose to his feet while keeping Crow in a kneeling position, arms raised as if in surrender.

Crow looked up at Ruger and even in the darkness he could see those fiery red eyes—those impossible eyes—and see the cuts and lacerations on the killer's face. Even the worst one barely bled a drop.

Crow knelt there, held by overwhelming strength, looking up at Ruger, trying to make sense out of what he was seeing. None of this was possible. Was he still dreaming? Was he lost somewhere in a nightmare? For one wild moment Crow wondered if he had really been shot worse than he thought back there on Val's farm. Could everything that had happened since then be part of some trauma-induced coma?

Ruger's fists were tightening and the pressure was making Crow's arm bones grind together. He had to do something, dream or not, impossible or not.

Using Ruger's iron grip as a support, Crow picked up both of his legs at once, poised for the split part of a second like a gymnast hanging from the rings, and then pulled his knees up to his chest so his feet could clear the floor as he brought them up and kicked out with every ounce of strength he could manage. He tried to break Ruger's knees, but the angle was bad and instead his heels struck Ruger in the hard muscle of both thighs.

It was enough. Ruger howled in pain—the first concession to humanity that he had made—and dropped Crow. Ruger staggered back with bad balance and had to grab the footrest of the bed to keep from falling.

Instantly Crow made a dive for Shanks's pistol and had it out when Ruger lunged at him again, howling with rage. Crow swung the gun up but Ruger swatted it out of his hand and the gun flew across the room where it struck the window, creating a vast spiderweb fracture. Ruger again reached down for Crow but Crow threw himself backward and kicked upward, catching

Ruger under the chin. Once more Ruger was staggered backward, but again he somehow managed to shake it off.

"What's going on?" someone yelled and Crow was vaguely aware of shapes in the doorway—nurses, patients.

"Get the cops!" Crow yelled, but he had no idea if anyone went to get help. Ruger reached over and swung the door shut with such force that Crow could hear cries of surprise and pain as it struck faces and hands.

Then Ruger turned and leered at Crow, showing the uneven row of teeth—the teeth Crow had shattered after they'd fought in the rain—and his grin looked like the mouth of a shark. All of those jagged teeth seemed unnaturally sharp and unnaturally long.

"I'm going to kill you and everything you love," Ruger hissed. He was not even breathing hard as he closed in again, bone-white fingers reaching to grab.

Crow kicked up again and caught Ruger in the chest, but it was like kicking a tree trunk. It didn't even slow him down. He tried it again and Ruger caught his ankle and dragged him forward like a fisherman reeling in a marlin. Crow tried every trick he knew to disengage his foot, but all he did was tear the skin on his ankle and twist his knee.

Ruger reached down to grab Crow's throat again when the loudest sound Crow had ever heard seemed to rip the whole room apart. Ruger was knocked forward and almost fell, but took a broad step to clear Crow and somehow remained on his feet. He turned and Crow looked up and there was Val on her knees, leaning against the far corner of the bed, holding Shanks's gun out as smoke curled up from the barrel.

With effort Ruger pulled himself erect and faced Val. He hissed at her like a snake and started to reach for her when she shot him again. The bullet caught him in the shoulder and spun him around. Crow covered his head with both arms and ducked out of the way as the bullet punched through Ruger's upper chest and struck the TV mounted on brackets above the bed. Metal and glass fragments showered down on Ruger, but he did not fall.

"You killed my father!" Val was screaming over and over again. She fired again, catching Ruger on the other shoulder and he did a wild pirouette before careening off the bed.

Crow reached over to Shanks and frantically patted down his legs until he found the backup pistol in a small holster strapped to his ankle. Above him Val fired again and Ruger was slammed back against the wall.

"You fucking bitch!" he screamed, but still he didn't go down.

Crow tore open the Velcro and clawed the pistol out of the holster. It was a .38 snub-nosed Smith & Wesson, and Crow rolled onto his back and raised the pistol with both hands and just as Val fired a shot into Ruger's stomach Crow opened fire and hit him again and again and again.

Caught between two fires, Ruger was a puppet dancing in the darkness, being jerked back and forth, either unwilling or unable to fall as Val hit him in the stomach and chest and groin and Crow hit him in the back and kidneys and shoulders.

Crow fired five times and the hammer clicked dry on the sixth chamber, which had been left empty. Val fired twice more and then there was the audible metallic snap of the breech locking open.

Ruger was chest-forward to the wall, and as Crow watched his legs buckled and he slid slowly down to his knees, lingered there for a second, and then toppled over onto his back. Mouth slack, eyes shut, muscles slack.

As Val knelt there her arm sagged to the floor and she dropped the gun. "You killed my father, you son of a bitch." She looked at Crow with dark and wild eyes and he could see the fresh dark bruise on her face where Ruger must have hit her when he'd slipped into the room during the blackout.

"Val . . . wait . . . I have to check." Holding the gun high, ready to use it as a club, Crow wormed his way over and with his other hand felt for a pulse in Ruger's throat. Nothing. He tried another spot. Absolutely nothing.

Crow bowed his head.

Karl Ruger was dead.

"Jesus Christ," Crow said, and then he struggled to his knees and reached across the corner of the bed toward her just as her eyes lost their focus and rolled up in their sockets. With a soft sigh she passed out and sagged down on the bed. Whimpering in fear, Crow crawled over the bed to her and pressed his ear to her chest, not breathing at all until he heard the steady thump-thump-thump of her heart.

"Thank God!" he breathed and kissed her over her heart and then kissed her sweet face. "Thank God. . . ."

Outside, there were yells and an official voice—Frank Ferro, Crow thought—was yelling, "Police! Police! Out of the way!" Footsteps were hurrying, getting louder, coming closer.

A hand clamped around his wrist with implacable force and Crow turned in absolute horror to see Karl Ruger leering up above the footrest, his eyes wide and red and hellish.

With irresistible force he pulled himself up and pulled Crow close and whispered in his graveyard voice, "Ubel Griswold sends his regards." Then he laughed the coldest laugh Crow had ever heard and the red light went out of his eyes and Karl Ruger sank back to the floor.

Crow was frozen there, his eyes wide and unblinking, his heart beating painfully in his chest, mouth agape as the horror of those five words plunged his entire world into madness.

Epilogue

Midnight came and went in Pine Deep and no one took notice as September died and a cold October was born amid shadows and sirens and flashing lights.

Detective Sergeant Frank Ferro took charge of the investigation and cleanup at Pinelands Hospital and slowly the story unfolded. The hospital lights had been shut off at the source by the simple act of the main breakers being thrown, and the auxiliary generator had been disabled with lines and wires cut. The maintenance supervisor, Carl Wilkerson, was found unconscious in the electrical shed behind the building—alive but badly injured with a cracked skull. The weapon was a pair of bolt cutters; the same cutters had been used to gain entry to the shed and disable the generator. The main breakers were turned back on and by morning the backup had been repaired as well. Wilkerson was admitted to the hospital in guarded condition, though when he regained consciousness two days later he had no memory at all of the event. "Traumatic amnesia," diagnosed Saul Weinstock.

Weinstock met with Ferro, LaMastra, and Gus in the doctors' lounge around two in the morning, as things were beginning to settle down. Over cups of coffee—Ferro's fourteenth of the day—Weinstock gave them a status report.

"Officer Shanks has a hell of a lump on his head and a very sore set of testicles—about which we can all sympathize—but will be fine. We're keeping him overnight for observation."

"How's Ms. Guthrie?" LaMastra asked. "She really came through in there."

Weinstock grinned. "Yeah, never leave Val out of the equation. She's known for rising to the occasion. And as far as her injuries go, we put two stitches in her cheek and in the morning we'll be doing a CT scan of her eye socket. X-rays showed that she has a hairline crack of the right orbit, but we need to rule out trauma to the eye itself."

"Jeez," said Gus. "She said all he did was backhand her."

Ferro shook his head. "And Crow?"

"I had to disappoint him about getting kicked loose tomorrow. He won't be going anywhere for at least two, three days. Fourteen stitches in his mouth. Both cheeks. Three loose molars. His left wrist has the weirdest compression bruise I've ever seen, like it was caught in a vise."

"He said Ruger just squeezed his wrists."

Weinstock shook his head. "No. He had to have caught it in a door or something. The human hand can't generate the kind of PSI needed to do that. But with all the jolts he took I doubt he remembers things clearly."

"Yeah," said LaMastra, "he also said Ruger's eyes turned red for a while."

"As I said, he's disoriented."

Ferro sipped his coffee. It was horrible. Reheated, probably, though that wasn't why his face was sour. "And our boy Ruger?"

"Karl Ruger's body was taken to the morgue where an autopsy will be performed tomorrow by yours truly. Though I'd rather just run him through a composter and let it be."

"Amen to that," said Gus and LaMastra at the same time.

"Here's the part I don't get, gentlemen, and maybe there's some new street drug that can turn someone into Superman, but cursory examination showed that Ruger had been shot over two dozen times," Weinstock said, pausing to let that sink in. "There were five original wounds, which had all started to close. Yes, you heard me. They were healing. Since the day before yesterday. And then there were all of the shots collectively fired by Crow and Val. You want to tell me how a man with five bullets in him eludes your police manhunt for two days and then breaks in here, knocks out our maintenance guy, knocks out a cop and beats the living shit out of two more people, and then only goes down after they empty two guns into him from a range of about six feet?" He looked at them, his mouth smiling but his eyes very hard and, perhaps, a little afraid. "You want to tell me how that's possible, guys, and I'll get us all on the cover of the *Journal of the American Medical Association* 'cause it'll be the medical miracle of the century."

Gus just looked into his coffee cup. LaMastra was staring at Ferro, and Ferro was meeting the doctor's flat stare, but after a few seconds all he could do was shake his head.

"He is dead, though, right?" asked Gus.

"Oh yes. Karl Ruger is very, very dead. He's wrapped in plastic and in the fridge. But to tell you the truth, fellas," Weinstock said, "I'm not even sure I want to do the autopsy on this guy. I'm not sure I know enough medicine to go in there and figure this out, and no, that's not a joke."

(2)

Vic Wingate listened to the news late into the night, then called Jim Polk for the inside word.

Polk said, "Yeah, he's dead. Crow and Val Guthrie shot the living hell out of him."

"Good," Vic said. "Good."

There was silence on the line for a moment and then Polk asked, "Vic?"

"Yeah?"

"Is this part of . . . you know? The *thing*?"

Vic laughed. "Everything's part of it, Jimmy. Everything."

"But—maybe I was reading this wrong, but I kind of had the impression that this Ruger clown was supposed to be on your side. I mean . . . our . . . side."

"He is."

"Not no more he ain't."

Vic just laughed and hung up.

He sat back in his lounger and crossed his ankles. The house above him was quiet. Lois was passed out on the couch and Mike had gone to bed on time. Vic had let him be tonight—there had been too much going on. Tomorrow he'd start working on some way to steer Mike back into Tow-Truck Eddie's path, but that could wait. There was still a whole month before Mike absolutely had to be killed. Plenty of time.

For now Vic could relax and revel in the fact that everything the Man had said would happen *had* happened. It was a shame Ruger hadn't managed to take Crow and Val Guthrie out of the equation, but there was still time for that. There was, he thought, time for the whole plan to unfold just the way Griswold wanted it to. Right up to Halloween night and the beginning of the Red Wave.

Happy, content, Vic Wingate drifted off to sleep.

(3)

Malcolm Crow lay in his bed and stared at the ceiling, eyes wide despite the pull of the morphine, cold sweat beading on his face. Everything was quiet now. Val was safe and protected. Even though Ruger was gone, there was now an officer stationed in her room, just as Jerry Head was now parked in his room.

Weinstock had let Crow stay with Val all the way up until the drugs knocked her out, and then he'd kissed her—kissed his *fiancée!*—and then allowed himself to be gently urged into a wheelchair and taken back to his room. Despite the painkillers, he hurt, but he didn't really care. Val was safe.

And Val was going to be his wife.

His *wife!*

Before she had drifted off to sleep Val had clutched his hand with hers—a small but strong hand now stained with powder burns—and in a desperate voice had asked, "Is it over, Crow?"

Crow had kissed her hand and her lips. "Yeah, it's over, baby.

He's dead." His mouth was full of stitches and it hurt to talk, but that was something they both needed to hear aloud. "He's dead. Gone."

Her lip curled as she said, "And I hope his soul burns in hell!" There was still fear in Val's eyes, but there was steel there, too, and Crow loved her for the strength he saw there. His heart swelled to the breaking point.

"For all eternity," Crow agreed heartily. He caressed her hair. "We did it, Val—we stopped him. You and me, baby. Your dad can rest now, Val. It's over."

"It's over," she echoed, and closed her eyes for so long Crow thought that the drugs finally had her, but then she opened her eyes and lifted her hand, looking at the engagement ring sparkling on her finger. "It's so beautiful . . ." she murmured and drifted off to sleep.

Crow kissed her forehead and her eyes and her lips and then let the orderly help him back to his wheelchair. His body felt ancient and badly used, but his heart was young. All the way back to his room joy at the prospect of a future with Val kept leaping up inside him, but it was like something on one end of a seesaw. As it peaked and dropped back down, another intense emotion soared up.

A total, abject, and penetrating terror. While he had been with Val he had forced it down into the recesses of his mind, but nothing would compel it to stay there. Ruger's last words kept echoing in his brain.

Ubel Griswold sends his regards.

How the hell had Ruger known about Griswold? How could he have found out about that killer and how had he known to use Griswold's name like a hammer to hit him? How? It made no sense at all.

Ubel Griswold sends his regards.

Griswold was dead—thirty years dead. At least, everyone thought he was dead. He had vanished off the face of the earth at the end of the Black Harvest. The Bone Man had been killed for his murder. Griswold couldn't be alive. It was impossible.

So . . . how had Ruger known about him, and why had he said what he said?

Ubel Griswold sends his regards.

Only two people in all of Pine Deep knew what kind of man Griswold had been—himself and Terry. Griswold had nearly killed Terry, and had in fact murdered Crow's older brother, just as he had murdered little Mandy Wolfe, and so many others. He had tried to kill Crow, but the Bone Man had been there. Had just chanced to be there, and had come after Griswold swinging a shovel and yelling fit to wake everyone in the neighborhood, and everyone had come running. Maybe Griswold could have killed them both, but when all the neighbors had come running—a mass of people who had been filled with grief and impotent rage all through that horrible season—Griswold had fled.

All those years ago young Malcolm Crow had seen Griswold very clearly in the bright spill of moonlight. He had seen Griswold's face, had seen it change. Had seen it become the true face of Griswold. He had told his father what he'd seen, and had been whipped for lying.

The Bone Man had seen it, too, and had gone hunting for both the man and the monster. Had he really killed him before the mob had beaten him to death and strung him up on the scarecrow post? Crow had always believed that . . . but now he wondered.

Ubel Griswold sends his regards.

Griswold had been a monster. So had Karl Ruger, and Crow had seen a change in him, too. The image of Ruger's eyes turning from brown to red would not leave Crow's mind. He hadn't imagined it. No way. Was it the same kind of change? Was Ruger the same kind of monster as Griswold? Or . . . was he something else? Something different? He thought about Ruger lying on a slab in the morgue down in the basement, and he wondered. Did the morgue drawers have locks? Was the morgue itself locked?

His stitched and battered mouth hurt abominably but he didn't want more painkillers. They'd just put him to sleep, and Crow was not sure he ever wanted to go to sleep again. Yesterday he had dreamed of Karl Ruger and last night Ruger had shown up. Not exactly the same as his dream, but so close as to be terrifying. If he let himself sleep now, what would he dream? His skin crawled at the thought.

Crow looked over to where Jerry Head sat slumped in the chair leafing through a magazine.

"Hey . . . Jerry . . . ?"

The officer looked up. He was bleary with lack of sleep, but his eyes were still cop eyes. "Yeah?"

"You . . . you won't fall asleep on me now, will you?"

For a moment Head looked surprised, and then a small compassionate smile formed on his lips. He sat up straighter in his chair. "Naw, man. I got your back. You get some sleep. I'll be here for another hour and then we got one of your local boys, Eddie Oswald, coming on and he'll sit with you until morning."

Crow felt relieved. Head was big and tough, and Tow-Truck Eddie was even bigger and tougher. "Thanks, man."

The morphine was taking him now and the edges of the room were getting hazy.

Ubel Griswold sends his regards.

Before the darkness closed in entirely, Malcolm Crow did something he had not done since he'd been a little boy. He crossed himself and said a bedtime prayer. For himself . . . and for Val.

As he faded off to sleep he heard, or dreamed that he heard, a sweet guitar playing sad old blues. It comforted him, and the night passed.

(4)

Four floors below where Crow slept, in the basement morgue of the Pinelands College Teaching Hospital, the body of Karl Ruger lay in a plastic body bag on the stainless steel table in drawer number 14. The remains of Tony Macchio were three drawers to his left. Henry Guthrie was his direct right-hand neighbor. There were more drawers occupied at one time than at any time since a three-car pile up in Crestville the previous April.

The wall clock ticked the seconds slowly as 3:00 a.m. turned to 4:00.

Inside drawer number 14 Ruger's body was still and cold. There was no blood moving through his veins. His lungs were collapsed, his heart as still and cold as a stone. His muscles, once so strong and deadly, were flaccid, and his brutal hands were limp.

Only his eyes were open. Wide and unblinking, staring up at the utter blackness of the inside of the drawer

Wait! a voice said in his mind, and Karl Ruger's dry tongue flicked out over his lips once, twice, then vanished back into his slack mouth. After a while he closed his eyes.

And waited.

ACKNOWLEDGMENTS

Authors who write long books need lots of help (take that any way you care to), as well as technical advice. I want to thank the following folks for their generous assistance in writing *Ghost Road Blues*.

Chief Pat Priore of Tullytown, Pennsylvania, for technical info on police procedure. If any of the law enforcement information is incorrect, the error rests purely with the author.

Arthur Mensch and Randy Kirsch for reading the book and giving me their unreserved and unflinching opinions.

My web design team, David Kramer and Geoff Strauss of www.careerdoctorforwriters.com, who are equal parts strange and wonderful and who created a terrific website for me.

John West for too many things to list.

The Bucks County Center for Writers in Doylestown, Pennsylvania (formerly the Writers Room of Bucks County) and my colleagues in the Philadelphia Writers Conference.

My agent Sara Crowe of the Harvey Klinger Agency.

My many friends and colleagues in Horror Writers Association, and the satellite chapters: the Garden State Horror Writers and the NJ-PA Horror Writers Association.

And as always, for my wife, Sara Jo and my son, Sam, for their constant support and enthusiasm during the process . . . and after.

To all: countless thanks!

**Don't miss the next exciting Pine Deep novel by
Jonathan Maberry**

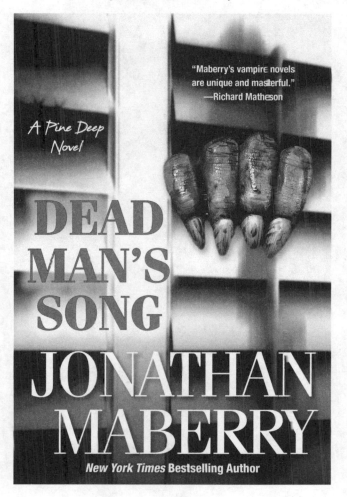

A Pine Deep
Novel

"Maberry's vampire novels
are unique and masterful."
—Richard Matheson

DEAD
MAN'S
SONG

JONATHAN
MABERRY

New York Times **Bestselling Author**

Available from Kensington Publishing Corp.

Keep reading to enjoy a teaser excerpt!

It was October when it happened. It should always be October when these things happen. In October you expect things to die.

In October the sun shrinks away, it hides behind mountains and throws long shadows over small towns like Pine Deep. Especially towns like Pine Deep. The wind grows new teeth and it learns to bite. The colors fade from deep summer greens to the mournful browns and desiccated yellows of autumn. In October the harvest blades are honed to sharpness, and that's when the sickles and scythes, the threshers and combines, maliciously attack the fields, leaving the long stalks of corn lying dead in haphazard piles along the beaten rows. Pumpkin growers come like headsmen to gather the gourds for the carvers' knives. The insects, so alive during the long months of July, August, and September, die in their thousands, their withered carcasses crunching under the feet of children hurrying home from school, children racing to beat the fall of night. Children do not play out of doors in the nights of Pine Deep.

There are shadows everywhere, even in places they have no right to be. The shadows range from the purple haze of twilit streets to the utter, bottomless black in the gaping mouths of sewers. Some of the shadows are cold, featureless—just blocks of lightless air; other shadows seem to possess an unnatural vitality; they seem to roil and writhe, especially as the young ones— the innocent ones—pass by. In those kinds of shadows something always seems to be waiting. Impatiently waiting. In those kinds of shadows something always seems to be watching. Hungrily watching. These are not the warm shadows of September, for in that month the darkness still remembers the warmth of summer suns; nor are they yet the utterly dead shadows of bleak November, to whom the sun's warmth is only a wan memory. These are the shadows of October, and they were hungry shadows. When the dying sun casts these kinds of shadows, well. . . .

This was Pine Deep, and it was October. A kind of October peculiar to Pine Deep. The spring and summer before had been lush; the autumn of the year before that had been bright and bountiful, yielding one of those rare and wonderful golden harvests that were written of in tourist books of the region; and though there had been shadows, there hadn't been shadows as dark as these. No, these shadows belonged to an autumn whose harvest was going to be far darker—these were the shadows of a Black Harvest October in Pine Deep.

And it was October when it happened. It should always be October when these things happen.

In October you expect things to die.

(2)

"They said they'd send us some coffee and hot sandwiches in about half an hour," called Jimmy Castle, as he trudged back into the clearing. He had his hands jammed deep into the pockets of his jacket, fists balled tight to try and clutch some warmth. He walked briskly, shoulders rounded to keep the wind off his ears, his straw-colored hair snapping in the stiff breeze. "I told them to send some of those pocket hand-warmers, too . . . getting pretty fuckin' cold out. . . ."

His words trailed off to nothing as he entered the clearing; and all thoughts of warmth were slammed out of his brain.

He stopped walking, stopped talking, stopped breathing. The world imploded down into one tiny quarter-acre of unreality; time and order and logic all smashed into one chunk of madness. All sound in the world died; all movement failed. All that existed was the scene that filled his eyes as Jimmy Castle saw the two *things* that occupied the clearing. His mouth sagged open as he stood there rooted to the spot, feeling all sensation and awareness evaporate into smoke as the seconds fell dead around him.

Nels Cowan lay on the muddy ground, arms and legs spread in an ecstasy of agony, head thrown back and lolling on what little was left of his throat. Cowan's mouth was open, but any scream he uttered echoed only in the dark vastness of death. His eyes were open, beholding horror, but now it was the horror of the soul, for the body possessed awareness no longer. Blood glistened as black as oil in the moonlight, and Castle could even see the taut gray cords of half-severed tendons and the sharp white edge of a cracked vertebra.

Jimmy Castle opened his mouth, mimicking the silent scream of Nels Cowan. However, his scream escaped, ran shrieking out into the night air and soared disjointedly up into the night. He sagged to his knees, still screaming, as his fingers scrabbled at the butt of his gun, his fingernails making audible scratching sounds in the silence.

The dark shape hunched over Nels Cowan raised its head and looked at him. Pulpy chunks of pumpkin still clung to its white flesh, sliding in the ooze made of equal parts pumpkin meat and human blood. The white face stared at him, expressionless for a long moment, and then the bloody mouth opened in a great smile full of immense darkness and hunger, lips parting to reveal hideous teeth that were grimed with pink-white tatters of flesh. The teeth gleamed white through the red as the smile broadened into a feral snarl; a mask of lust and hate, the nose wrinkled like a dog's, the black eyes becoming lost in pits of gristle. A tongue, impossibly long, lolled from the mouth and licked drops of blood from the thing's chin.

Jimmy Castle sagged back, his screams dying away in a sick, small little mewling sound as he continued to claw at his gun, which he was only distantly aware was coming free of the holster. With no mindful awareness of his actions he racked the slide, flicked off the safety, held the gun out and up in both hands, pointed. Fired. Actions performed a thousand times in practice, performed now with absolutely no conscious control, machine-like and correct. The barrel of the heavy 9mm rose, sought its target and screamed defiance at the man-shape that was rising, tensing, readying itself to spring.

Thunder boomed and lightning flashed in the clearing as Jimmy Castle tried to blast the thing back into nightmares.

He fired straight, aiming by instinct alone at the centerline of the creature's body. He fired fast.

He fired true.

He fired nine times, each boom as loud as all the noise in the world.

He sent nine tumbling lead slugs directly into the thing, catching it as it rose, catching it in belly and groin and chest.

He hit it every single time.

And it did him no damn good at all.